CHUNKY

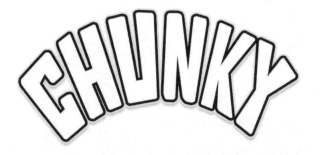

This book is dedicated to
drama teacher Mrs. Miller

Katherine Tegen Books is an imprint of HarperCollins Publishers.
HarperAlley is an imprint of HarperCollins Publishers.

Chunky
Copyright © 2021 by Yehudi Mercado

Library of Congress Control Number: 2020949371
ISBN 978-0-06-297279-8 – ISBN 978-0-06-297278-1 (pbk.)

The artist used Adobe Photoshop to create the digital illustrations for
this book.
Typography by Yehudi Mercado and Laura Mock
21 22 23 24 25   EP   10 9 8 7 6 5 4 3 2 1
❖
First Edition

YEHUDI MERCADO

CHUNKY

YAY

KATHERINE TEGEN BOOKS
Imprints of HarperCollins Publishers

HARPER
alley

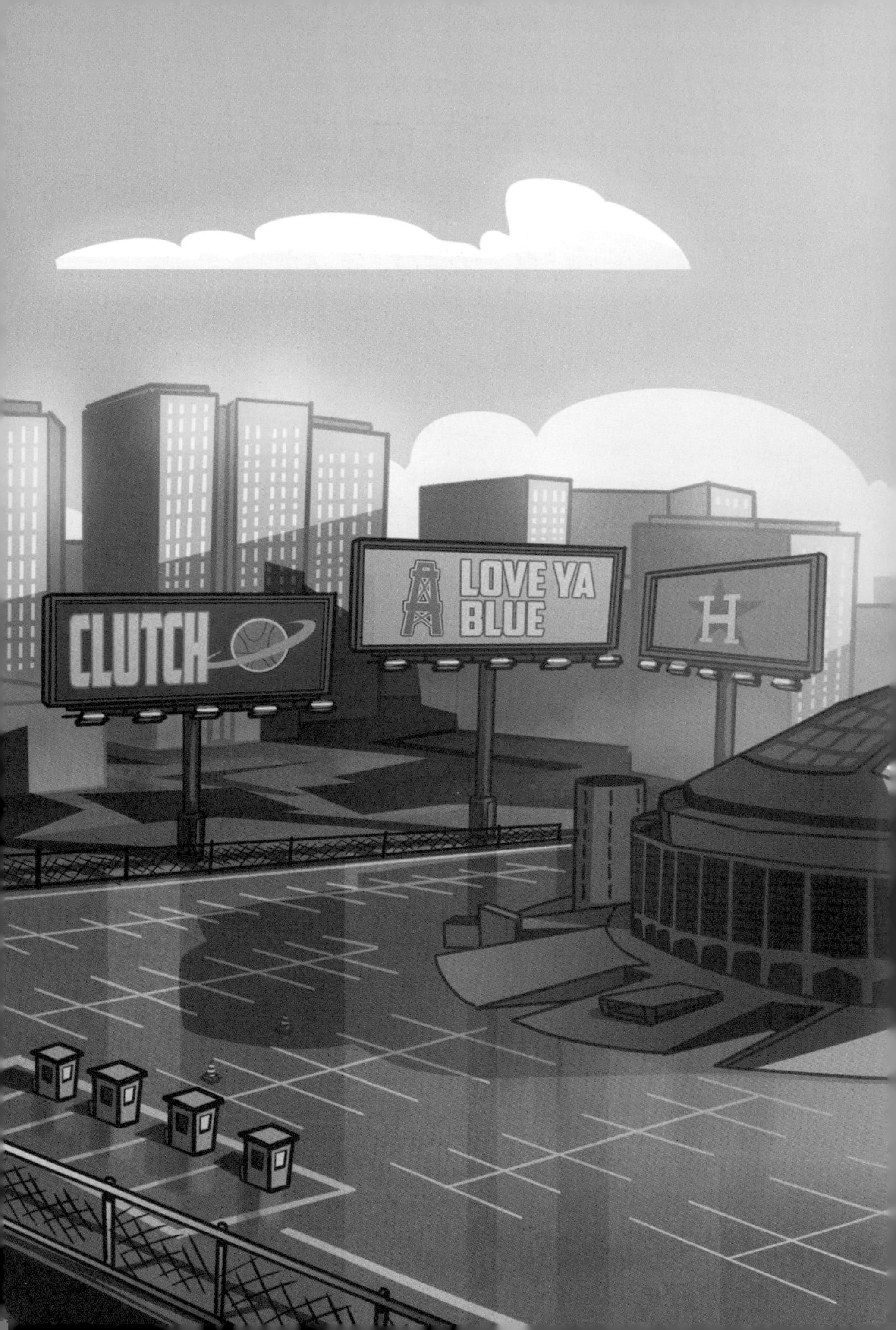
CLUTCH
LOVE YA BLUE
H

CHAPTER ONE
Pregame

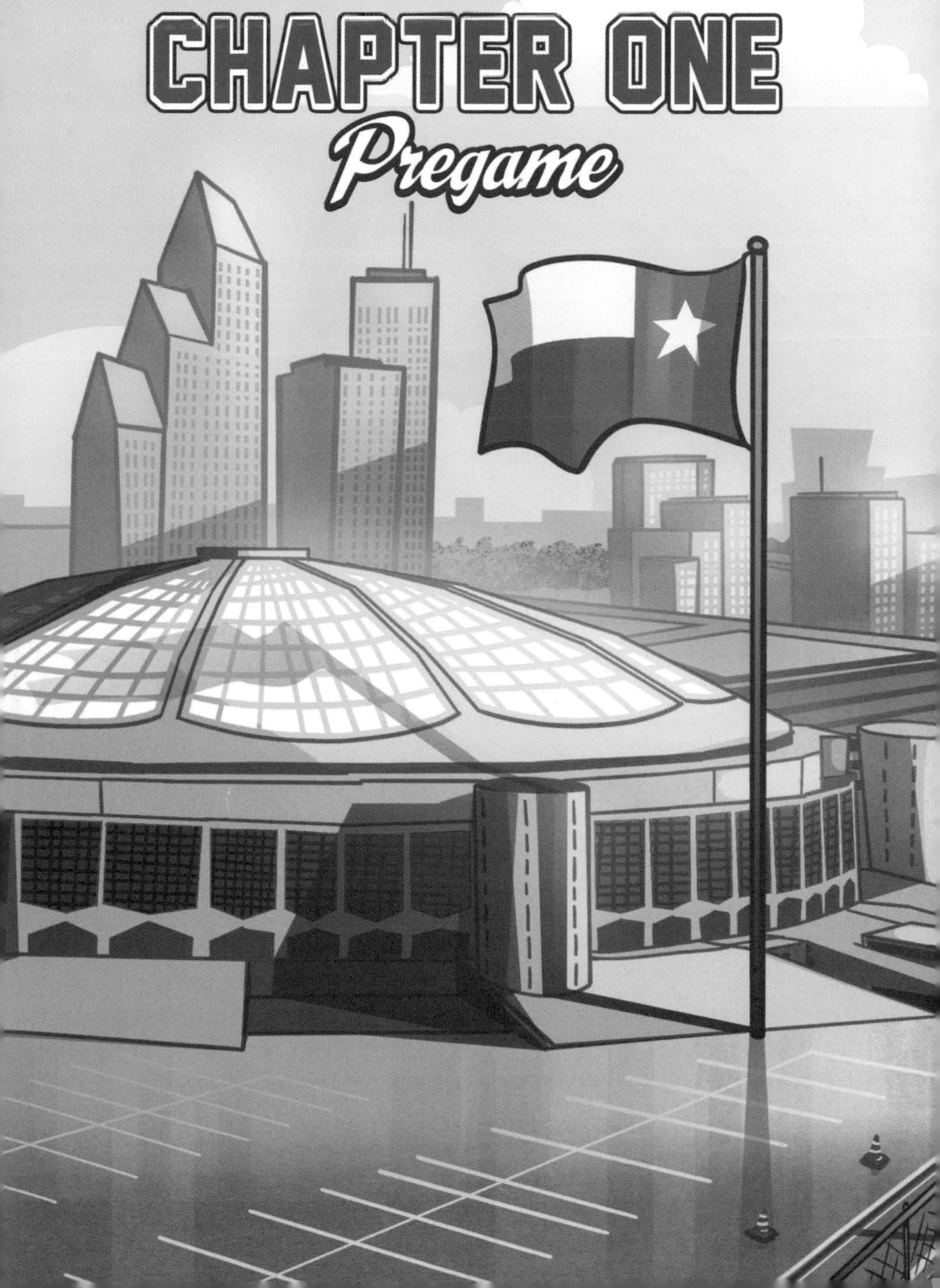

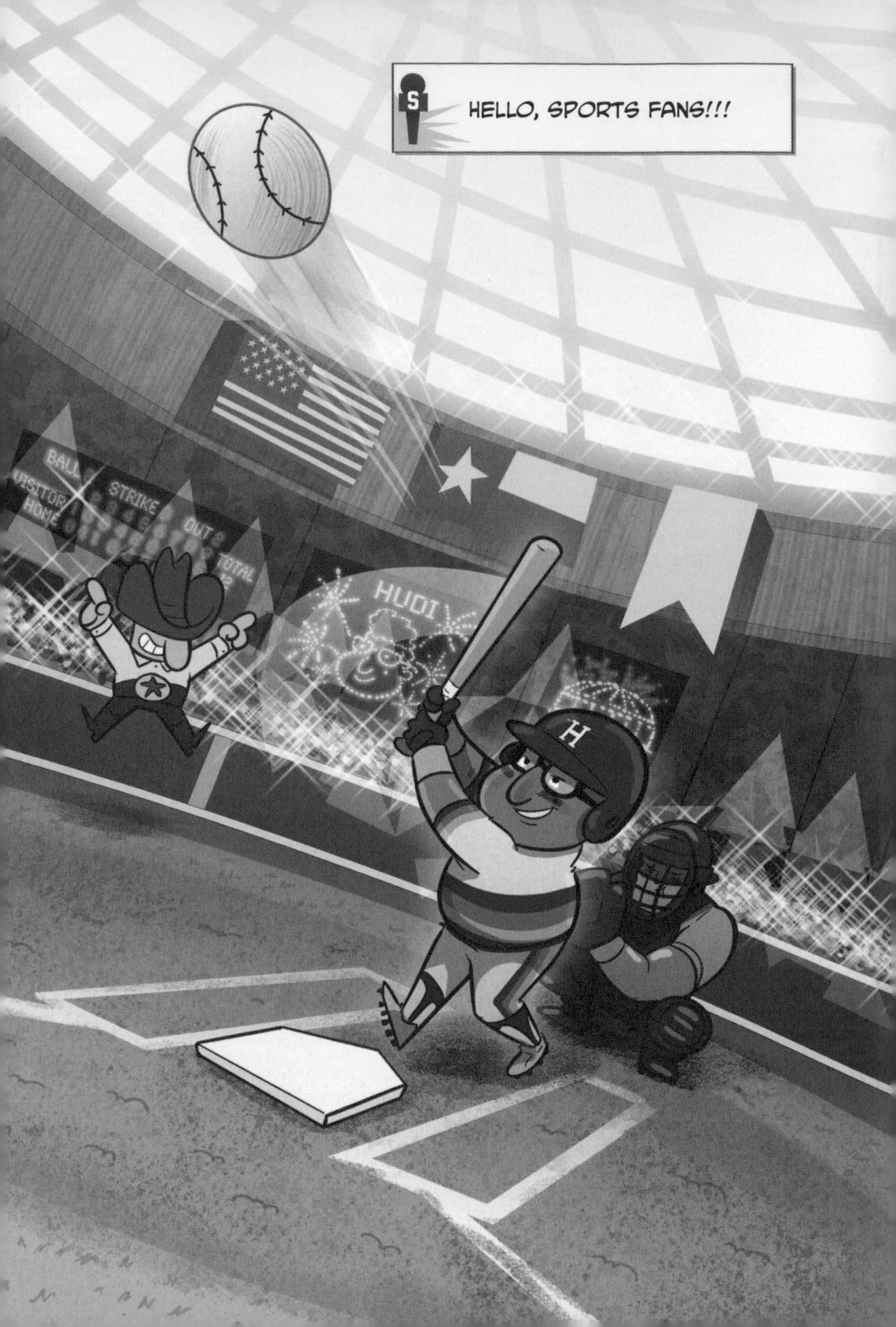
HELLO, SPORTS FANS!!!
BALL
STRIKE
VISITOR
HOME
OUT
TOTAL

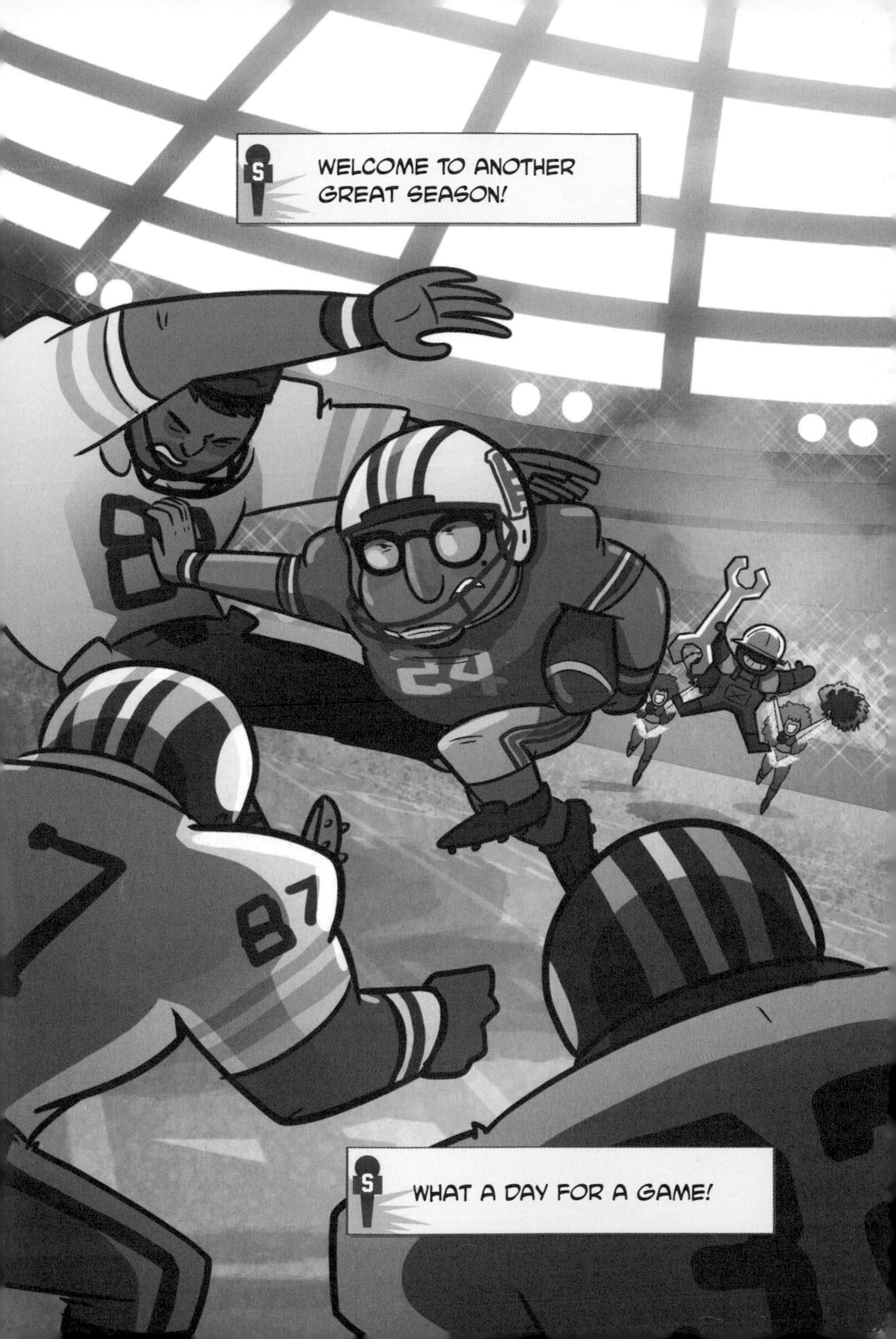
WELCOME TO ANOTHER GREAT SEASON!
WHAT A DAY FOR A GAME!

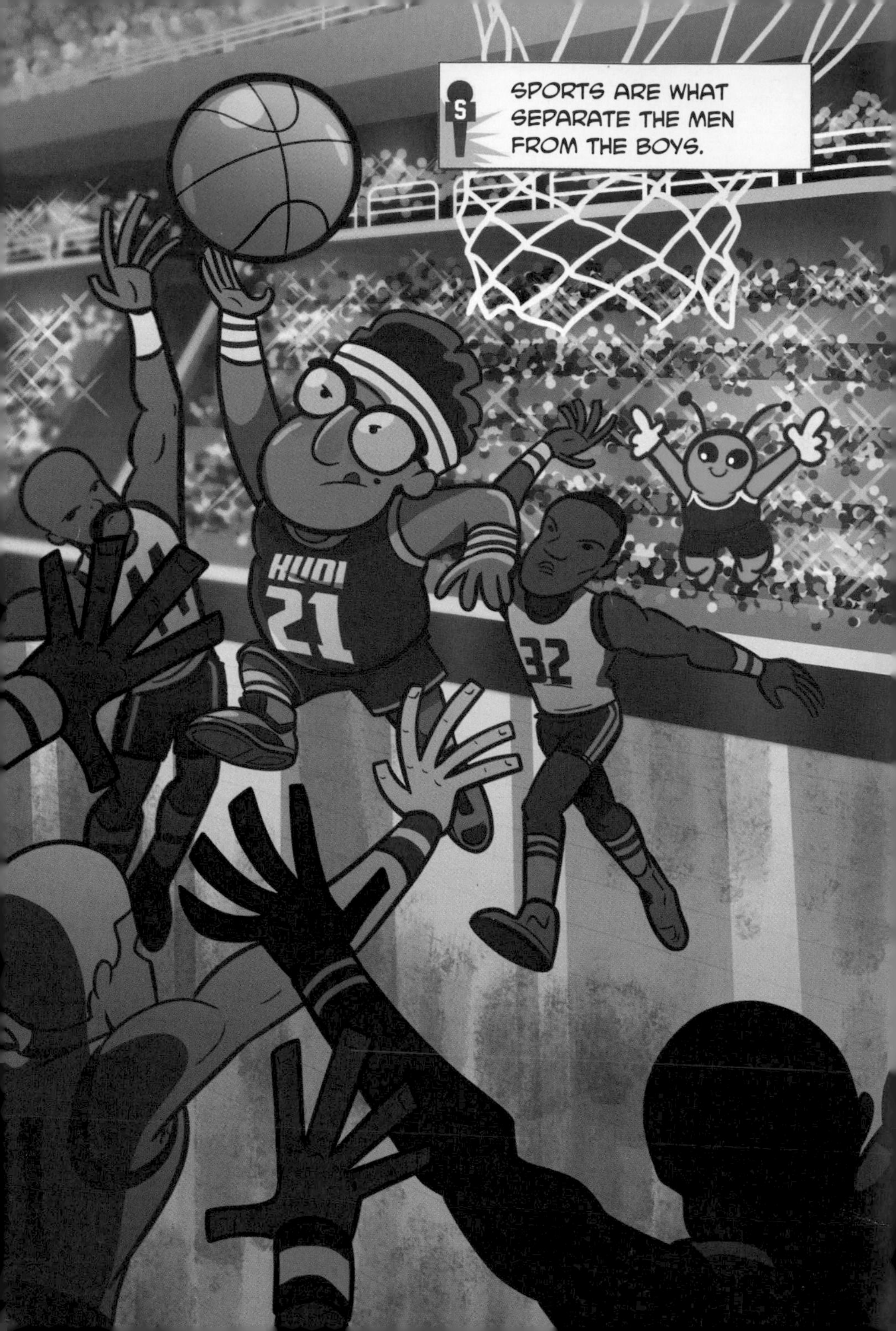

S
SPORTS ARE WHAT SEPARATE THE MEN FROM THE BOYS.
HUDI
21
32

A WIN CAN MAKE YOUR DAY . . .
HUDI!
HUDI!
HUDI!
HUDI!
HUDI!
HUDI!
HUDI!
HUDI!
HUDI!
HUD
. . . BUT A LOSS CAN RUIN YOUR LIFE.

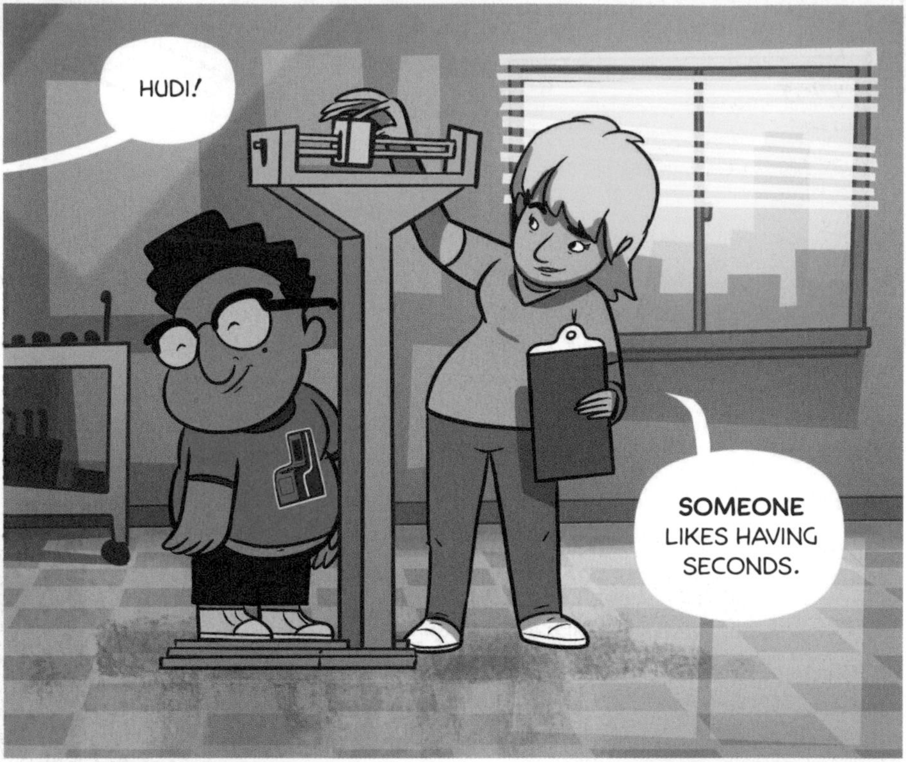
HUDI!
SOMEONE LIKES HAVING SECONDS.

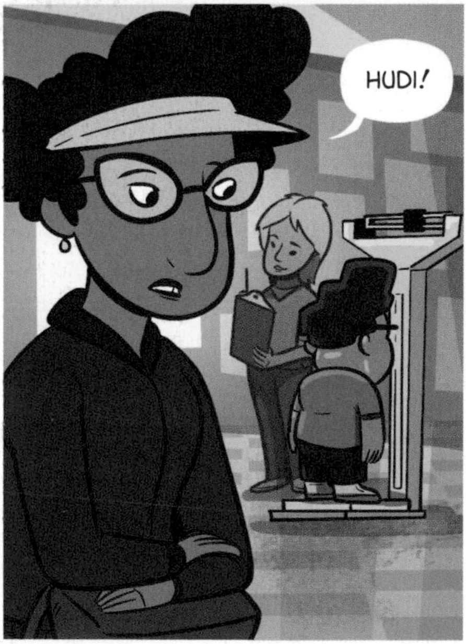
HUDI!

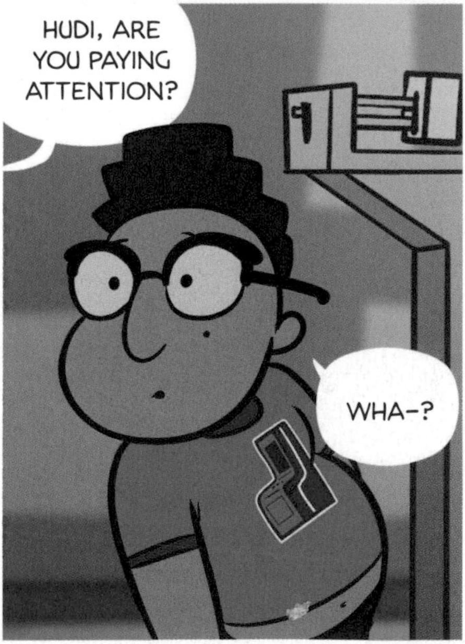
HUDI, ARE YOU PAYING ATTENTION?
WHA-?

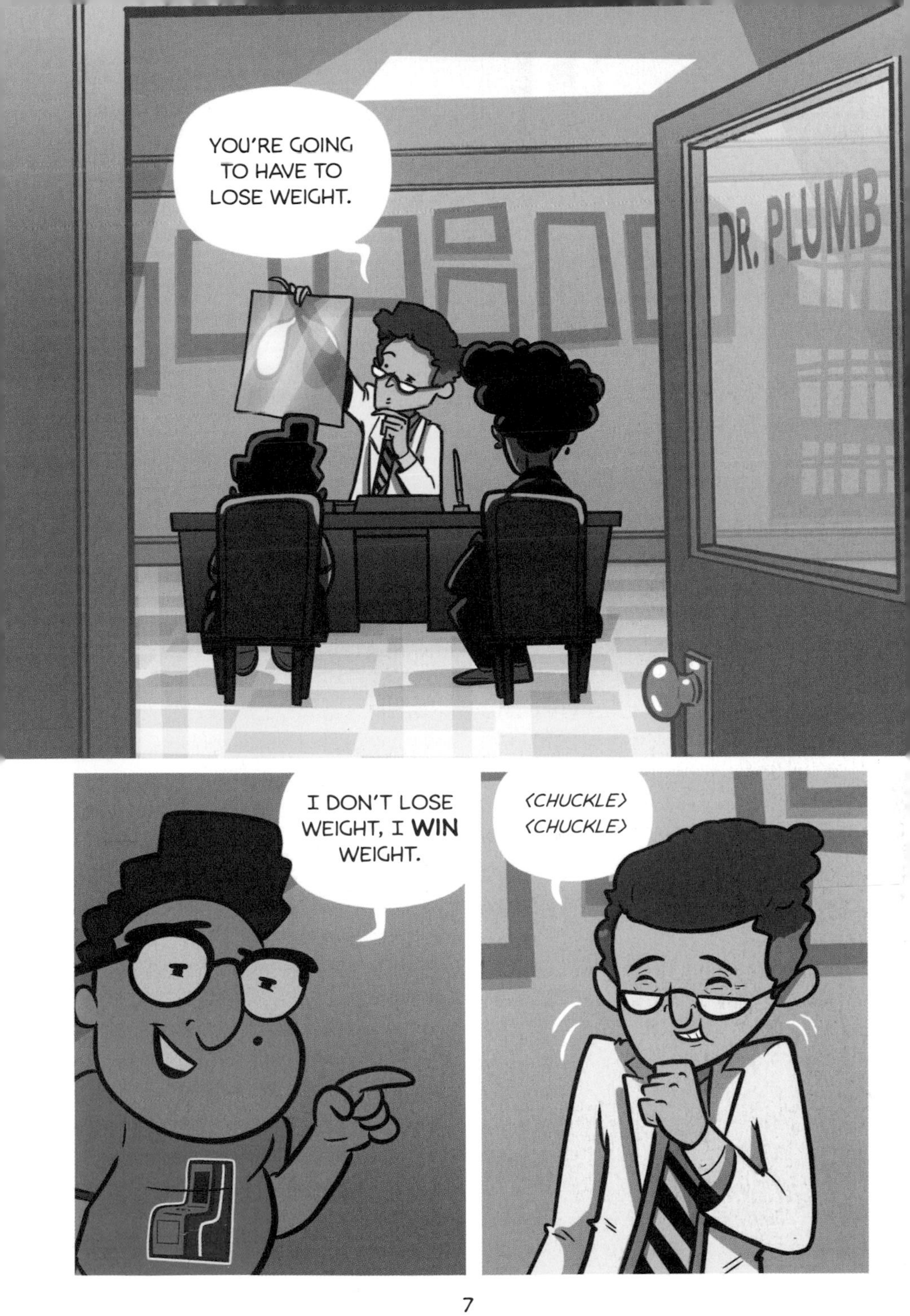
YOU'RE GOING TO HAVE TO LOSE WEIGHT.
DR. PLUMB
I DON'T LOSE WEIGHT, I **WIN** WEIGHT.
<CHUCKLE>
<CHUCKLE>

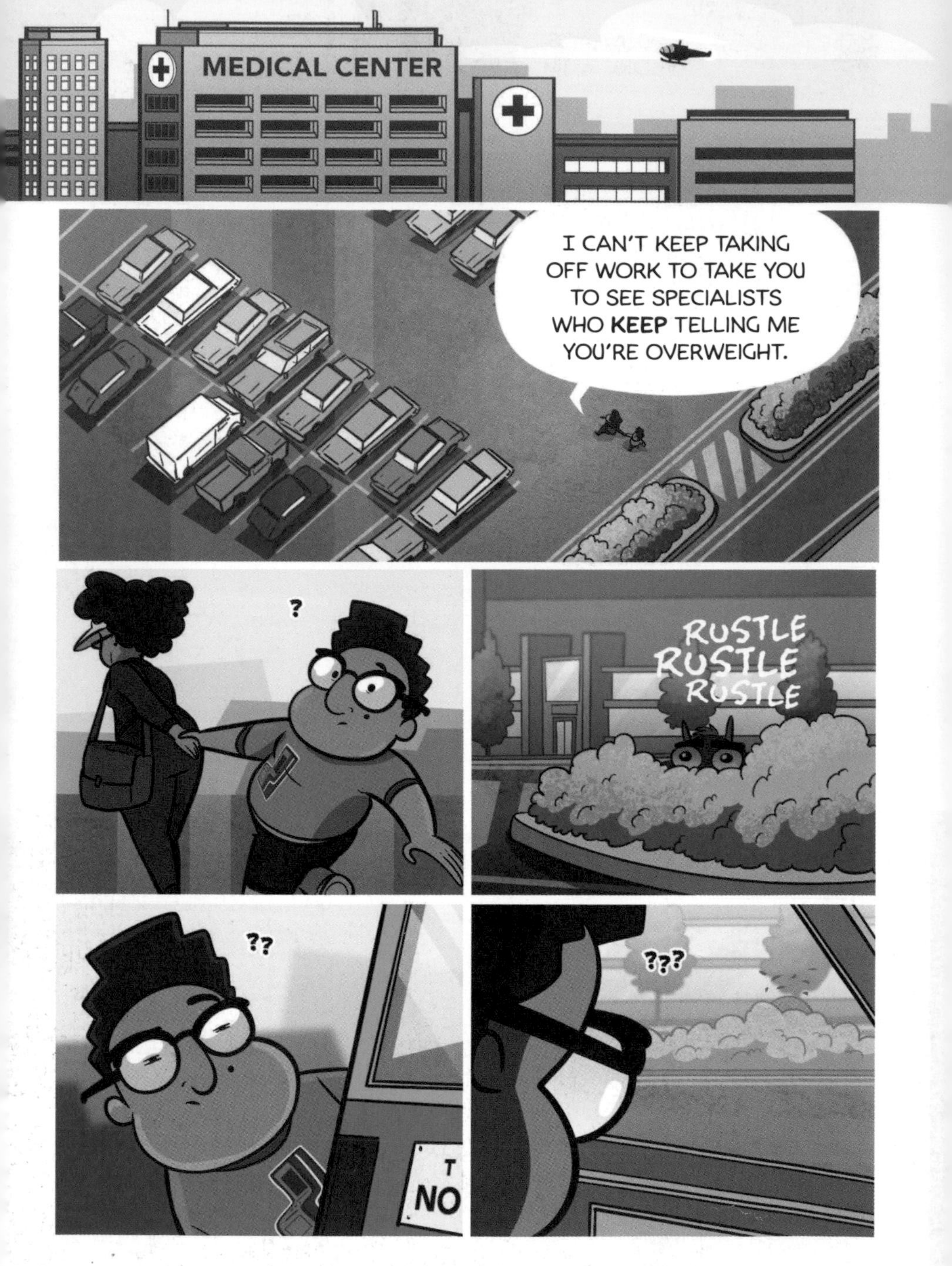
MEDICAL CENTER
I CAN'T KEEP TAKING OFF WORK TO TAKE YOU TO SEE SPECIALISTS WHO **KEEP** TELLING ME YOU'RE OVERWEIGHT.
?
RUSTLE
RUSTLE
RUSTLE
??
T
NO
???

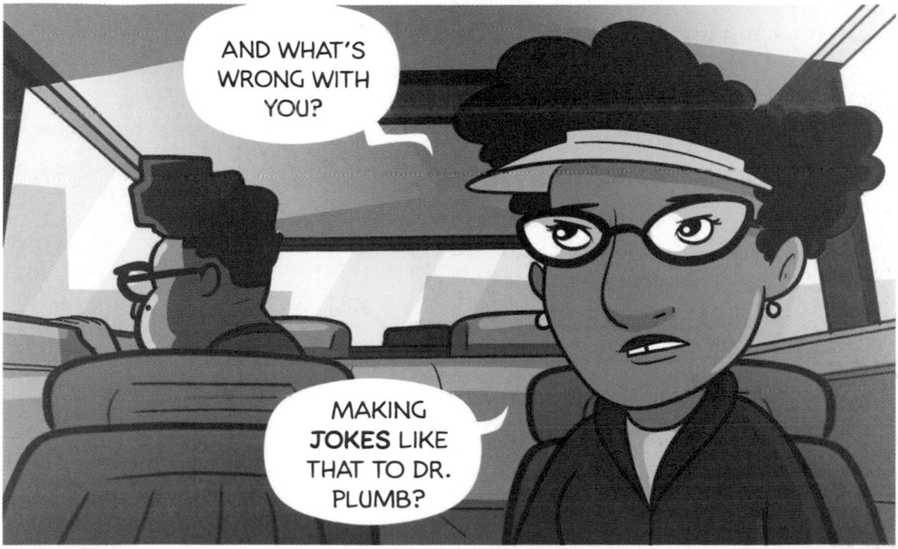
AND WHAT'S WRONG WITH YOU?
MAKING JOKES LIKE THAT TO DR. PLUMB?

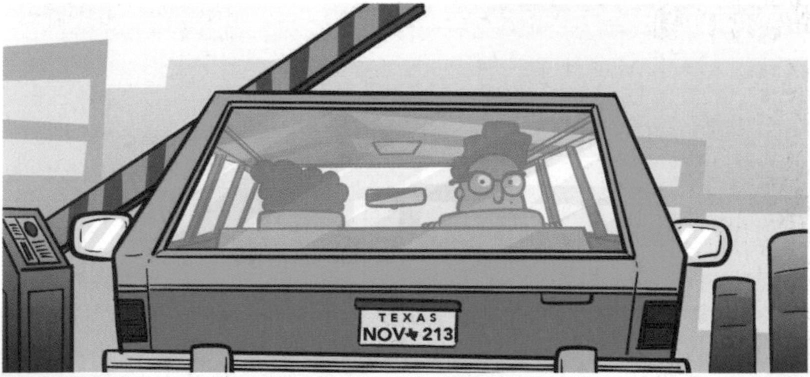
TEXAS
NOV 213

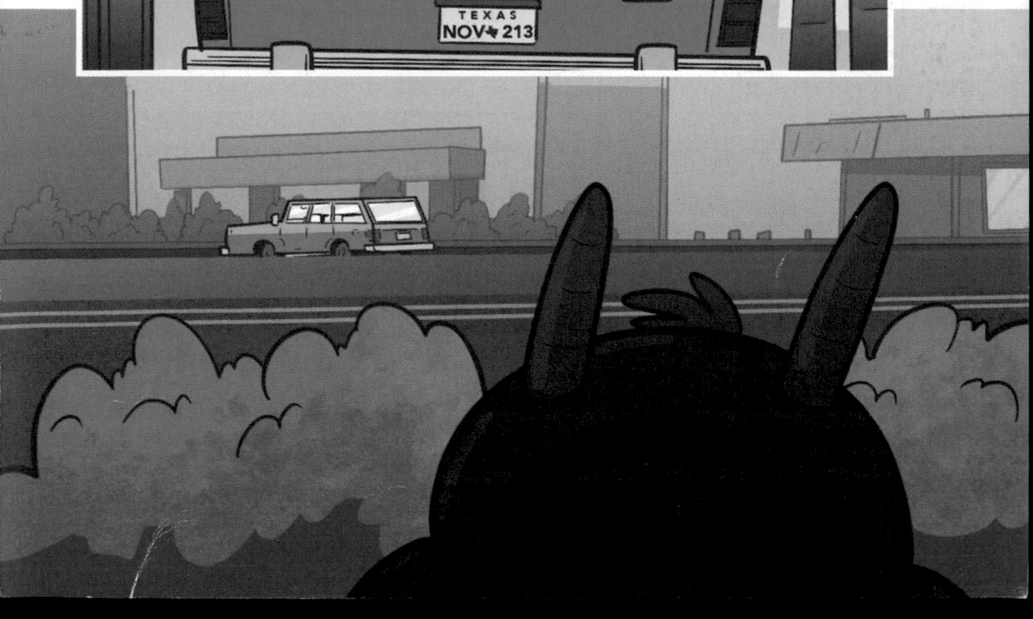

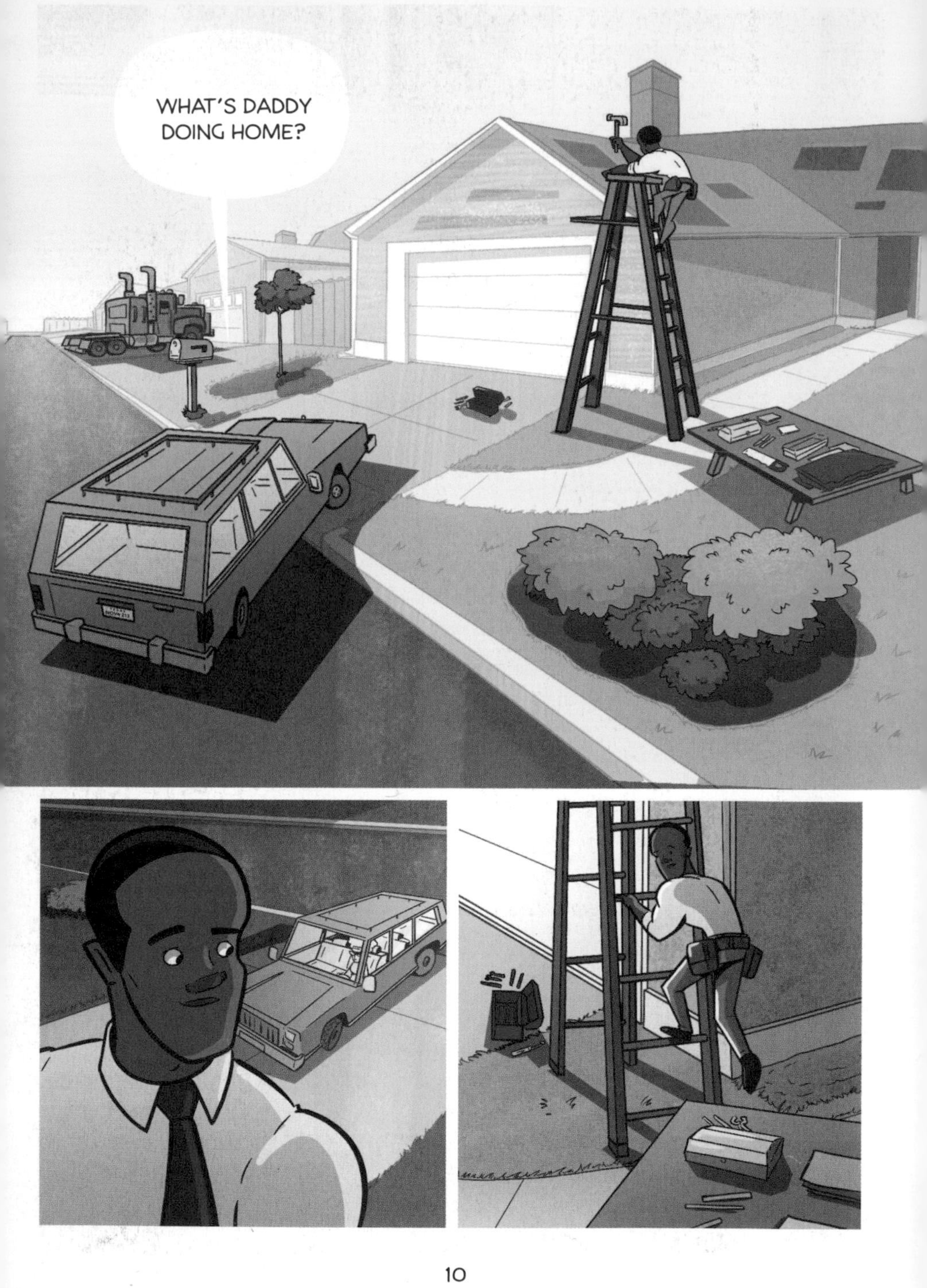
WHAT'S DADDY DOING HOME?

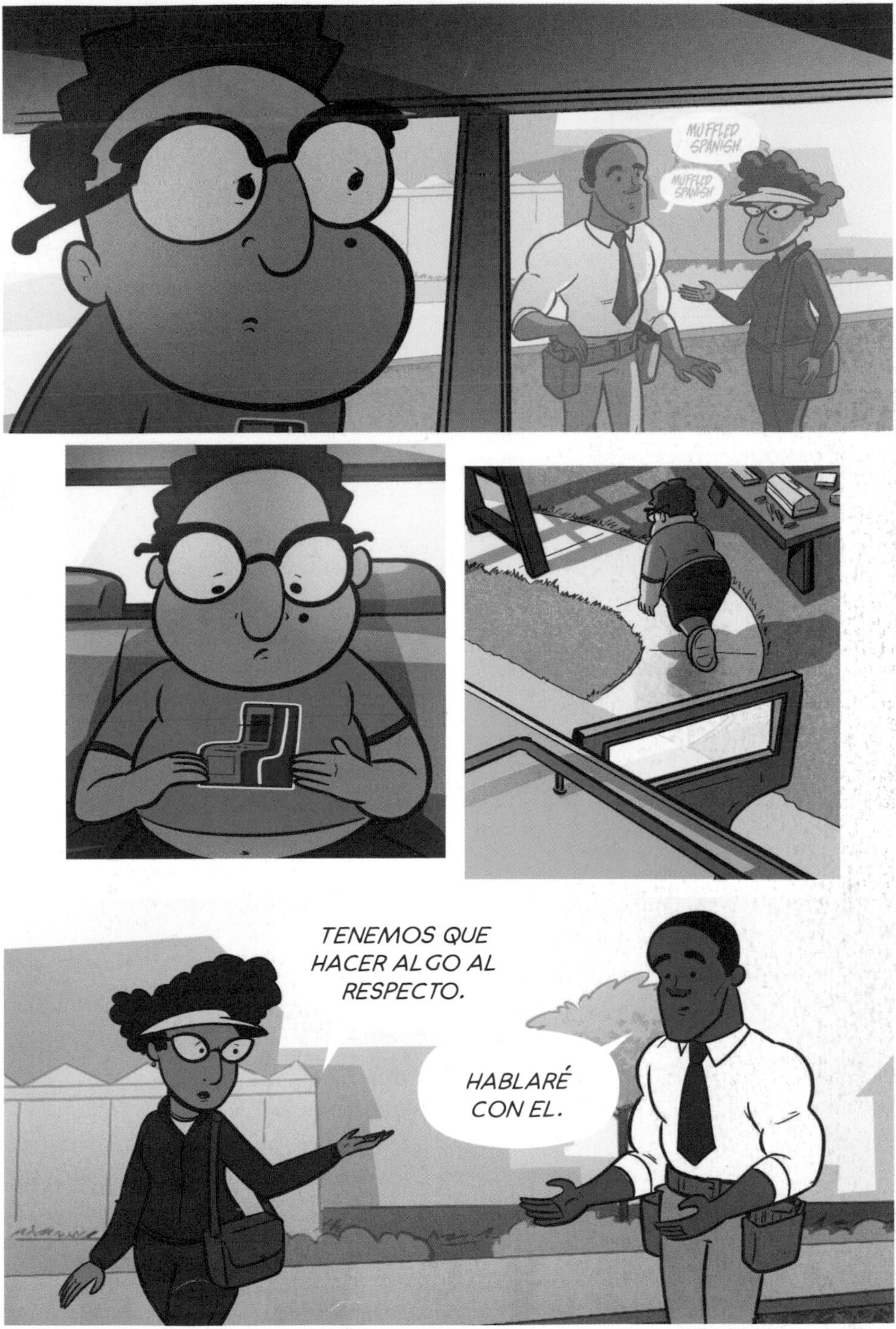
MUFFLED SPANISH
MUFFLED SPANISH
TENEMOS QUE HACER ALGO AL RESPECTO.
HABLARÉ CON EL.

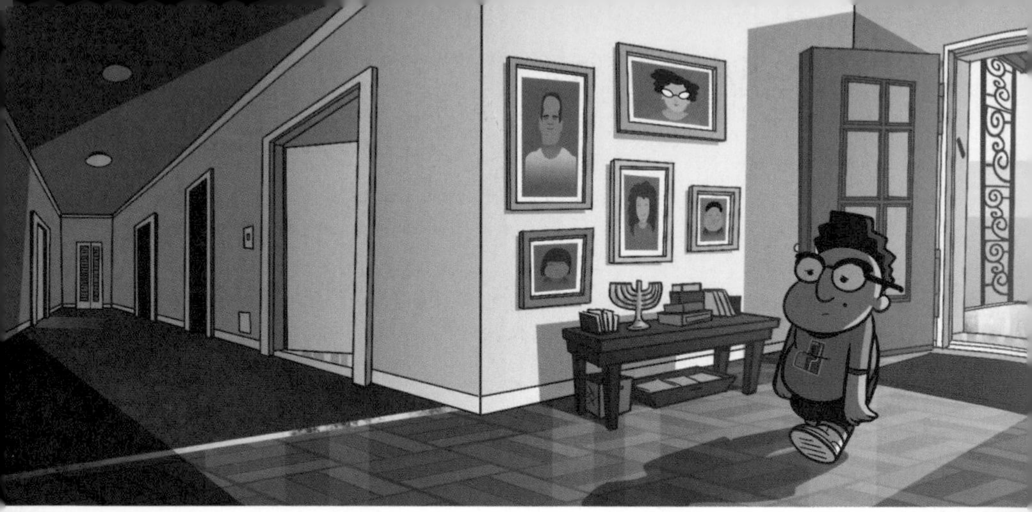

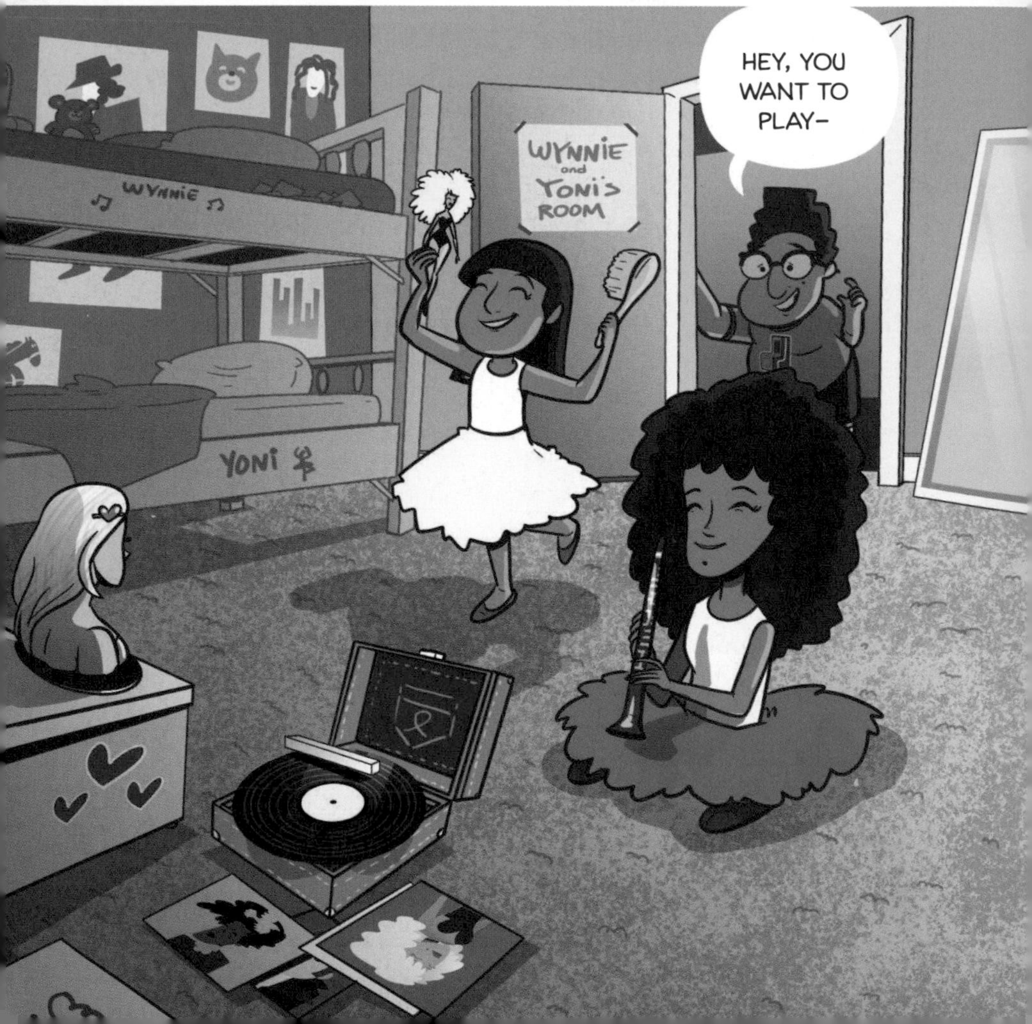
HEY, YOU WANT TO PLAY–
WYNNIE and TONI'S ROOM
WYNNIE
YONI

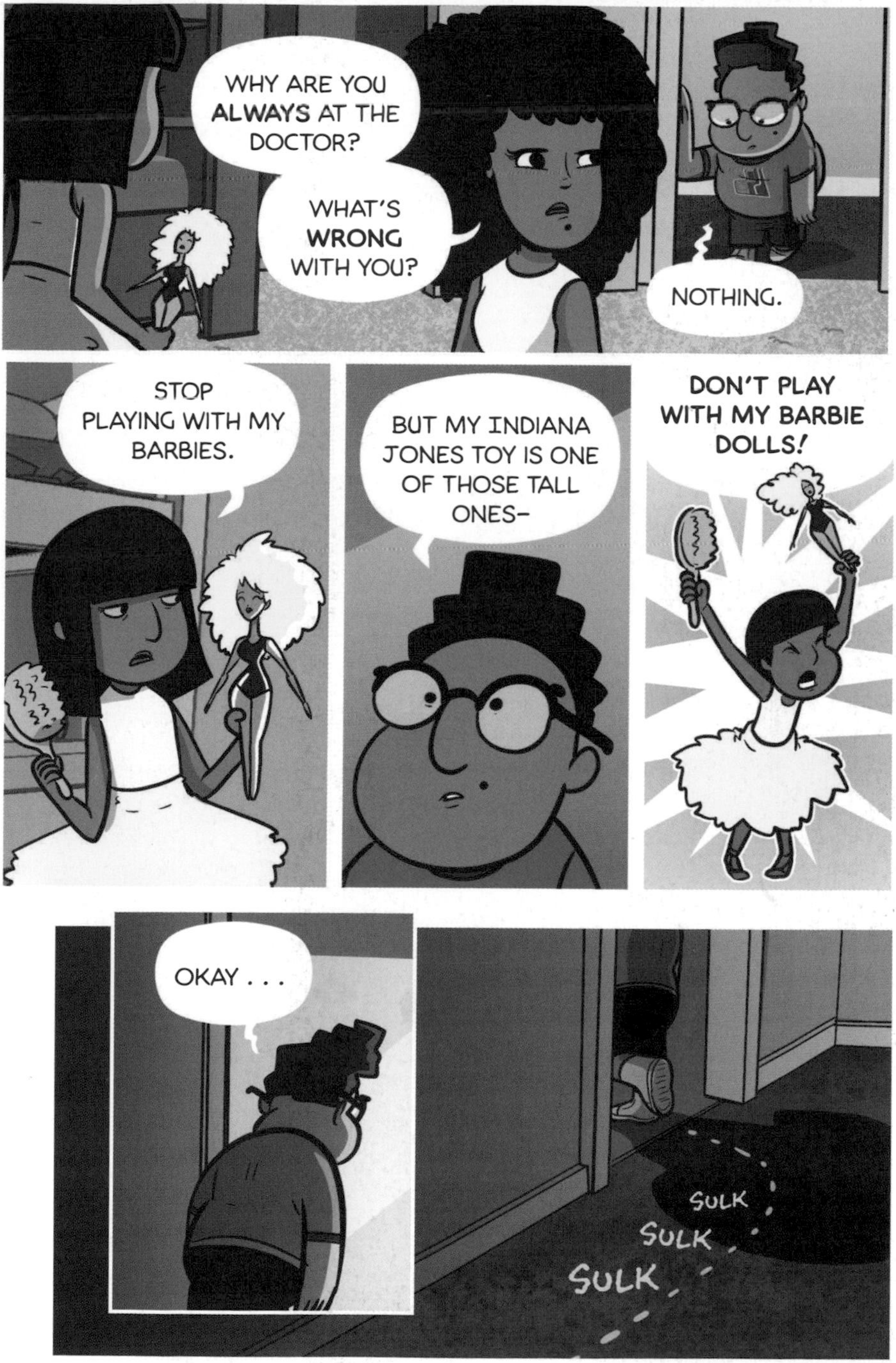
WHY ARE YOU ALWAYS AT THE DOCTOR?
WHAT'S WRONG WITH YOU?
NOTHING.
STOP PLAYING WITH MY BARBIES.
BUT MY INDIANA JONES TOY IS ONE OF THOSE TALL ONES–
DON'T PLAY WITH MY BARBIE DOLLS!
OKAY . . .
SULK
SULK
SULK

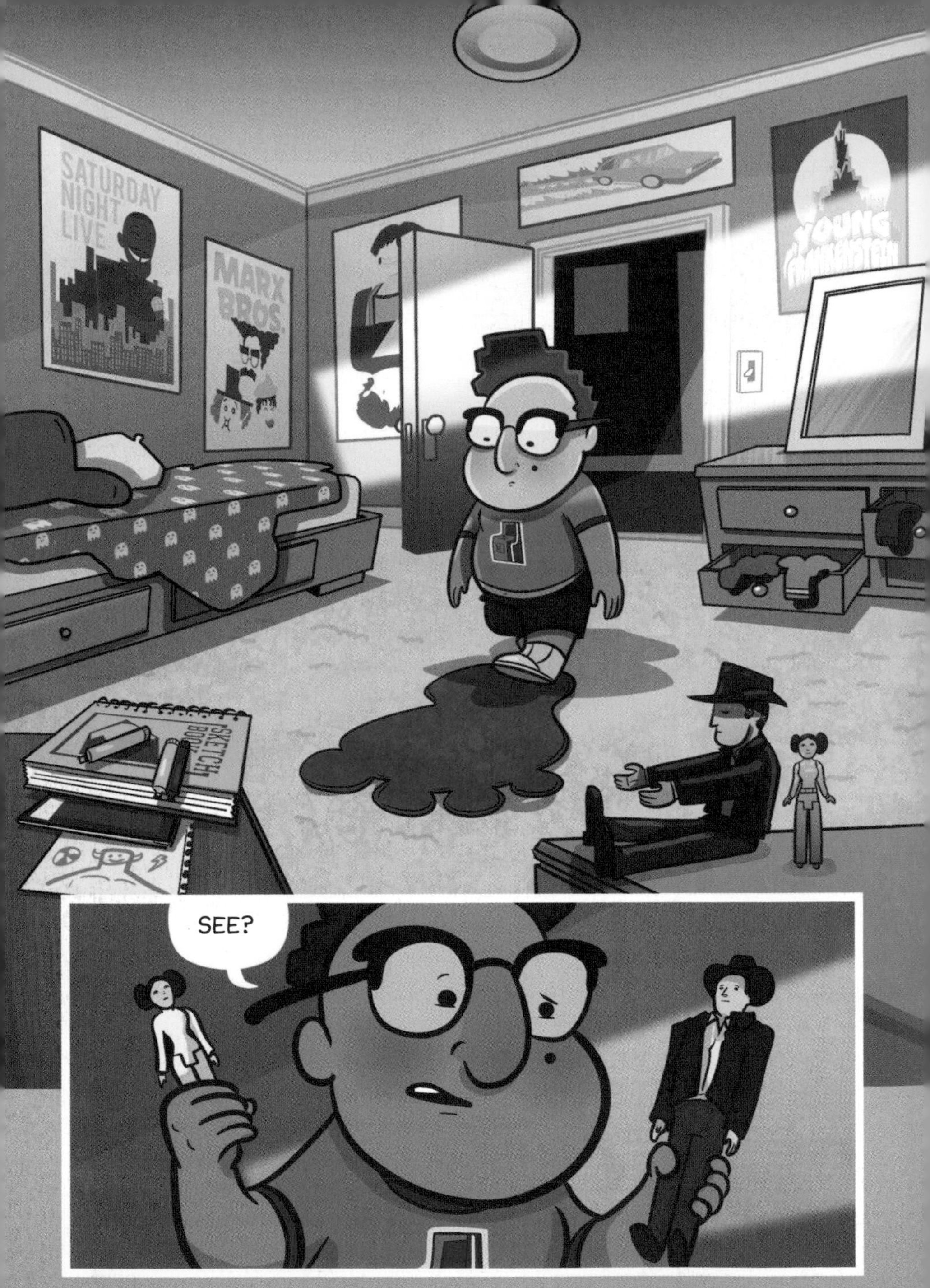
SATURDAY NIGHT LIVE
MARX BROS.
YOUNG FRANKENSTEIN
SKETCH BOOK
SEE?

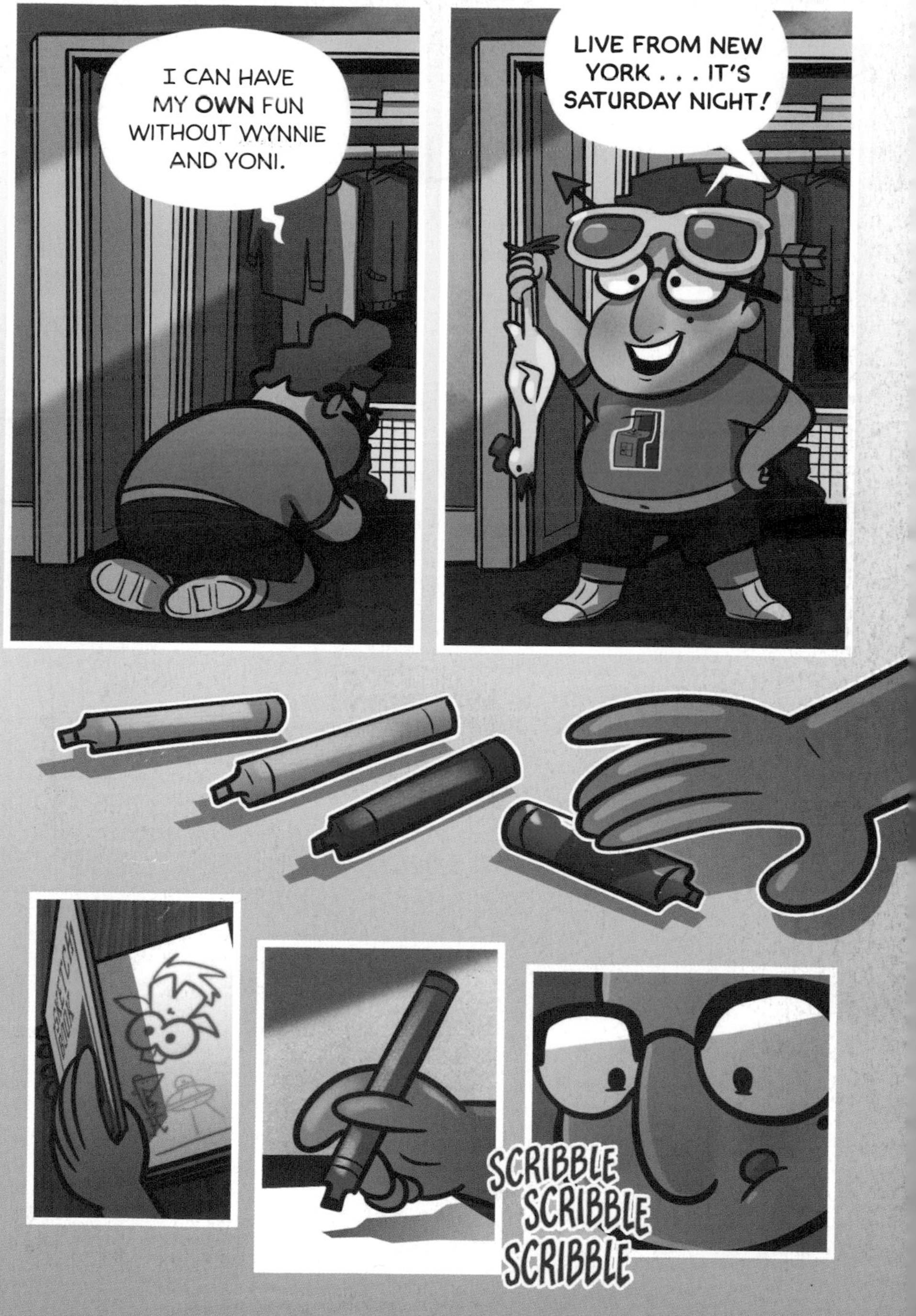
I CAN HAVE MY OWN FUN WITHOUT WYNNIE AND YONI.
LIVE FROM NEW YORK . . . IT'S SATURDAY NIGHT!
SCRIBBLE
SCRIBBLE
SCRIBBLE

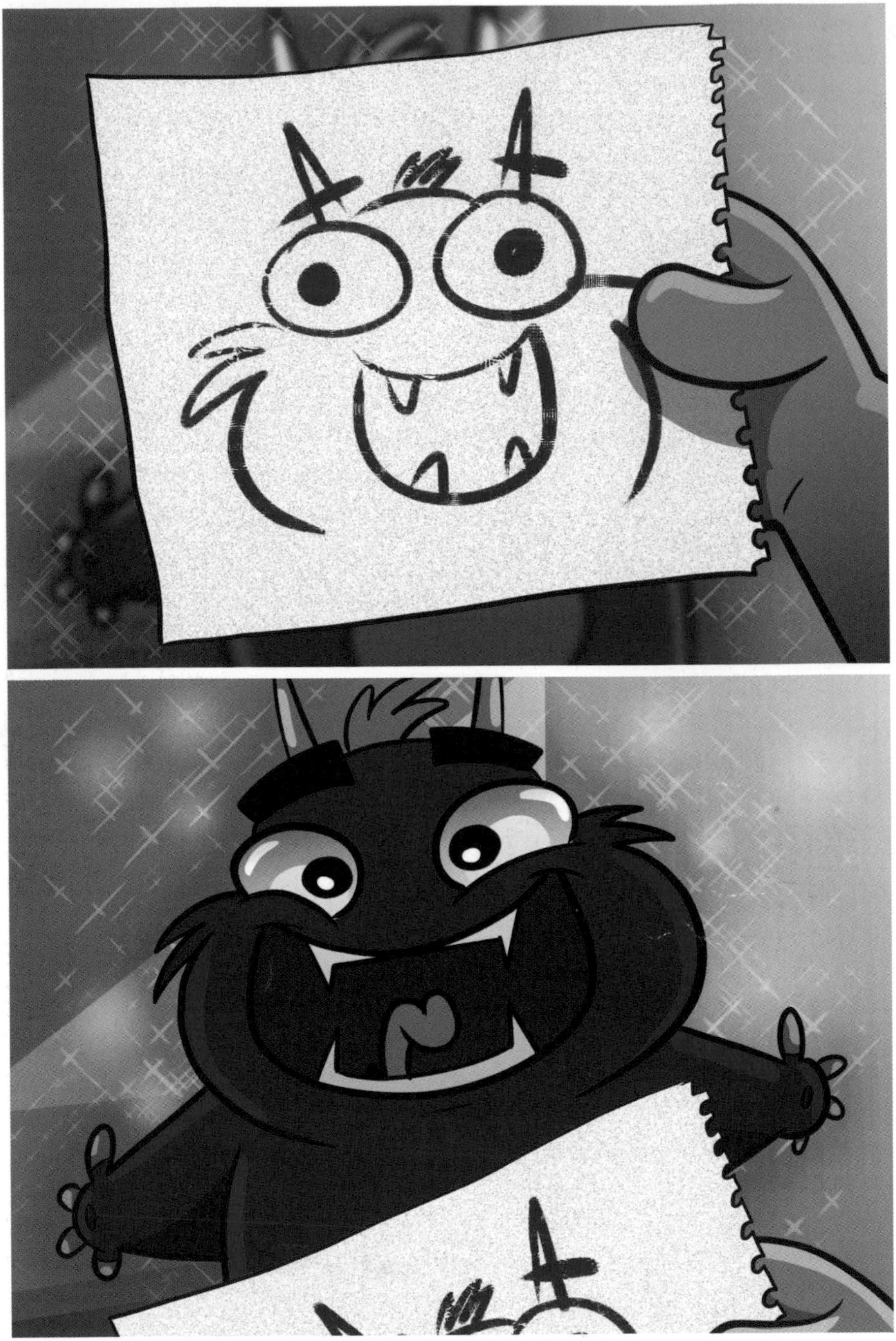

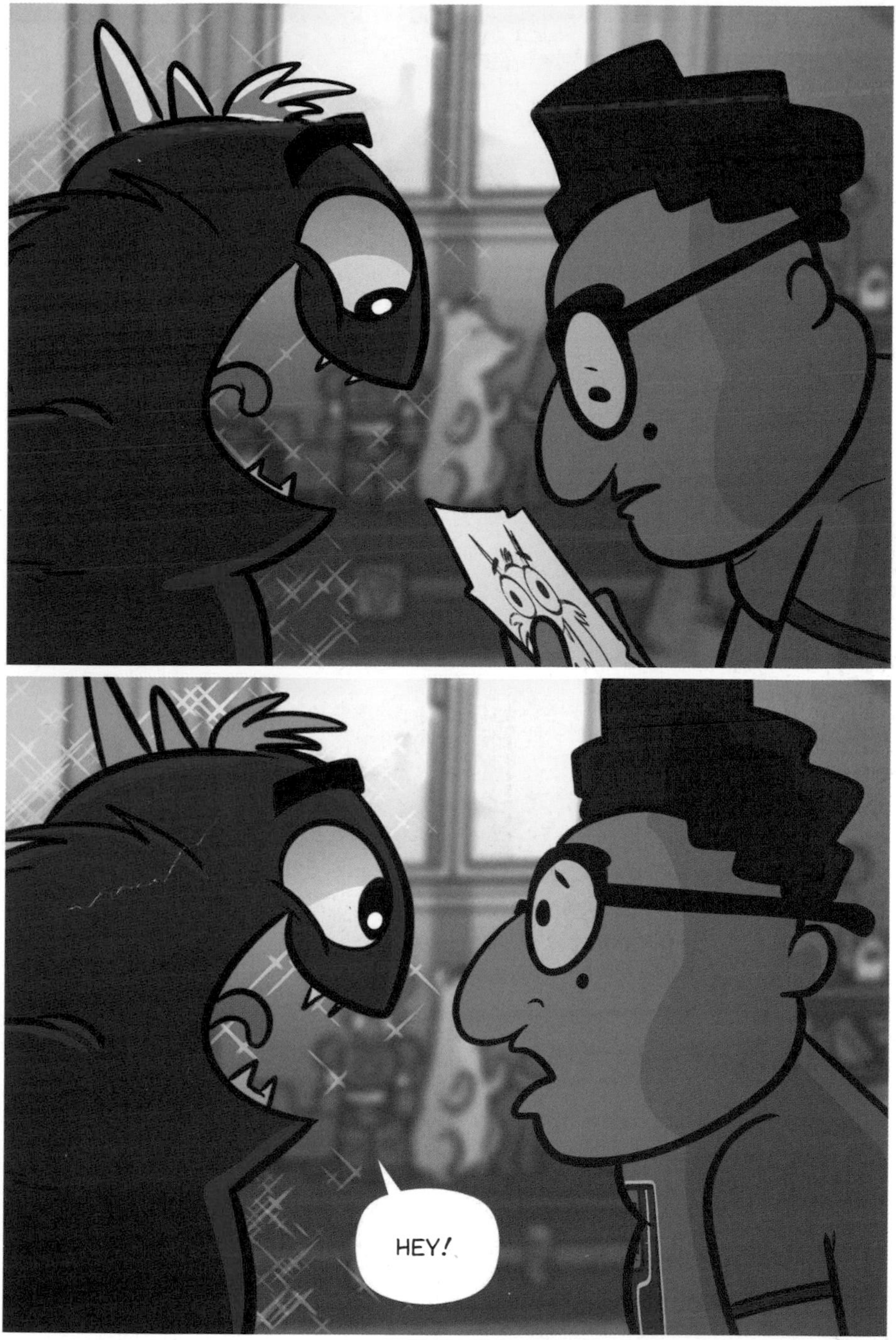
HEY!

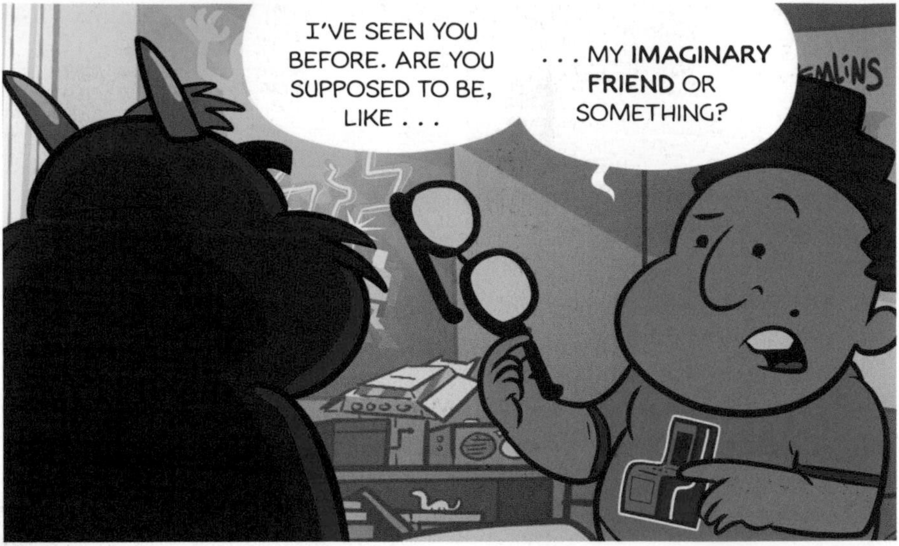
I'VE SEEN YOU BEFORE. ARE YOU SUPPOSED TO BE, LIKE . . .
. . . MY **IMAGINARY FRIEND** OR SOMETHING?
EMLINS

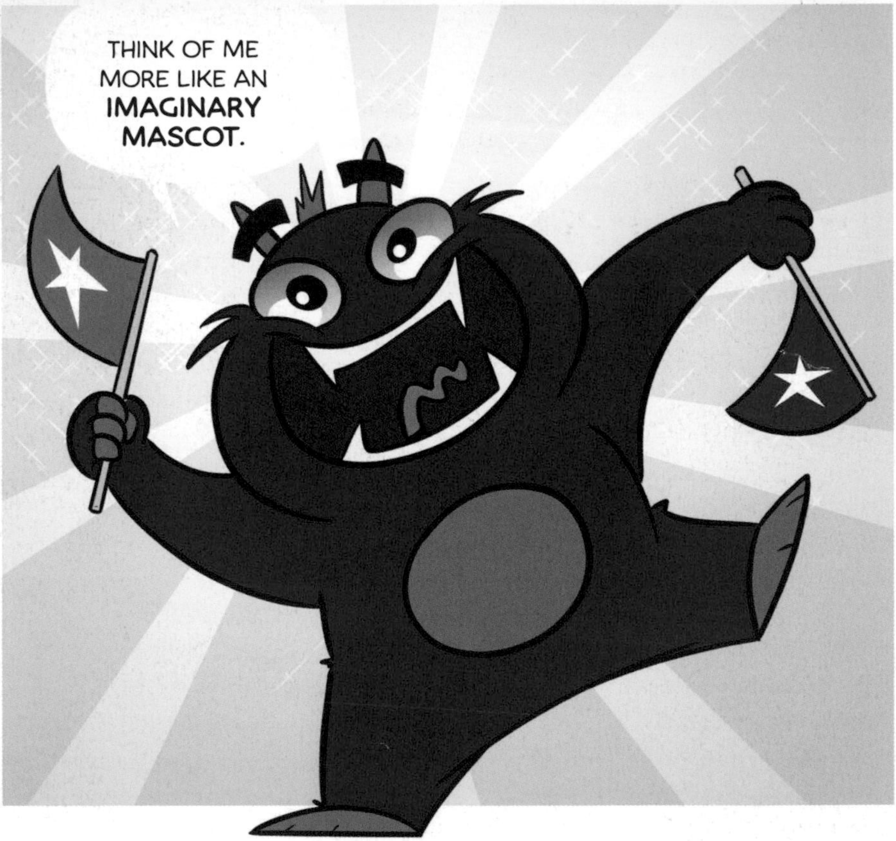
THINK OF ME MORE LIKE AN **IMAGINARY MASCOT.**

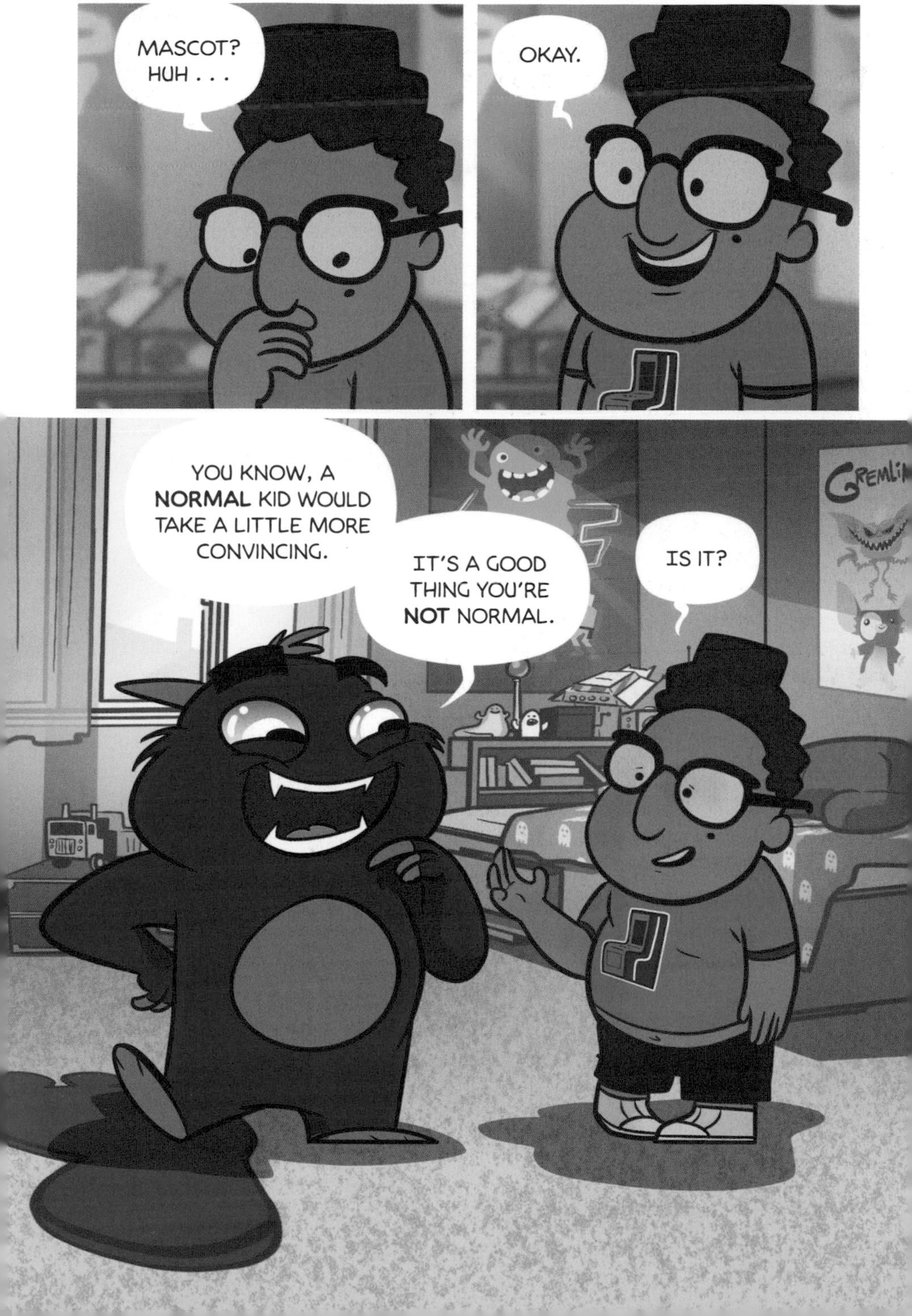
MASCOT? HUH . . .
OKAY.
YOU KNOW, A **NORMAL** KID WOULD TAKE A LITTLE MORE CONVINCING.
IT'S A GOOD THING YOU'RE **NOT** NORMAL.
IS IT?

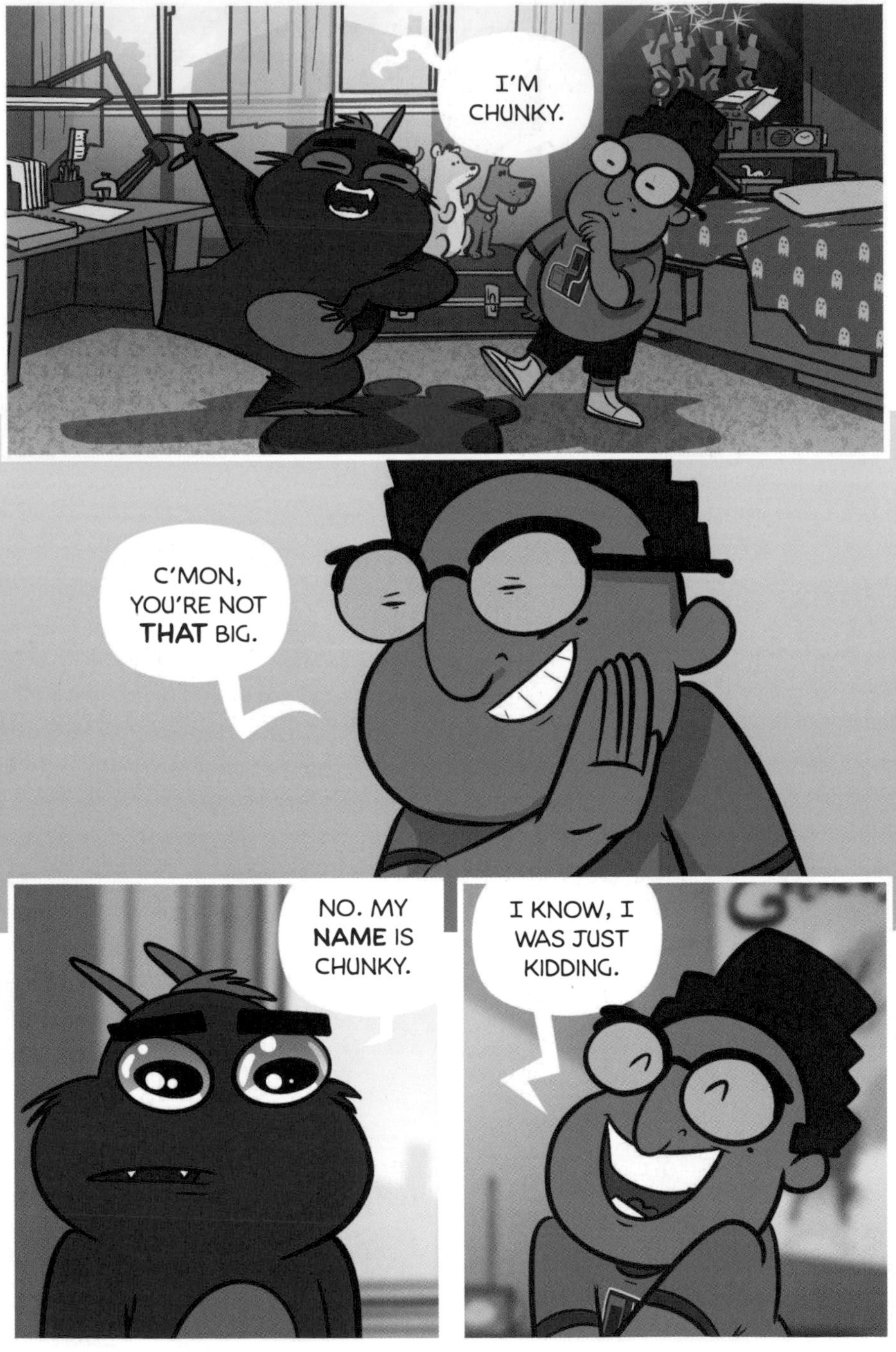
I'M CHUNKY.
C'MON, YOU'RE NOT **THAT** BIG.
NO. MY **NAME** IS CHUNKY.
I KNOW, I WAS JUST KIDDING.

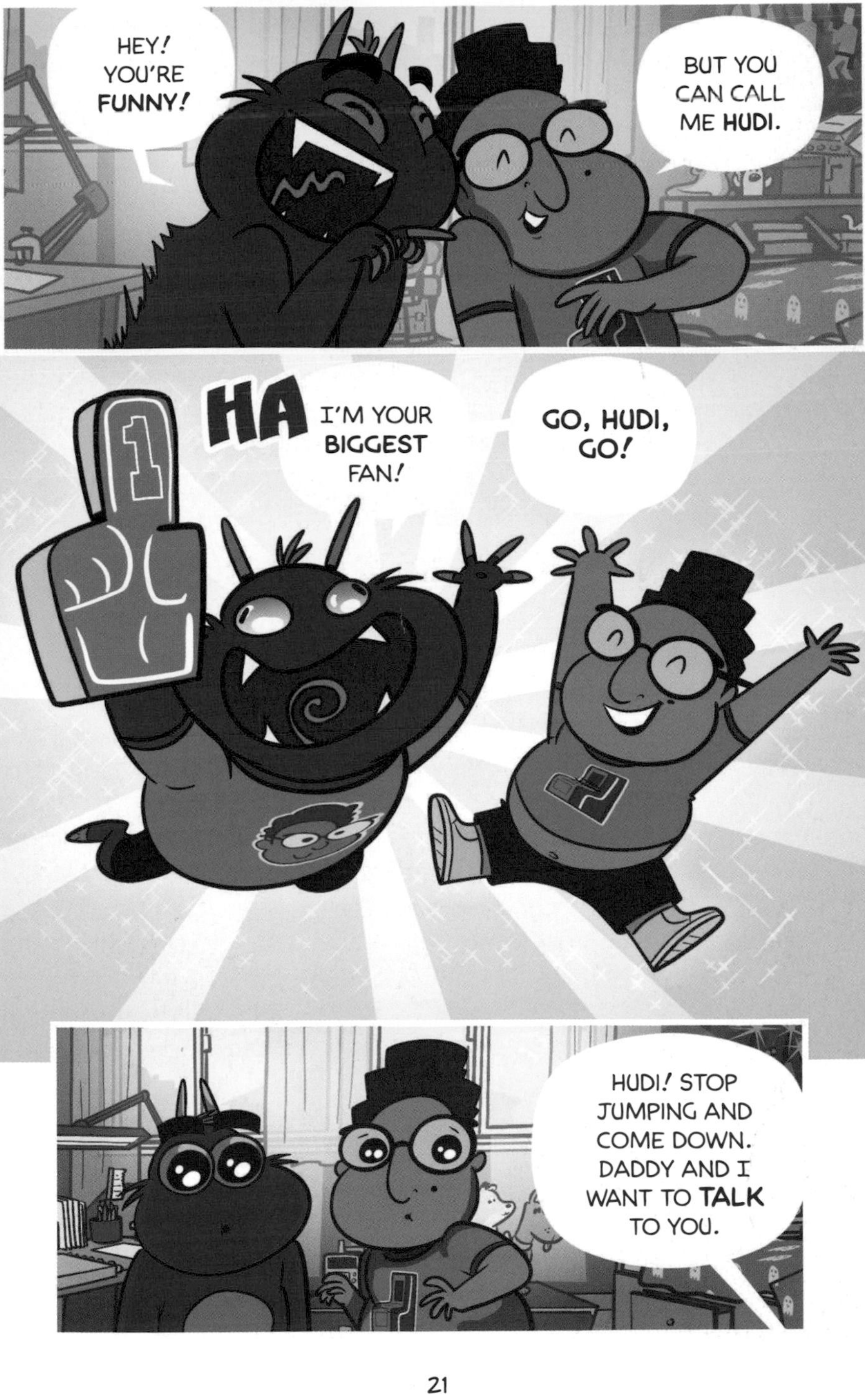

HEY! YOU'RE FUNNY!
BUT YOU CAN CALL ME HUDI.
HA
I'M YOUR BIGGEST FAN!
GO, HUDI, GO!
HUDI! STOP JUMPING AND COME DOWN. DADDY AND I WANT TO TALK TO YOU.

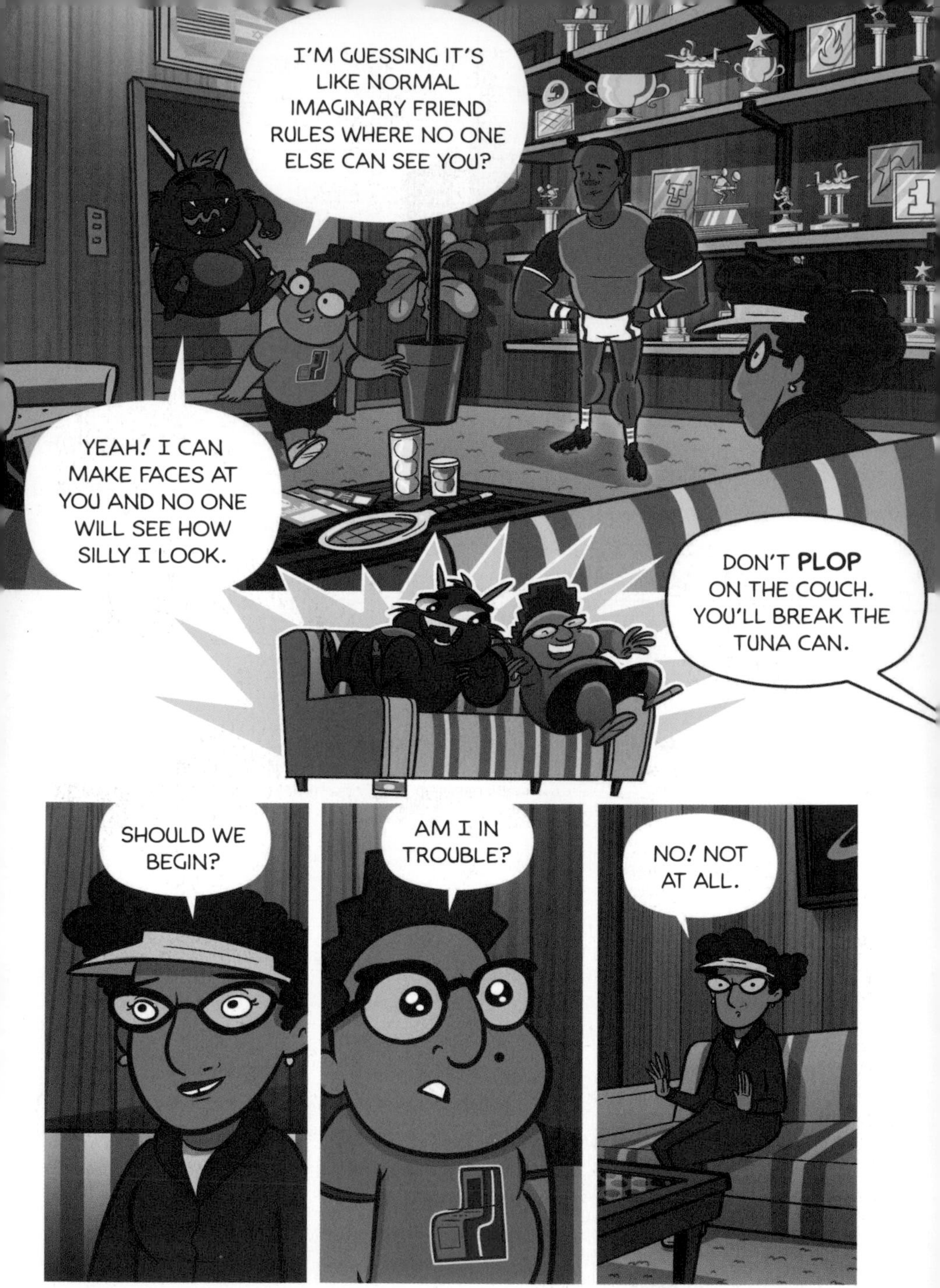
I'M GUESSING IT'S LIKE NORMAL IMAGINARY FRIEND RULES WHERE NO ONE ELSE CAN SEE YOU?
YEAH! I CAN MAKE FACES AT YOU AND NO ONE WILL SEE HOW SILLY I LOOK.
DON'T **PLOP** ON THE COUCH. YOU'LL BREAK THE TUNA CAN.
SHOULD WE BEGIN?
AM I IN TROUBLE?
NO! NOT AT ALL.

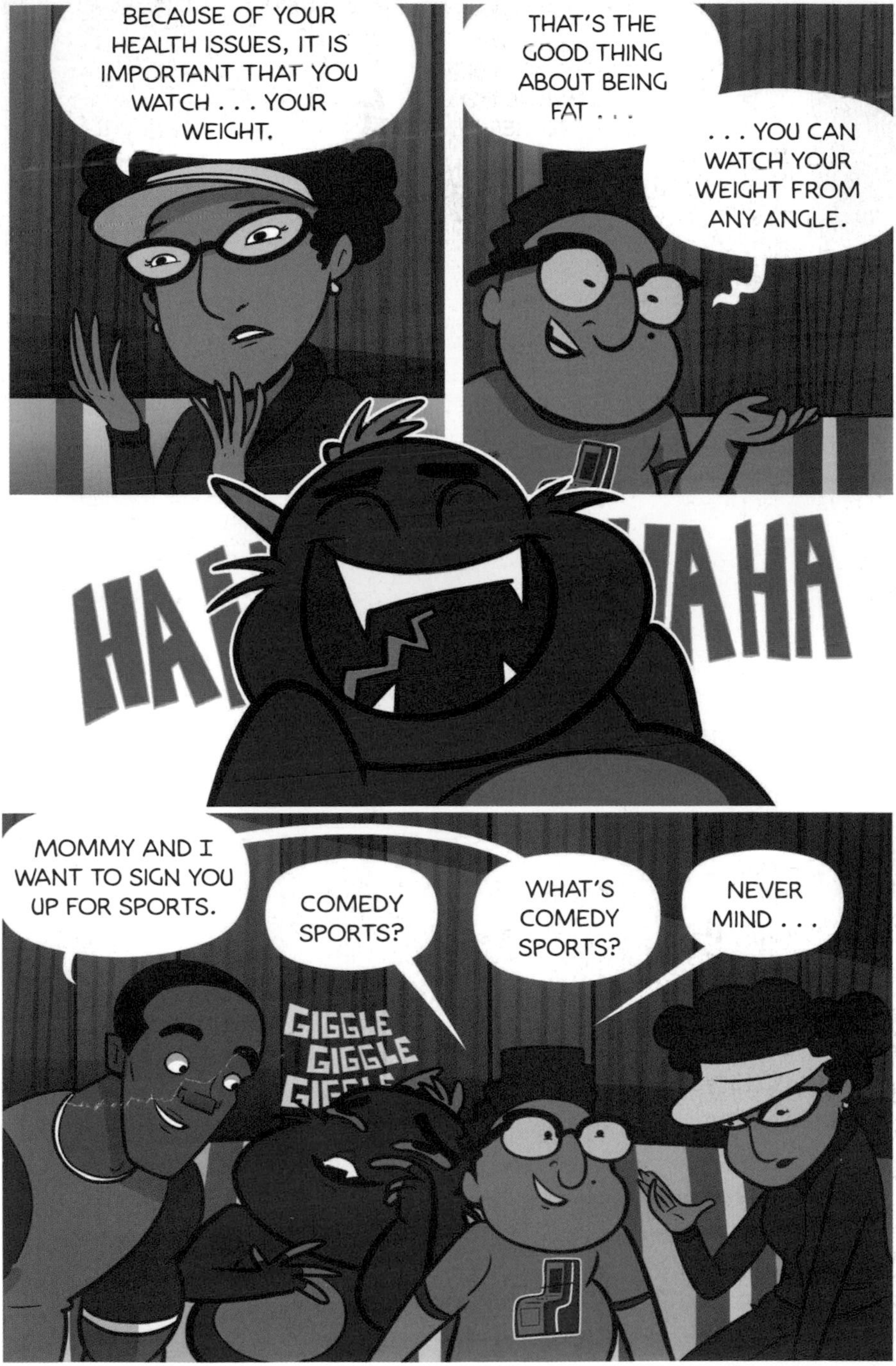
BECAUSE OF YOUR HEALTH ISSUES, IT IS IMPORTANT THAT YOU WATCH . . . YOUR WEIGHT.
THAT'S THE GOOD THING ABOUT BEING FAT . . .
. . . YOU CAN WATCH YOUR WEIGHT FROM ANY ANGLE.
HA
AHA
MOMMY AND I WANT TO SIGN YOU UP FOR SPORTS.
GIGGLE
GIGGLE
COMEDY SPORTS?
WHAT'S COMEDY SPORTS?
NEVER MIND . . .

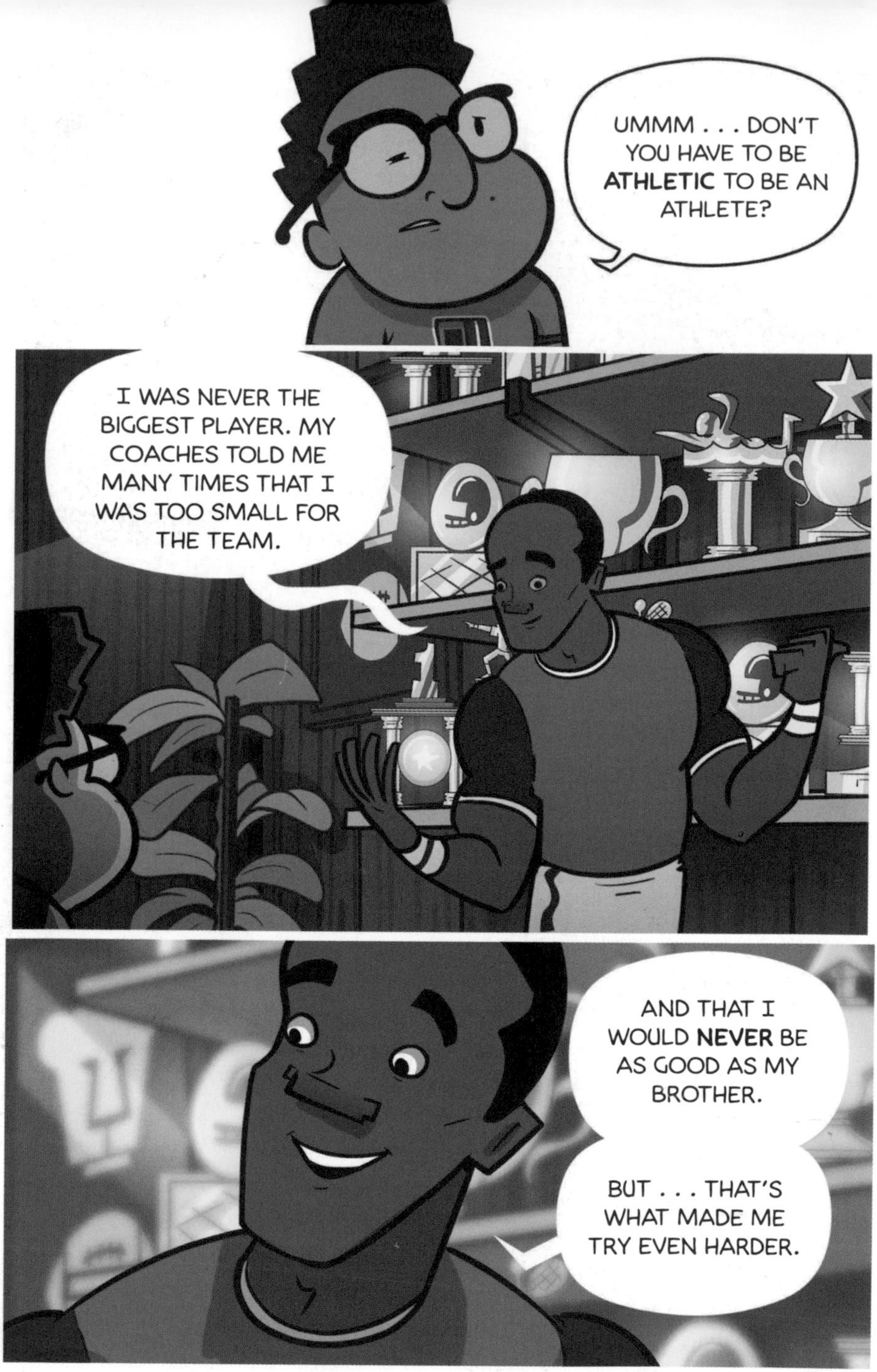

UMMM . . . DON'T YOU HAVE TO BE **ATHLETIC** TO BE AN ATHLETE?
I WAS NEVER THE BIGGEST PLAYER. MY COACHES TOLD ME MANY TIMES THAT I WAS TOO SMALL FOR THE TEAM.
AND THAT I WOULD **NEVER** BE AS GOOD AS MY BROTHER.
BUT . . . THAT'S WHAT MADE ME TRY EVEN HARDER.

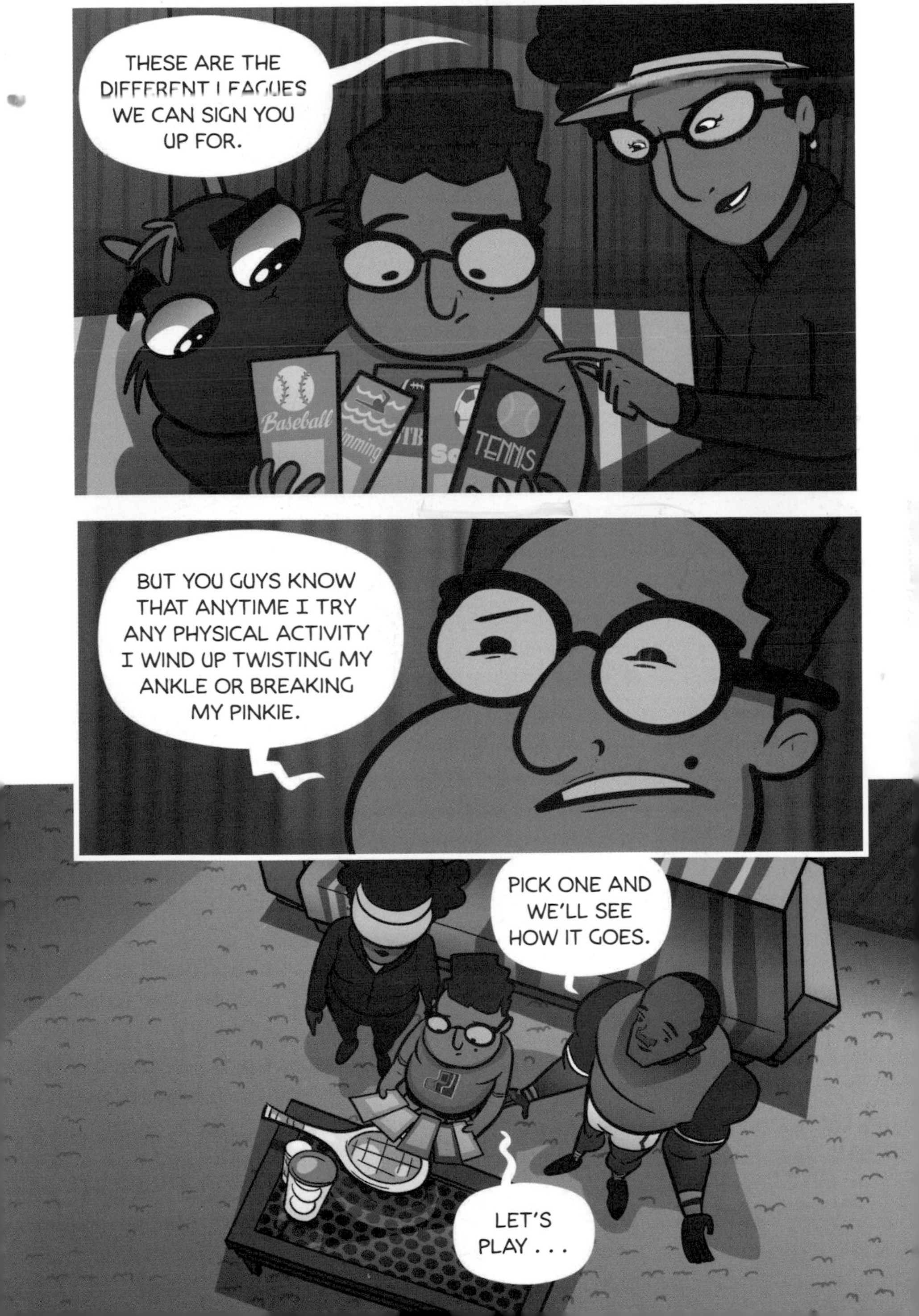
THESE ARE THE DIFFERENT LEAGUES WE CAN SIGN YOU UP FOR.
Baseball
TENNIS
BUT YOU GUYS KNOW THAT ANYTIME I TRY ANY PHYSICAL ACTIVITY I WIND UP TWISTING MY ANKLE OR BREAKING MY PINKIE.
PICK ONE AND WE'LL SEE HOW IT GOES.
LET'S PLAY . . .

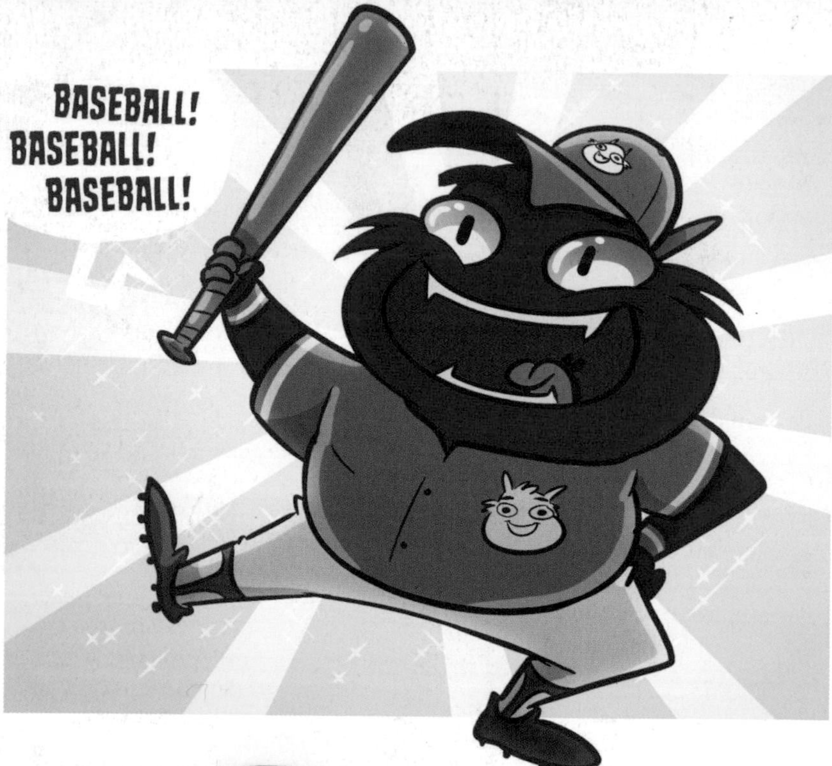
BASEBALL! BASEBALL! BASEBALL!

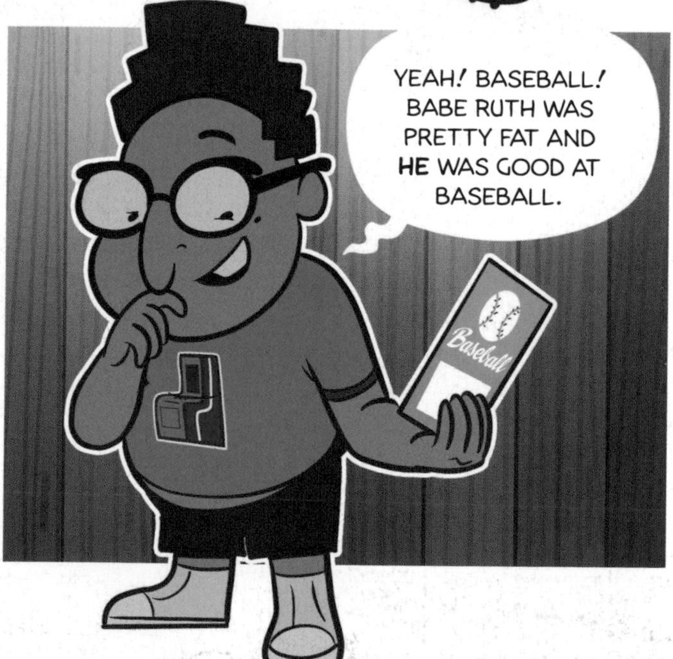
YEAH! BASEBALL! BABE RUTH WAS PRETTY FAT AND HE WAS GOOD AT BASEBALL.
Baseball

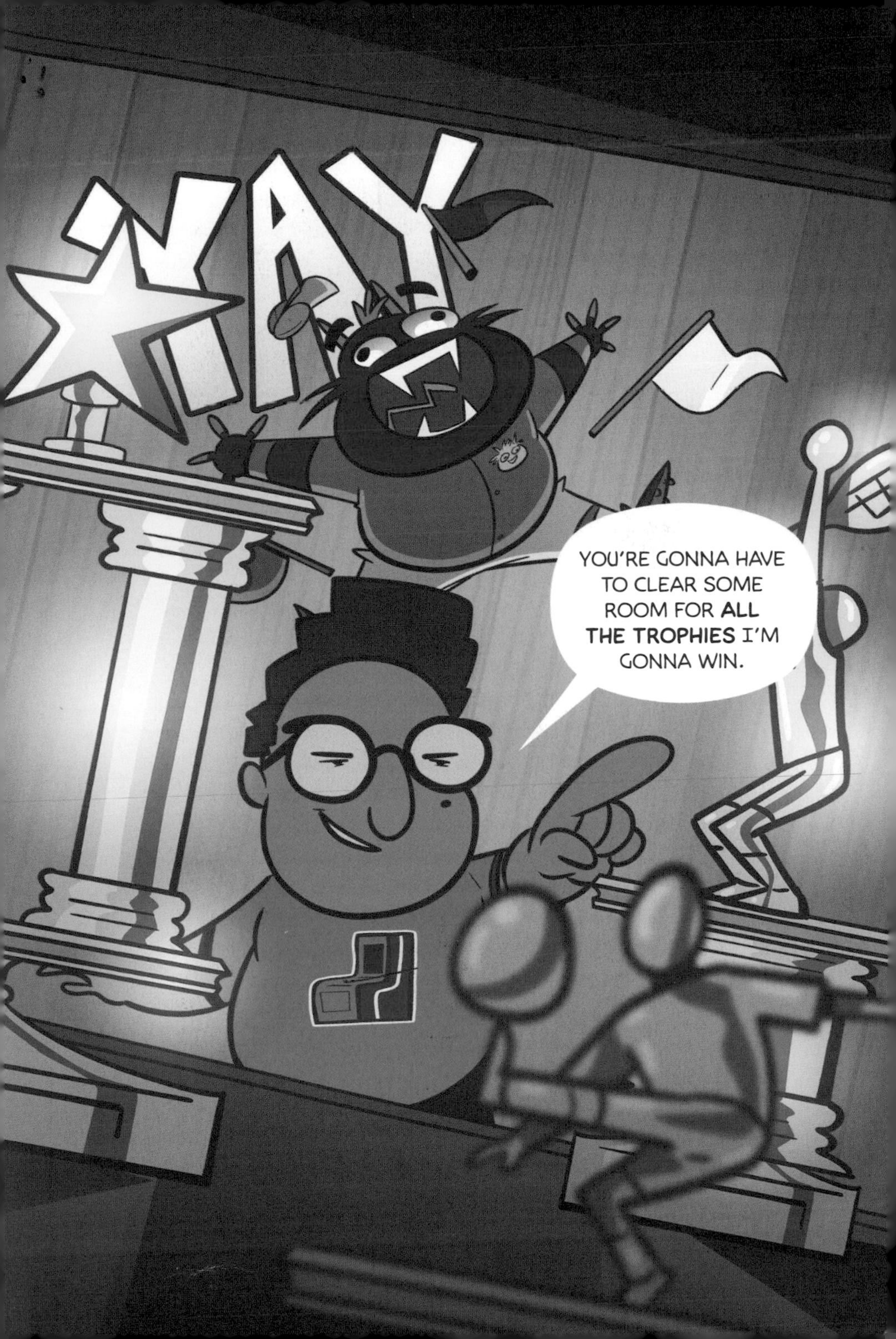
YAY
YOU'RE GONNA HAVE TO CLEAR SOME ROOM FOR **ALL THE TROPHIES** I'M GONNA WIN.

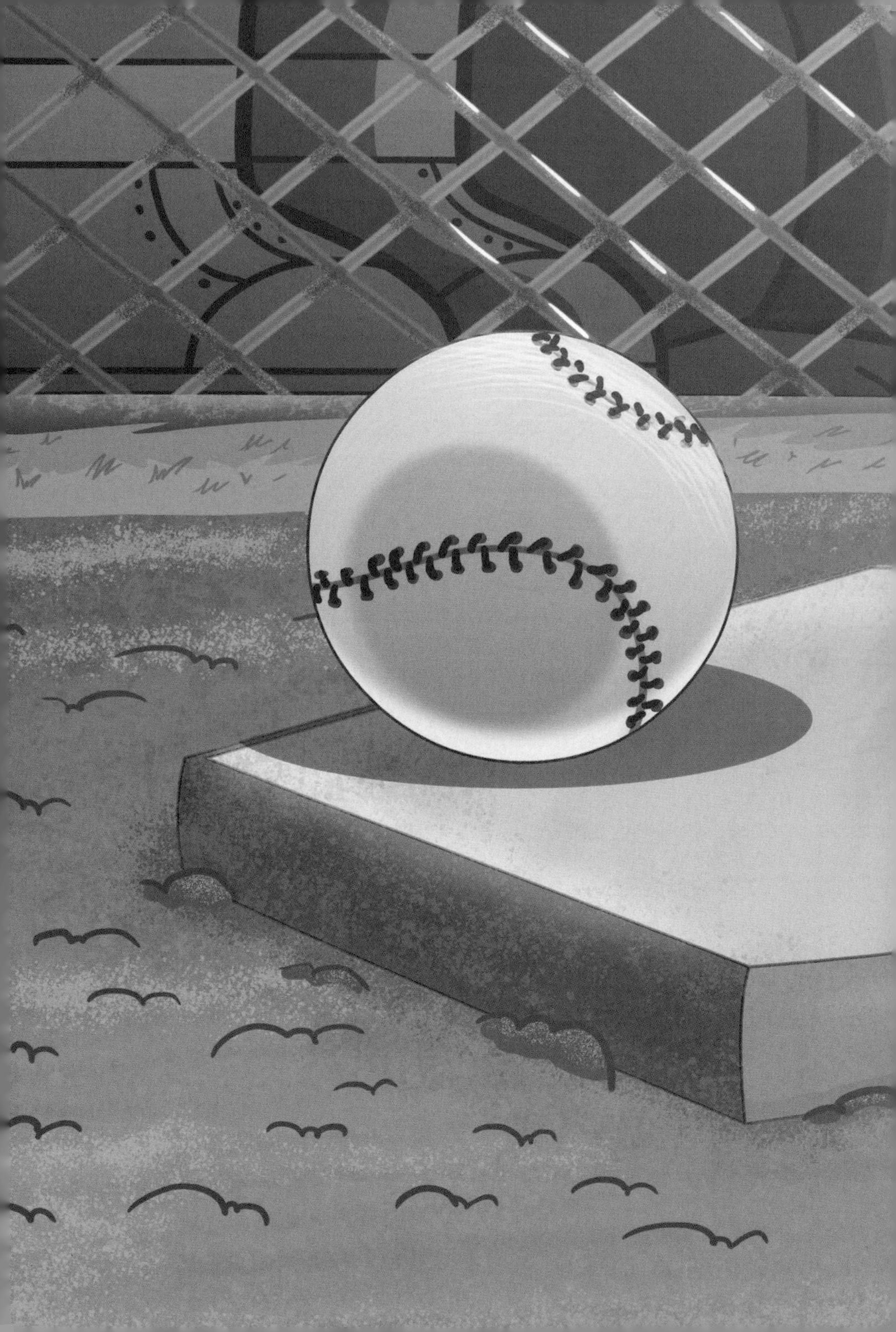

CHAPTER TWO
Baseball

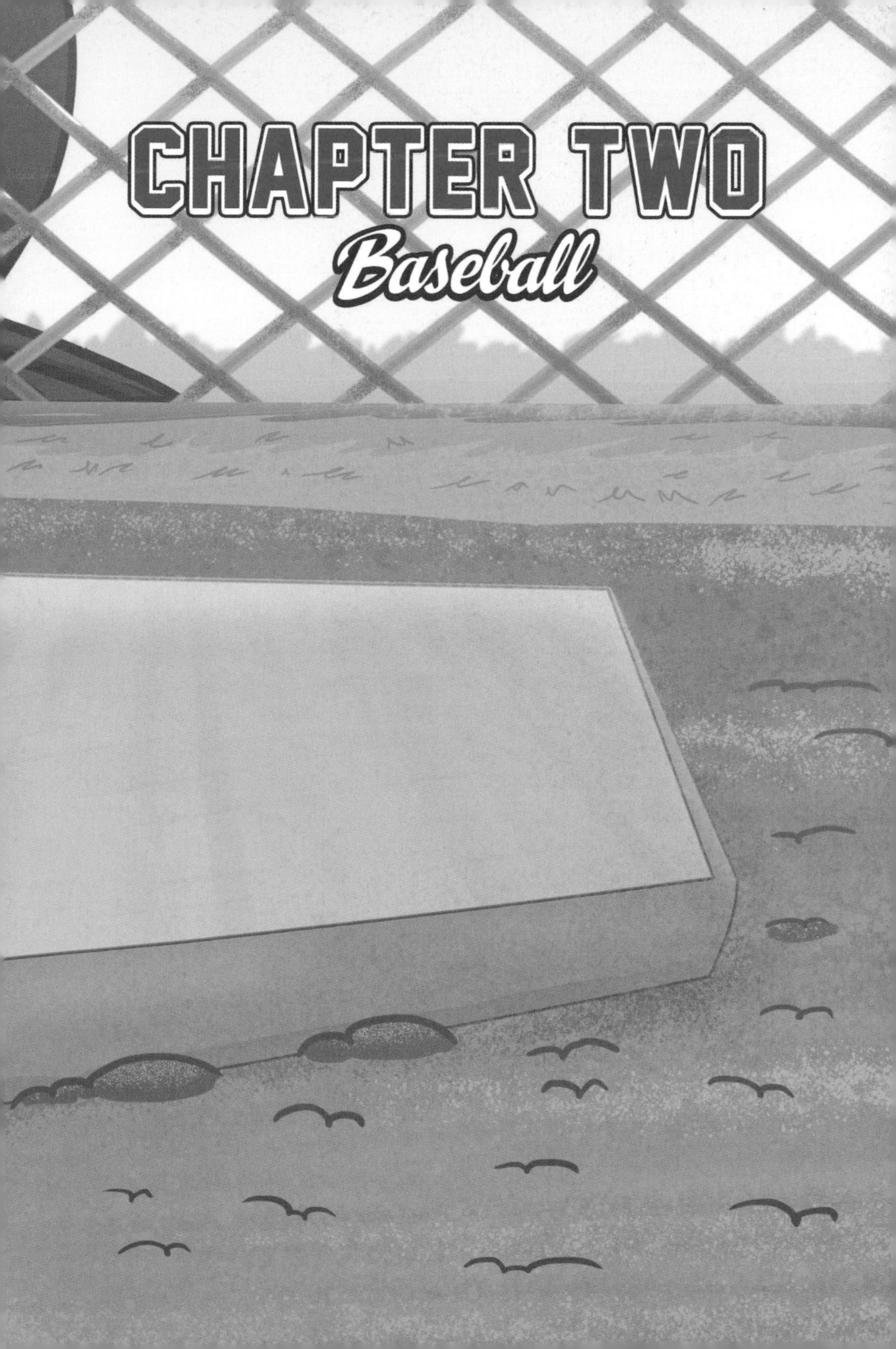

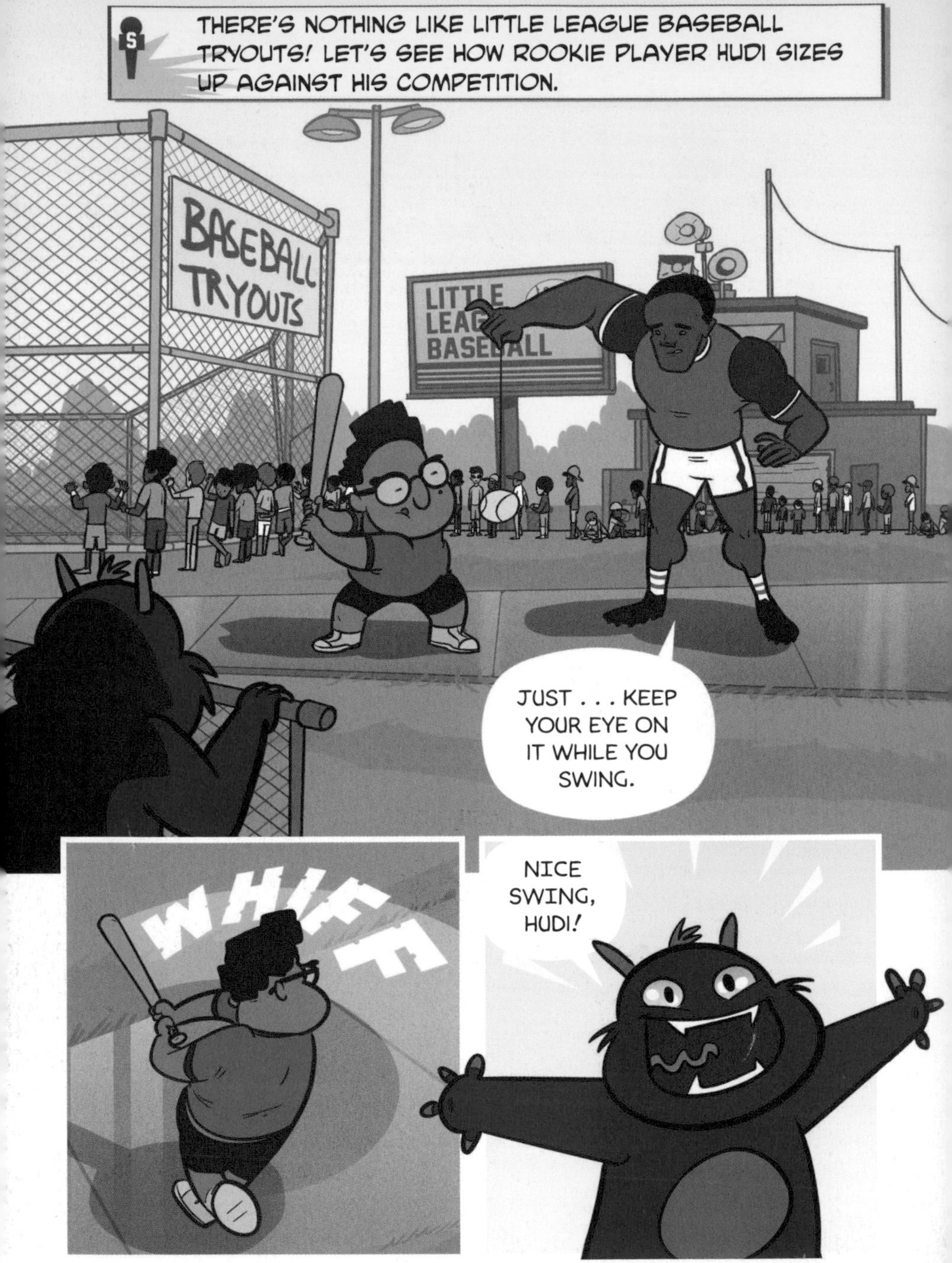
THERE'S NOTHING LIKE LITTLE LEAGUE BASEBALL TRYOUTS! LET'S SEE HOW ROOKIE PLAYER HUDI SIZES UP AGAINST HIS COMPETITION.
BASEBALL TRYOUTS
LITTLE LEAGUE BASEBALL
JUST . . . KEEP YOUR EYE ON IT WHILE YOU SWING.
WHIFF
NICE SWING, HUDI!

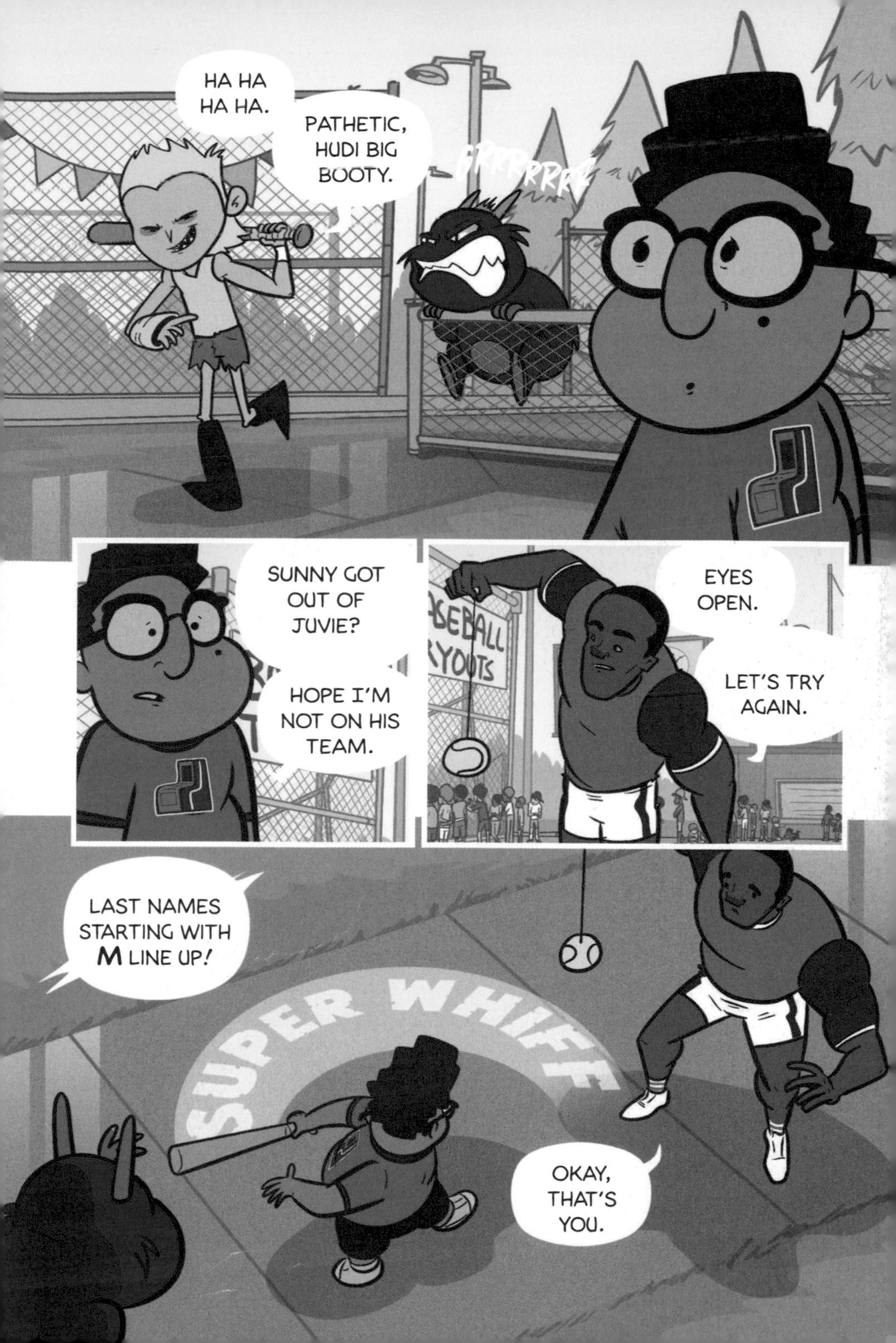
HA HA HA HA.
PATHETIC, HUDI BIG BOOTY.
GRRRRRRR
SUNNY GOT OUT OF JUVIE?
HOPE I'M NOT ON HIS TEAM.
EYES OPEN.
LET'S TRY AGAIN.
LAST NAMES STARTING WITH **M** LINE UP!
SUPER WHIFF
OKAY, THAT'S YOU.

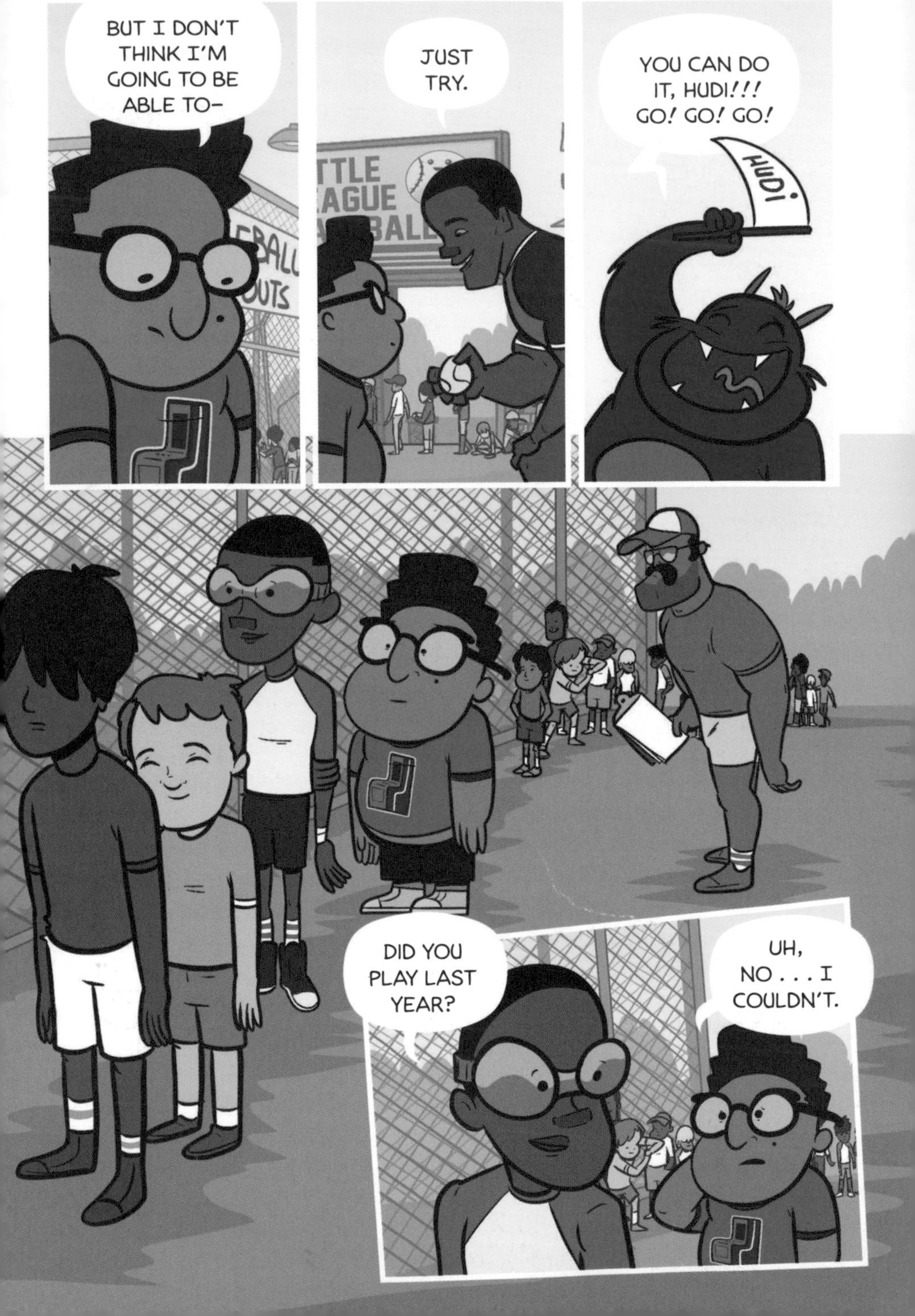
BUT I DON'T THINK I'M GOING TO BE ABLE TO–
JUST TRY.
YOU CAN DO IT, HUDI!!! GO! GO! GO!
HUDI
DID YOU PLAY LAST YEAR?
UH, NO . . . I COULDN'T.

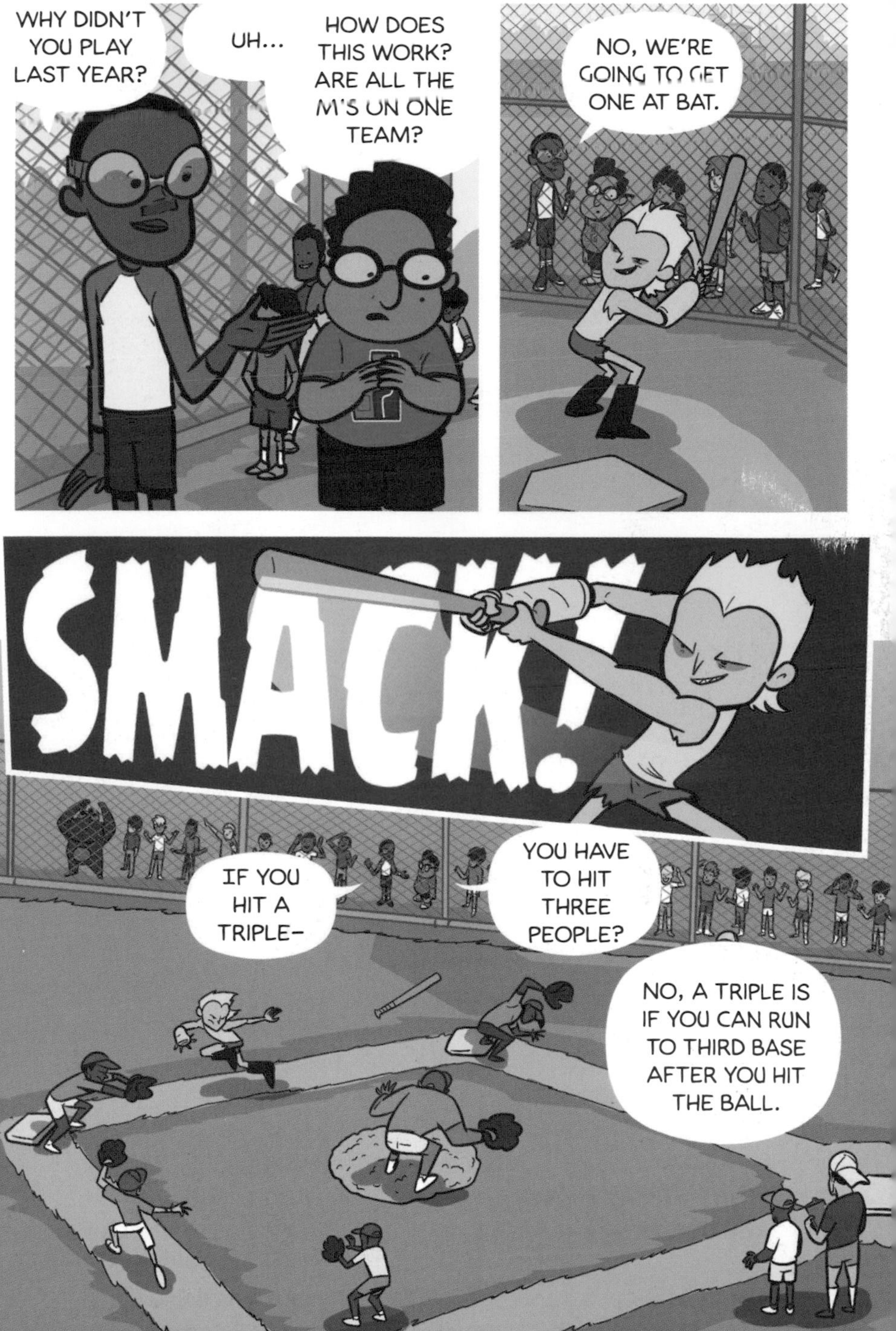
WHY DIDN'T YOU PLAY LAST YEAR?
UH...
HOW DOES THIS WORK? ARE ALL THE M'S ON ONE TEAM?
NO, WE'RE GOING TO GET ONE AT BAT.
SMACK!
IF YOU HIT A TRIPLE-
YOU HAVE TO HIT THREE PEOPLE?
NO, A TRIPLE IS IF YOU CAN RUN TO THIRD BASE AFTER YOU HIT THE BALL.

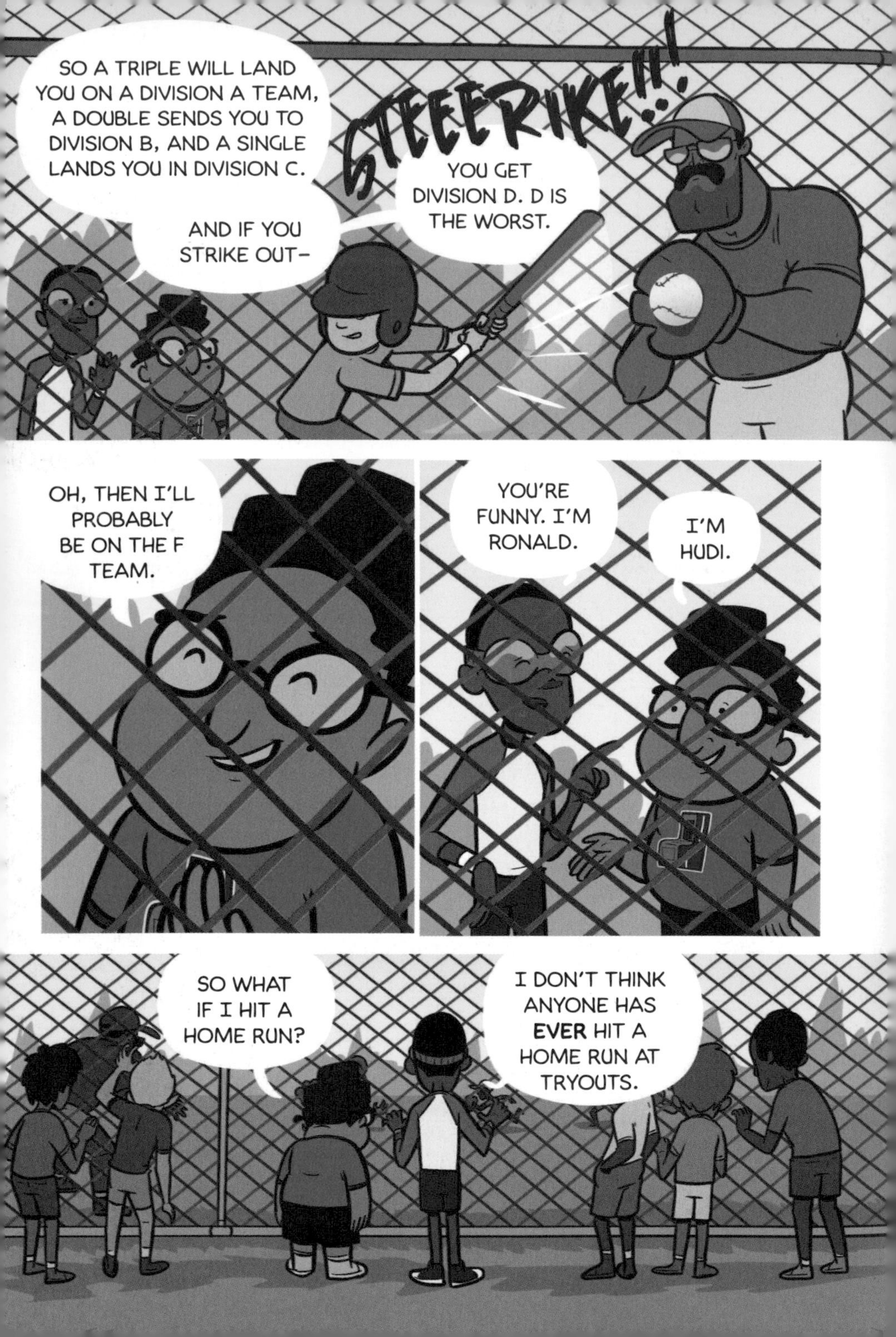
SO A TRIPLE WILL LAND YOU ON A DIVISION A TEAM, A DOUBLE SENDS YOU TO DIVISION B, AND A SINGLE LANDS YOU IN DIVISION C.
AND IF YOU STRIKE OUT–
STEEERIKE!!!
YOU GET DIVISION D. D IS THE WORST.
OH, THEN I'LL PROBABLY BE ON THE F TEAM.
YOU'RE FUNNY. I'M RONALD.
I'M HUDI.
SO WHAT IF I HIT A HOME RUN?
I DON'T THINK ANYONE HAS **EVER** HIT A HOME RUN AT TRYOUTS.

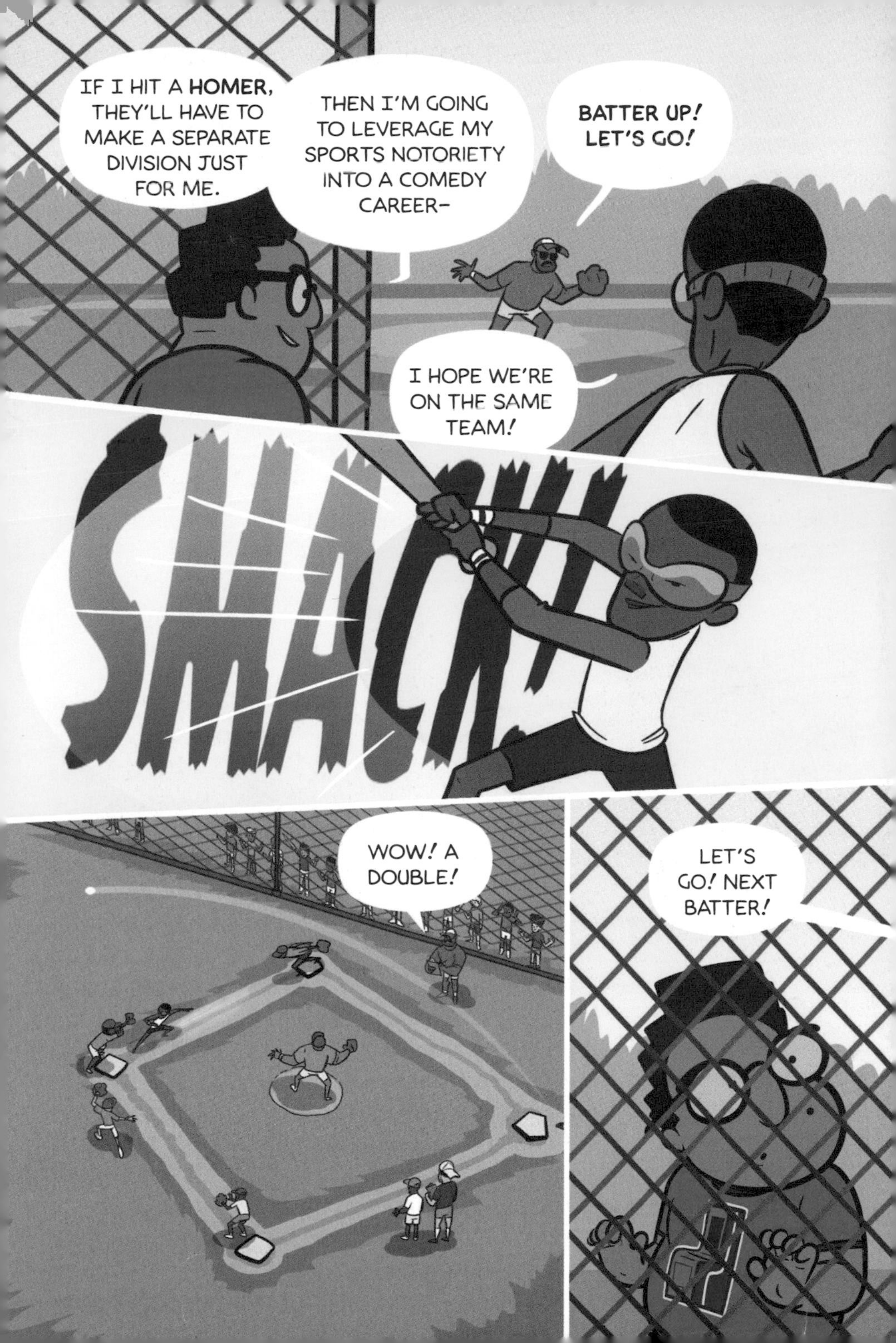
IF I HIT A **HOMER**, THEY'LL HAVE TO MAKE A SEPARATE DIVISION JUST FOR ME.
THEN I'M GOING TO LEVERAGE MY SPORTS NOTORIETY INTO A COMEDY CAREER–
BATTER UP! LET'S GO!
I HOPE WE'RE ON THE SAME TEAM!
SMACK!
WOW! A DOUBLE!
LET'S GO! NEXT BATTER!

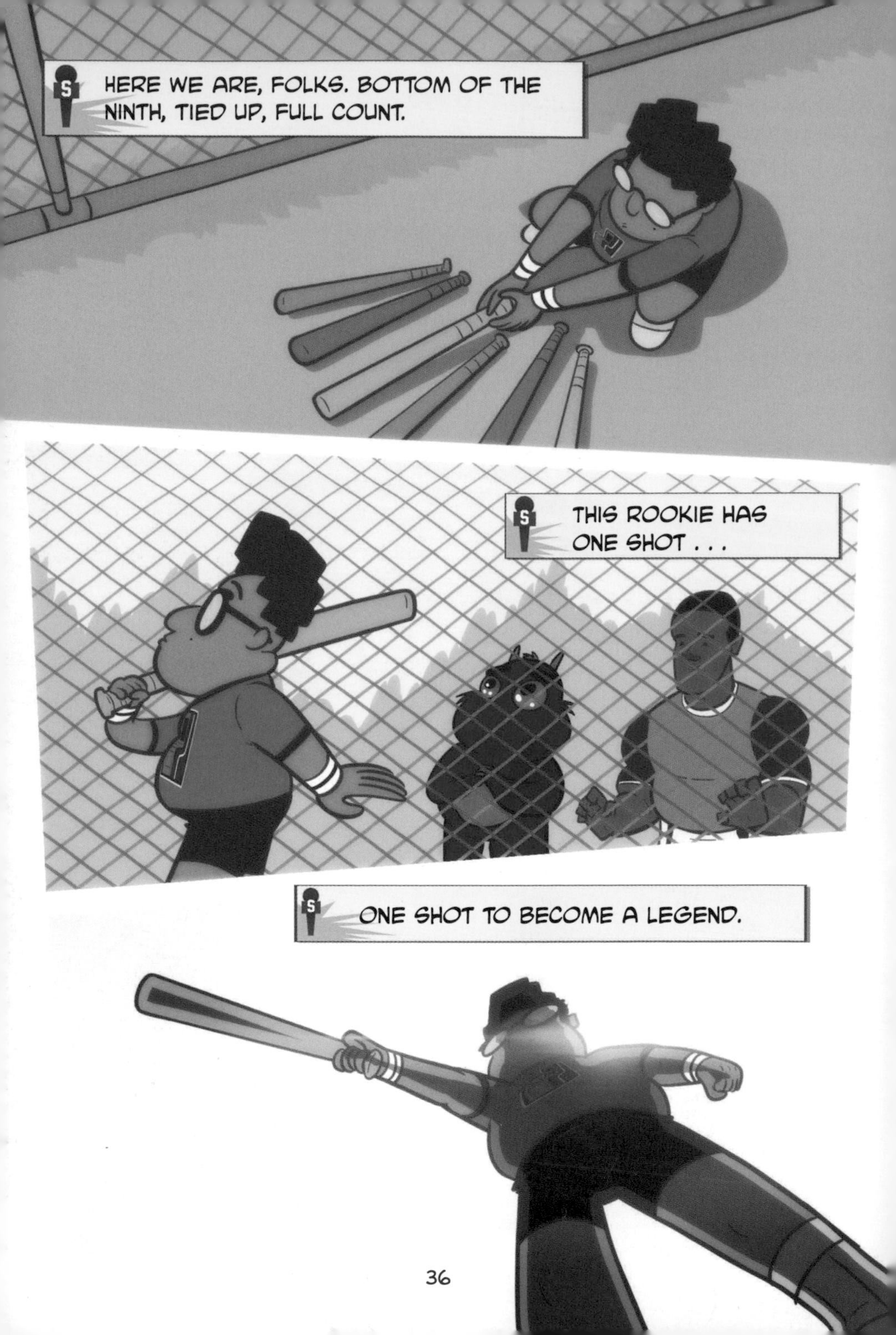
HERE WE ARE, FOLKS. BOTTOM OF THE NINTH, TIED UP, FULL COUNT.
THIS ROOKIE HAS ONE SHOT . . .
ONE SHOT TO BECOME A LEGEND.

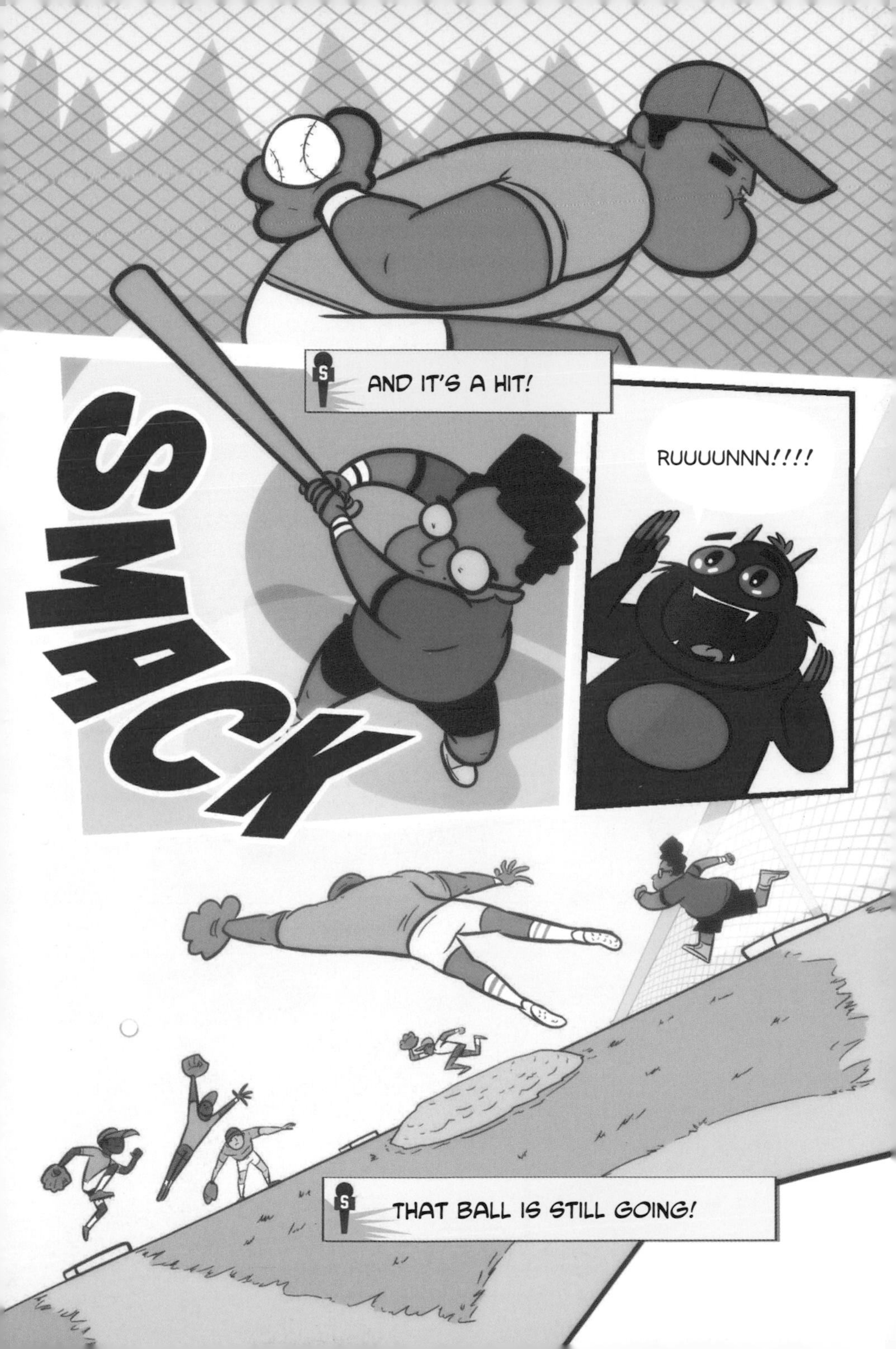
AND IT'S A HIT!
SMACK
RUUUUNNN!!!!
THAT BALL IS STILL GOING!

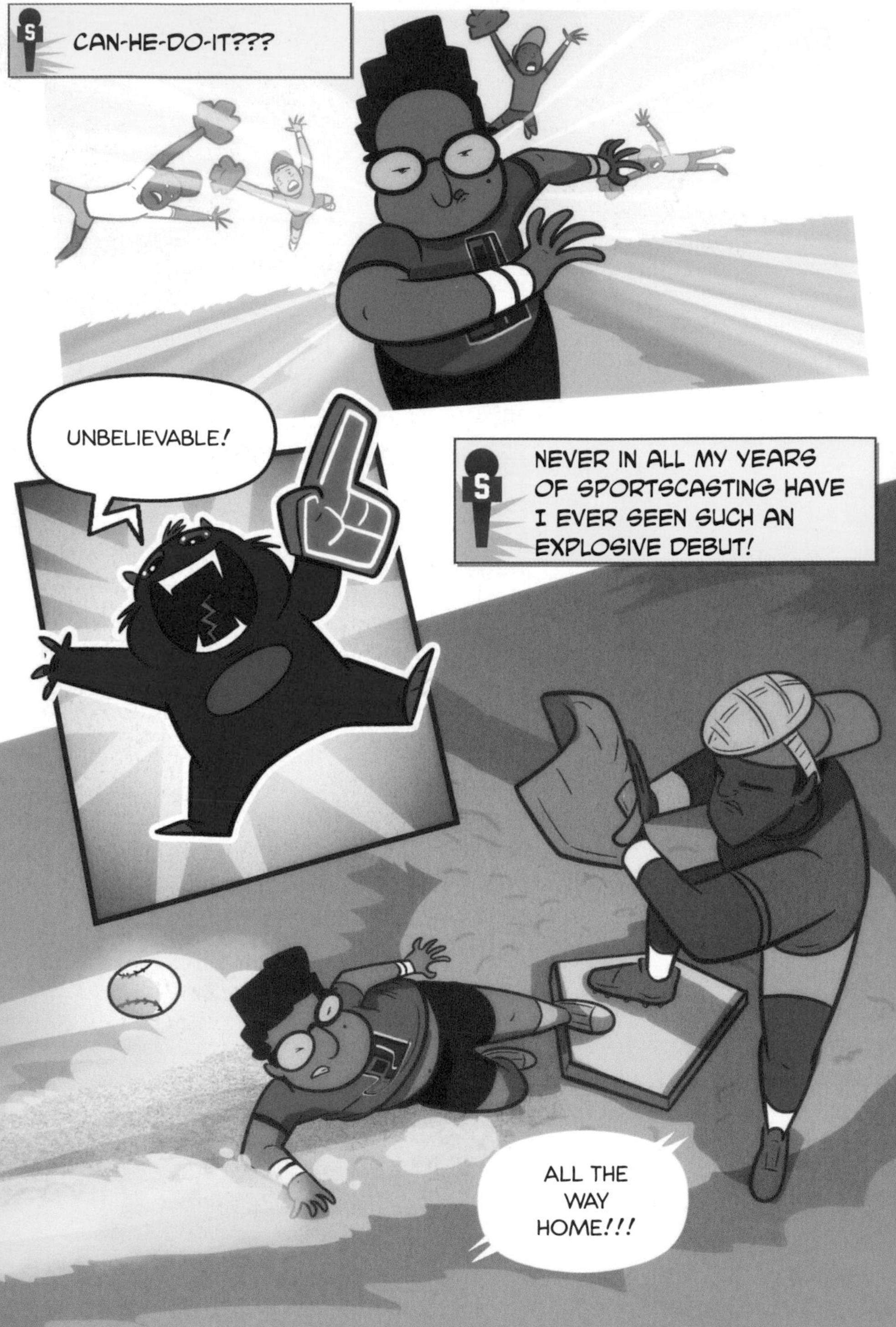

CAN-HE-DO-IT???
UNBELIEVABLE!
NEVER IN ALL MY YEARS OF SPORTSCASTING HAVE I EVER SEEN SUCH AN EXPLOSIVE DEBUT!
ALL THE WAY HOME!!!

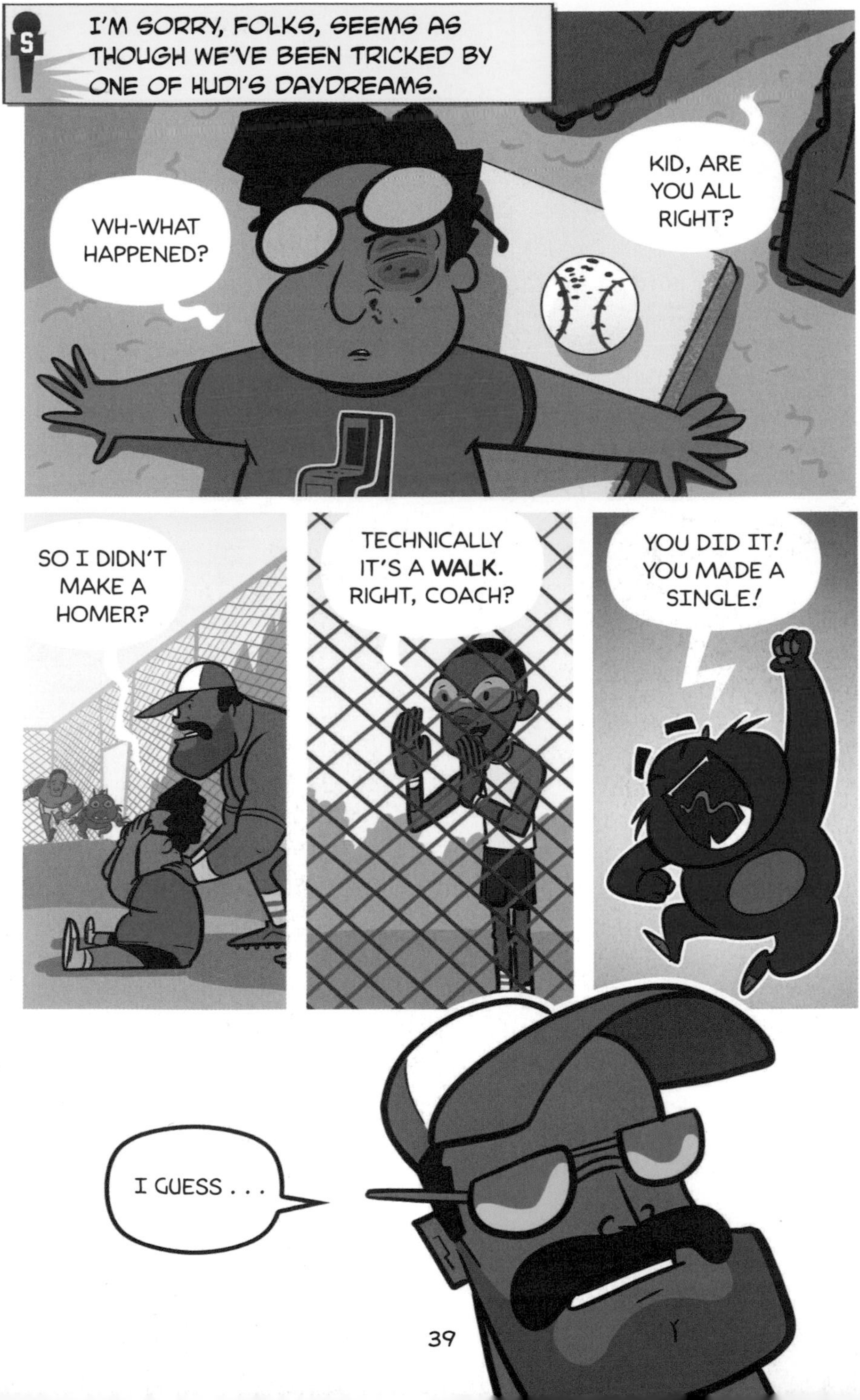
I'M SORRY, FOLKS, SEEMS AS THOUGH WE'VE BEEN TRICKED BY ONE OF HUDI'S DAYDREAMS.
WH-WHAT HAPPENED?
KID, ARE YOU ALL RIGHT?
SO I DIDN'T MAKE A HOMER?
TECHNICALLY IT'S A **WALK**. RIGHT, COACH?
YOU DID IT! YOU MADE A SINGLE!
I GUESS . . .

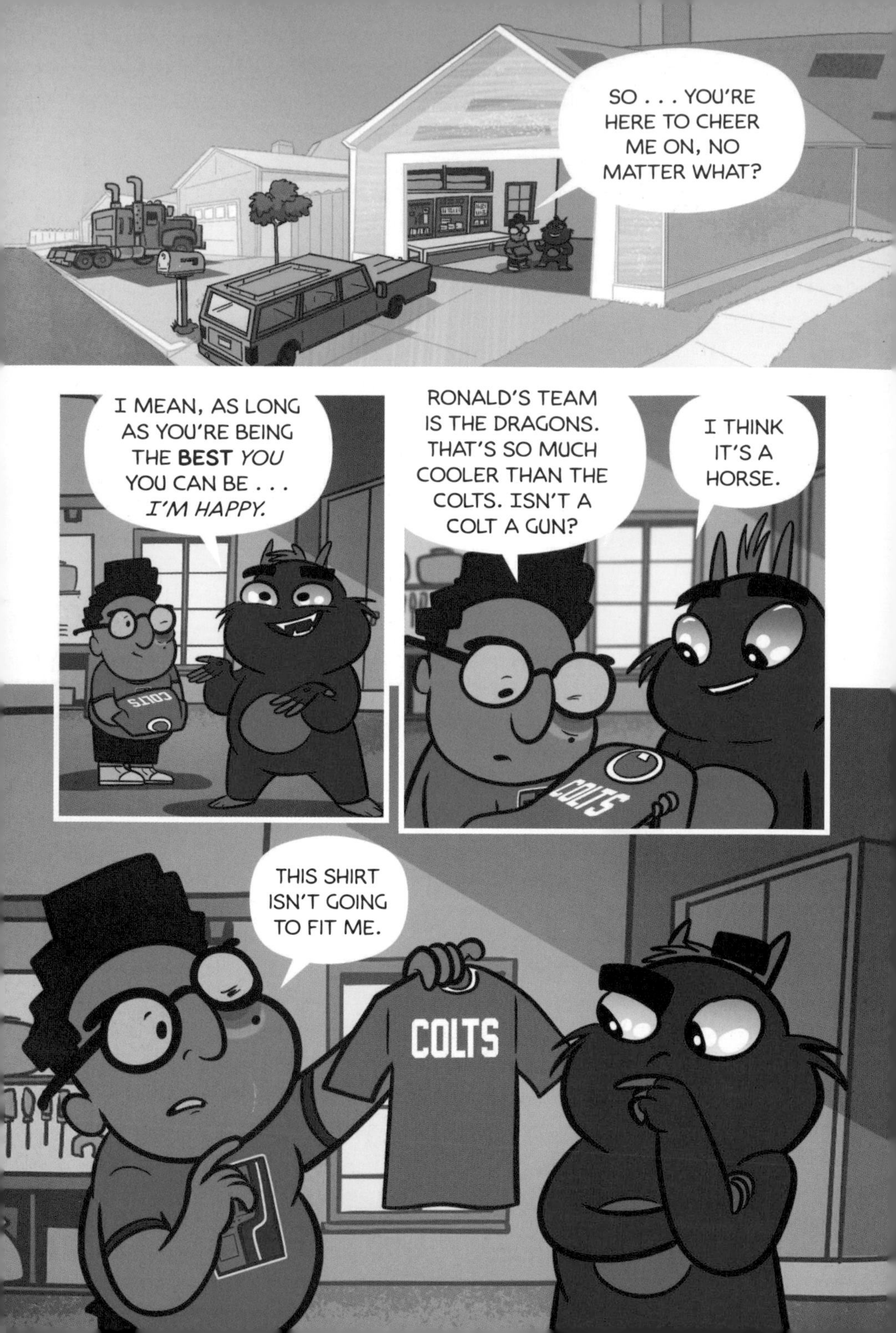
SO . . . YOU'RE HERE TO CHEER ME ON, NO MATTER WHAT?
I MEAN, AS LONG AS YOU'RE BEING THE **BEST** *YOU* YOU CAN BE . . . *I'M HAPPY.*
COLTS
RONALD'S TEAM IS THE DRAGONS. THAT'S SO MUCH COOLER THAN THE COLTS. ISN'T A COLT A GUN?
I THINK IT'S A HORSE.
COLTS
THIS SHIRT ISN'T GOING TO FIT ME.
COLTS

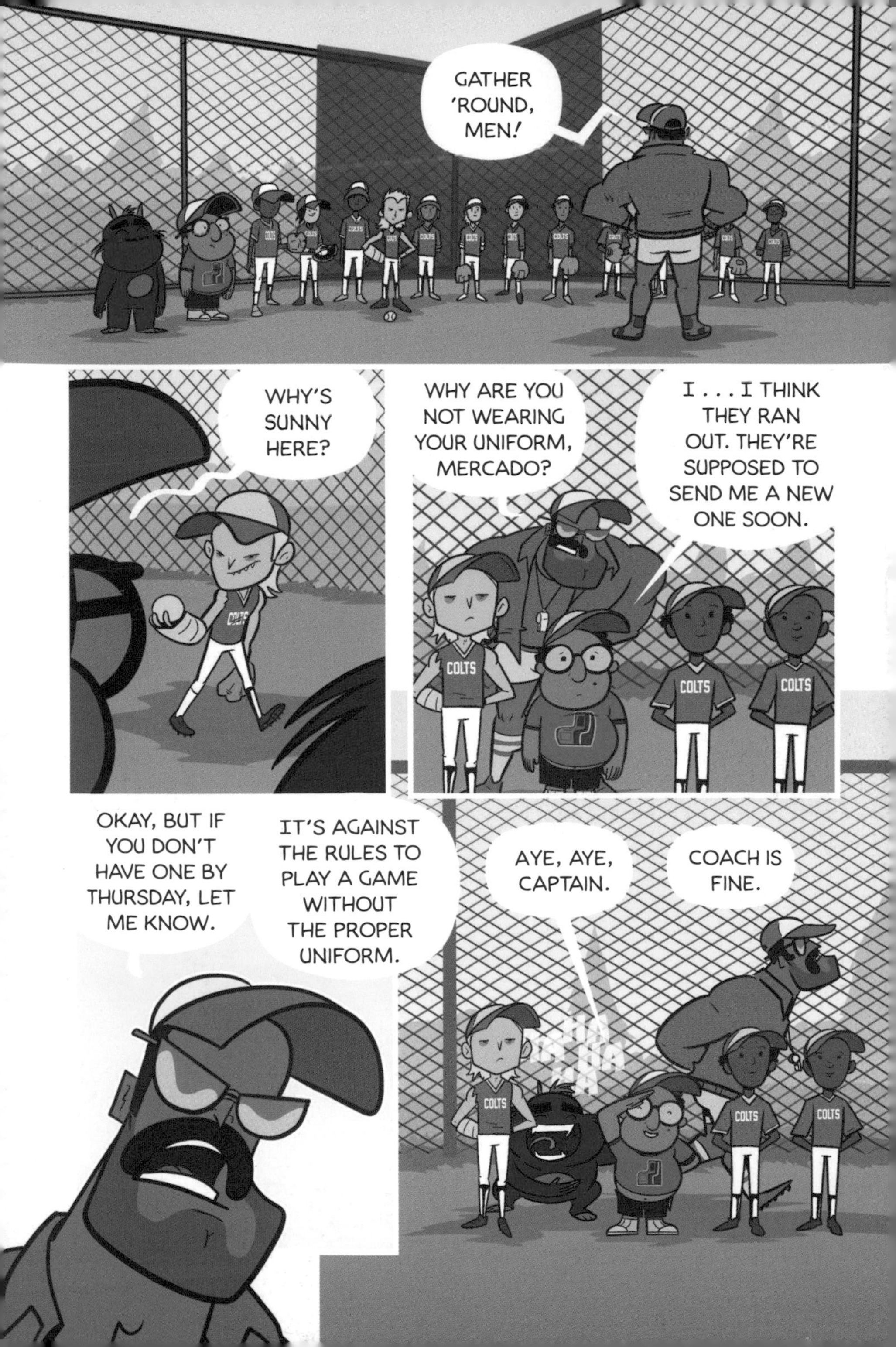
GATHER 'ROUND, MEN!
WHY'S SUNNY HERE?
WHY ARE YOU NOT WEARING YOUR UNIFORM, MERCADO?
I . . . I THINK THEY RAN OUT. THEY'RE SUPPOSED TO SEND ME A NEW ONE SOON.
OKAY, BUT IF YOU DON'T HAVE ONE BY THURSDAY, LET ME KNOW.
IT'S AGAINST THE RULES TO PLAY A GAME WITHOUT THE PROPER UNIFORM.
AYE, AYE, CAPTAIN.
COACH IS FINE.

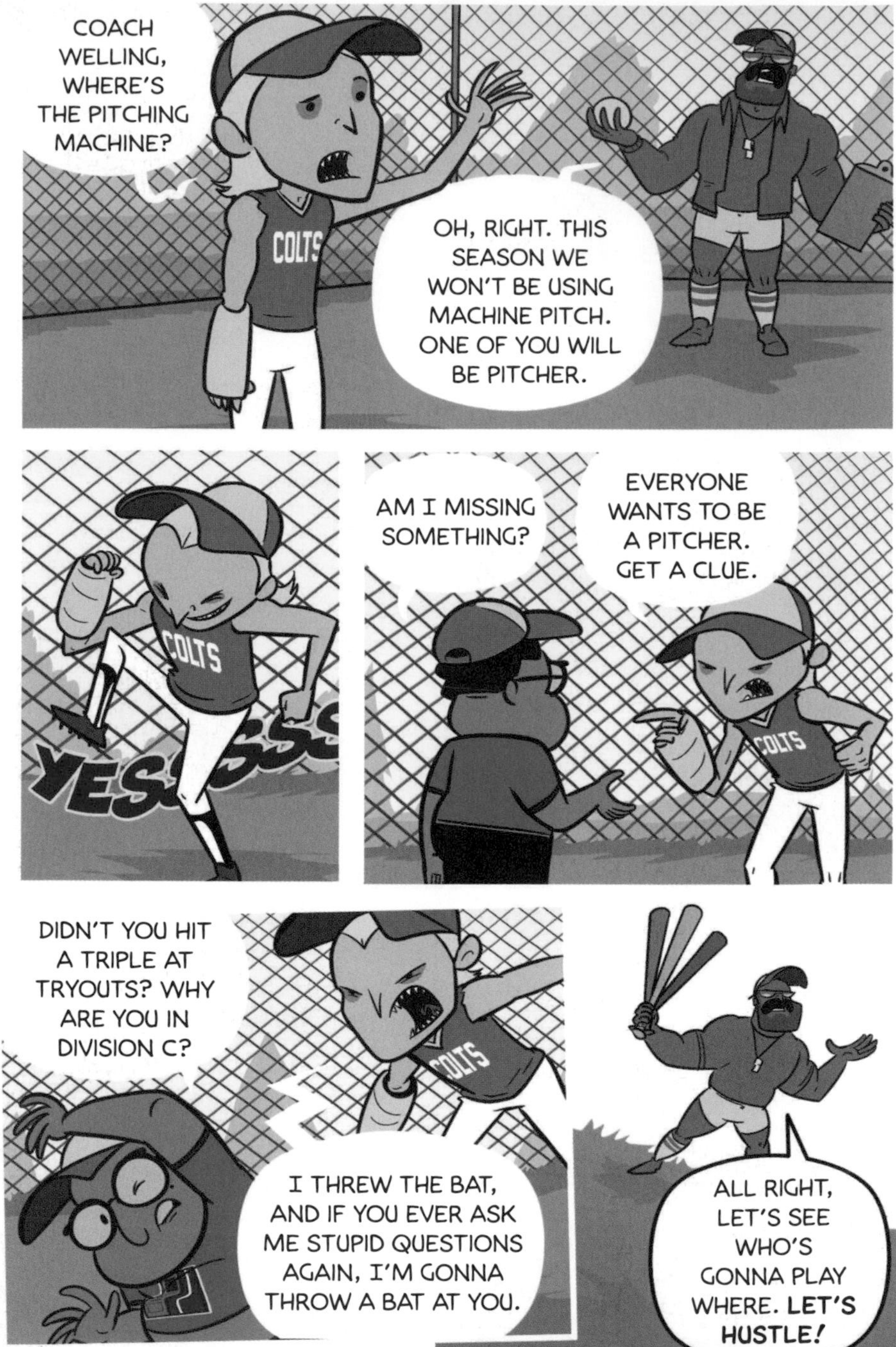
COACH WELLING, WHERE'S THE PITCHING MACHINE?
OH, RIGHT. THIS SEASON WE WON'T BE USING MACHINE PITCH. ONE OF YOU WILL BE PITCHER.
COLTS
YESSSS
COLTS
AM I MISSING SOMETHING?
EVERYONE WANTS TO BE A PITCHER. GET A CLUE.
COLTS
DIDN'T YOU HIT A TRIPLE AT TRYOUTS? WHY ARE YOU IN DIVISION C?
COLTS
I THREW THE BAT, AND IF YOU EVER ASK ME STUPID QUESTIONS AGAIN, I'M GONNA THROW A BAT AT YOU.
ALL RIGHT, LET'S SEE WHO'S GONNA PLAY WHERE. **LET'S HUSTLE!**

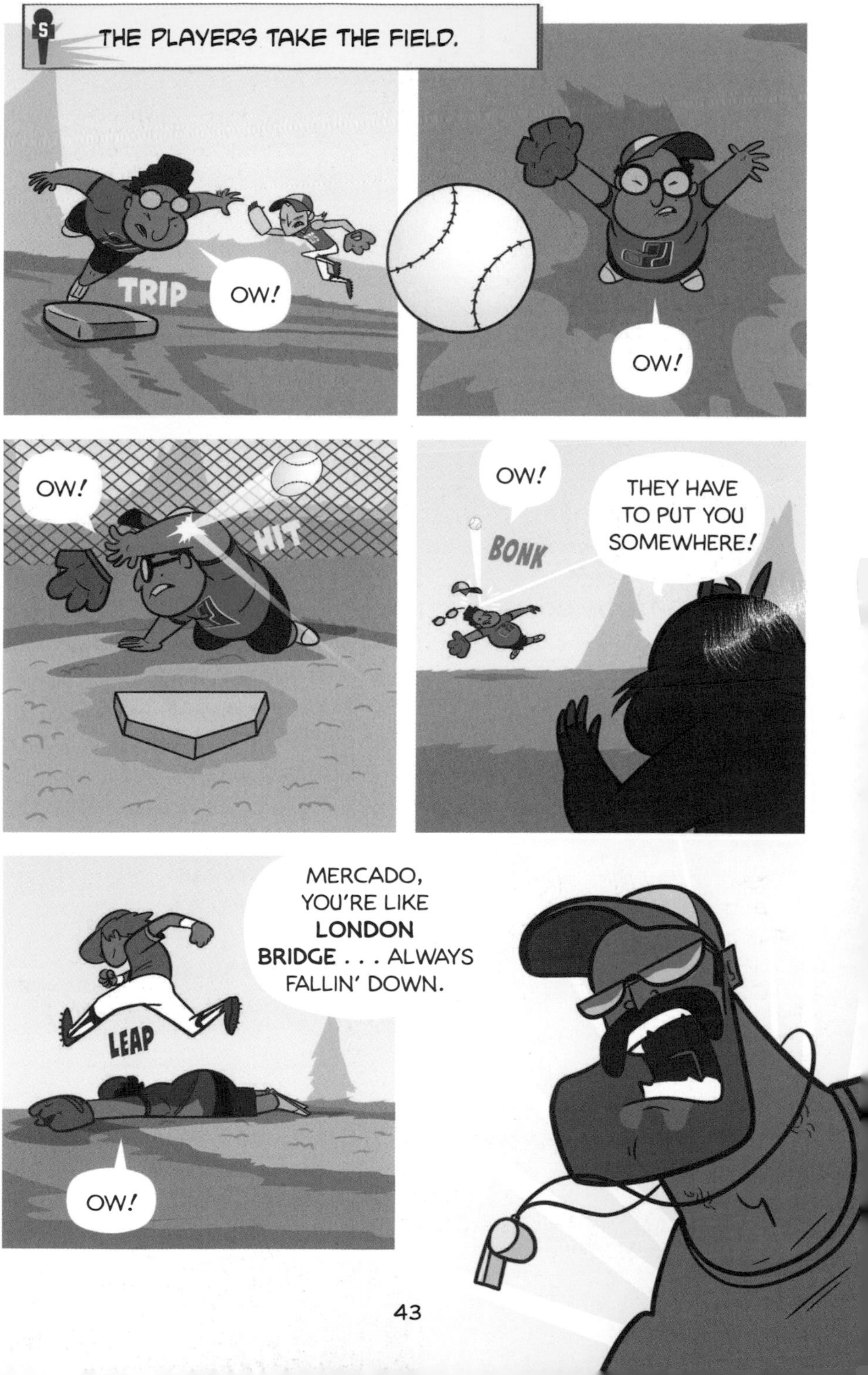
THE PLAYERS TAKE THE FIELD.
TRIP
OW!
OW!
OW!
HIT
OW!
BONK
THEY HAVE TO PUT YOU SOMEWHERE!
LEAP
OW!
MERCADO, YOU'RE LIKE **LONDON BRIDGE** . . . ALWAYS FALLIN' DOWN.

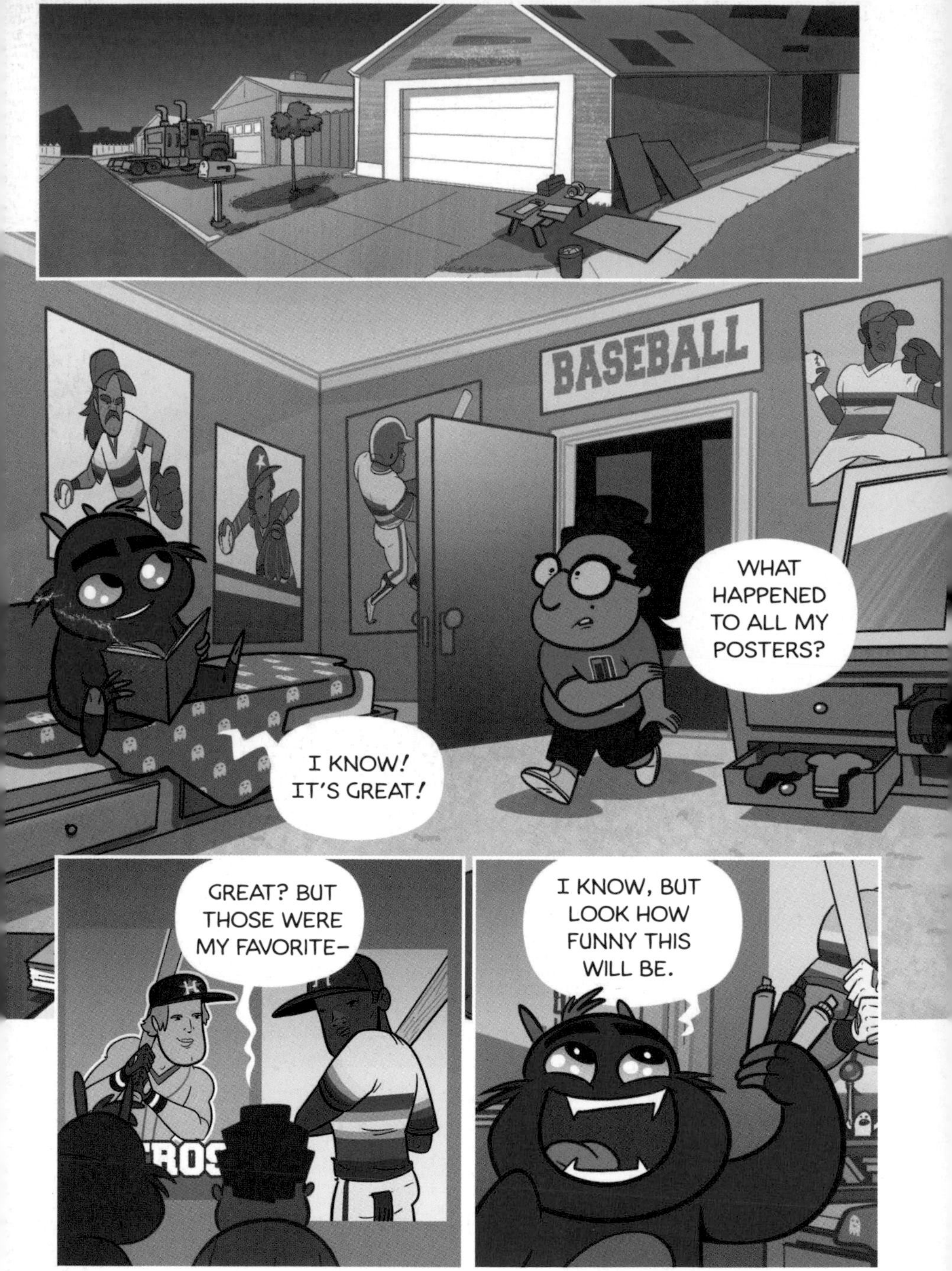
BASEBALL
WHAT HAPPENED TO ALL MY POSTERS?
I KNOW! IT'S GREAT!
GREAT? BUT THOSE WERE MY FAVORITE–
I KNOW, BUT LOOK HOW FUNNY THIS WILL BE.

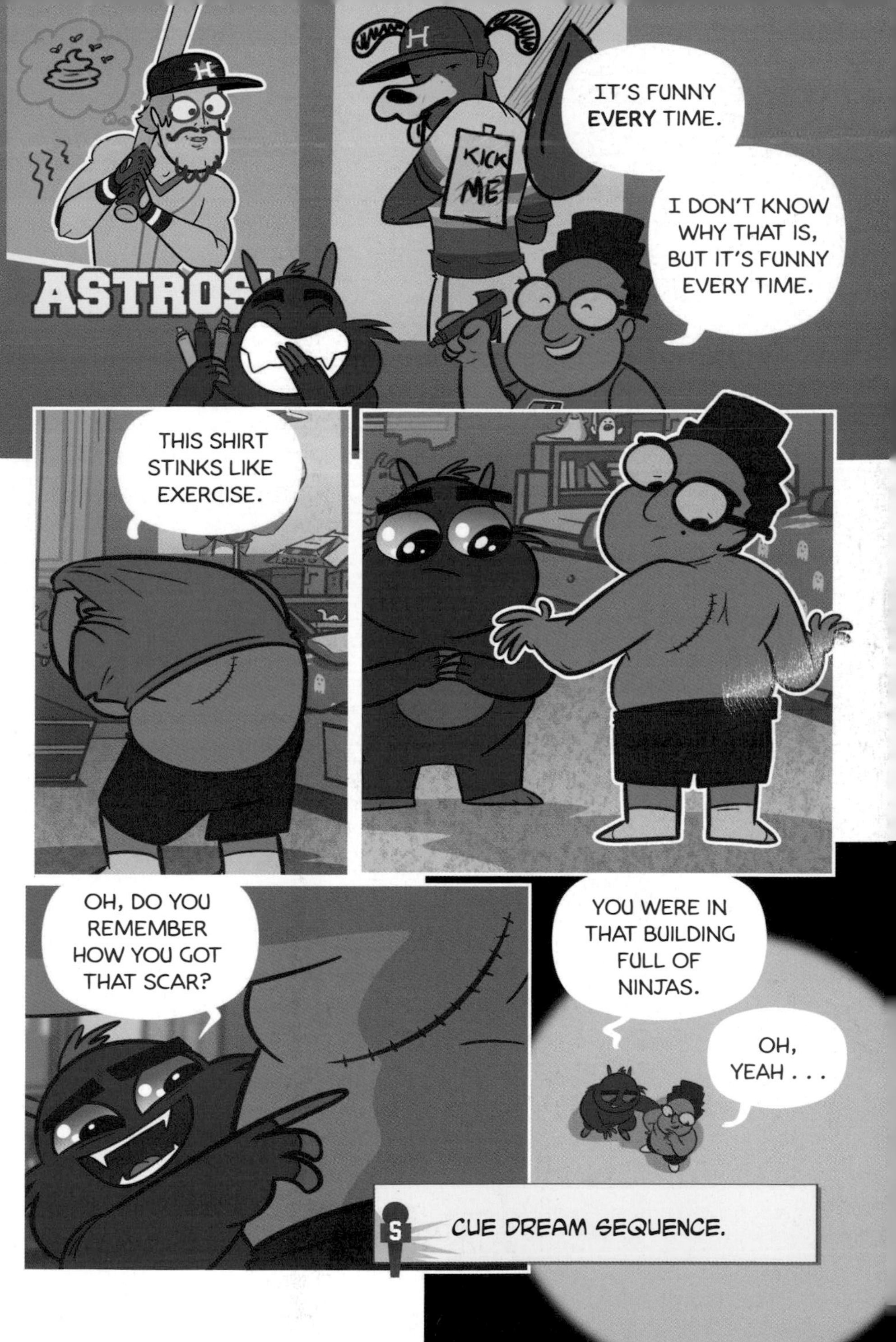
ASTROS!
KICK ME
IT'S FUNNY EVERY TIME.
I DON'T KNOW WHY THAT IS, BUT IT'S FUNNY EVERY TIME.
THIS SHIRT STINKS LIKE EXERCISE.
OH, DO YOU REMEMBER HOW YOU GOT THAT SCAR?
YOU WERE IN THAT BUILDING FULL OF NINJAS.
OH, YEAH . . .
CUE DREAM SEQUENCE.

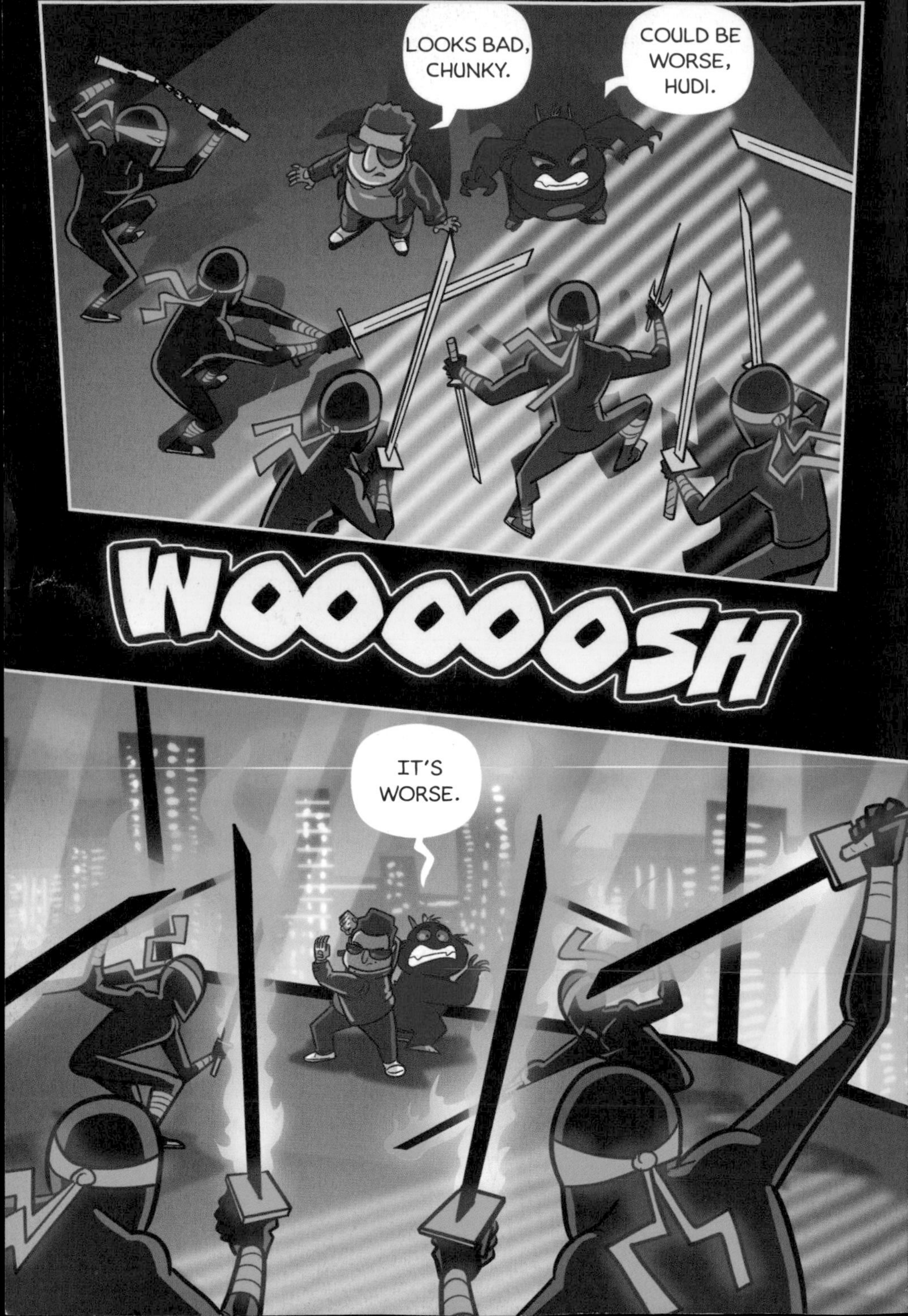
LOOKS BAD, CHUNKY.
COULD BE WORSE, HUDI.
WOOOOOSH
IT'S WORSE.

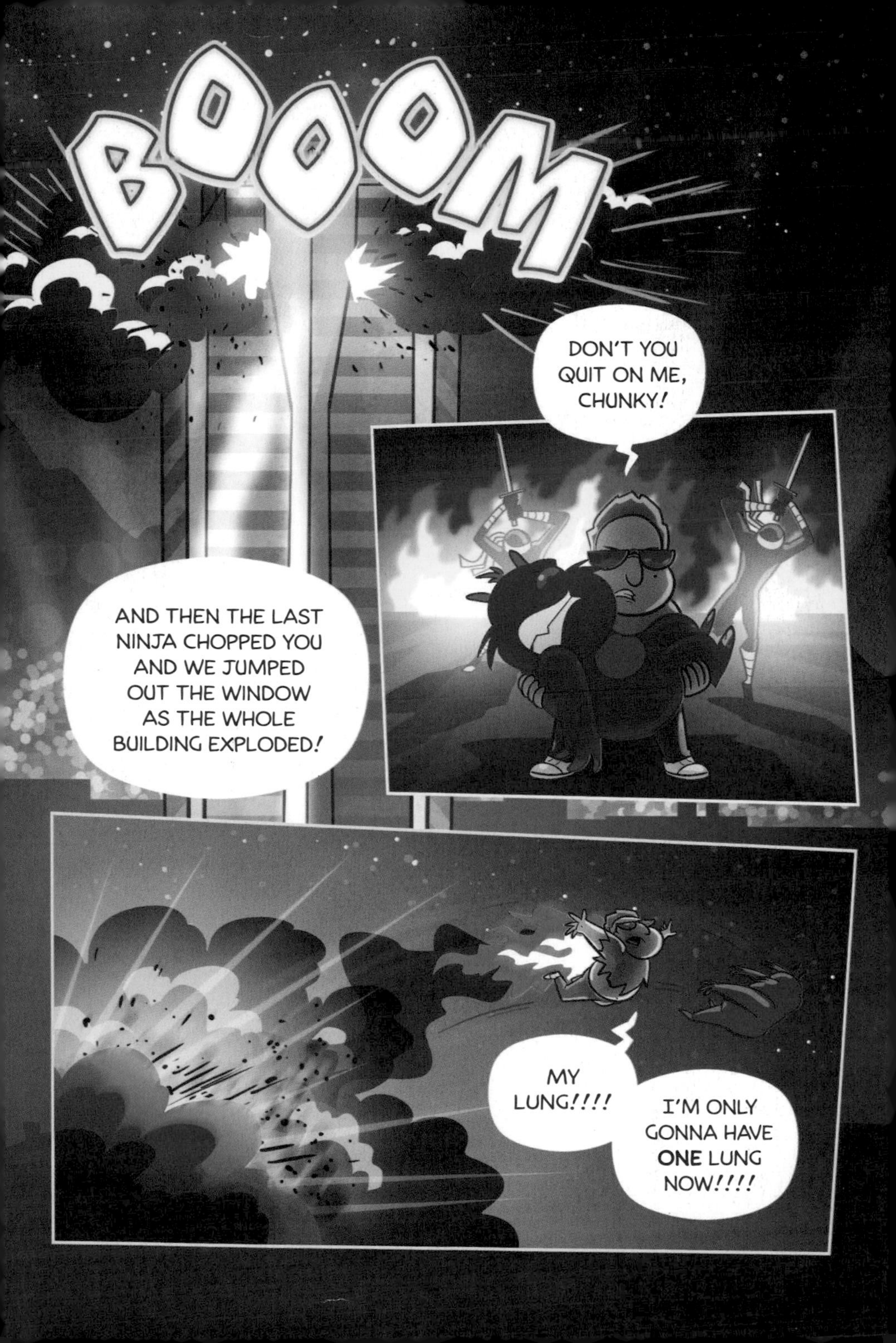
BOOOM
DON'T YOU QUIT ON ME, CHUNKY!
AND THEN THE LAST NINJA CHOPPED YOU AND WE JUMPED OUT THE WINDOW AS THE WHOLE BUILDING EXPLODED!
MY LUNG!!!!
I'M ONLY GONNA HAVE ONE LUNG NOW!!!!

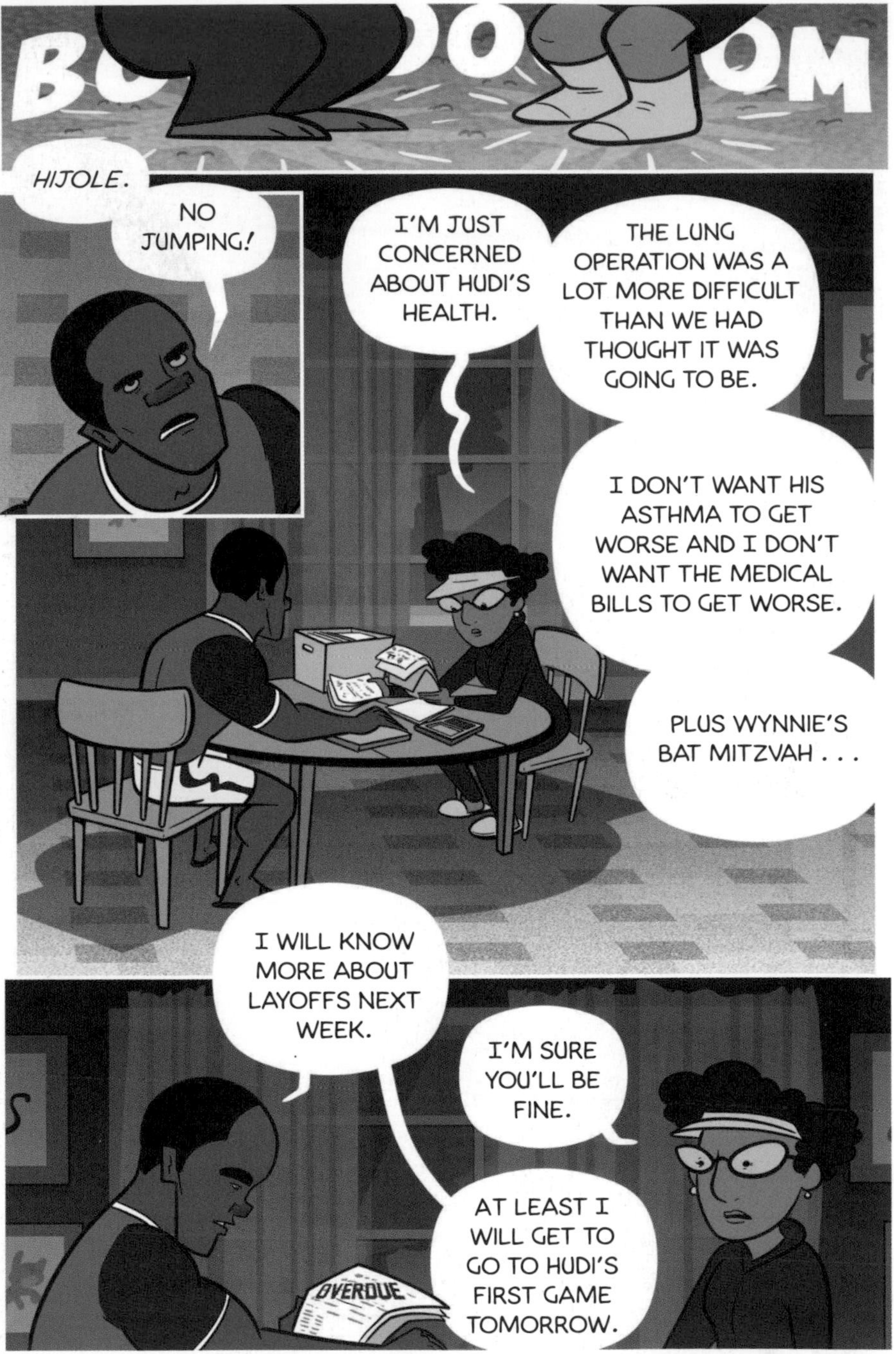
BOOOOM
HIJOLE.
NO JUMPING!
I'M JUST CONCERNED ABOUT HUDI'S HEALTH.
THE LUNG OPERATION WAS A LOT MORE DIFFICULT THAN WE HAD THOUGHT IT WAS GOING TO BE.
I DON'T WANT HIS ASTHMA TO GET WORSE AND I DON'T WANT THE MEDICAL BILLS TO GET WORSE.
PLUS WYNNIE'S BAT MITZVAH . . .
I WILL KNOW MORE ABOUT LAYOFFS NEXT WEEK.
I'M SURE YOU'LL BE FINE.
AT LEAST I WILL GET TO GO TO HUDI'S FIRST GAME TOMORROW.
OVERDUE

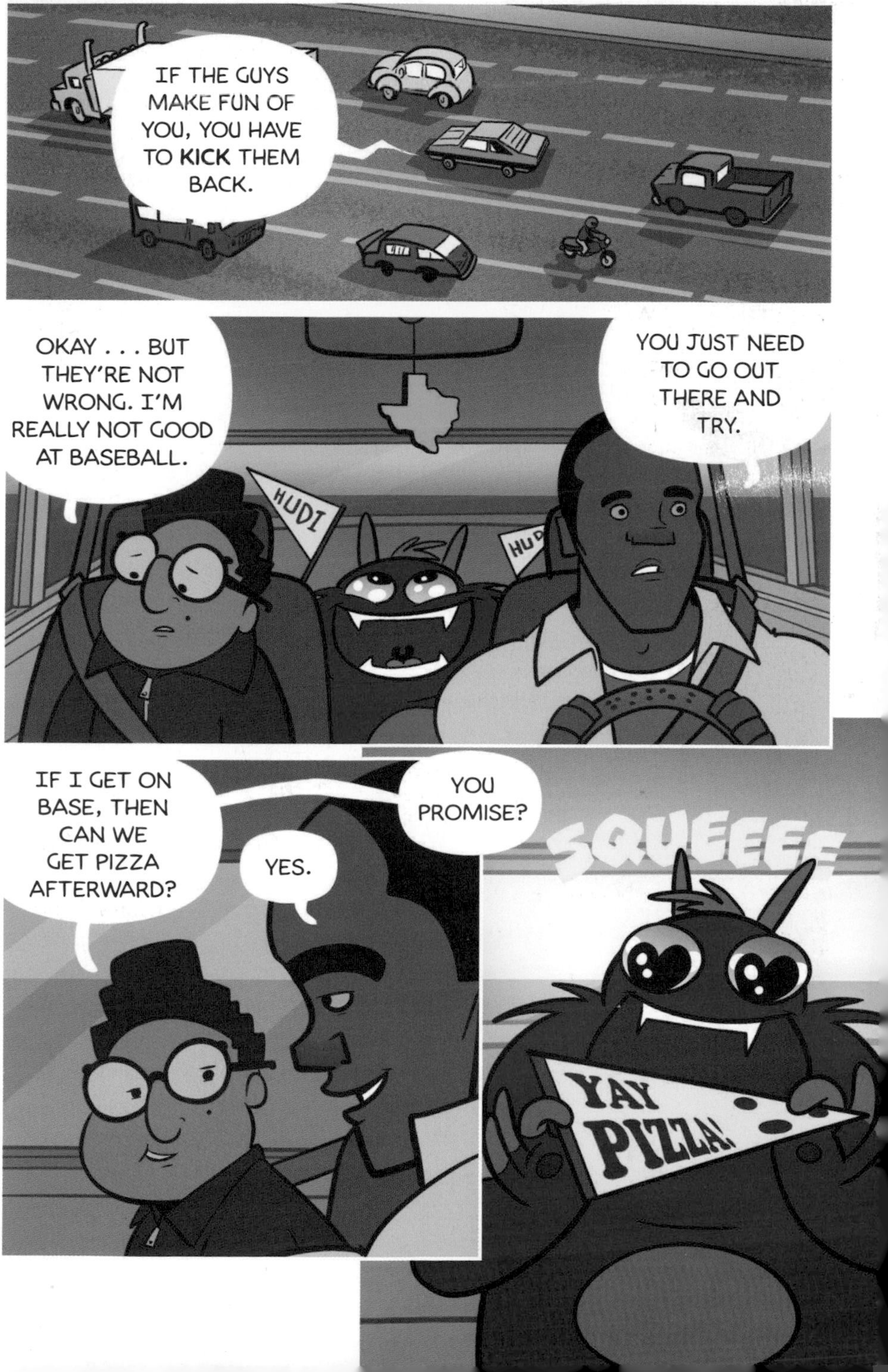
IF THE GUYS MAKE FUN OF YOU, YOU HAVE TO **KICK** THEM BACK.
OKAY . . . BUT THEY'RE NOT WRONG. I'M REALLY NOT GOOD AT BASEBALL.
YOU JUST NEED TO GO OUT THERE AND TRY.
HUDI
IF I GET ON BASE, THEN CAN WE GET PIZZA AFTERWARD?
YES.
YOU PROMISE?
SQUEEEE
YAY PIZZA!

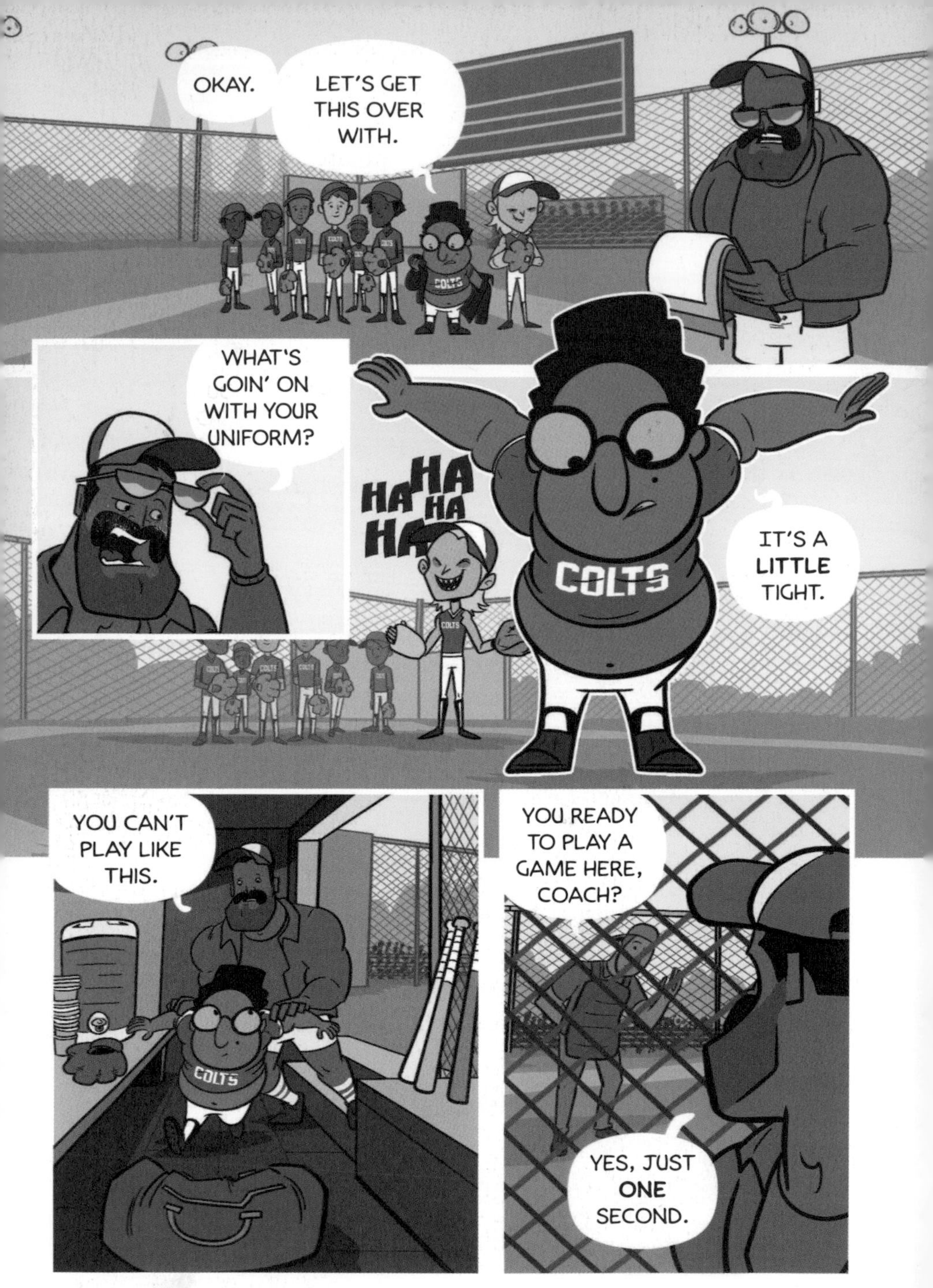
OKAY.
LET'S GET THIS OVER WITH.
WHAT'S GOIN' ON WITH YOUR UNIFORM?
HA HA HA HA
IT'S A **LITTLE** TIGHT.
COLTS
YOU CAN'T PLAY LIKE THIS.
COLTS
YOU READY TO PLAY A GAME HERE, COACH?
YES, JUST **ONE** SECOND.

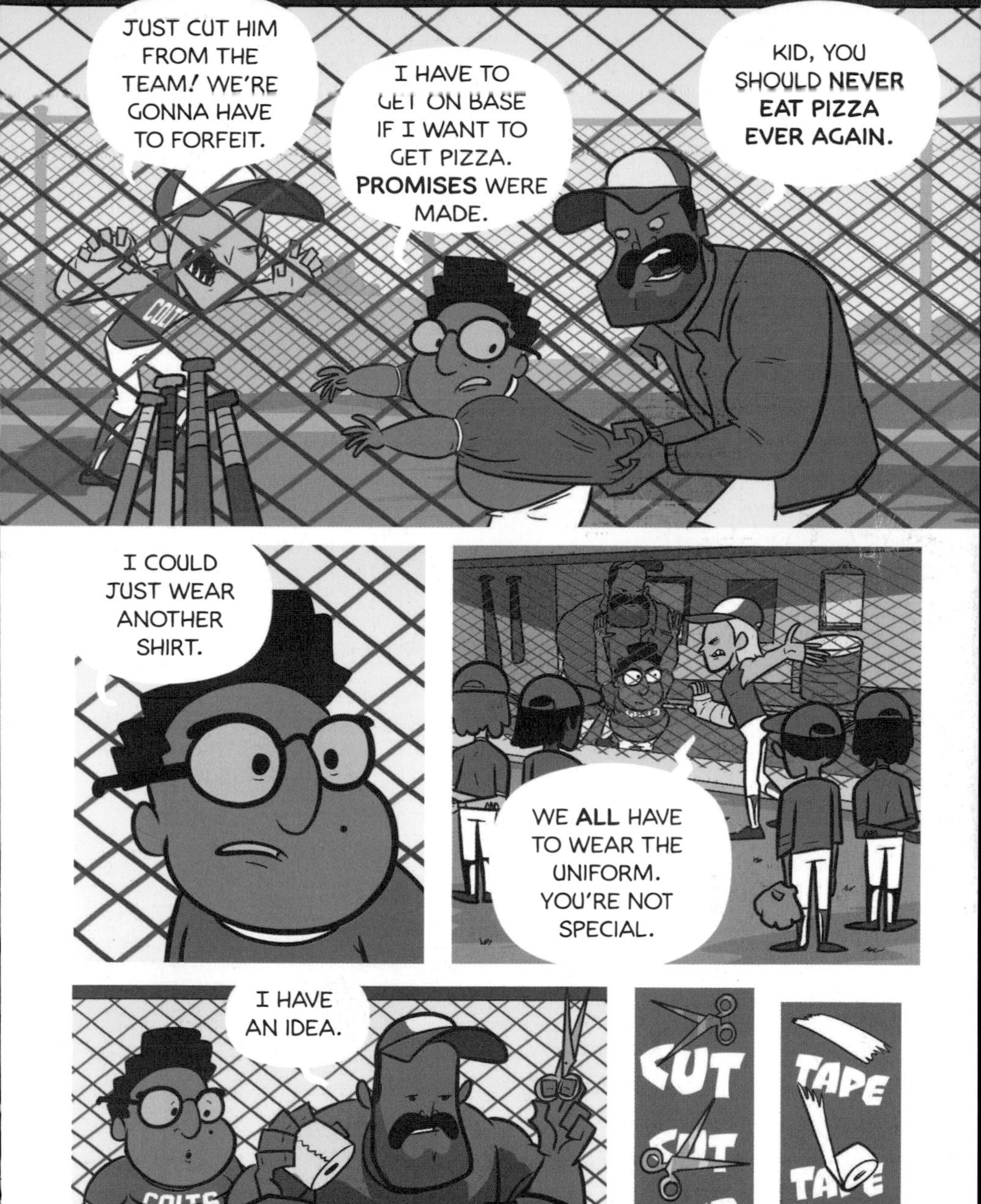
JUST CUT HIM FROM THE TEAM! WE'RE GONNA HAVE TO FORFEIT.
I HAVE TO GET ON BASE IF I WANT TO GET PIZZA. PROMISES WERE MADE.
KID, YOU SHOULD NEVER EAT PIZZA EVER AGAIN.
I COULD JUST WEAR ANOTHER SHIRT.
WE ALL HAVE TO WEAR THE UNIFORM. YOU'RE NOT SPECIAL.
I HAVE AN IDEA.
COLTS
<GULP>
CUT
CUT
SNIP
TAPE
TAPE
STRETCH

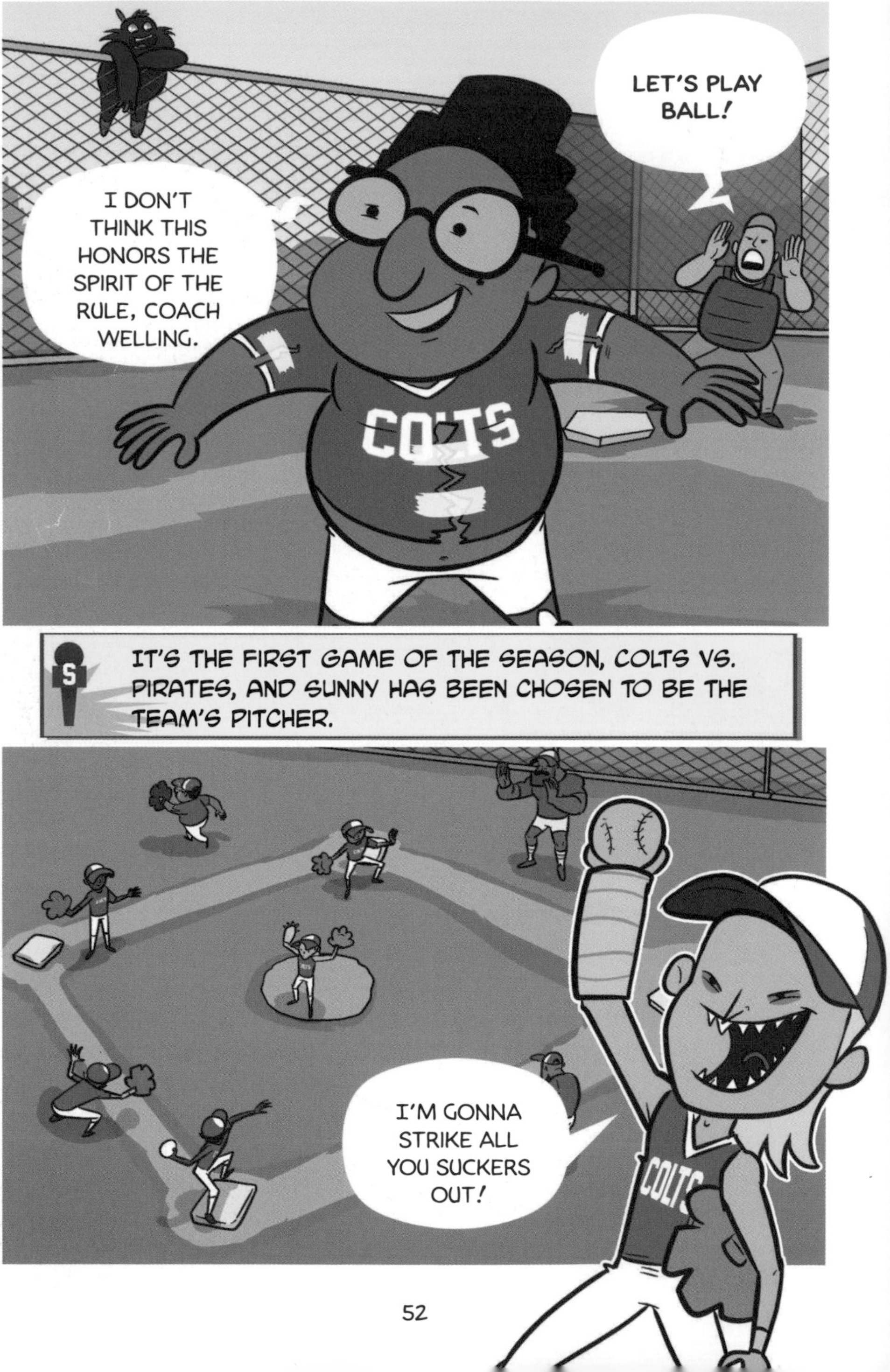
I DON'T THINK THIS HONORS THE SPIRIT OF THE RULE, COACH WELLING.
LET'S PLAY BALL!
COLTS
IT'S THE FIRST GAME OF THE SEASON, COLTS VS. PIRATES, AND SUNNY HAS BEEN CHOSEN TO BE THE TEAM'S PITCHER.
I'M GONNA STRIKE ALL YOU SUCKERS OUT!

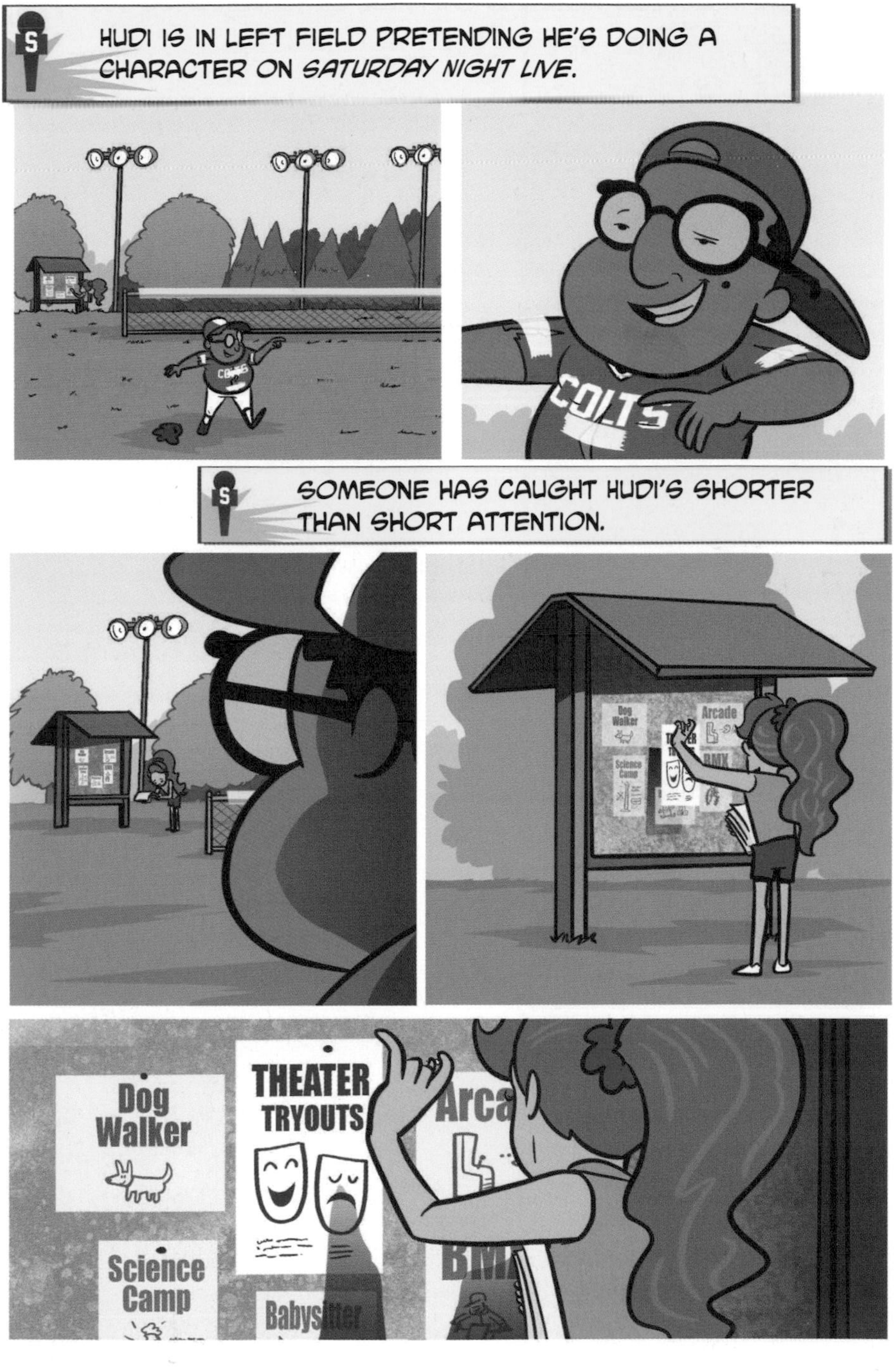
HUDI IS IN LEFT FIELD PRETENDING HE'S DOING A CHARACTER ON *SATURDAY NIGHT LIVE*.
COLTS
SOMEONE HAS CAUGHT HUDI'S SHORTER THAN SHORT ATTENTION.
Dog Walker
Arcade
Science Camp
BMX
Dog Walker
THEATER TRYOUTS
Science Camp

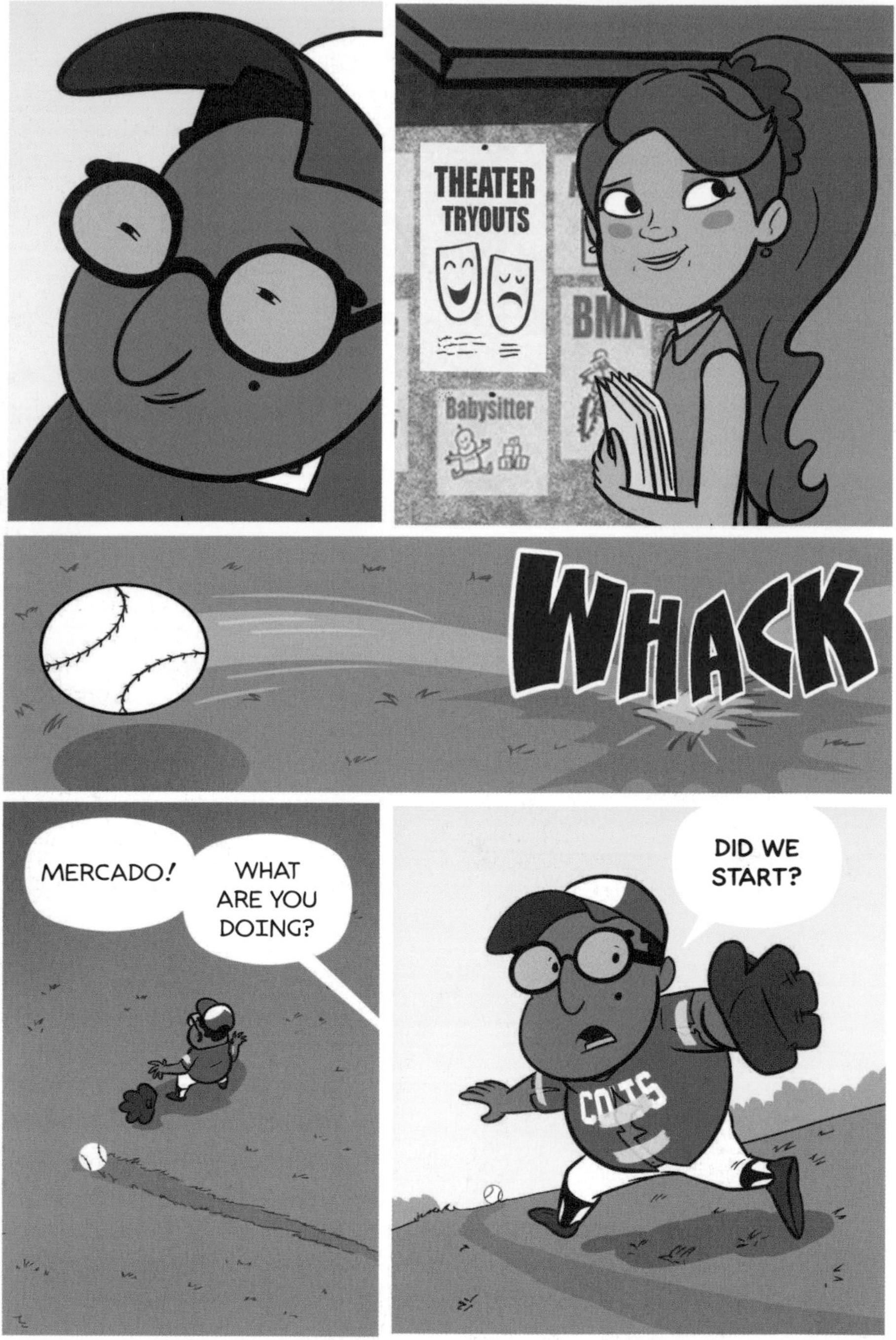
THEATER TRYOUTS
BabySitter
BMX
WHACK
MERCADO!
WHAT ARE YOU DOING?
DID WE START?
COLTS

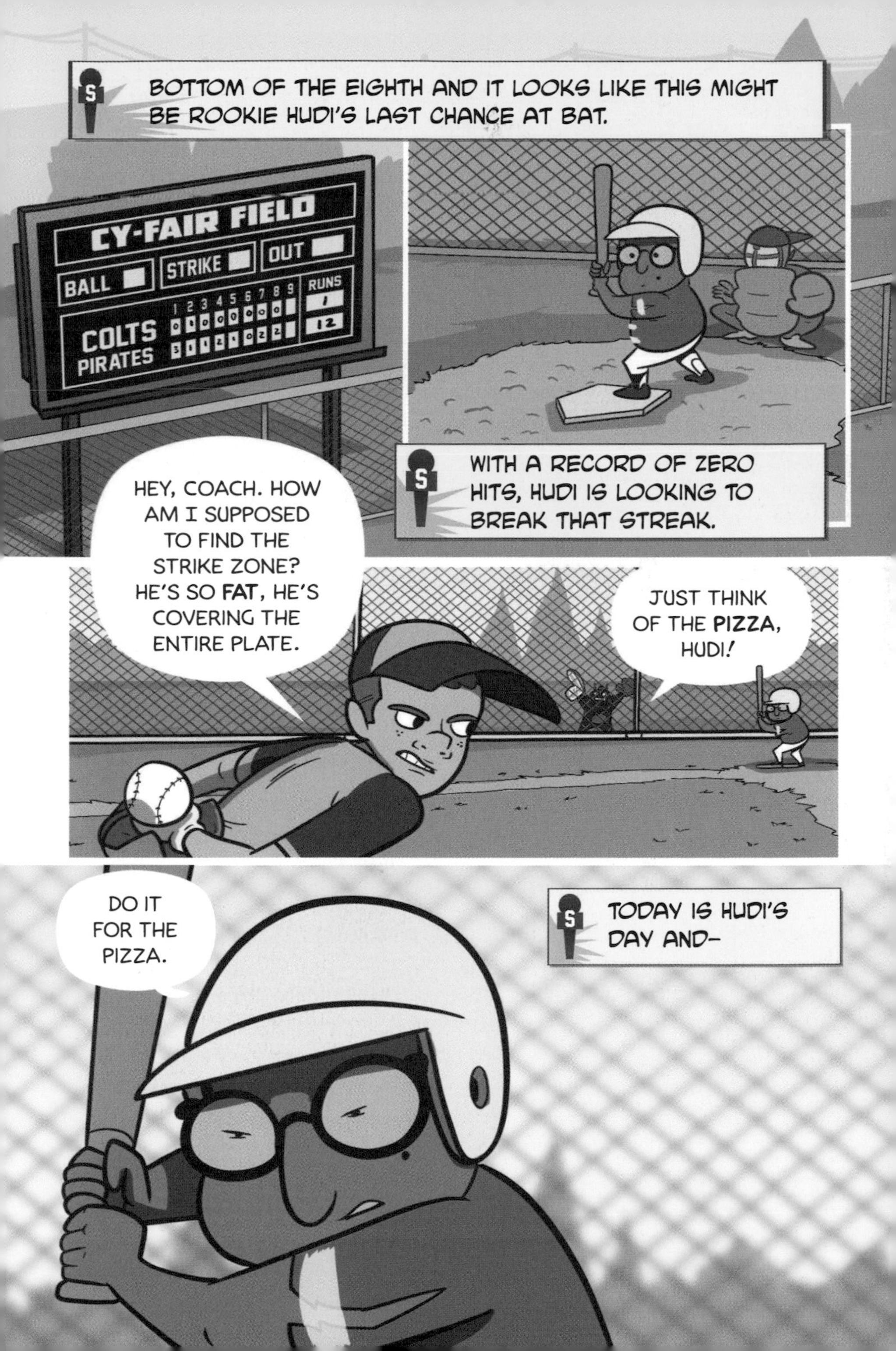

BOTTOM OF THE EIGHTH AND IT LOOKS LIKE THIS MIGHT BE ROOKIE HUDI'S LAST CHANCE AT BAT.
CY-FAIR FIELD
BALL
STRIKE
OUT
RUNS
COLTS
PIRATES
WITH A RECORD OF ZERO HITS, HUDI IS LOOKING TO BREAK THAT STREAK.
HEY, COACH. HOW AM I SUPPOSED TO FIND THE STRIKE ZONE? HE'S SO **FAT**, HE'S COVERING THE ENTIRE PLATE.
JUST THINK OF THE **PIZZA**, HUDI!
DO IT FOR THE PIZZA.
TODAY IS HUDI'S DAY AND—

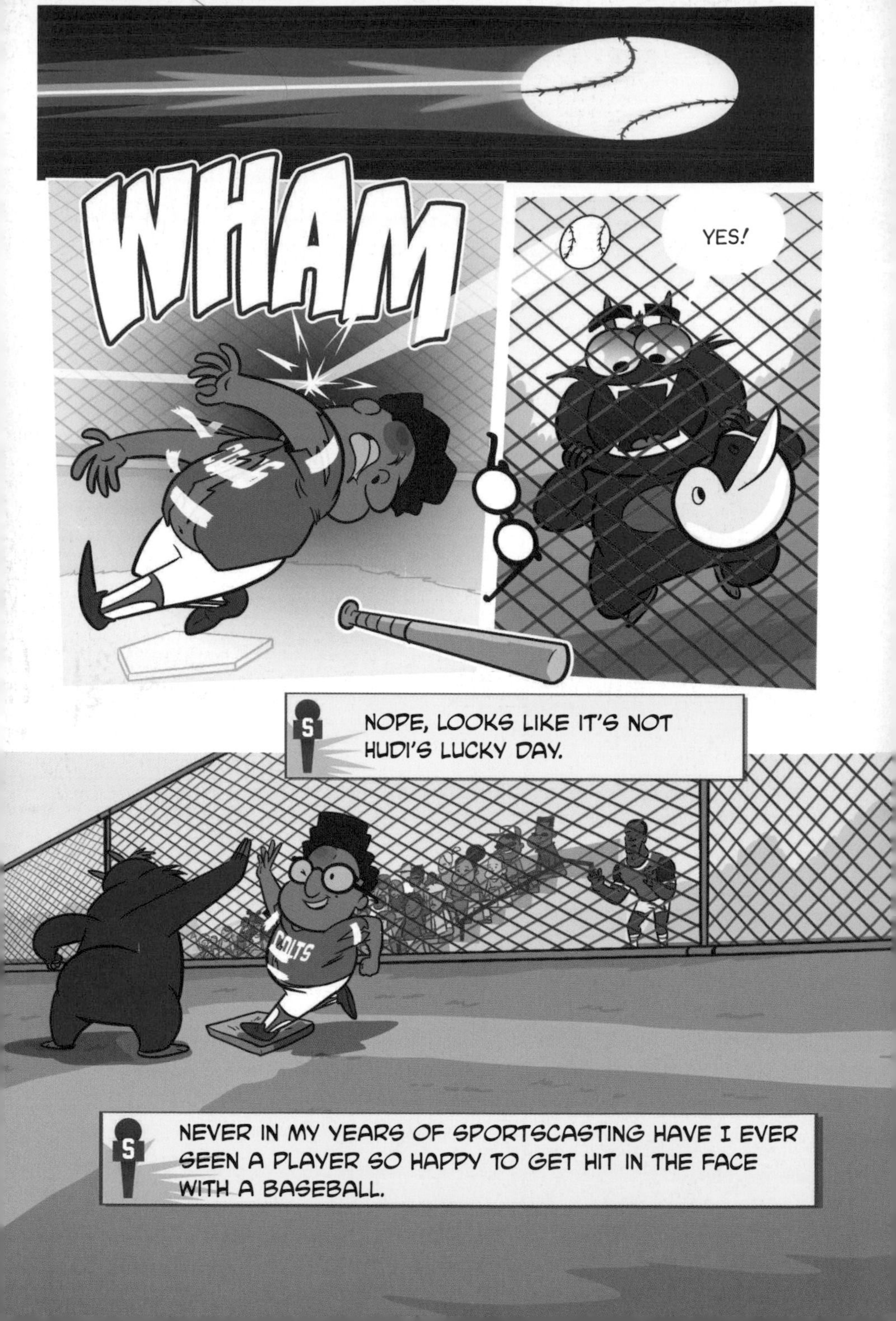
WHAM
YES!
NOPE, LOOKS LIKE IT'S NOT HUDI'S LUCKY DAY.
COLTS
NEVER IN MY YEARS OF SPORTSCASTING HAVE I EVER SEEN A PLAYER SO HAPPY TO GET HIT IN THE FACE WITH A BASEBALL.

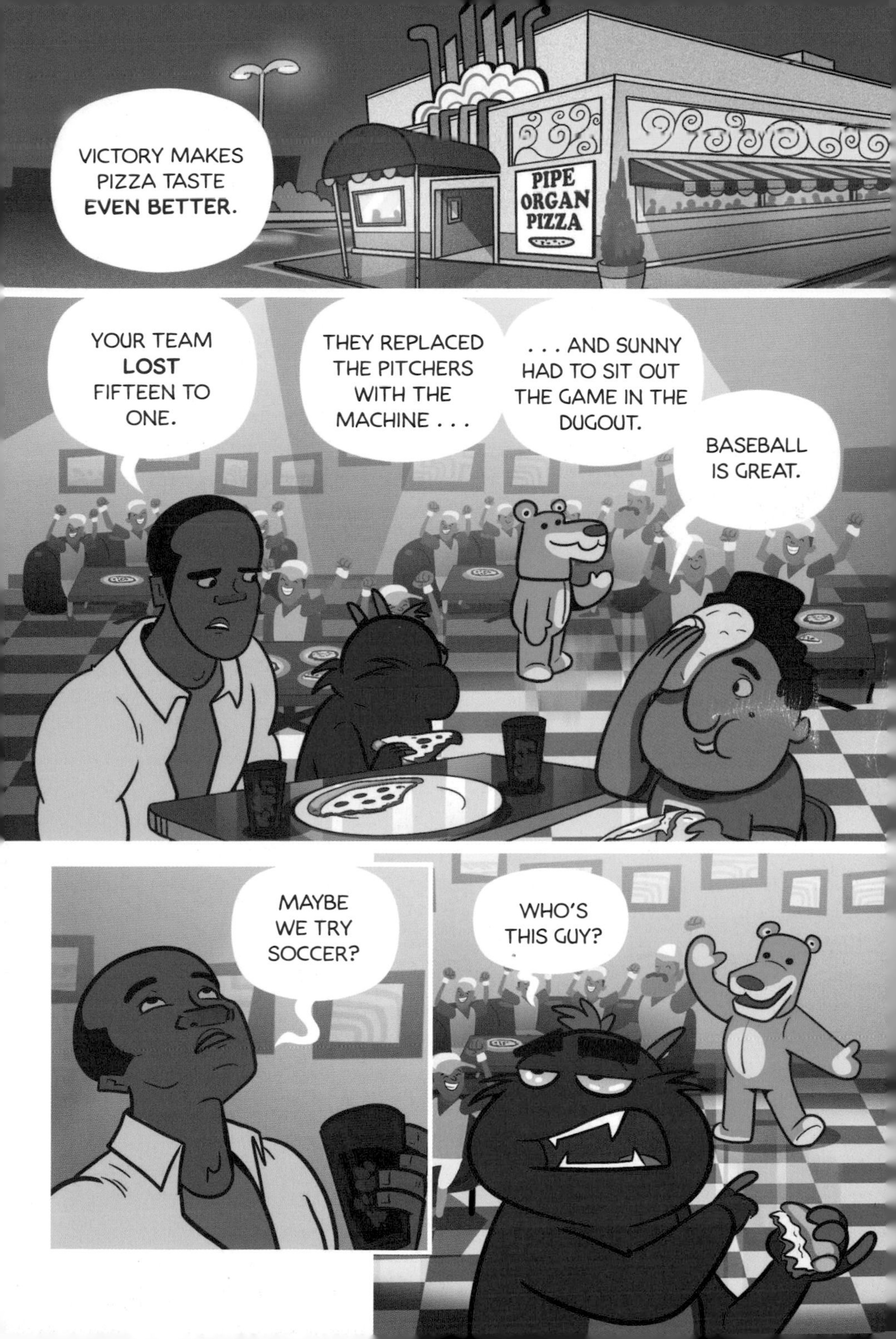
VICTORY MAKES PIZZA TASTE **EVEN BETTER.**
PIPE ORGAN PIZZA
YOUR TEAM **LOST** FIFTEEN TO ONE.
THEY REPLACED THE PITCHERS WITH THE MACHINE . . .
. . . AND SUNNY HAD TO SIT OUT THE GAME IN THE DUGOUT.
BASEBALL IS GREAT.
MAYBE WE TRY SOCCER?
WHO'S THIS GUY?

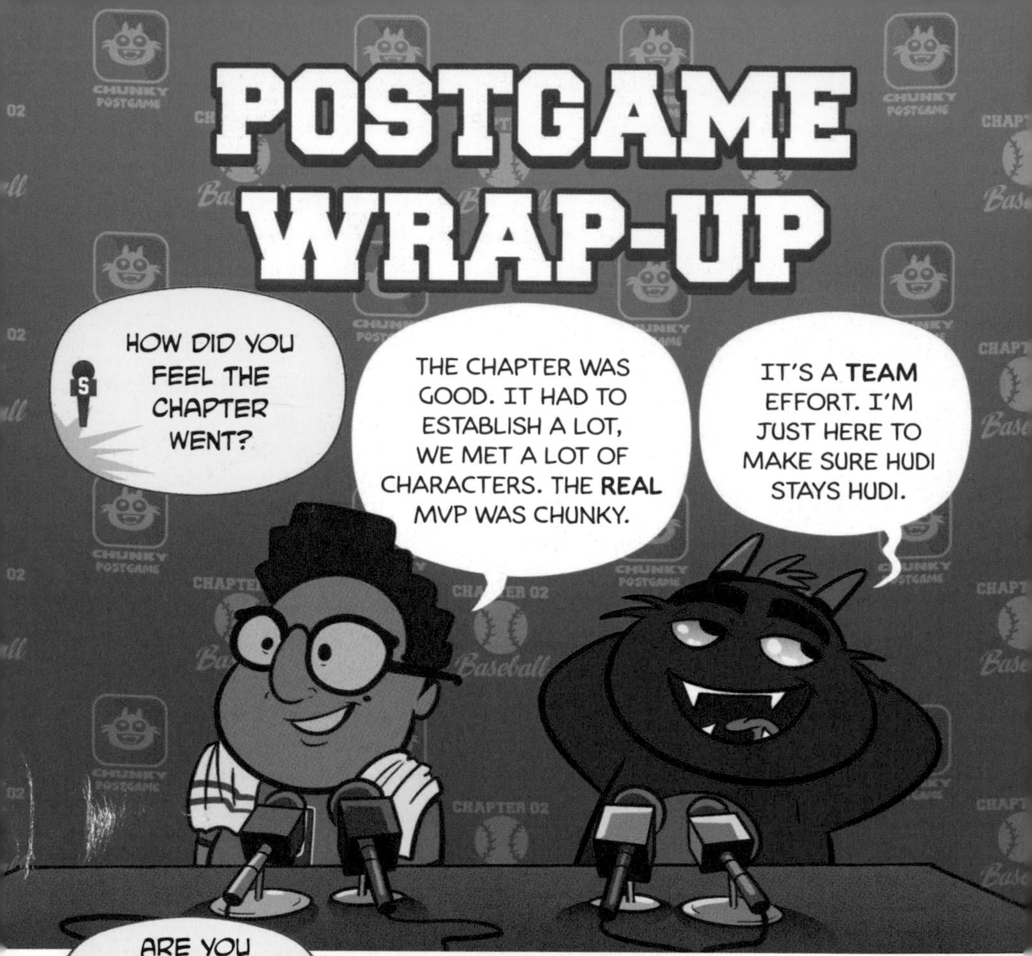
POSTGAME WRAP-UP
HOW DID YOU FEEL THE CHAPTER WENT?
THE CHAPTER WAS GOOD. IT HAD TO ESTABLISH A LOT, WE MET A LOT OF CHARACTERS. THE **REAL** MVP WAS CHUNKY.
IT'S A **TEAM** EFFORT. I'M JUST HERE TO MAKE SURE HUDI STAYS HUDI.

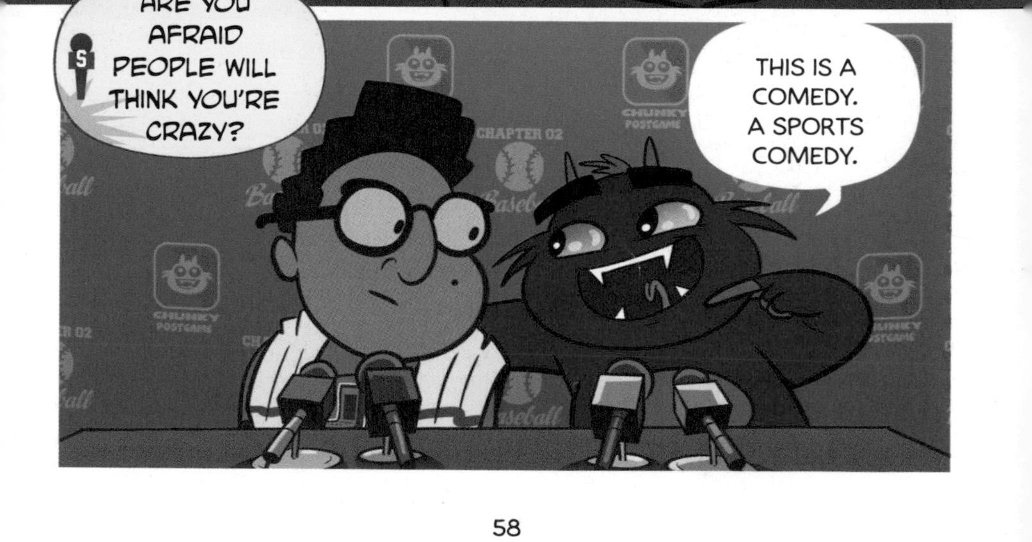
ARE YOU AFRAID PEOPLE WILL THINK YOU'RE CRAZY?
THIS IS A COMEDY. A SPORTS COMEDY.

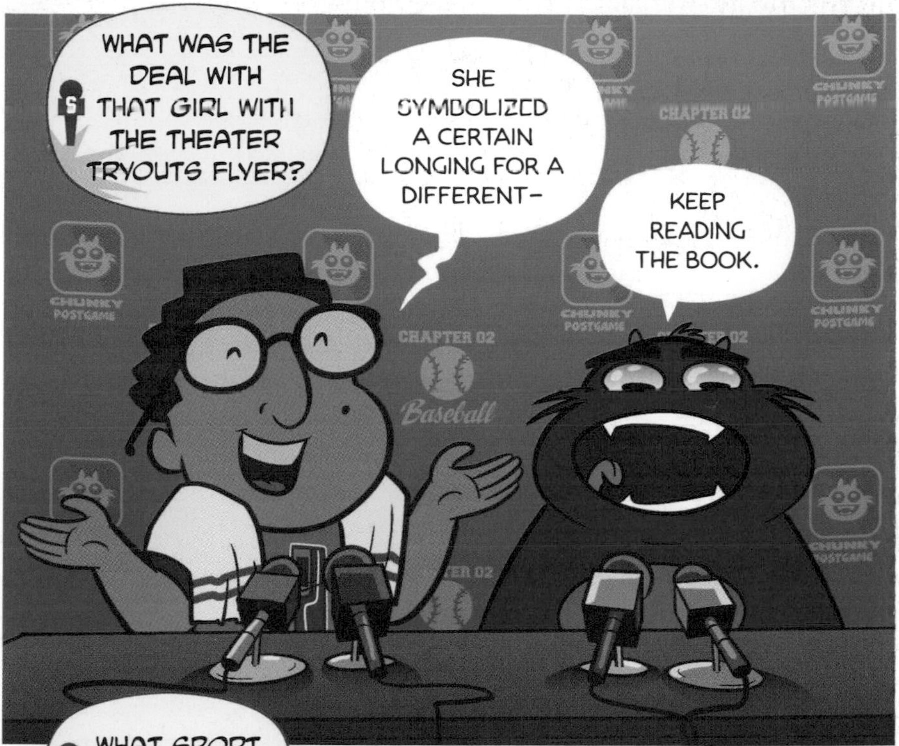
WHAT WAS THE DEAL WITH THAT GIRL WITH THE THEATER TRYOUTS FLYER?
SHE SYMBOLIZED A CERTAIN LONGING FOR A DIFFERENT–
KEEP READING THE BOOK.
CHUNKY POSTGAME
CHAPTER 02
Baseball

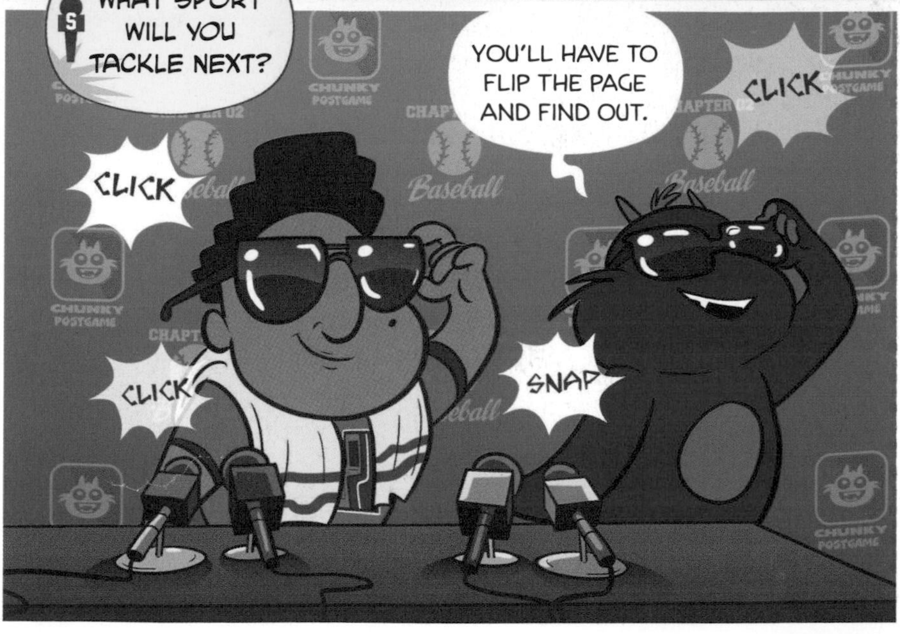
WHAT SPORT WILL YOU TACKLE NEXT?
YOU'LL HAVE TO FLIP THE PAGE AND FIND OUT.
CLICK
CLICK
CLICK
SNAP
Baseball

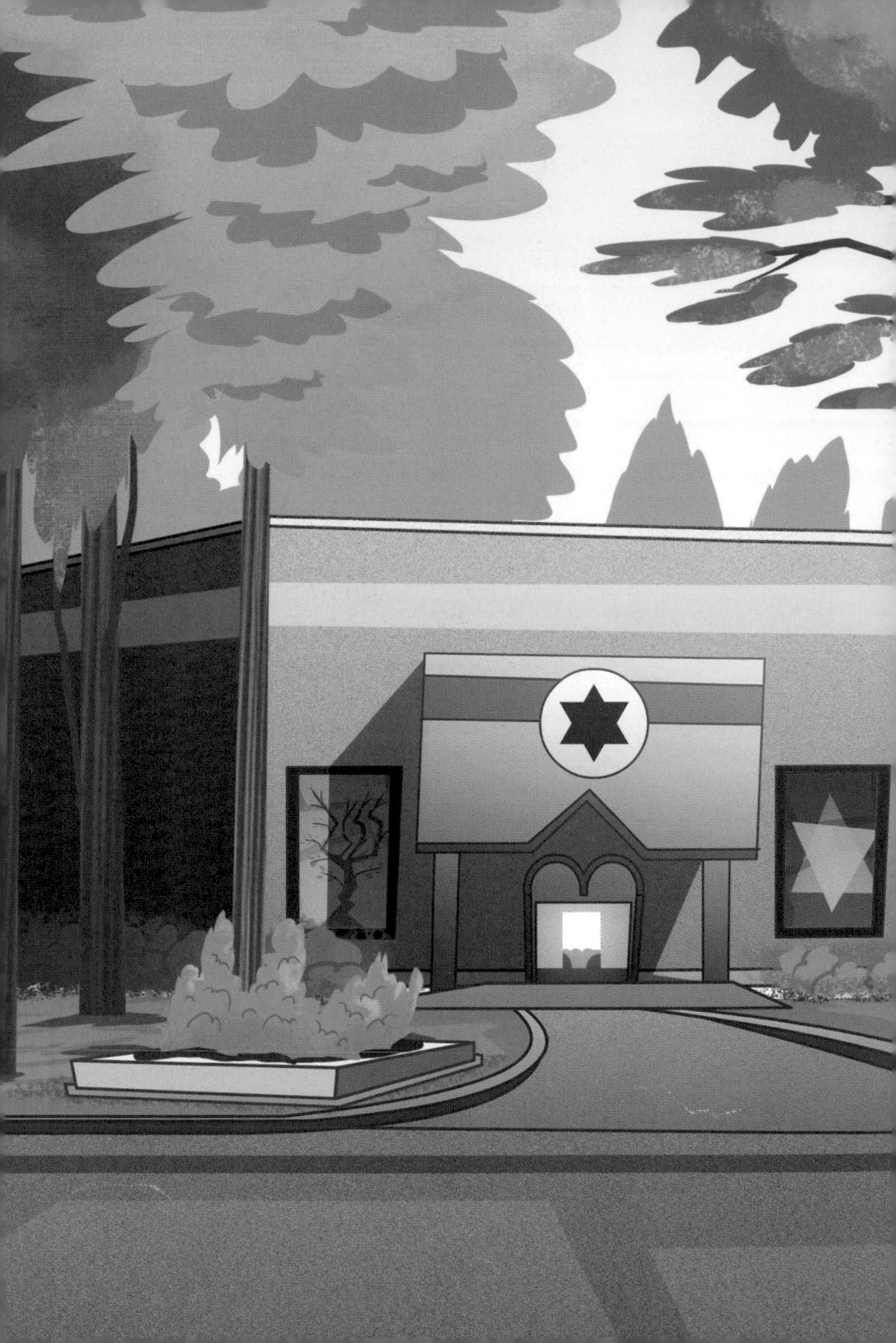

CHAPTER THREE

Soccer

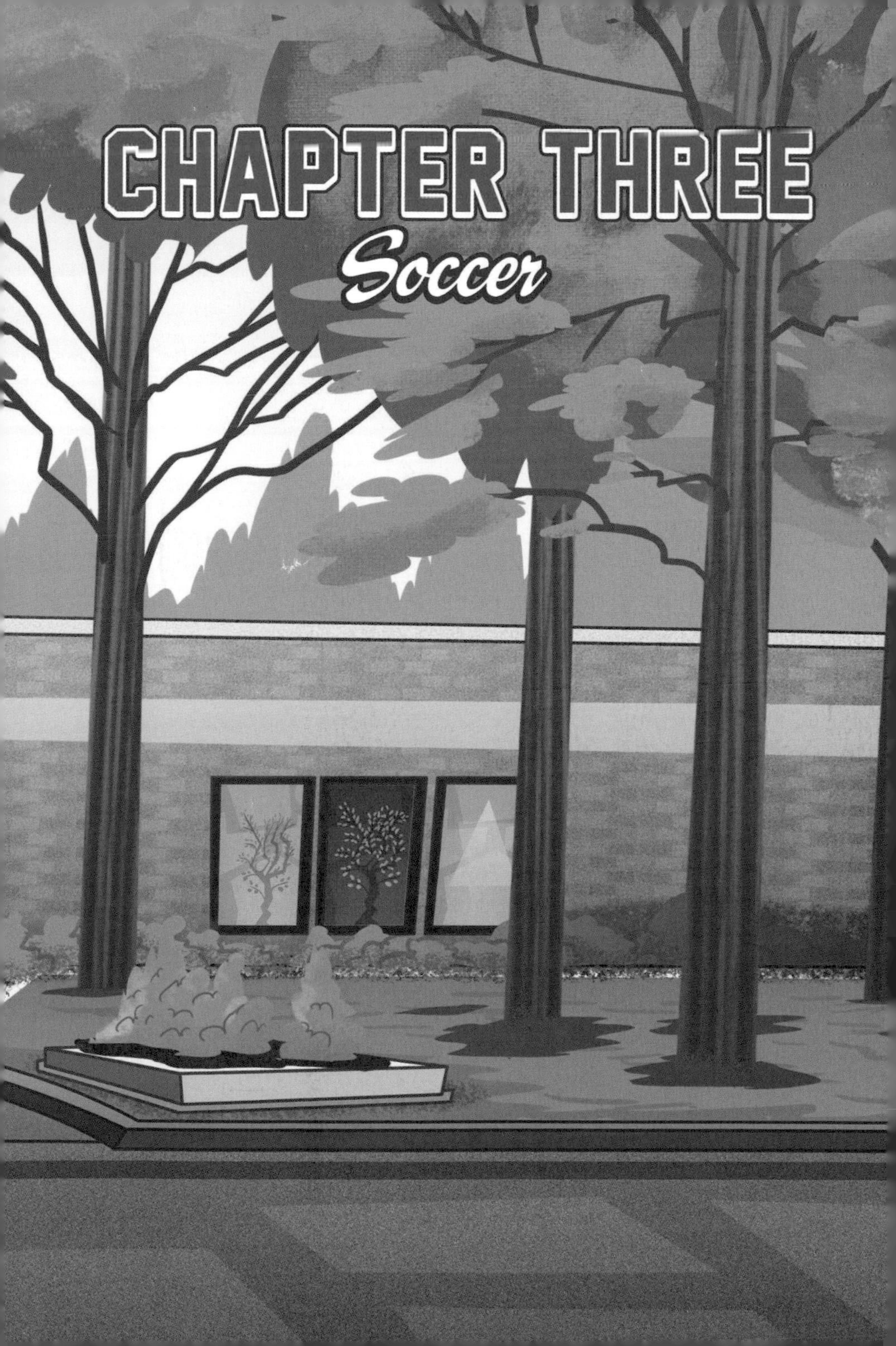

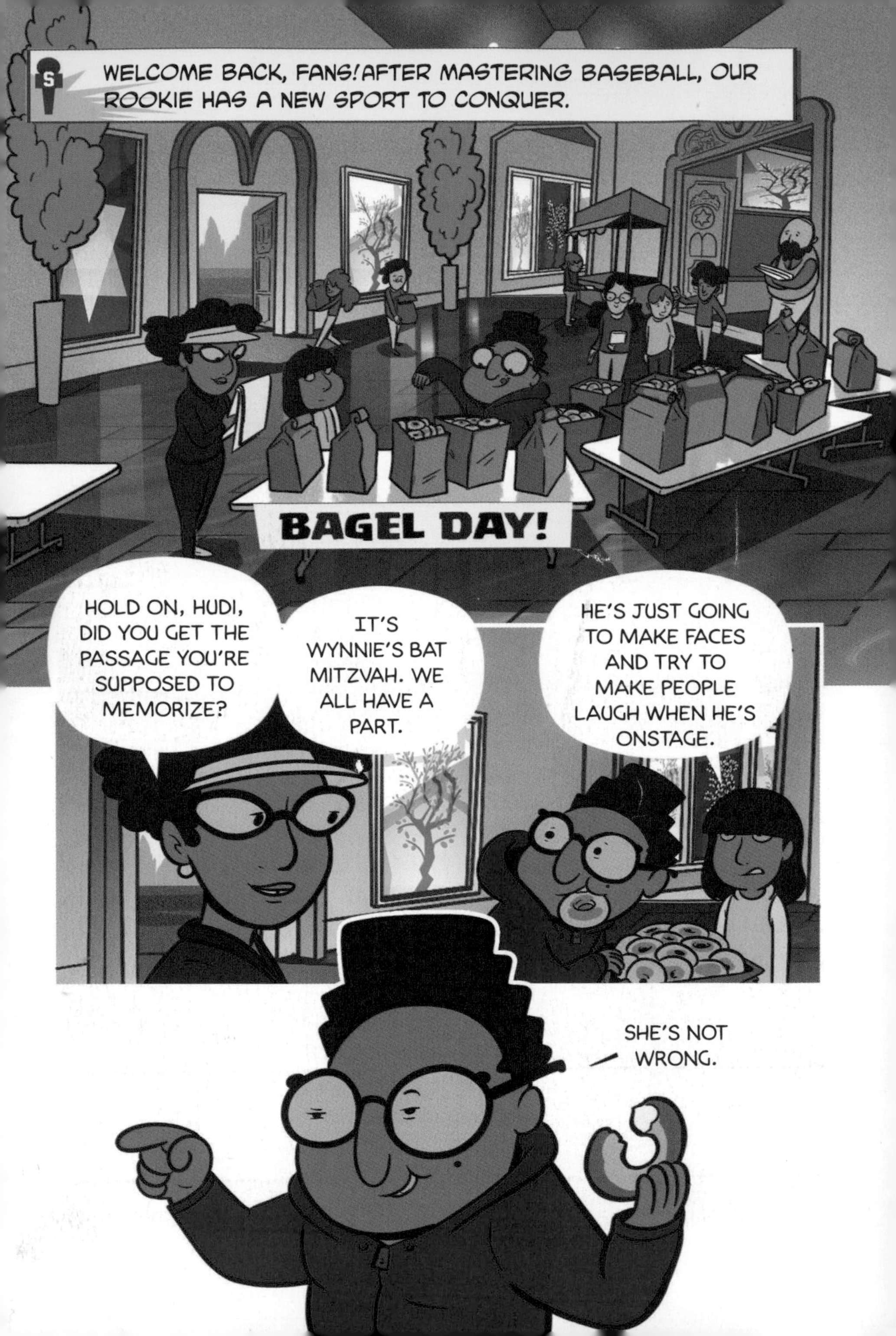
WELCOME BACK, FANS! AFTER MASTERING BASEBALL, OUR ROOKIE HAS A NEW SPORT TO CONQUER.
BAGEL DAY!
HOLD ON, HUDI, DID YOU GET THE PASSAGE YOU'RE SUPPOSED TO MEMORIZE?
IT'S WYNNIE'S BAT MITZVAH. WE ALL HAVE A PART.
HE'S JUST GOING TO MAKE FACES AND TRY TO MAKE PEOPLE LAUGH WHEN HE'S ONSTAGE.
SHE'S NOT WRONG.

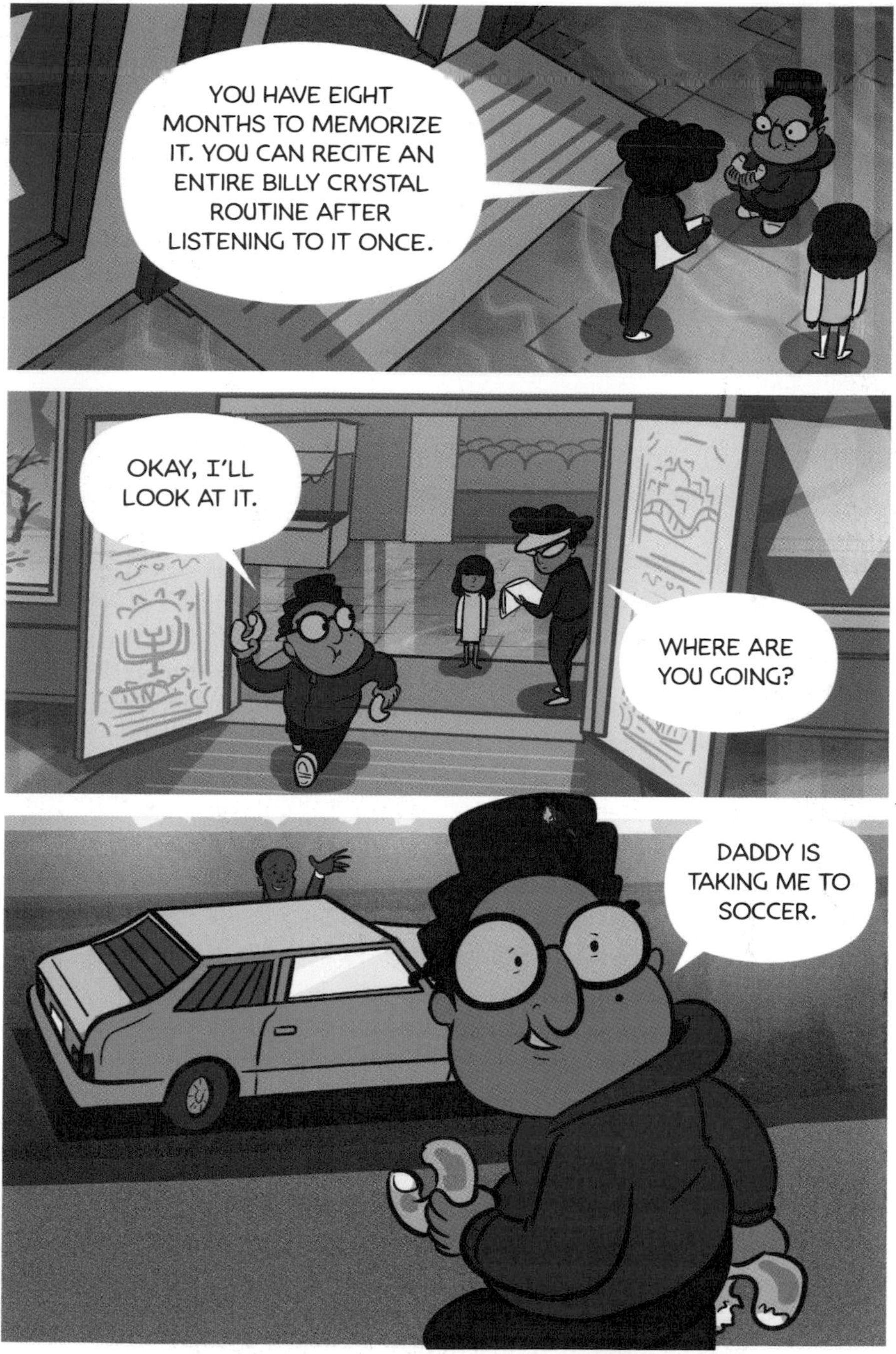
YOU HAVE EIGHT MONTHS TO MEMORIZE IT. YOU CAN RECITE AN ENTIRE BILLY CRYSTAL ROUTINE AFTER LISTENING TO IT ONCE.
OKAY, I'LL LOOK AT IT.
WHERE ARE YOU GOING?
DADDY IS TAKING ME TO SOCCER.

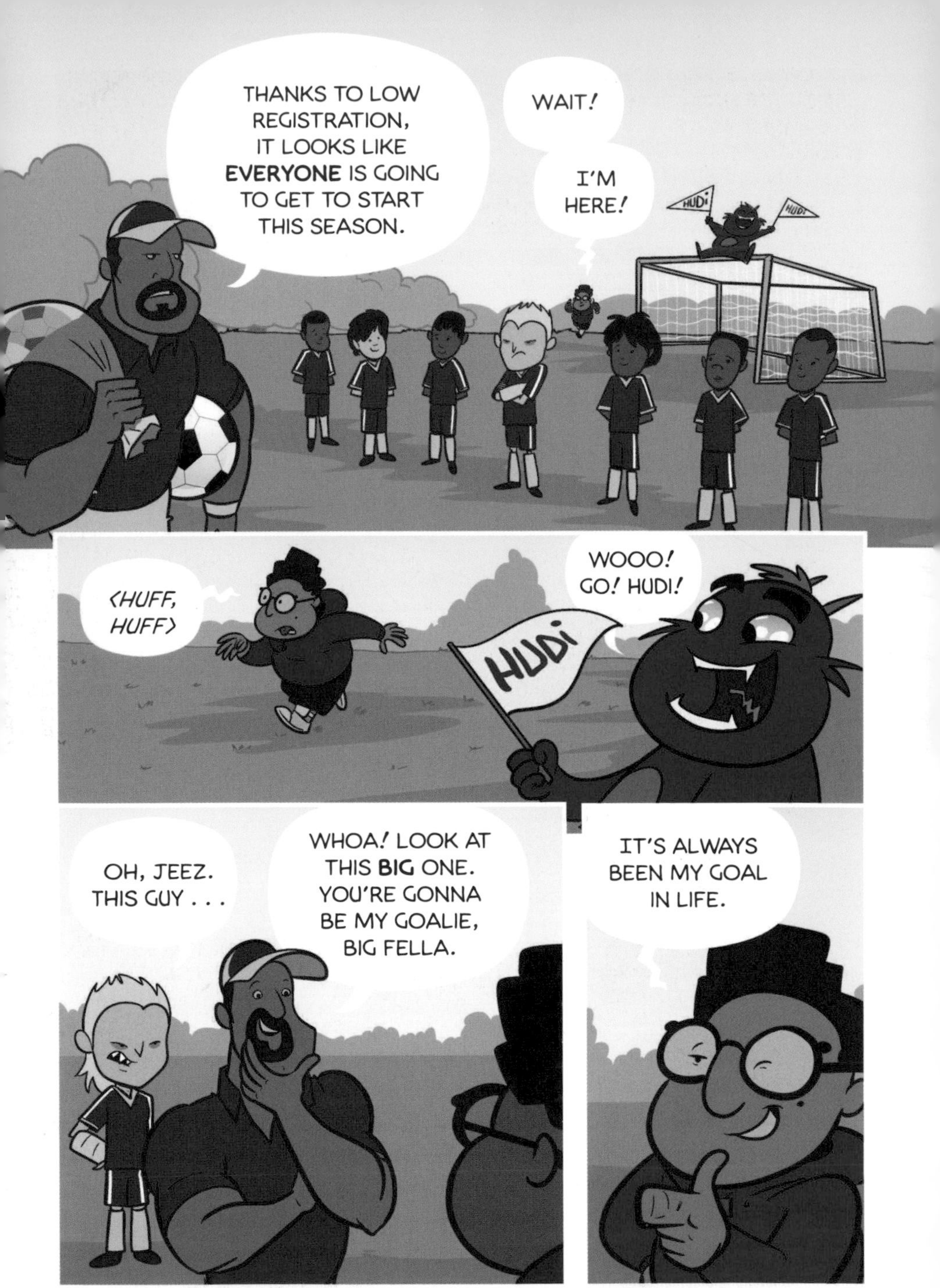
THANKS TO LOW REGISTRATION, IT LOOKS LIKE **EVERYONE** IS GOING TO GET TO START THIS SEASON.
WAIT!
I'M HERE!
HUDI
HUDI
<HUFF, HUFF>
WOOO! GO! HUDI!
HUDI
OH, JEEZ. THIS GUY . . .
WHOA! LOOK AT THIS **BIG** ONE. YOU'RE GONNA BE MY GOALIE, BIG FELLA.
IT'S ALWAYS BEEN MY GOAL IN LIFE.

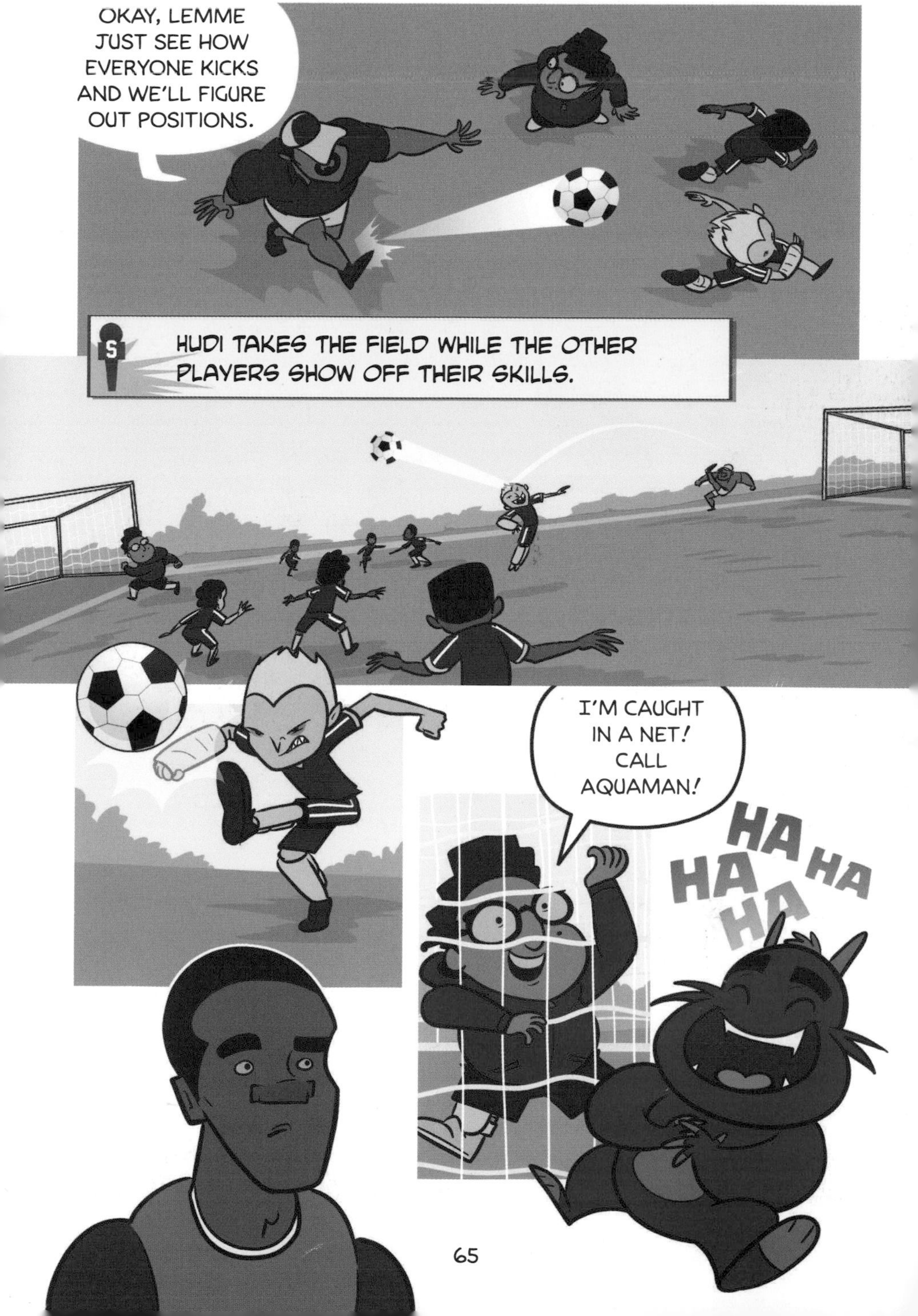
OKAY, LEMME JUST SEE HOW EVERYONE KICKS AND WE'LL FIGURE OUT POSITIONS.
HUDI TAKES THE FIELD WHILE THE OTHER PLAYERS SHOW OFF THEIR SKILLS.
I'M CAUGHT IN A NET! CALL AQUAMAN!
HA HA HA HA HA

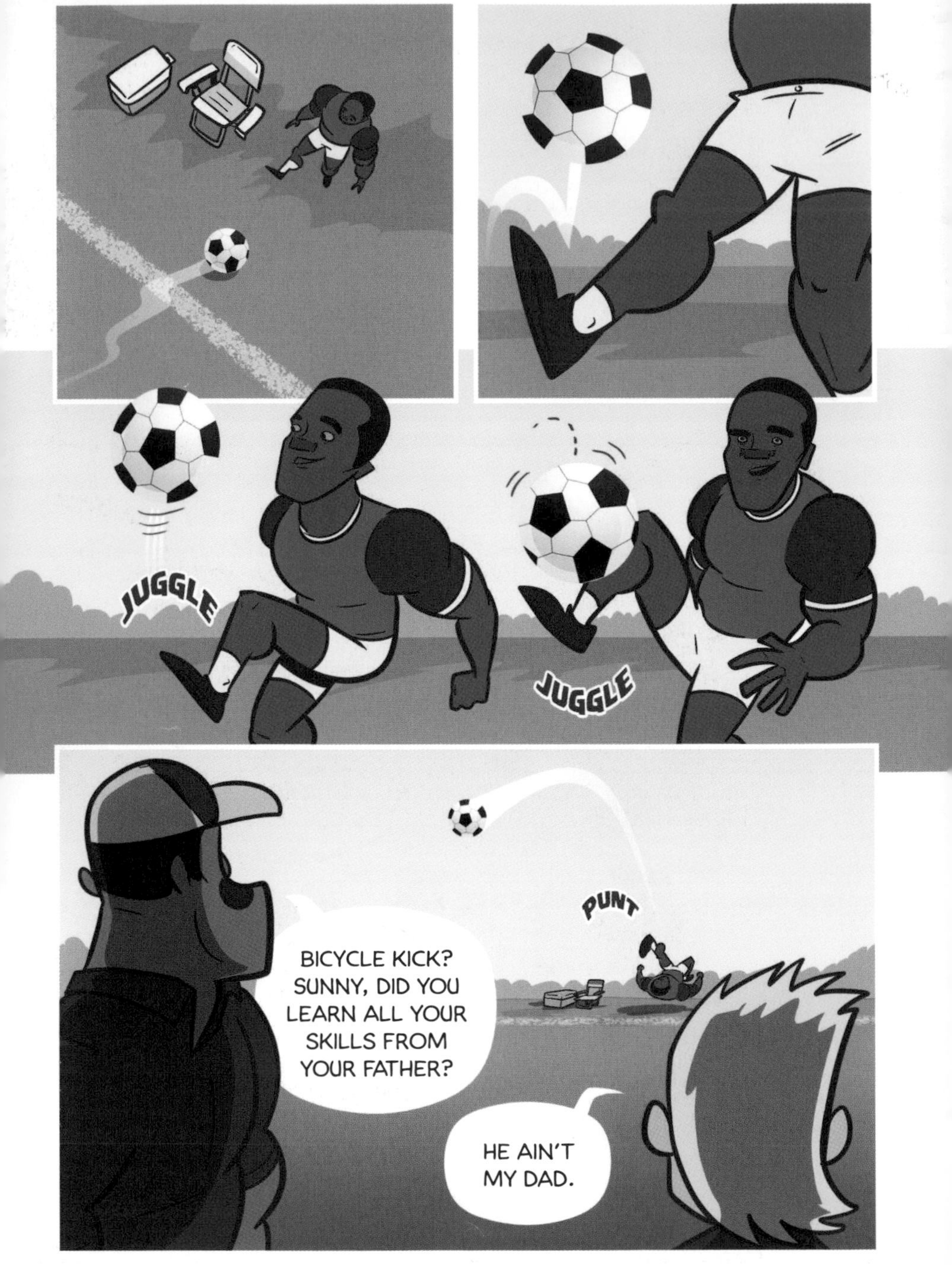
JUGGLE
JUGGLE
PUNT
BICYCLE KICK? SUNNY, DID YOU LEARN ALL YOUR SKILLS FROM YOUR FATHER?
HE AIN'T MY DAD.

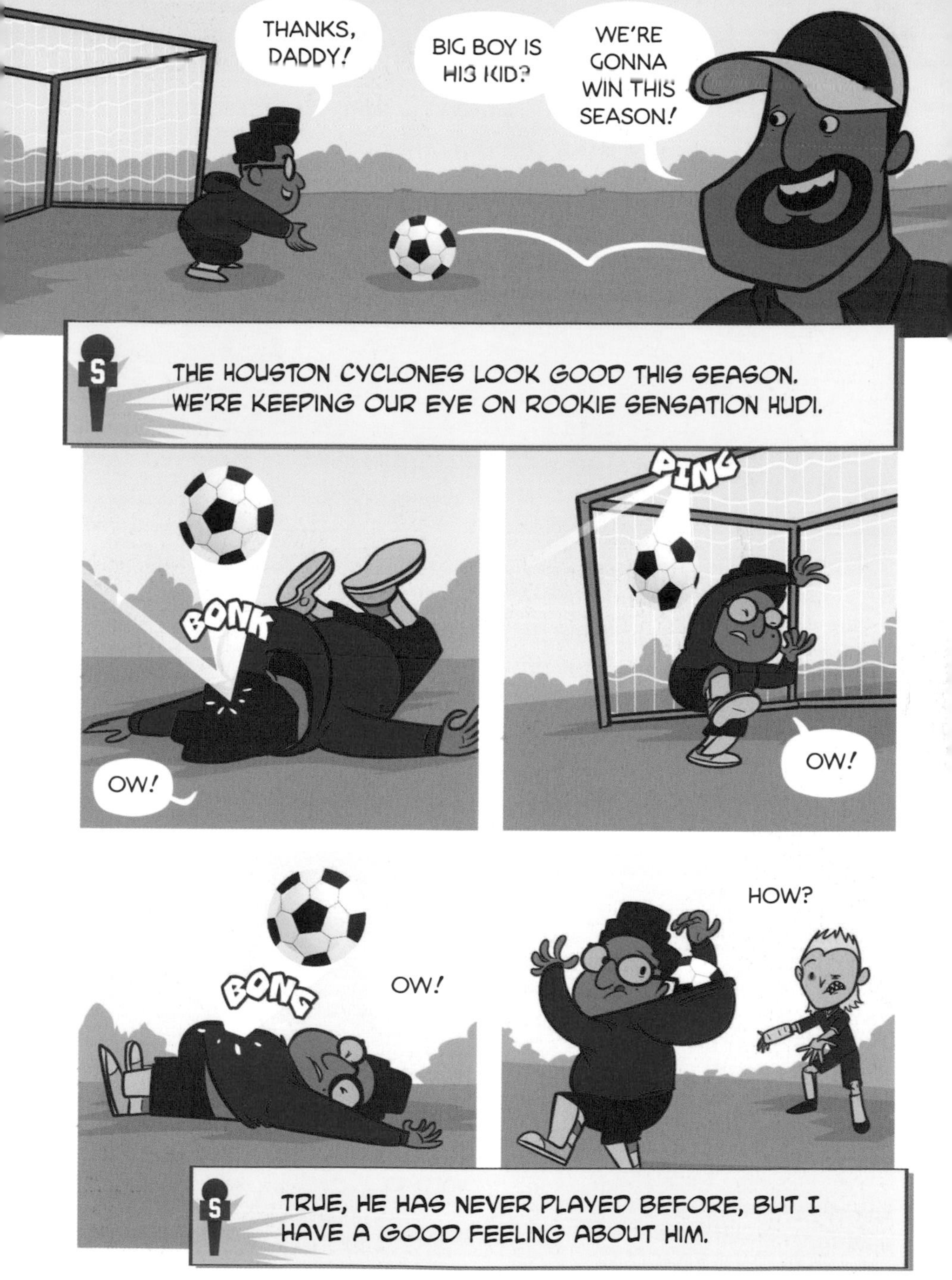
THANKS, DADDY!
BIG BOY IS HIS KID?
WE'RE GONNA WIN THIS SEASON!
THE HOUSTON CYCLONES LOOK GOOD THIS SEASON. WE'RE KEEPING OUR EYE ON ROOKIE SENSATION HUDI.
BONK
OW!
PING
OW!
BONG
OW!
HOW?
TRUE, HE HAS NEVER PLAYED BEFORE, BUT I HAVE A GOOD FEELING ABOUT HIM.

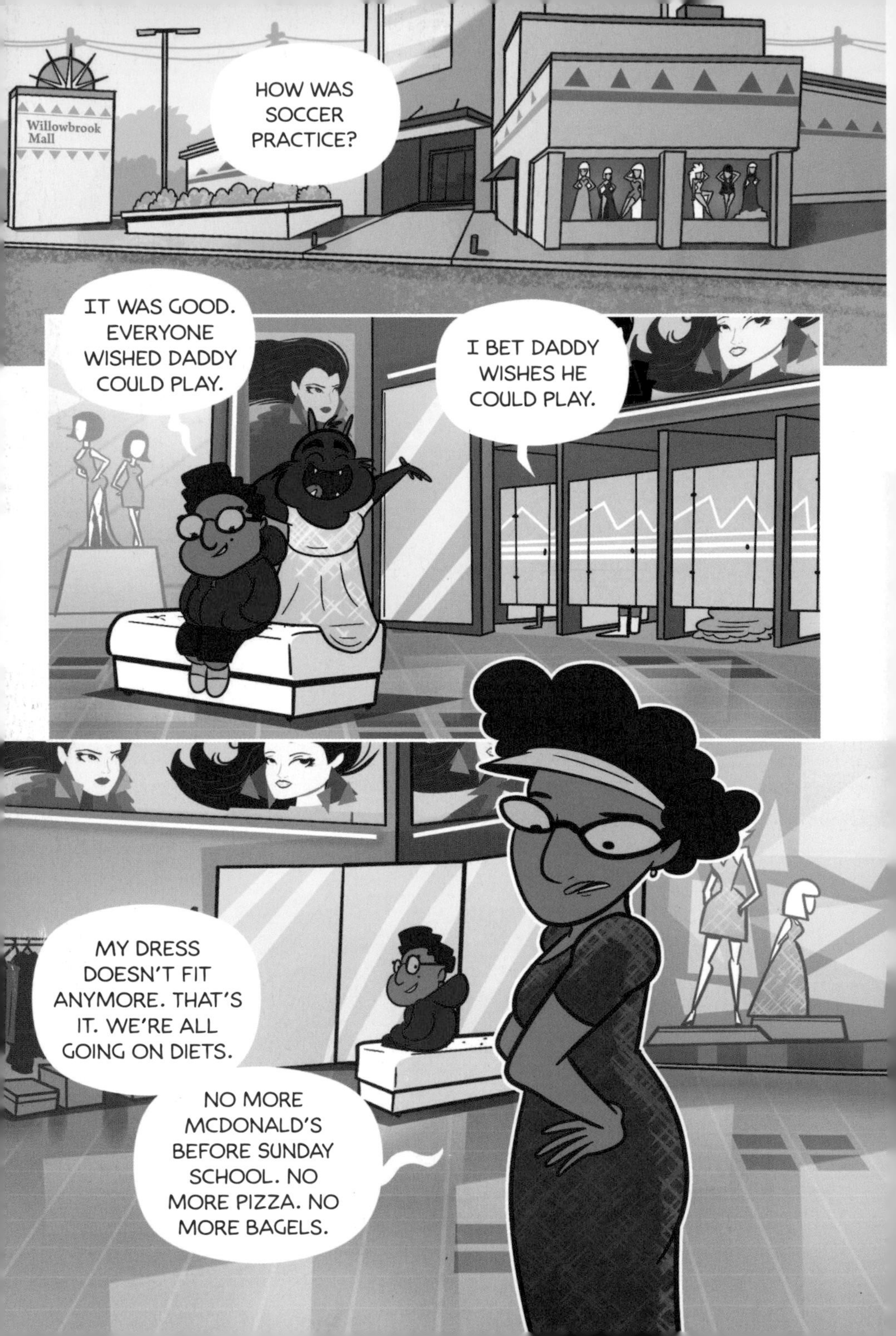
Willowbrook Mall
HOW WAS SOCCER PRACTICE?
IT WAS GOOD. EVERYONE WISHED DADDY COULD PLAY.
I BET DADDY WISHES HE COULD PLAY.
MY DRESS DOESN'T FIT ANYMORE. THAT'S IT. WE'RE ALL GOING ON DIETS.
NO MORE MCDONALD'S BEFORE SUNDAY SCHOOL. NO MORE PIZZA. NO MORE BAGELS.

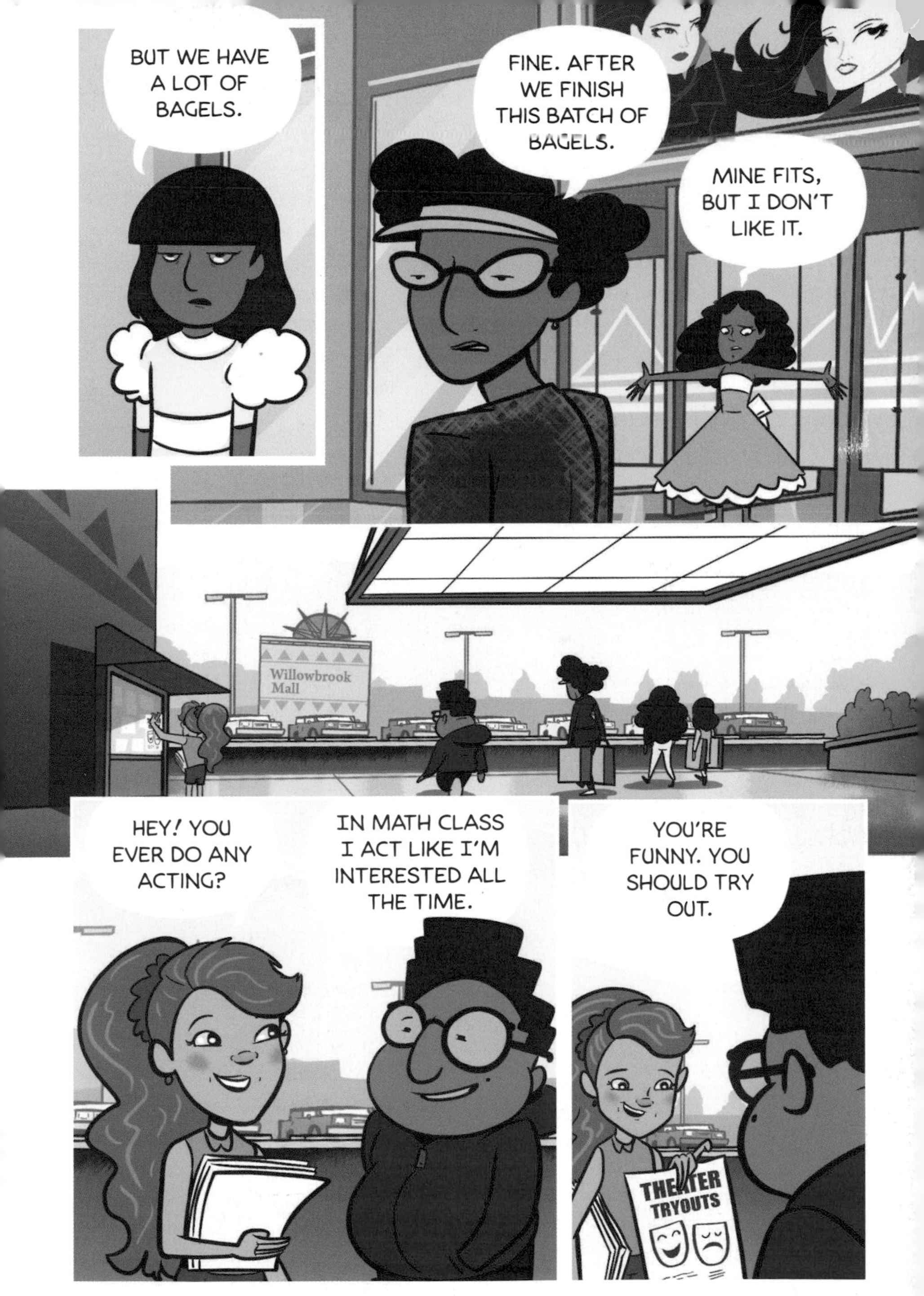

BUT WE HAVE A LOT OF BAGELS.
FINE. AFTER WE FINISH THIS BATCH OF BAGELS.
MINE FITS, BUT I DON'T LIKE IT.
Willowbrook Mall
HEY! YOU EVER DO ANY ACTING?
IN MATH CLASS I ACT LIKE I'M INTERESTED ALL THE TIME.
YOU'RE FUNNY. YOU SHOULD TRY OUT.
THEATER TRYOUTS

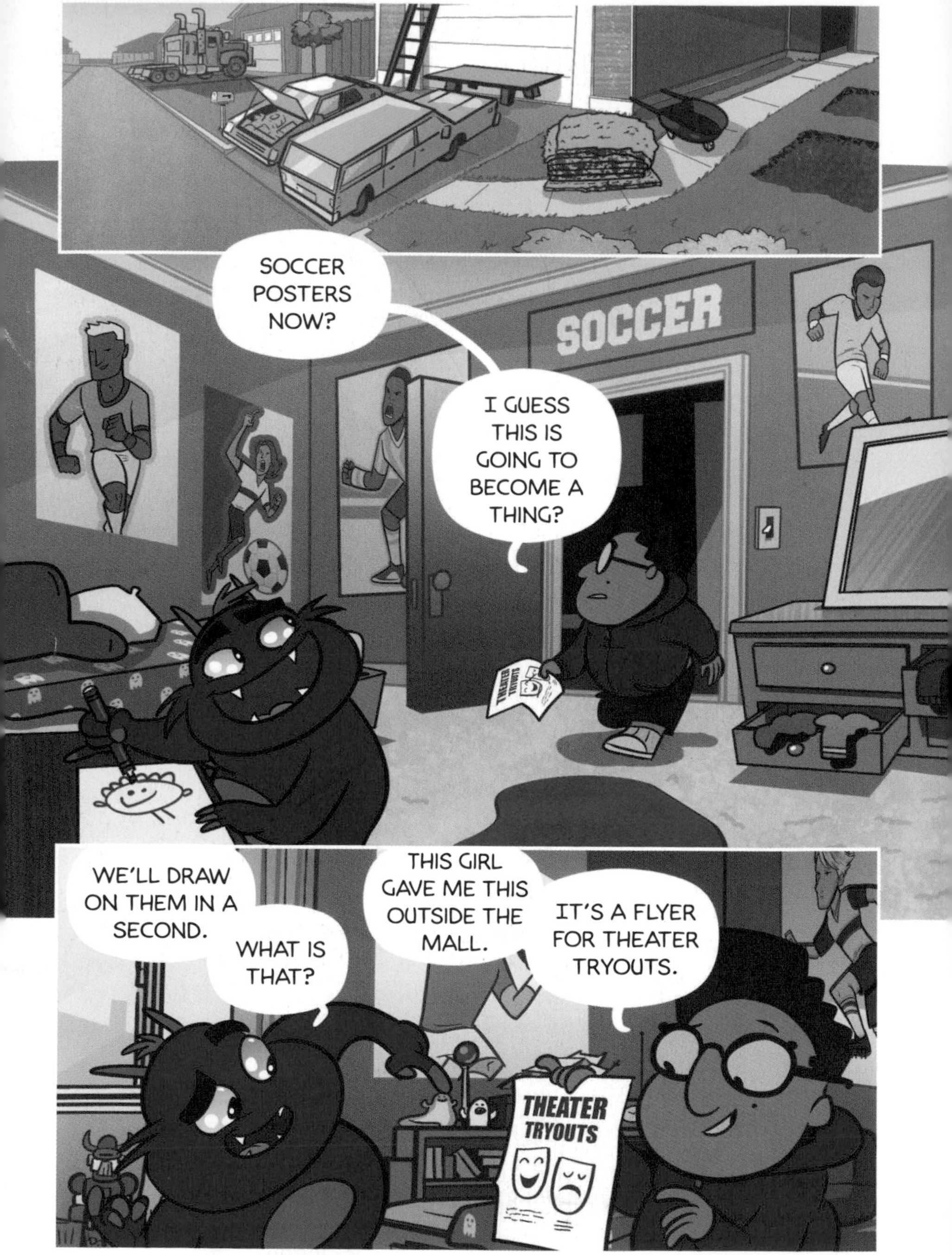
SOCCER POSTERS NOW?
I GUESS THIS IS GOING TO BECOME A THING?
SOCCER
WE'LL DRAW ON THEM IN A SECOND.
WHAT IS THAT?
THIS GIRL GAVE ME THIS OUTSIDE THE MALL.
IT'S A FLYER FOR THEATER TRYOUTS.
THEATER TRYOUTS

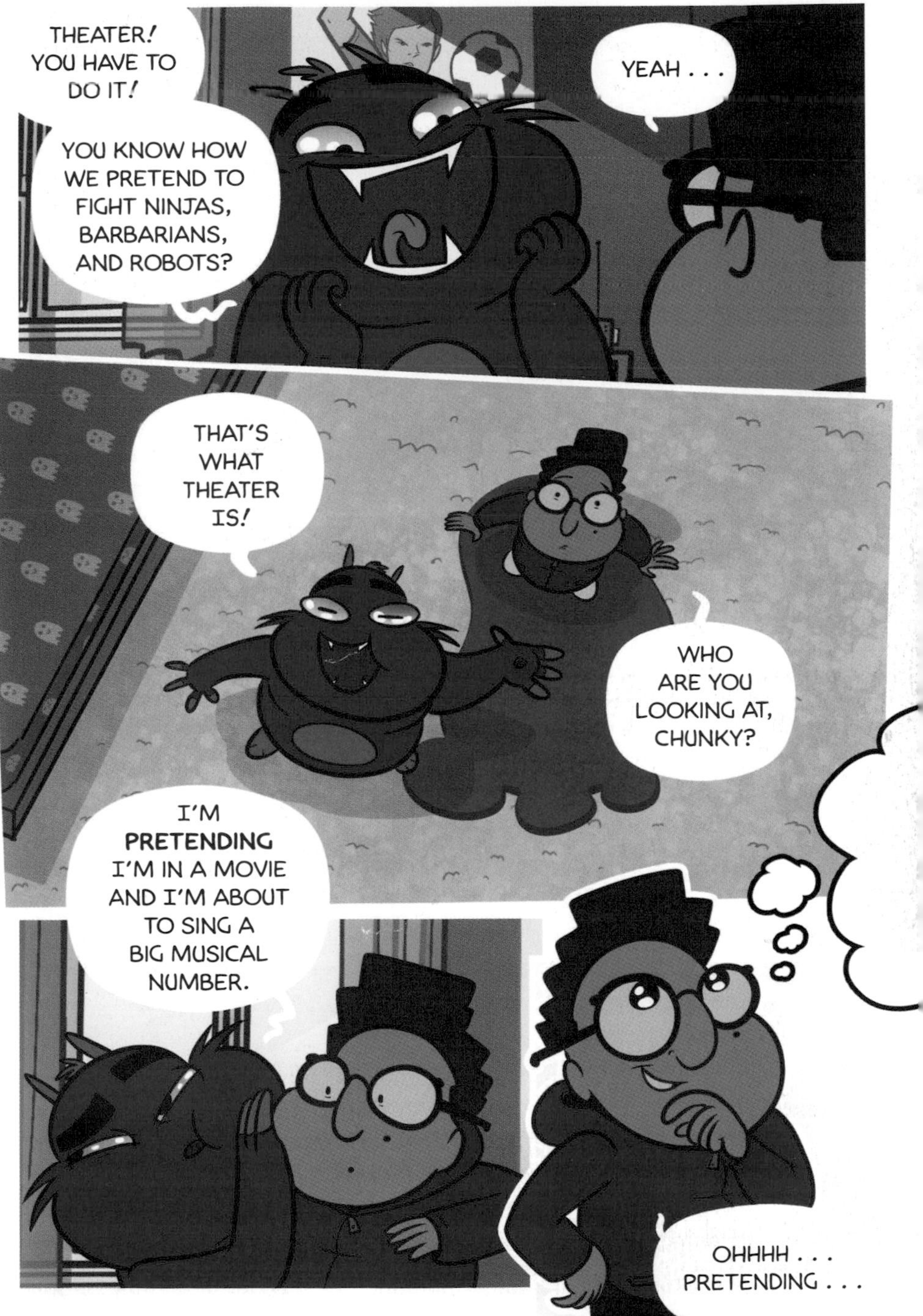
THEATER! YOU HAVE TO DO IT!
YOU KNOW HOW WE PRETEND TO FIGHT NINJAS, BARBARIANS, AND ROBOTS?
YEAH . . .
THAT'S WHAT THEATER IS!
WHO ARE YOU LOOKING AT, CHUNKY?
I'M **PRETENDING** I'M IN A MOVIE AND I'M ABOUT TO SING A BIG MUSICAL NUMBER.
OHHHH . . . PRETENDING . . .

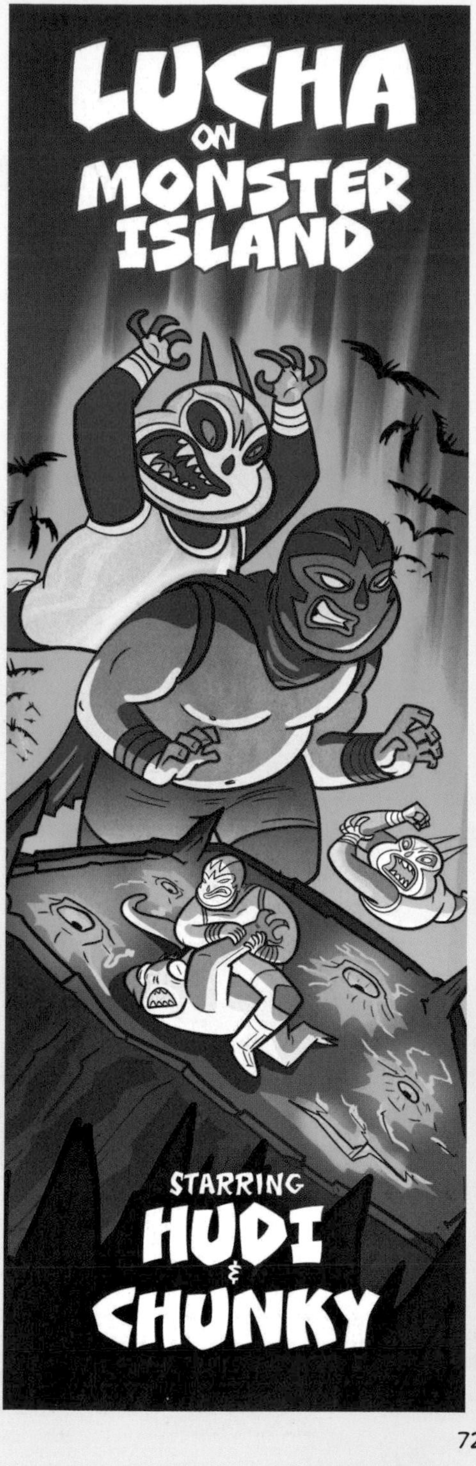
LUCHA
ON
MONSTER
ISLAND
STARRING
HUDI
&
CHUNKY

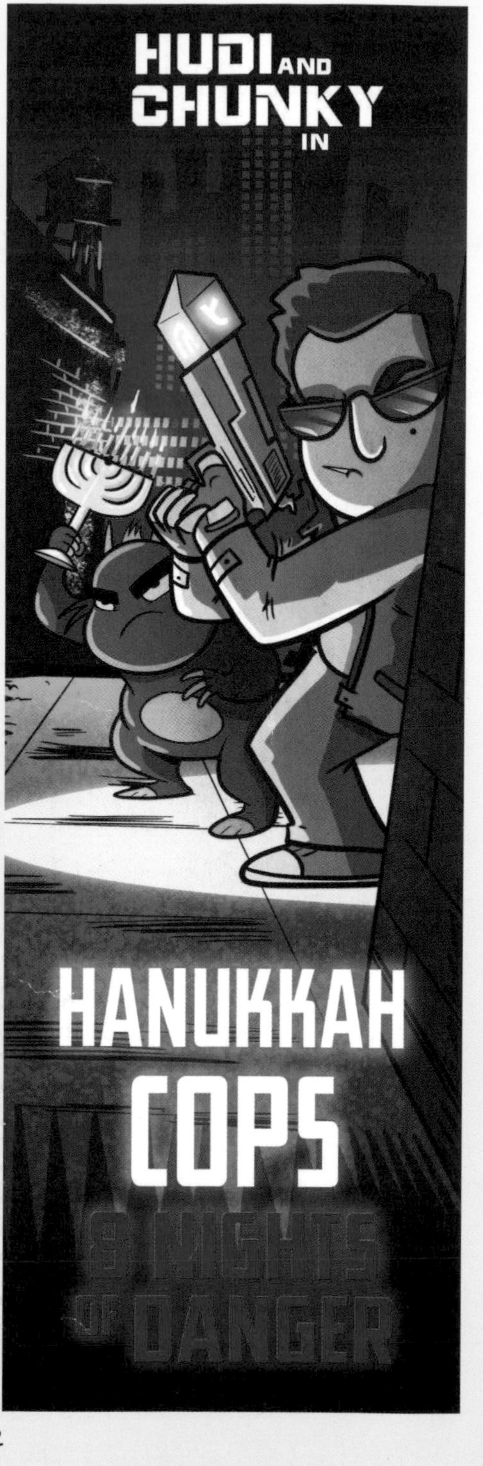
HUDI AND
CHUNKY
IN
HANUKKAH
COPS
8 NIGHTS
OF DANGER

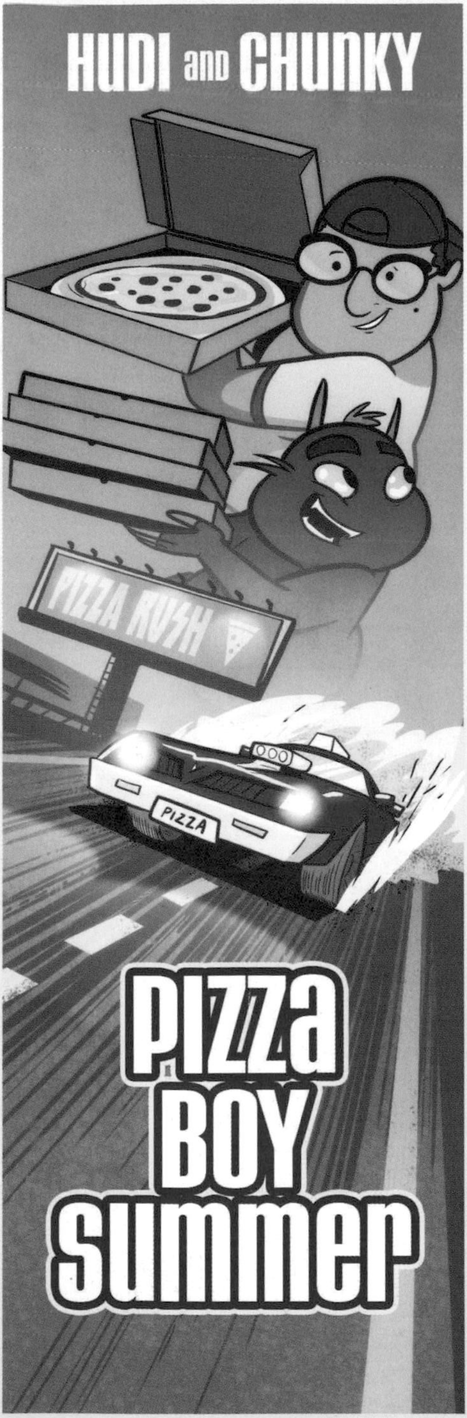
HUDI and CHUNKY
PIZZA RUSH
PIZZA
pizza
BOY
summer

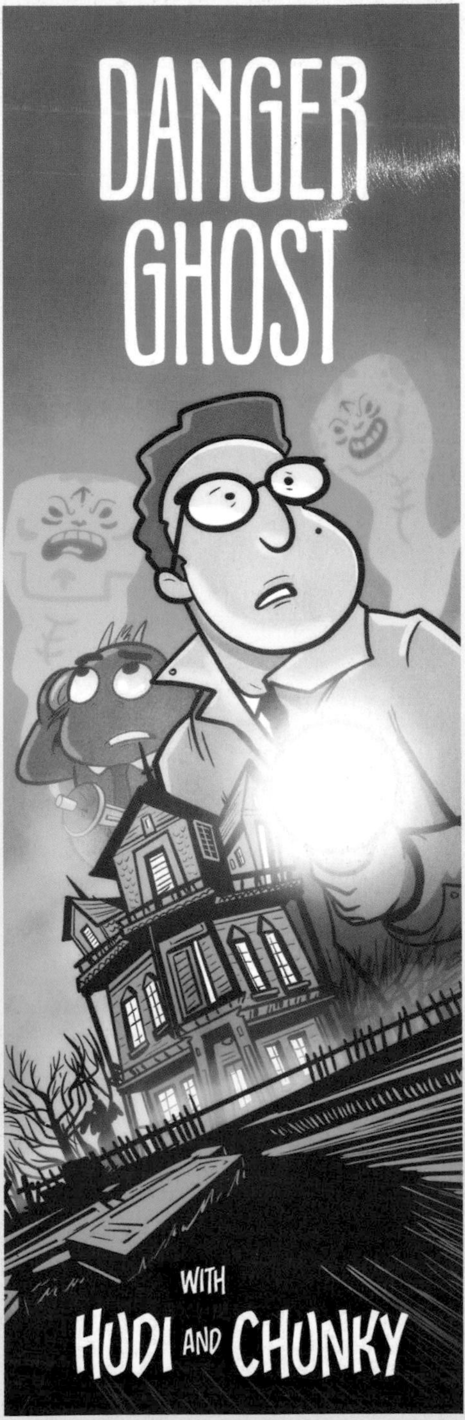
DANGER
GHOST
WITH
HUDI AND CHUNKY

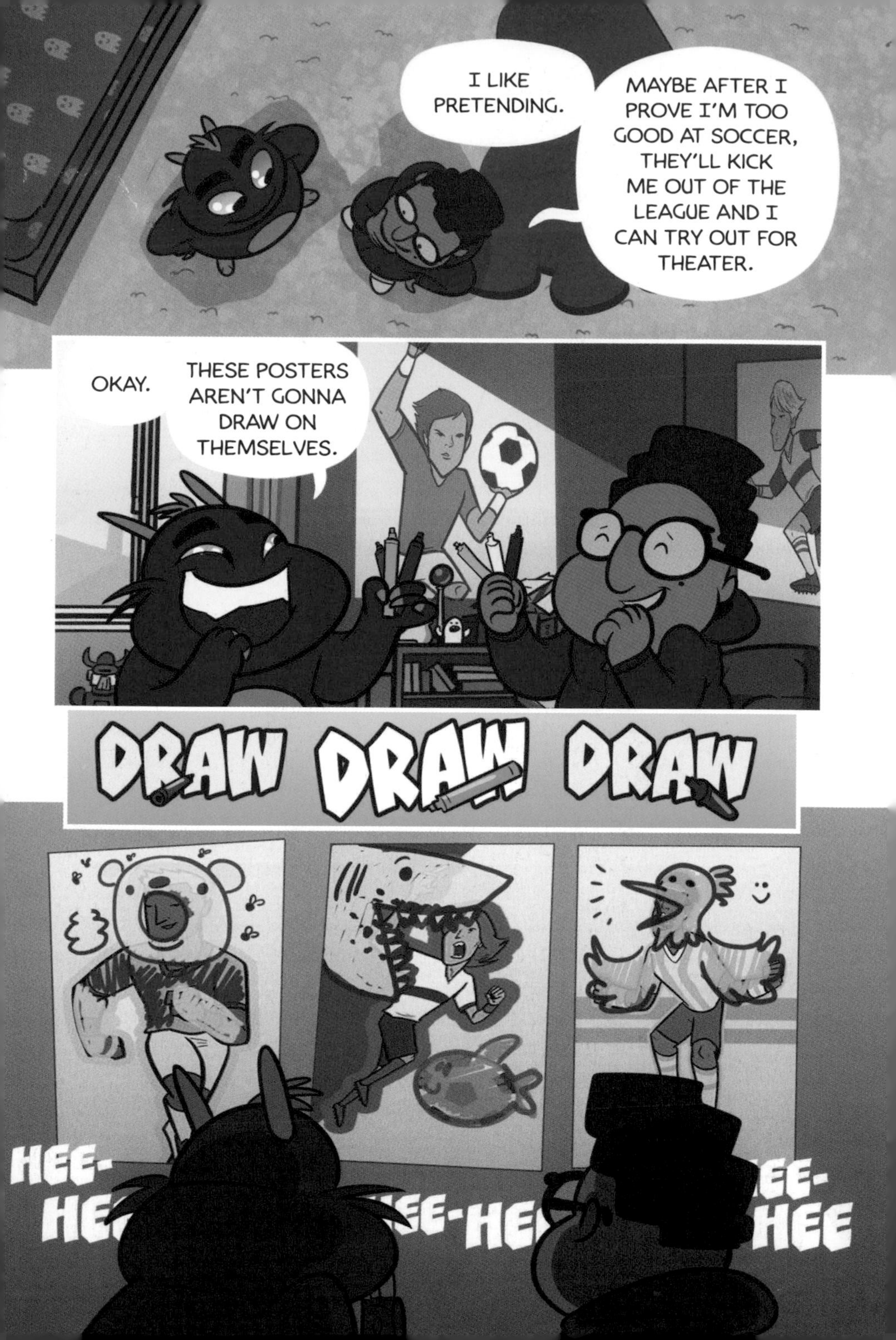
I LIKE PRETENDING.
MAYBE AFTER I PROVE I'M TOO GOOD AT SOCCER, THEY'LL KICK ME OUT OF THE LEAGUE AND I CAN TRY OUT FOR THEATER.
OKAY.
THESE POSTERS AREN'T GONNA DRAW ON THEMSELVES.
DRAW DRAW DRAW
HEE-

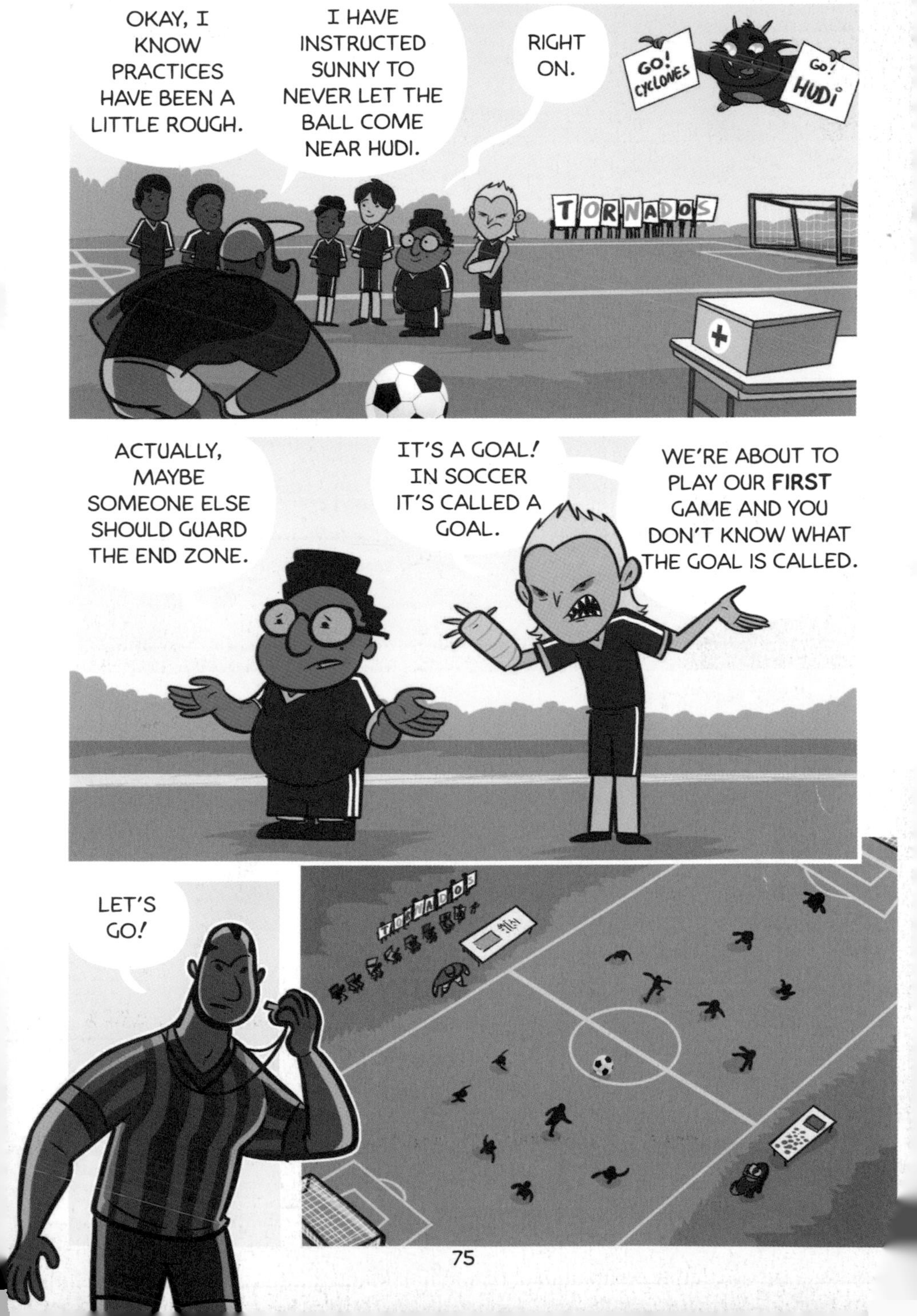
OKAY, I KNOW PRACTICES HAVE BEEN A LITTLE ROUGH.
I HAVE INSTRUCTED SUNNY TO NEVER LET THE BALL COME NEAR HUDI.
RIGHT ON.
GO! CYCLONES
GO! HUDI
TORNADOS
ACTUALLY, MAYBE SOMEONE ELSE SHOULD GUARD THE END ZONE.
IT'S A GOAL! IN SOCCER IT'S CALLED A GOAL.
WE'RE ABOUT TO PLAY OUR **FIRST** GAME AND YOU DON'T KNOW WHAT THE GOAL IS CALLED.
LET'S GO!

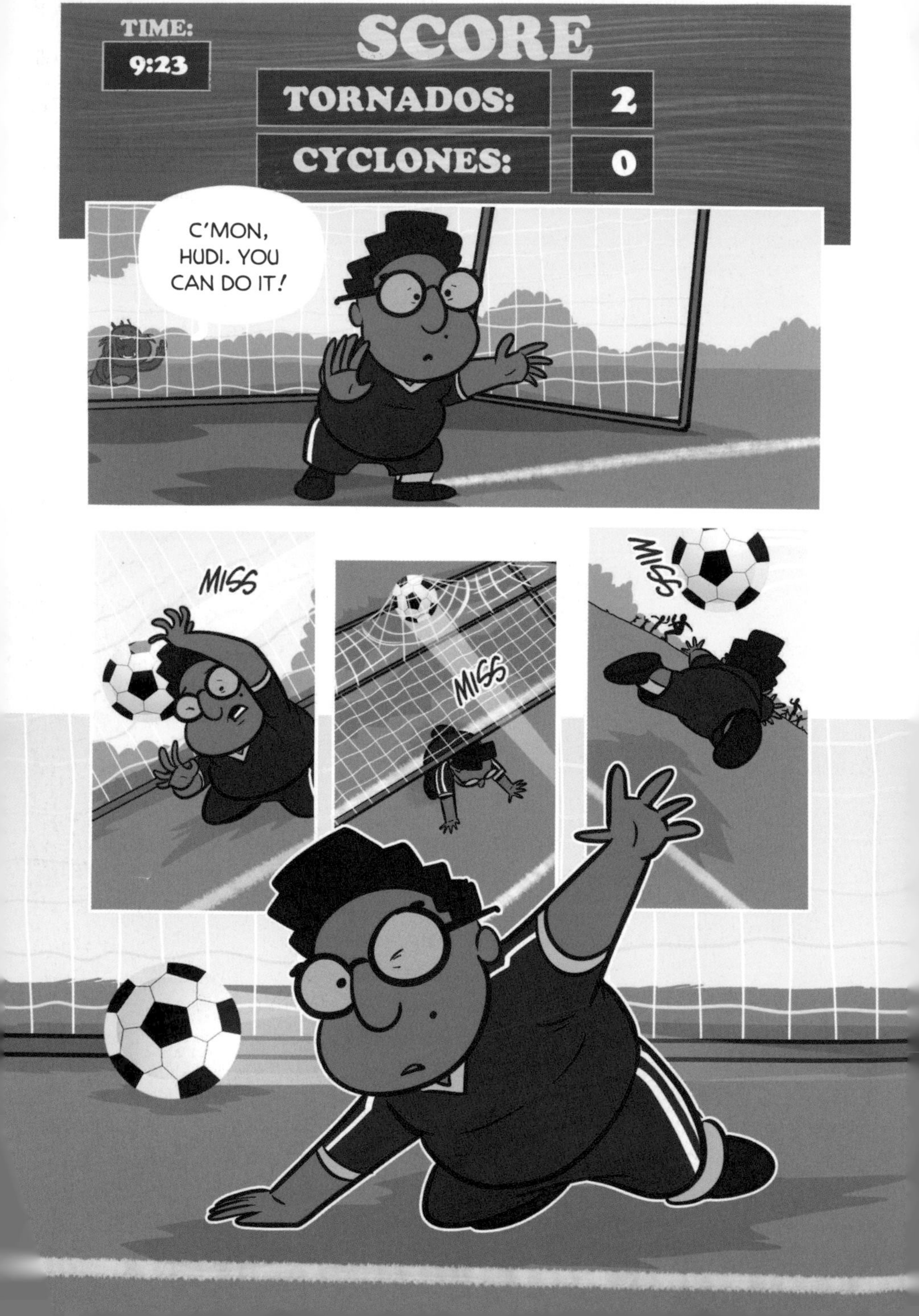
TIME:
9:23
SCORE
TORNADOS: 2
CYCLONES: 0
C'MON, HUDI. YOU CAN DO IT!
MISS
MISS
MISS

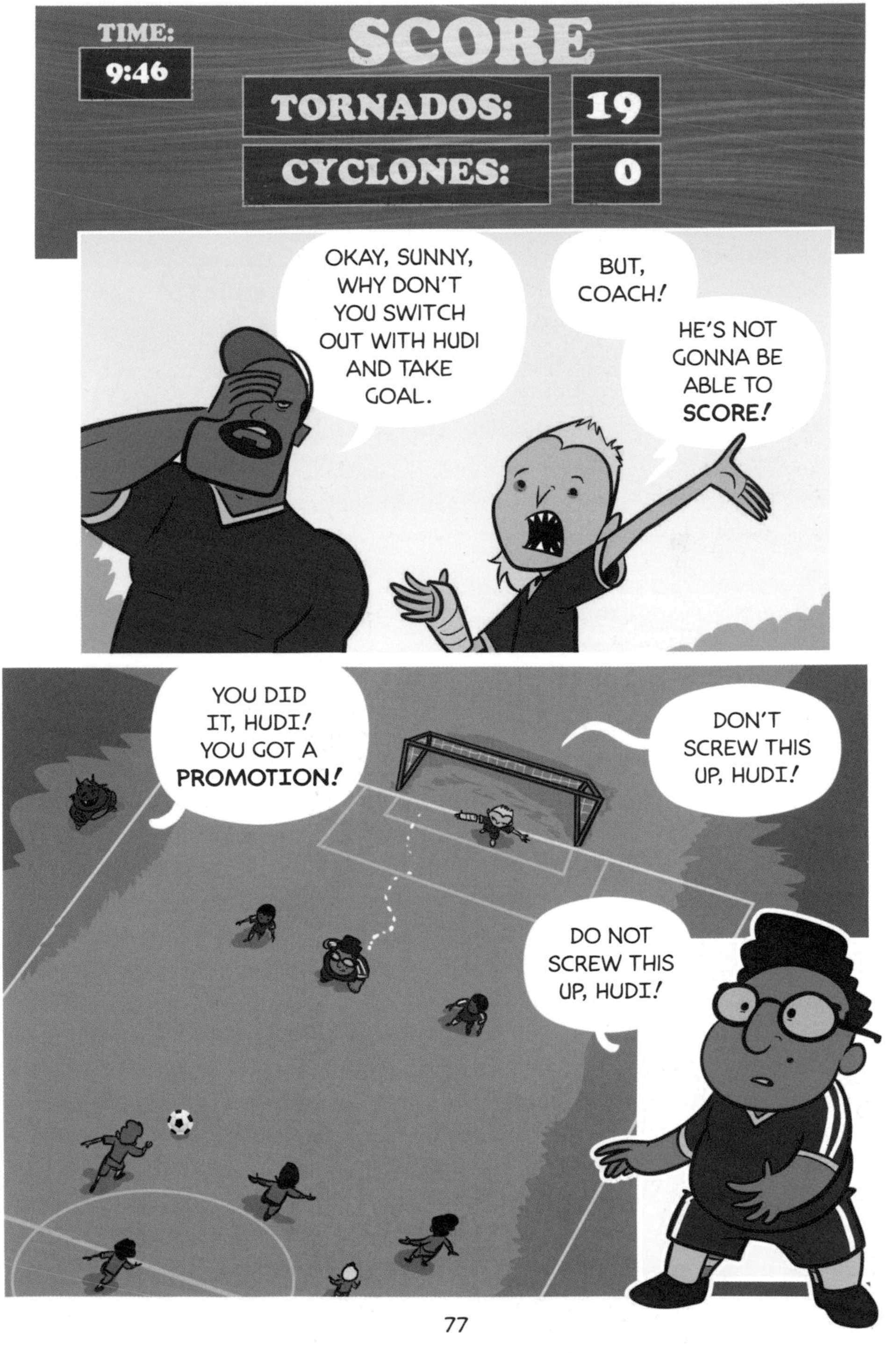
TIME:
9:46
SCORE
TORNADOS: 19
CYCLONES: 0
OKAY, SUNNY, WHY DON'T YOU SWITCH OUT WITH HUDI AND TAKE GOAL.
BUT, COACH!
HE'S NOT GONNA BE ABLE TO SCORE!
YOU DID IT, HUDI! YOU GOT A PROMOTION!
DON'T SCREW THIS UP, HUDI!
DO NOT SCREW THIS UP, HUDI!

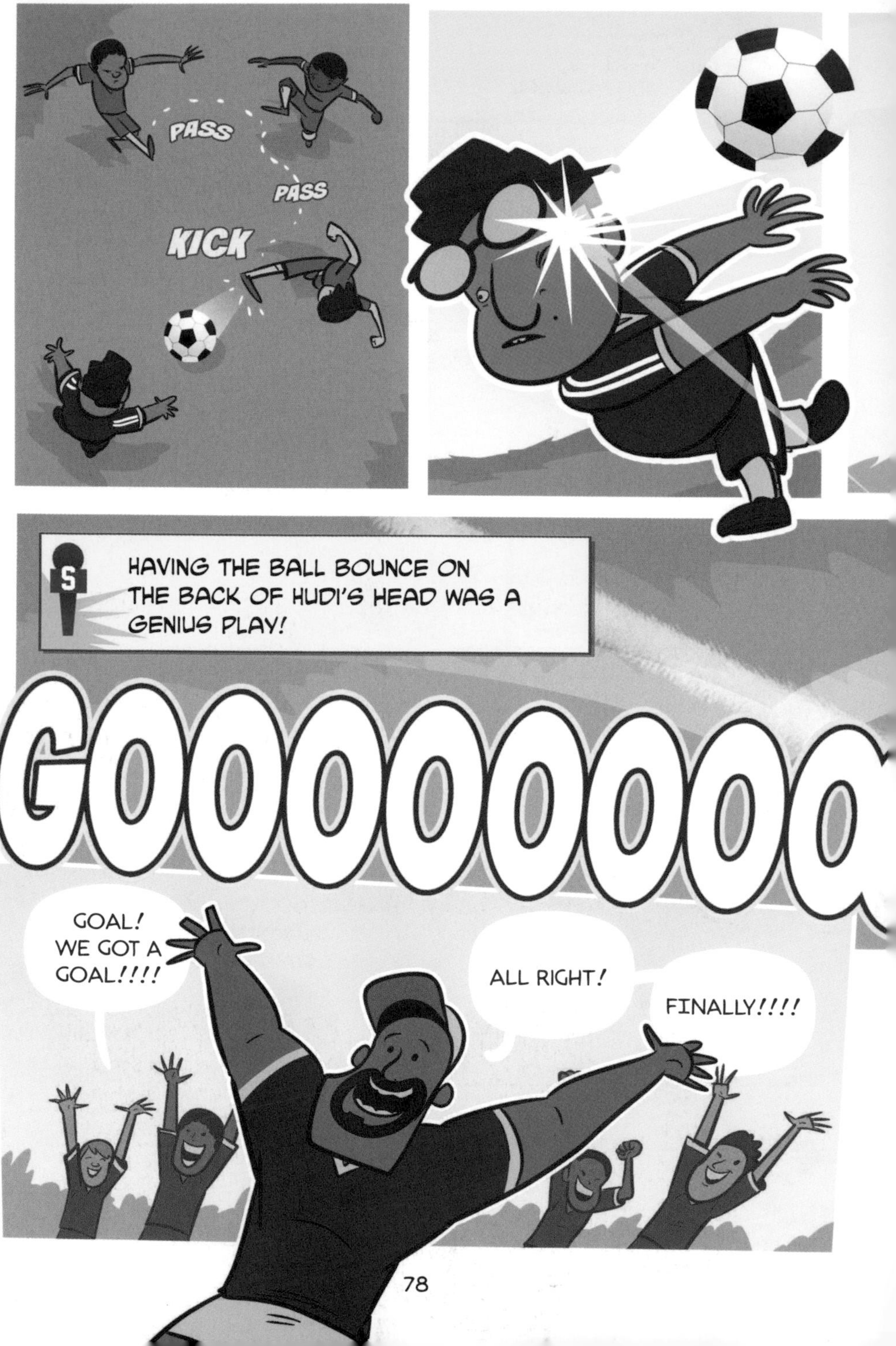
PASS
PASS
KICK
HAVING THE BALL BOUNCE ON THE BACK OF HUDI'S HEAD WAS A GENIUS PLAY!
GOOOOOOOA
GOAL! WE GOT A GOAL!!!!
ALL RIGHT!
FINALLY!!!!

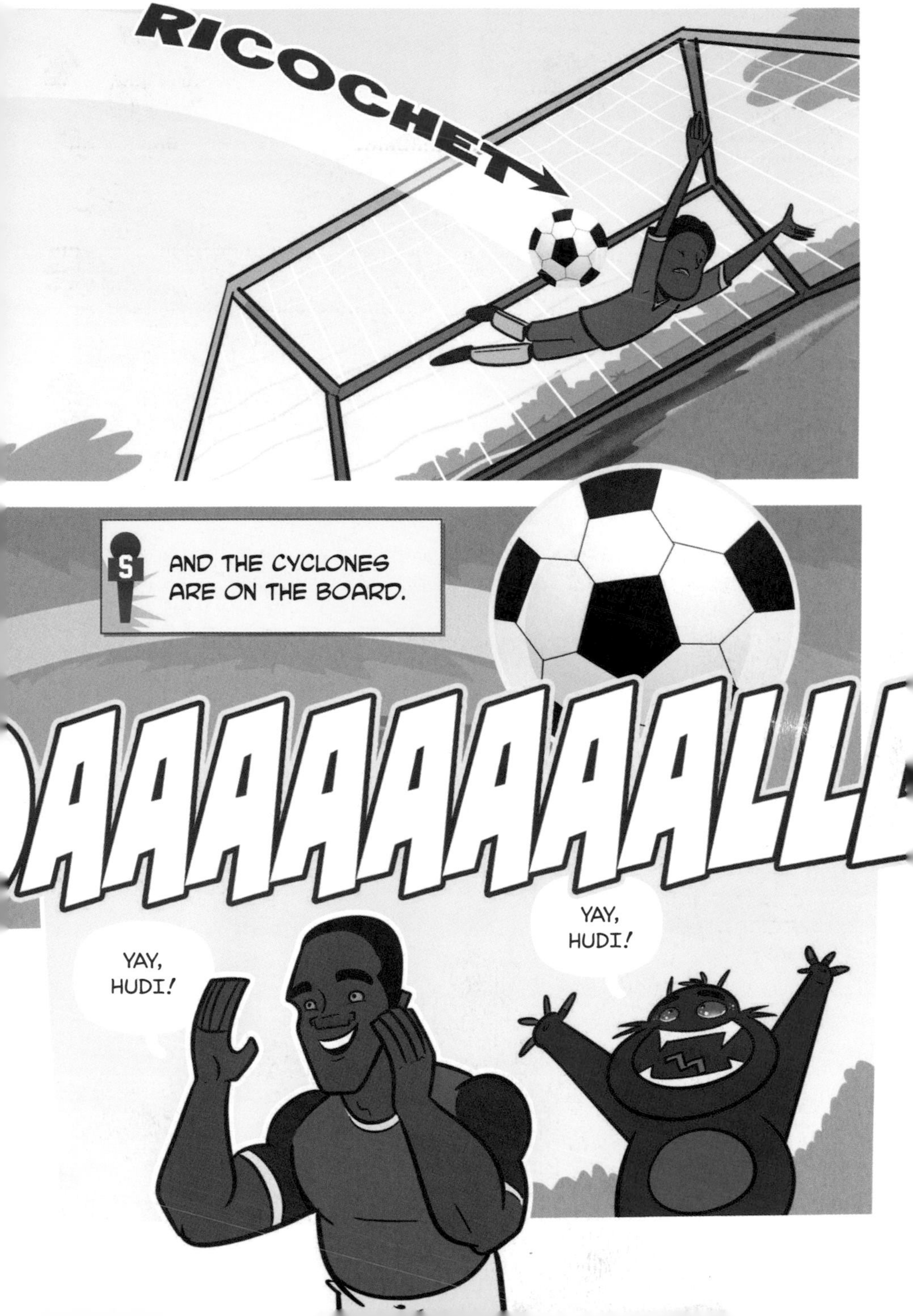
RICOCHET
AND THE CYCLONES ARE ON THE BOARD.
AAAAAAAAALL
YAY, HUDI!
YAY, HUDI!

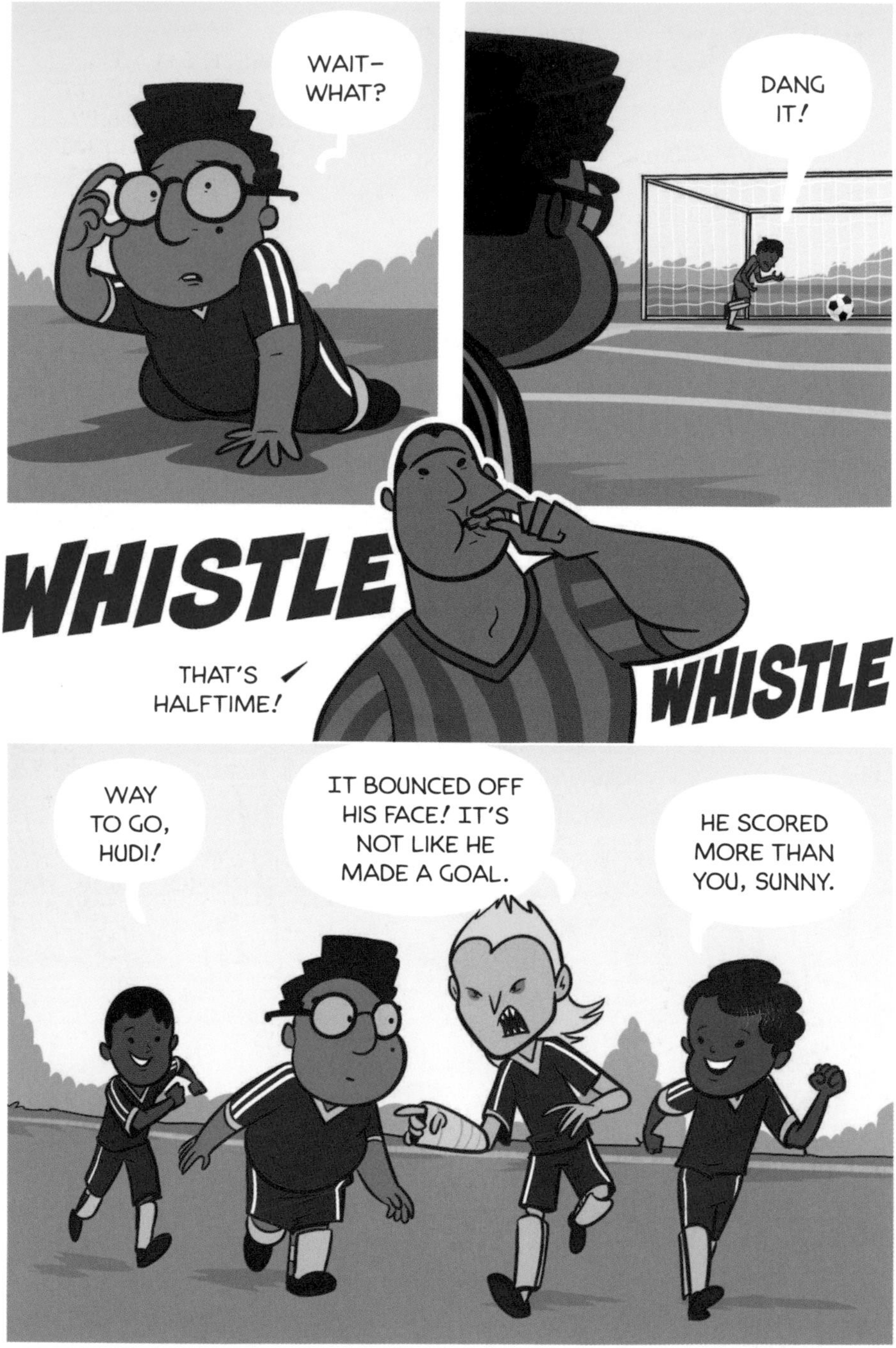
WAIT—
WHAT?
DANG IT!
WHISTLE
THAT'S HALFTIME!
WHISTLE
WAY TO GO, HUDI!
IT BOUNCED OFF HIS FACE! IT'S NOT LIKE HE MADE A GOAL.
HE SCORED MORE THAN YOU, SUNNY.

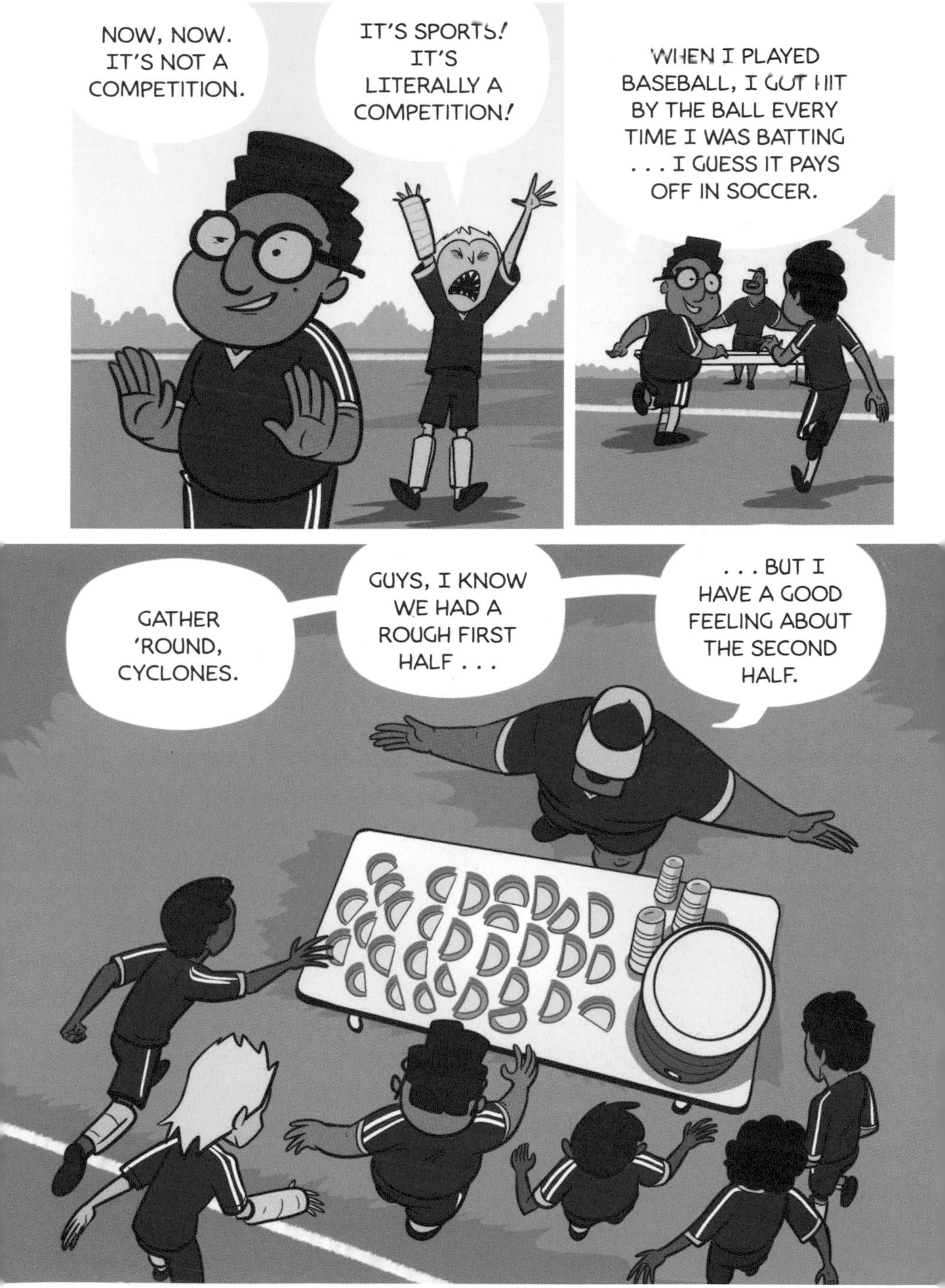
NOW, NOW. IT'S NOT A COMPETITION.
IT'S SPORTS! IT'S LITERALLY A COMPETITION!
WHEN I PLAYED BASEBALL, I GOT HIT BY THE BALL EVERY TIME I WAS BATTING . . . I GUESS IT PAYS OFF IN SOCCER.
GATHER 'ROUND, CYCLONES.
GUYS, I KNOW WE HAD A ROUGH FIRST HALF . . .
. . . BUT I HAVE A GOOD FEELING ABOUT THE SECOND HALF.

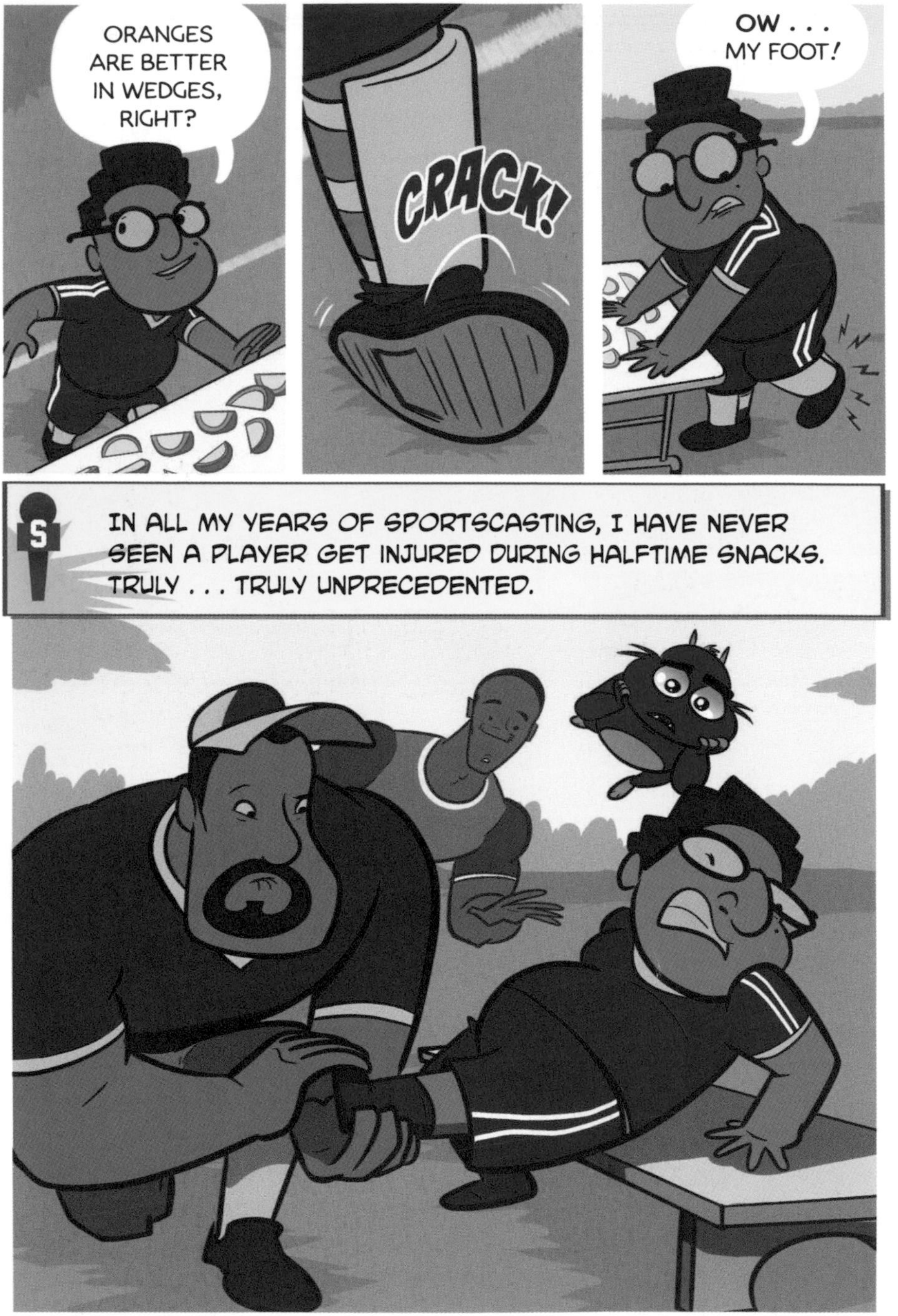
ORANGES ARE BETTER IN WEDGES, RIGHT?
CRACK!
OW . . . MY FOOT!
S
IN ALL MY YEARS OF SPORTSCASTING, I HAVE NEVER SEEN A PLAYER GET INJURED DURING HALFTIME SNACKS. TRULY . . . TRULY UNPRECEDENTED.

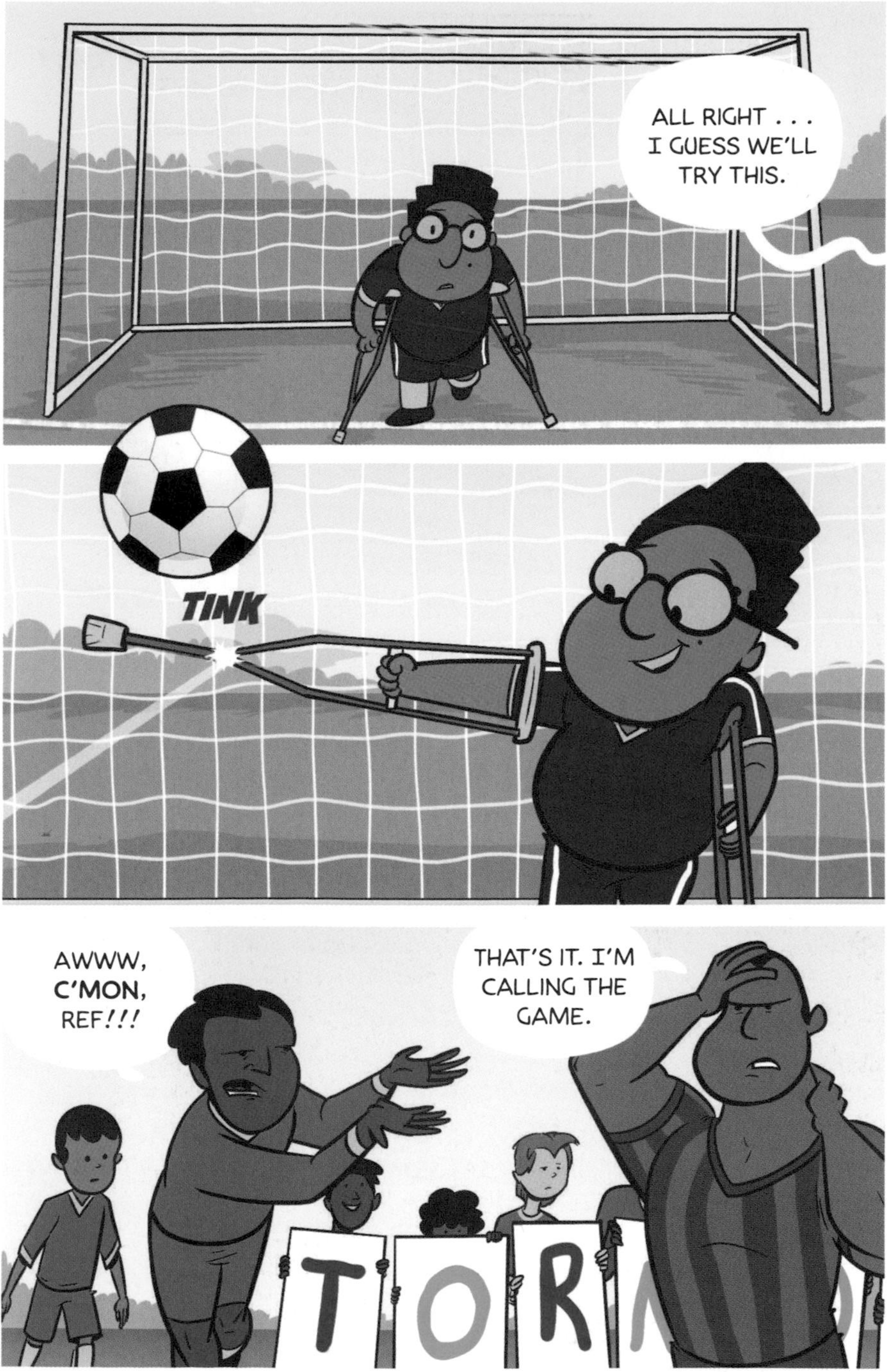
ALL RIGHT . . . I GUESS WE'LL TRY THIS.
TINK
AWWW, **C'MON,** REF*!!!*
THAT'S IT. I'M CALLING THE GAME.

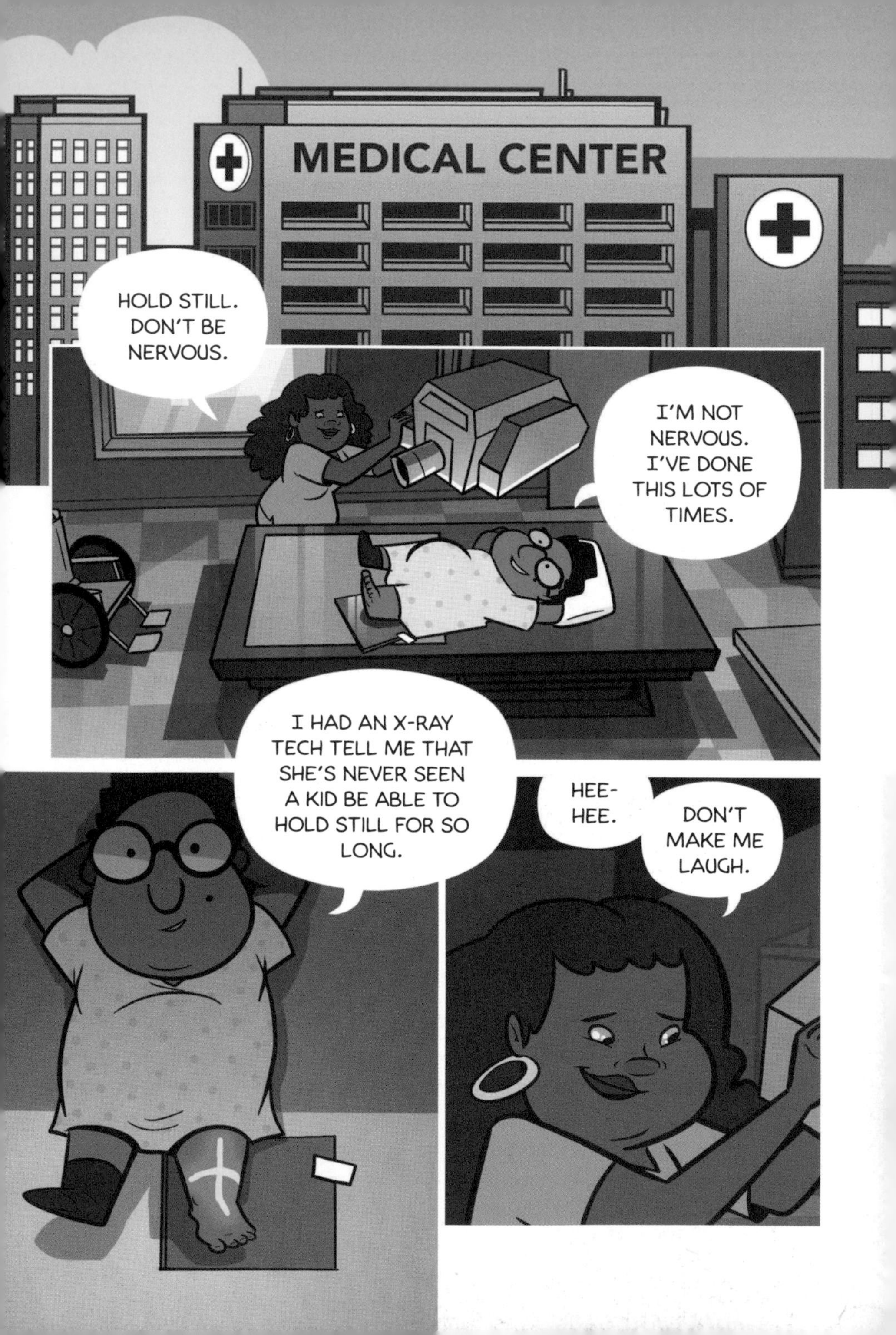
MEDICAL CENTER
HOLD STILL. DON'T BE NERVOUS.
I'M NOT NERVOUS. I'VE DONE THIS LOTS OF TIMES.
I HAD AN X-RAY TECH TELL ME THAT SHE'S NEVER SEEN A KID BE ABLE TO HOLD STILL FOR SO LONG.
HEE-HEE.
DON'T MAKE ME LAUGH.

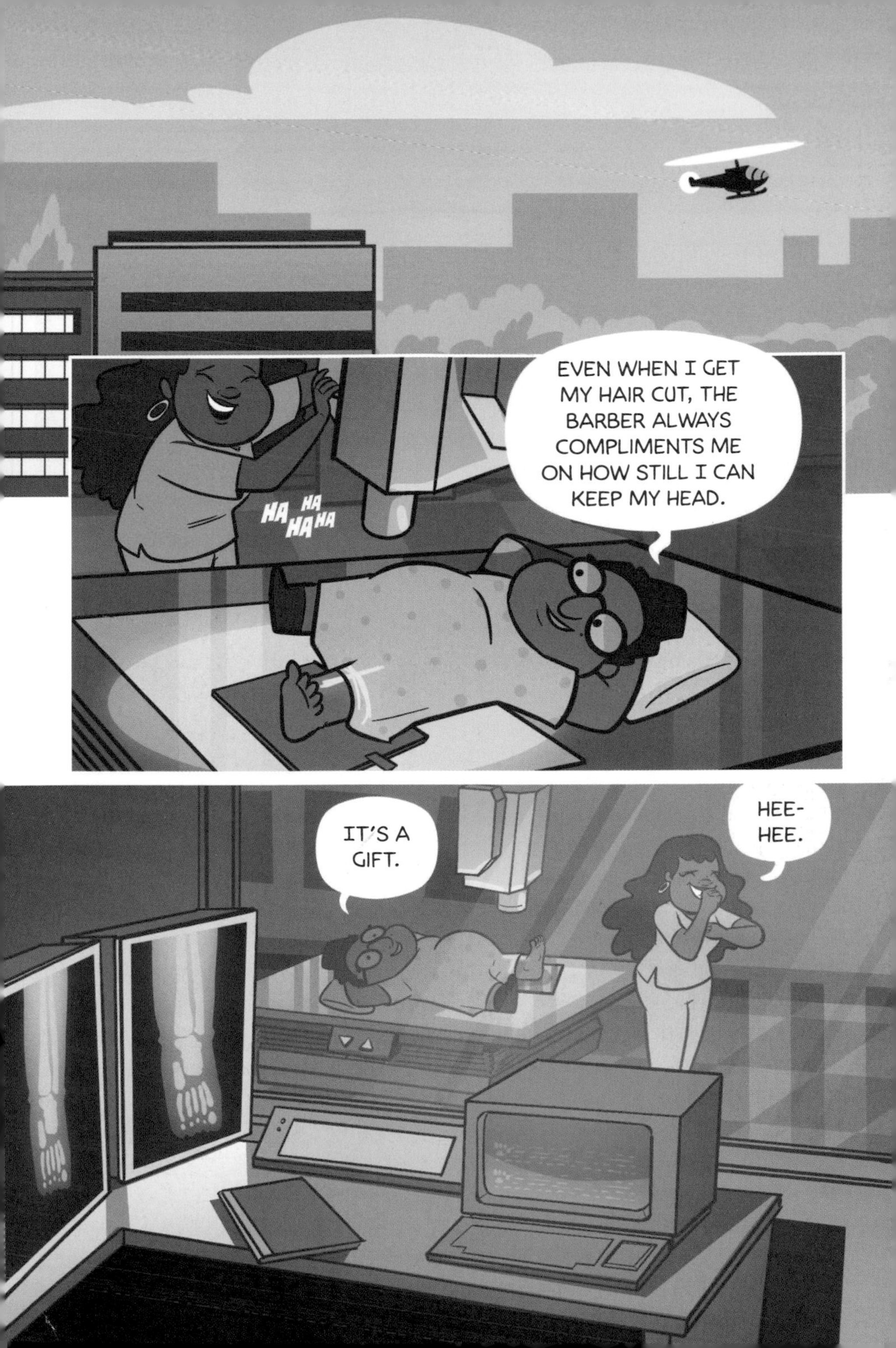

EVEN WHEN I GET MY HAIR CUT, THE BARBER ALWAYS COMPLIMENTS ME ON HOW STILL I CAN KEEP MY HEAD.
HA HA HA HA
IT'S A GIFT.
HEE-HEE.

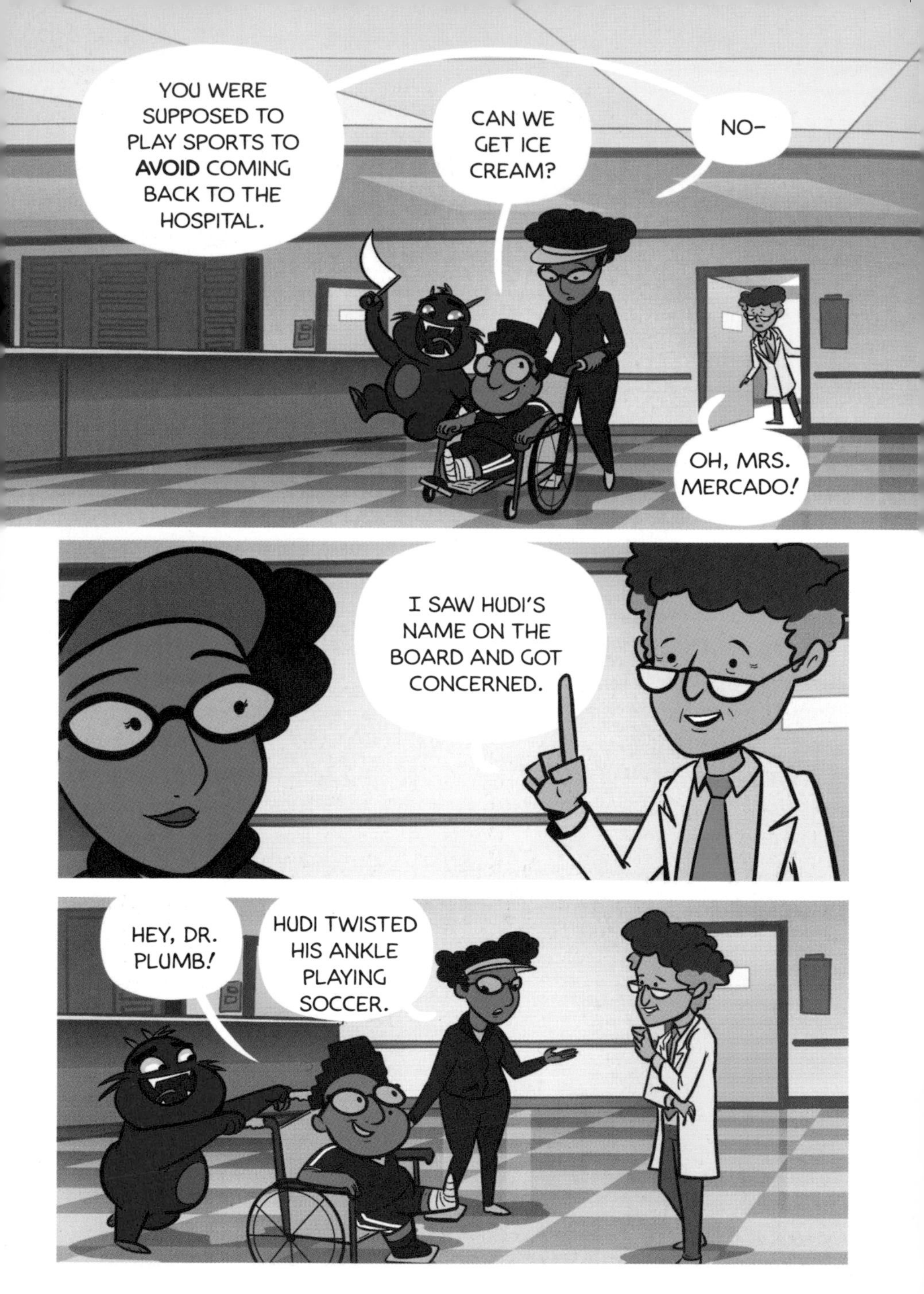
YOU WERE SUPPOSED TO PLAY SPORTS TO AVOID COMING BACK TO THE HOSPITAL.
CAN WE GET ICE CREAM?
NO–
OH, MRS. MERCADO!
I SAW HUDI'S NAME ON THE BOARD AND GOT CONCERNED.
HEY, DR. PLUMB!
HUDI TWISTED HIS ANKLE PLAYING SOCCER.

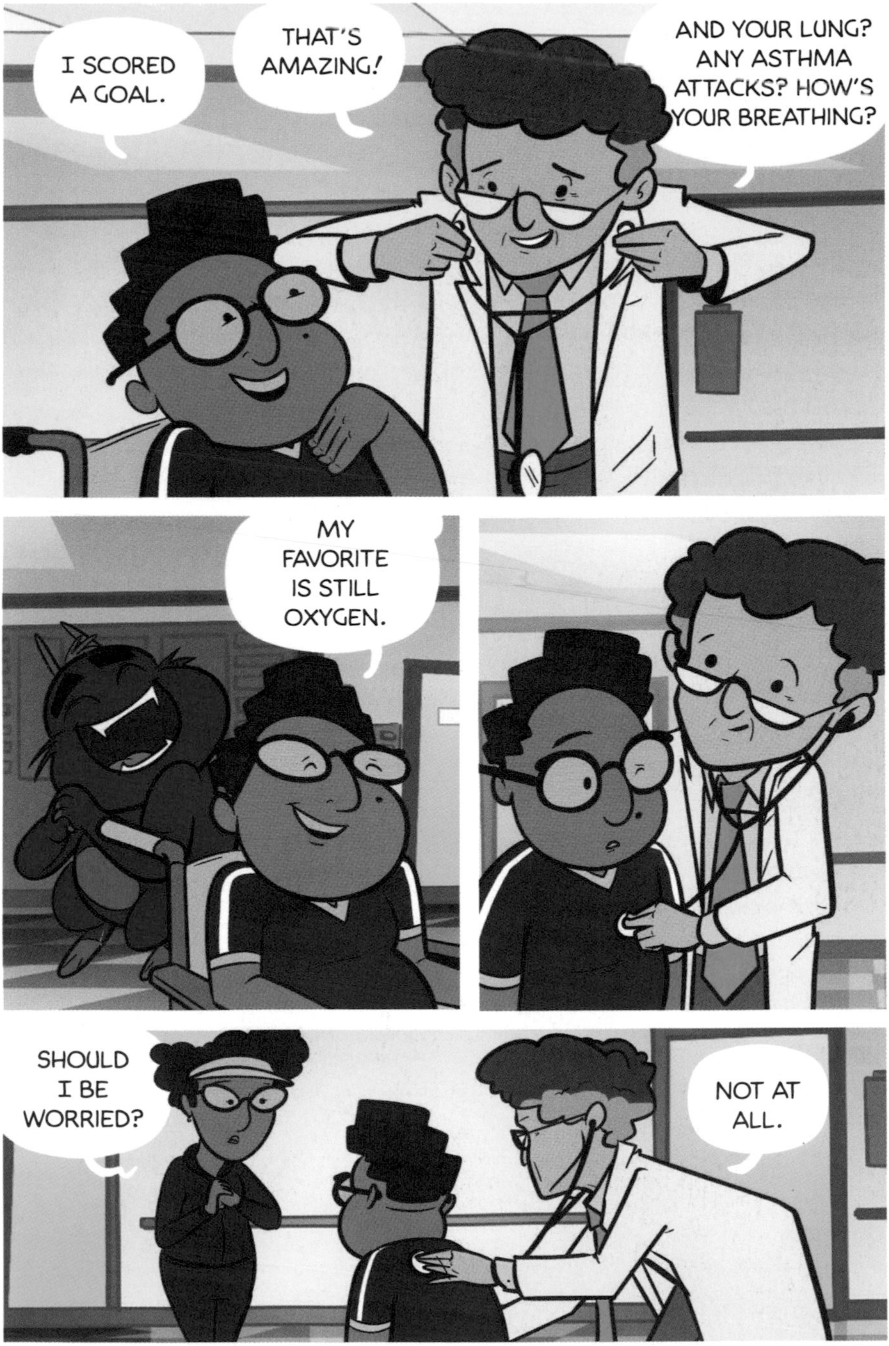
I SCORED A GOAL.
THAT'S AMAZING!
AND YOUR LUNG? ANY ASTHMA ATTACKS? HOW'S YOUR BREATHING?
MY FAVORITE IS STILL OXYGEN.
SHOULD I BE WORRIED?
NOT AT ALL.

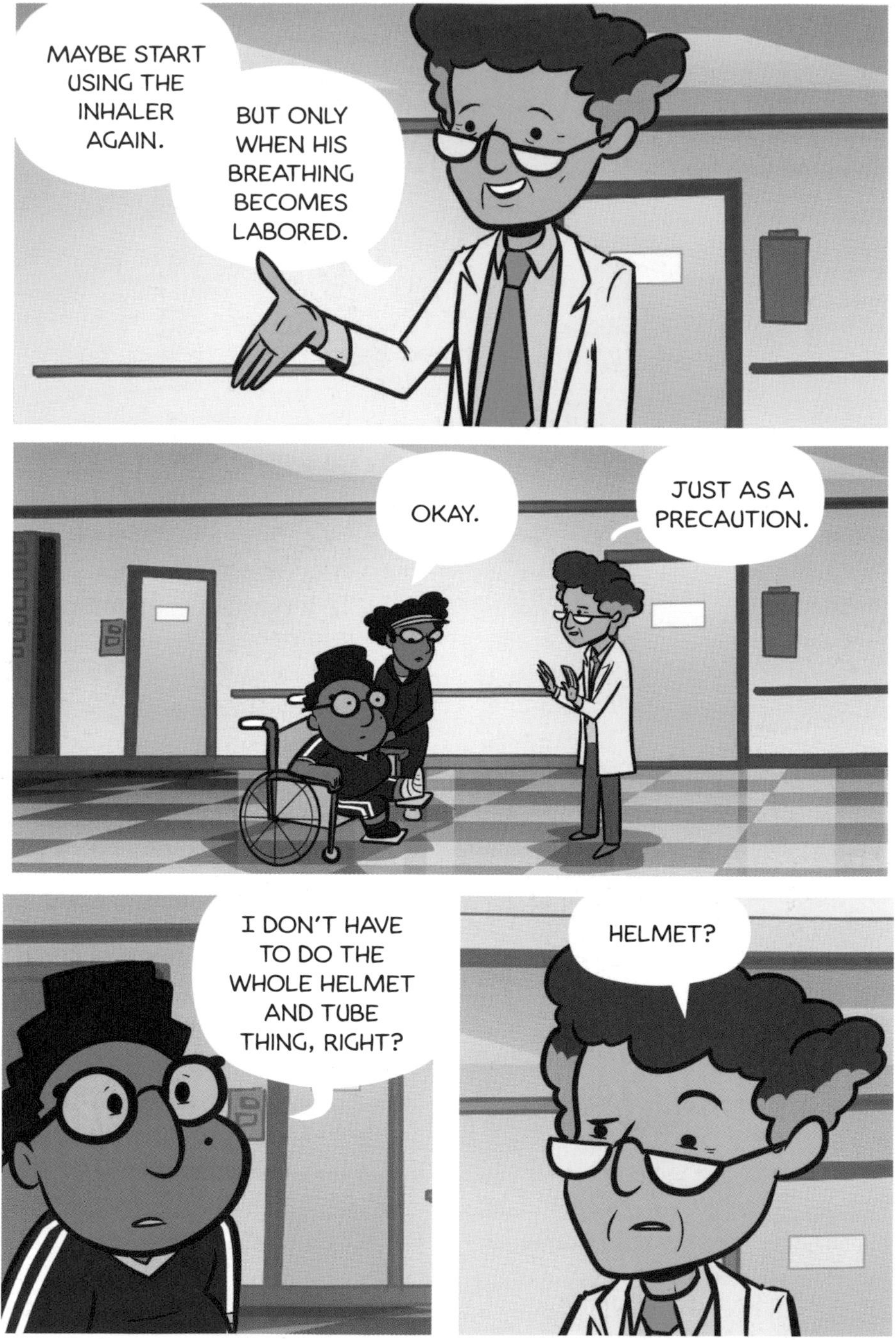
MAYBE START USING THE INHALER AGAIN.
BUT ONLY WHEN HIS BREATHING BECOMES LABORED.
OKAY.
JUST AS A PRECAUTION.
I DON'T HAVE TO DO THE WHOLE HELMET AND TUBE THING, RIGHT?
HELMET?

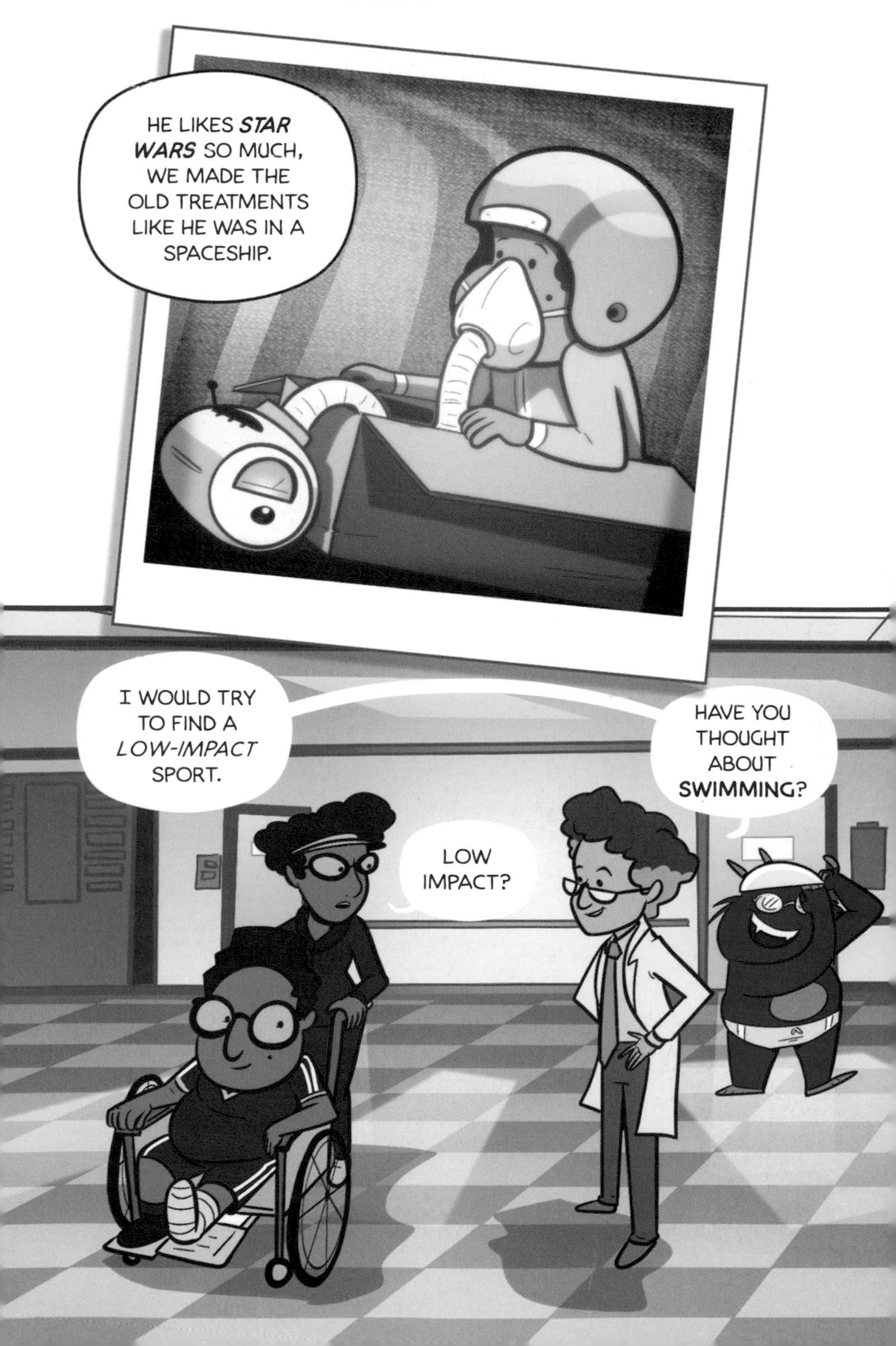
HE LIKES STAR WARS SO MUCH, WE MADE THE OLD TREATMENTS LIKE HE WAS IN A SPACESHIP.
I WOULD TRY TO FIND A LOW-IMPACT SPORT.
HAVE YOU THOUGHT ABOUT SWIMMING?
LOW IMPACT?

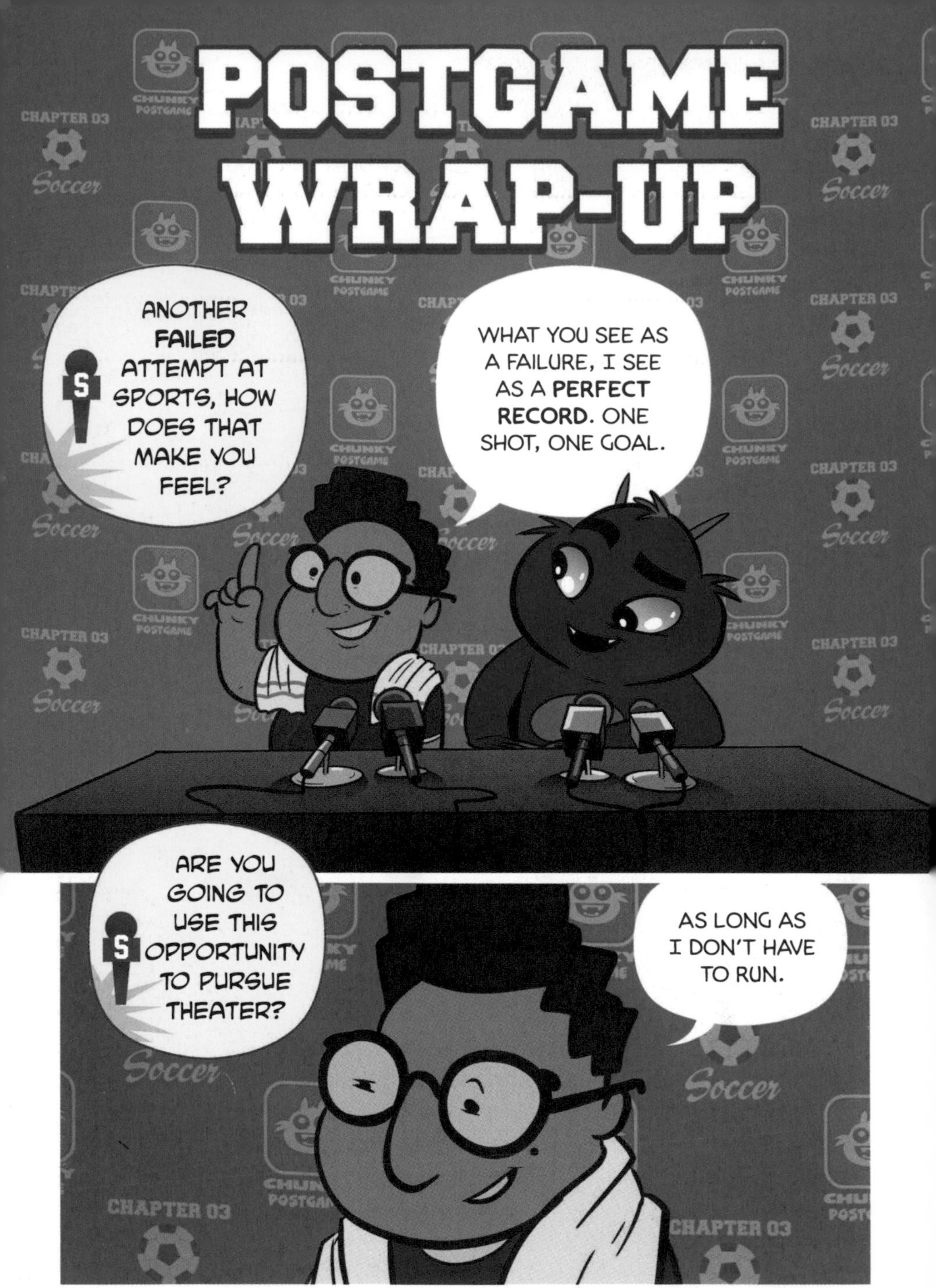
POSTGAME WRAP-UP
ANOTHER FAILED ATTEMPT AT SPORTS, HOW DOES THAT MAKE YOU FEEL?
WHAT YOU SEE AS A FAILURE, I SEE AS A PERFECT RECORD. ONE SHOT, ONE GOAL.
ARE YOU GOING TO USE THIS OPPORTUNITY TO PURSUE THEATER?
AS LONG AS I DON'T HAVE TO RUN.

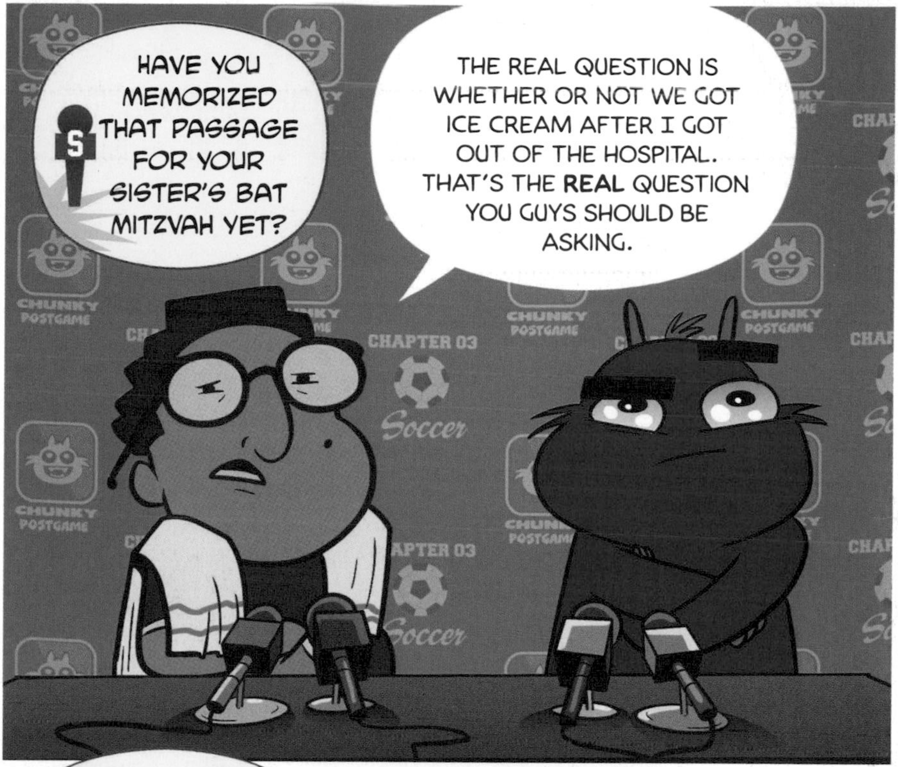
HAVE YOU MEMORIZED THAT PASSAGE FOR YOUR SISTER'S BAT MITZVAH YET?
THE REAL QUESTION IS WHETHER OR NOT WE GOT ICE CREAM AFTER I GOT OUT OF THE HOSPITAL. THAT'S THE REAL QUESTION YOU GUYS SHOULD BE ASKING.

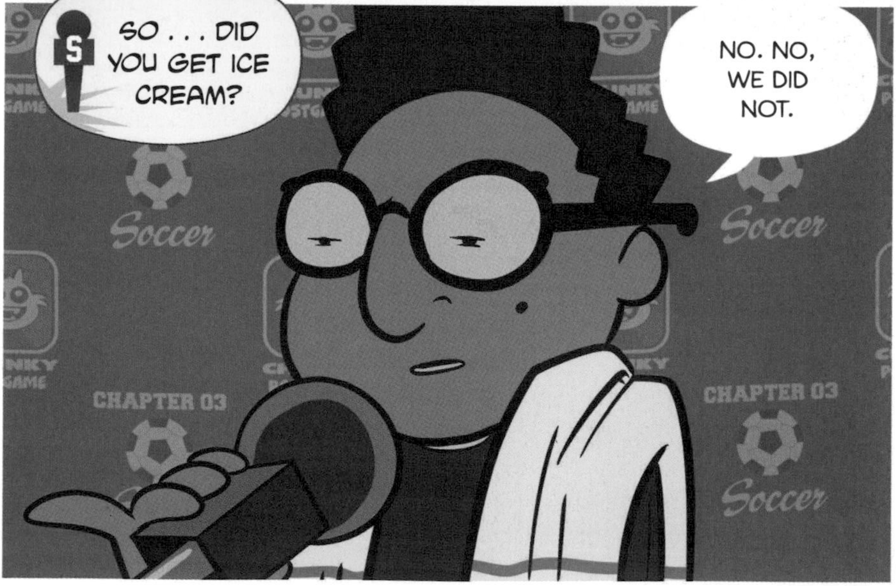
SO . . . DID YOU GET ICE CREAM?
NO. NO, WE DID NOT.

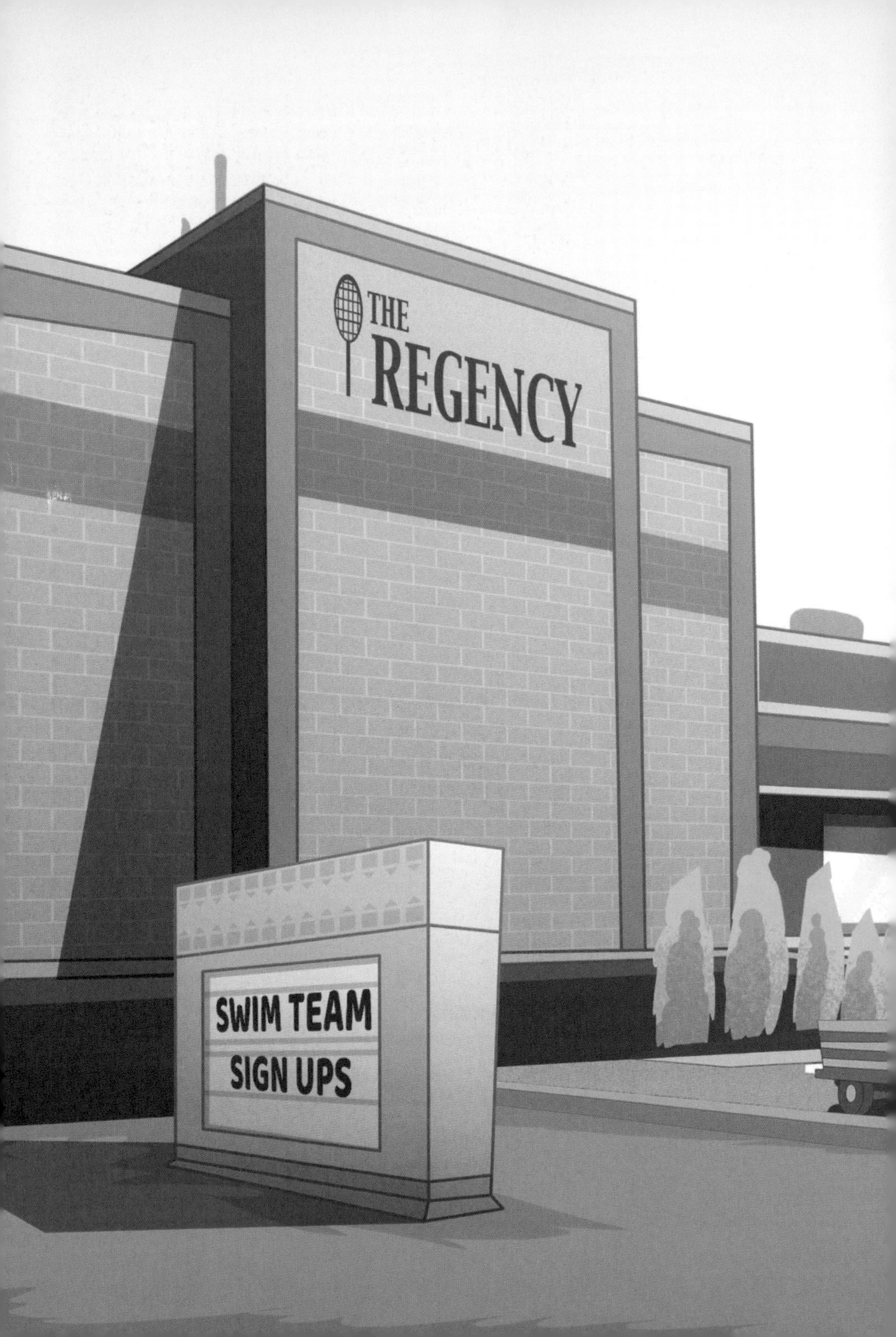
THE
REGENCY
SWIM TEAM
SIGN UPS

CHAPTER FOUR
Swimming

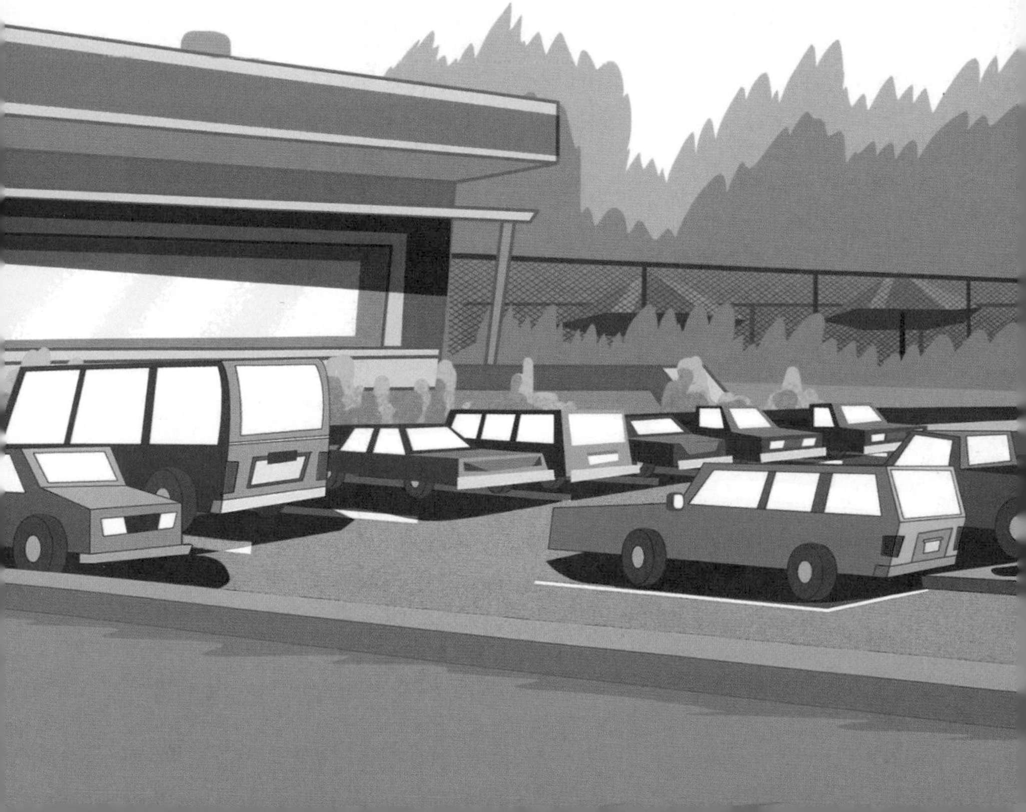

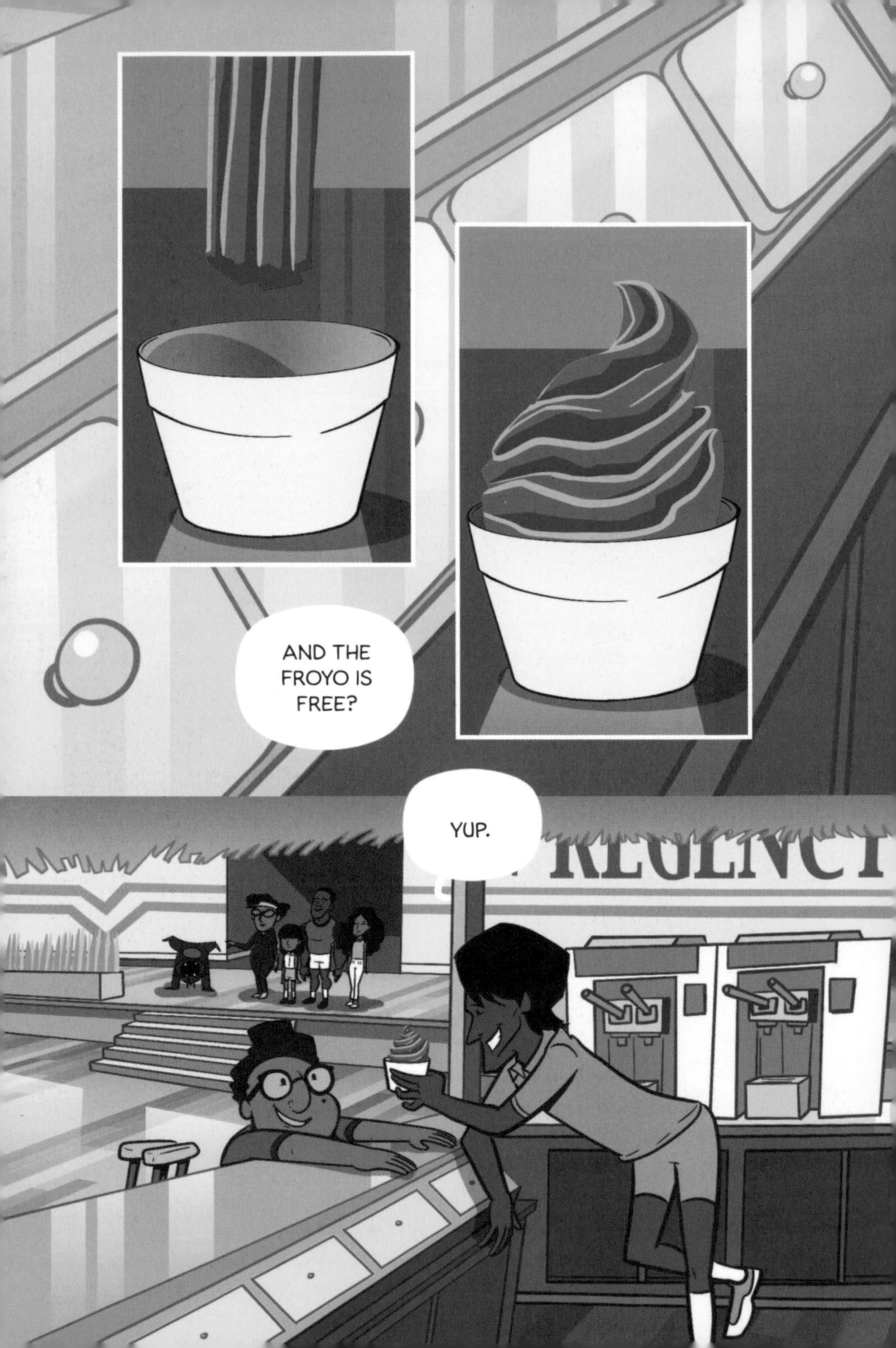
AND THE FROYO IS FREE?
YUP.
REGENCY

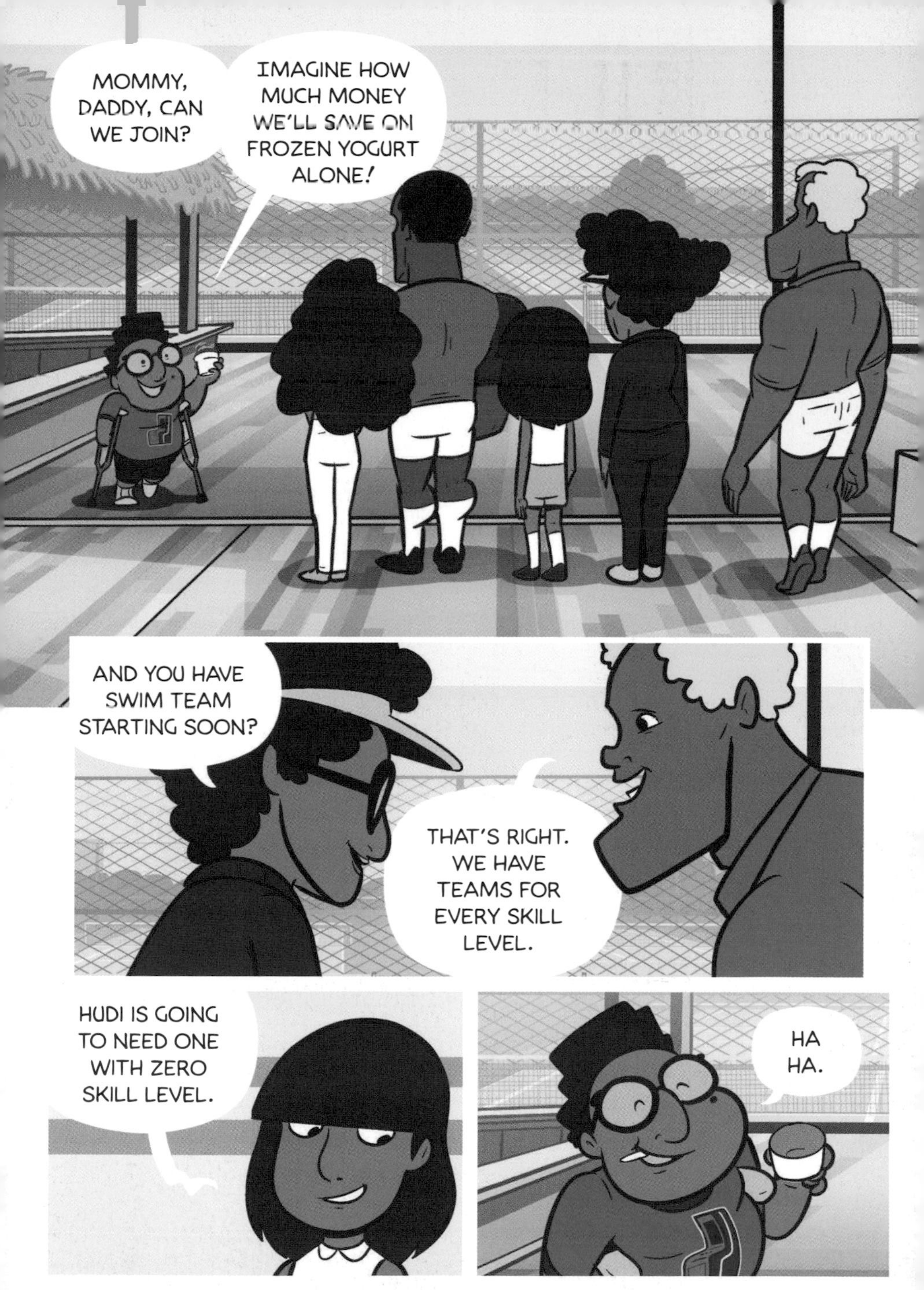
MOMMY, DADDY, CAN WE JOIN?
IMAGINE HOW MUCH MONEY WE'LL SAVE ON FROZEN YOGURT ALONE!
AND YOU HAVE SWIM TEAM STARTING SOON?
THAT'S RIGHT. WE HAVE TEAMS FOR EVERY SKILL LEVEL.
HUDI IS GOING TO NEED ONE WITH ZERO SKILL LEVEL.
HA HA.

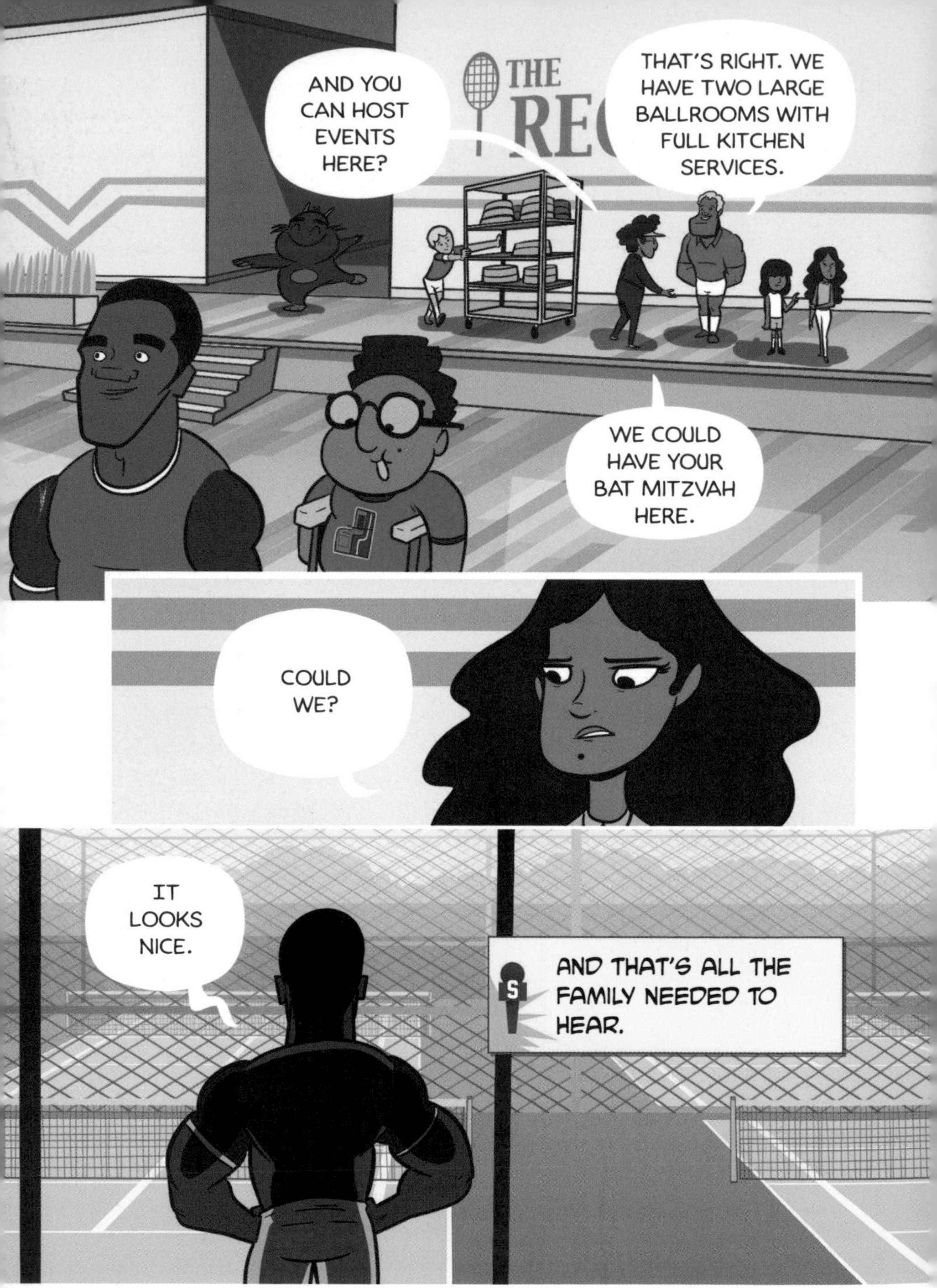
THE REC
AND YOU CAN HOST EVENTS HERE?
THAT'S RIGHT. WE HAVE TWO LARGE BALLROOMS WITH FULL KITCHEN SERVICES.
WE COULD HAVE YOUR BAT MITZVAH HERE.
COULD WE?
IT LOOKS NICE.
AND THAT'S ALL THE FAMILY NEEDED TO HEAR.

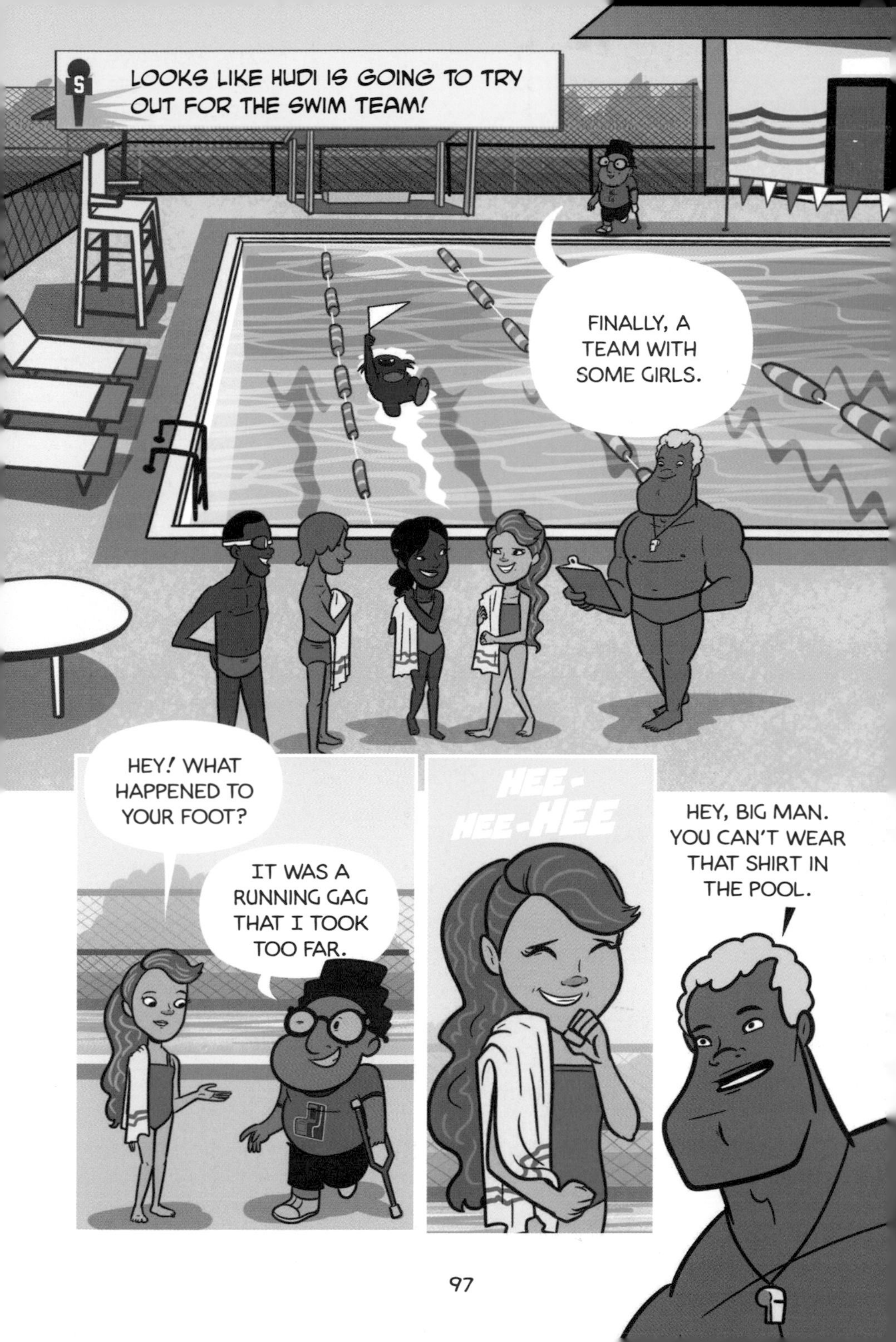
LOOKS LIKE HUDI IS GOING TO TRY OUT FOR THE SWIM TEAM!
FINALLY, A TEAM WITH SOME GIRLS.
HEY! WHAT HAPPENED TO YOUR FOOT?
IT WAS A RUNNING GAG THAT I TOOK TOO FAR.
HEE-HEE-HEE
HEY, BIG MAN. YOU CAN'T WEAR THAT SHIRT IN THE POOL.

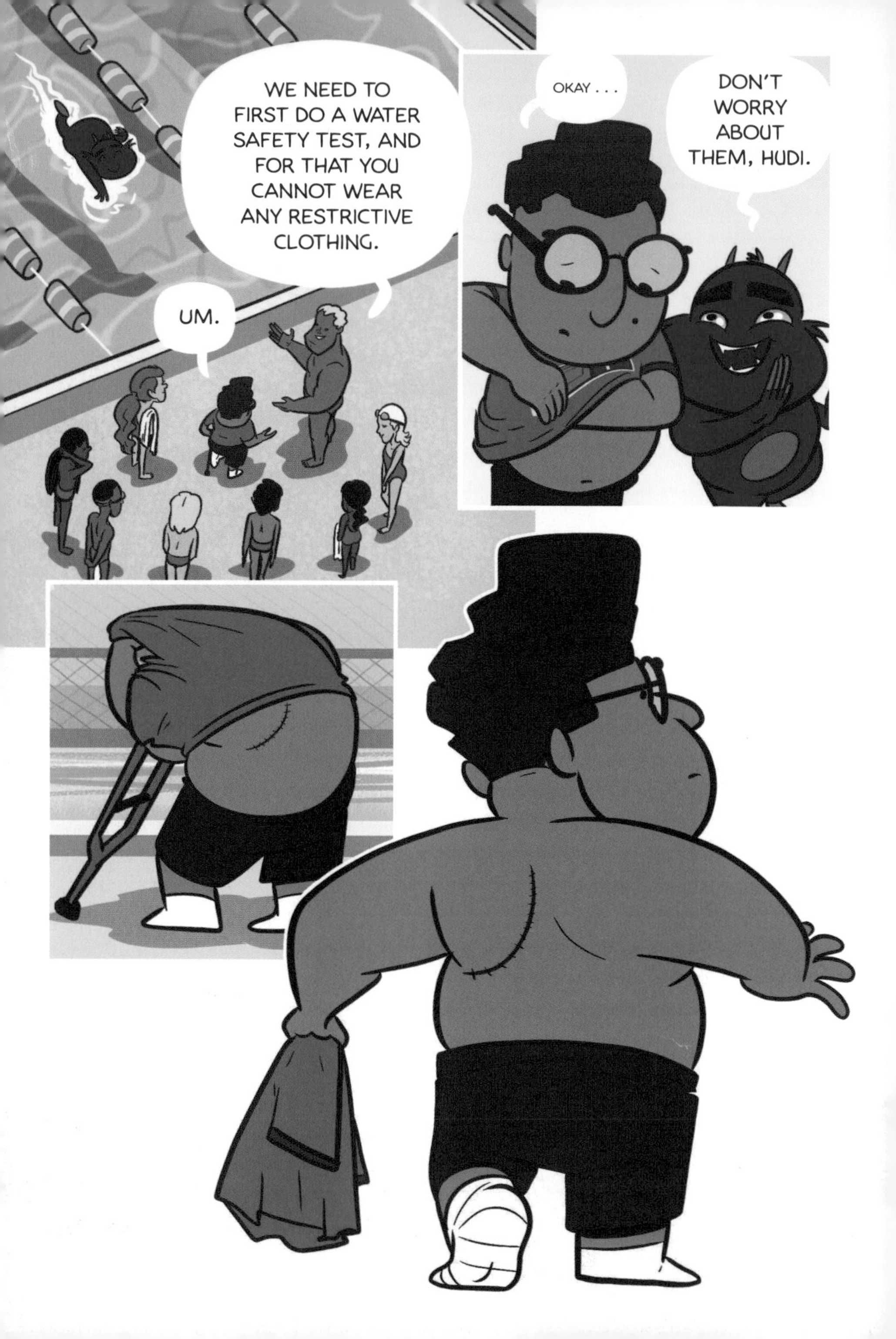
WE NEED TO FIRST DO A WATER SAFETY TEST, AND FOR THAT YOU CANNOT WEAR ANY RESTRICTIVE CLOTHING.
UM.
OKAY . . .
DON'T WORRY ABOUT THEM, HUDI.

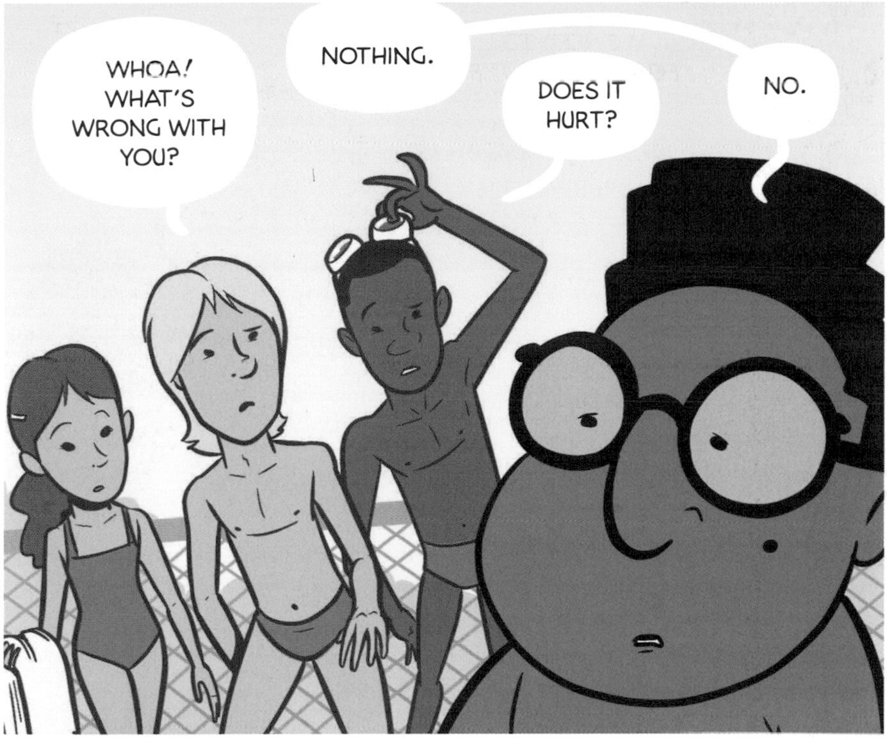
WHOA! WHAT'S WRONG WITH YOU?
NOTHING.
DOES IT HURT?
NO.

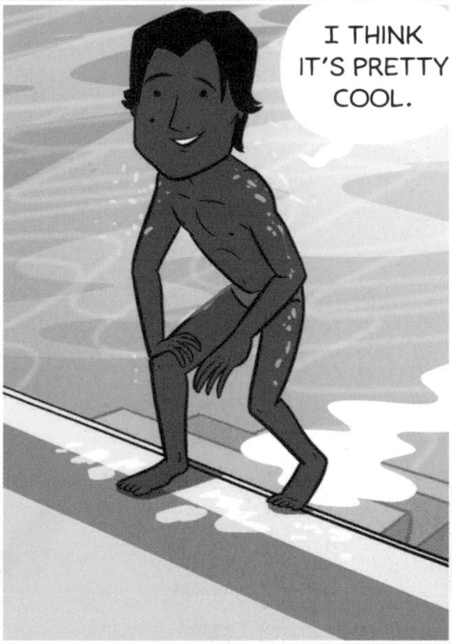
I THINK IT'S PRETTY COOL.

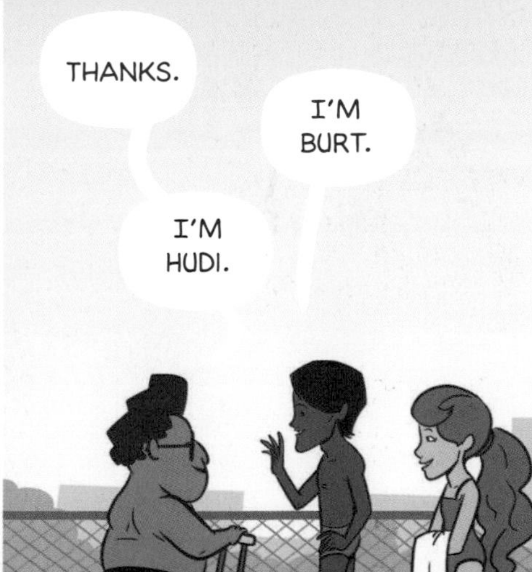
THANKS.
I'M BURT.
I'M HUDI.

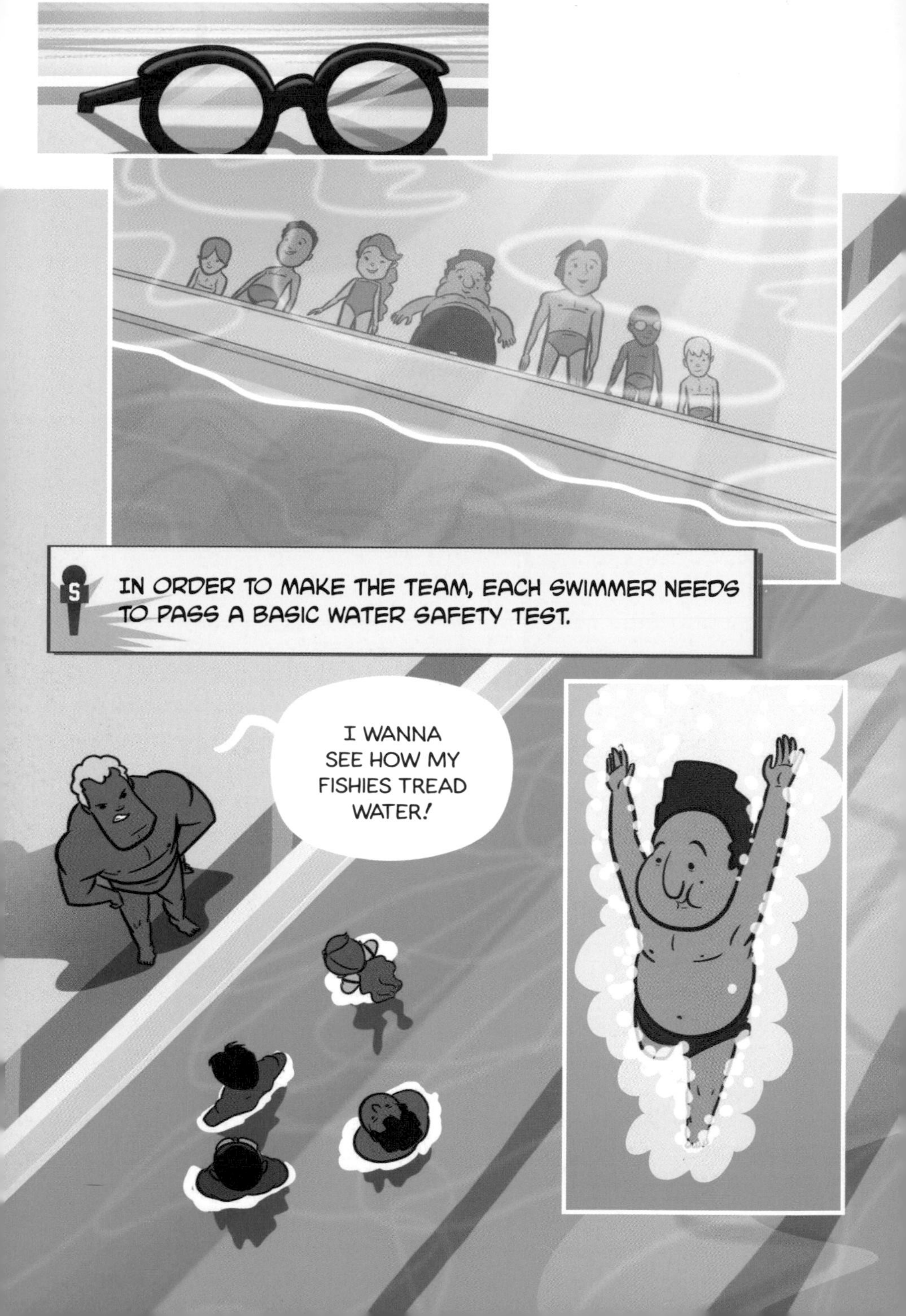
IN ORDER TO MAKE THE TEAM, EACH SWIMMER NEEDS TO PASS A BASIC WATER SAFETY TEST.
I WANNA SEE HOW MY FISHIES TREAD WATER!

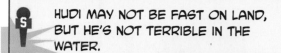
HUDI MAY NOT BE FAST ON LAND, BUT HE'S NOT TERRIBLE IN THE WATER.

HIS EXTREMELY FLAT FEET ACT ALMOST AS FINS. THEY MAKE HIM A DECENT SWIMMER.

GOOD JOB, FISHIES. LET'S TAKE A BREAK.

I LIKE SWIMMING. THERE'S NOTHING THAT'S GOING TO HIT ME IN THE FACE.

SO, HUDI, HOW DID YOU GET THAT COOL SCAR?

I HAD A REALLY BAD INFECTION IN MY LUNG AS A KID.

IT WAS A HARDENING OF THE BRONCHI.

I WAS ALWAYS SICK WITH RESPIRATORY INFECTIONS.

SO THEY DECIDED TO CHOP IT OUT.

I GUESS IT WAS PRETTY SCARY FOR MY PARENTS.

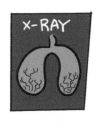

X-RAY

WHOA . . . YOU HAVE ONE LUNG?

YUP. HALF THE LUNGS, ALL THE CHARM.

ALL RIGHT, LET'S SEE YOUR BACKSTROKE, FISHIES!

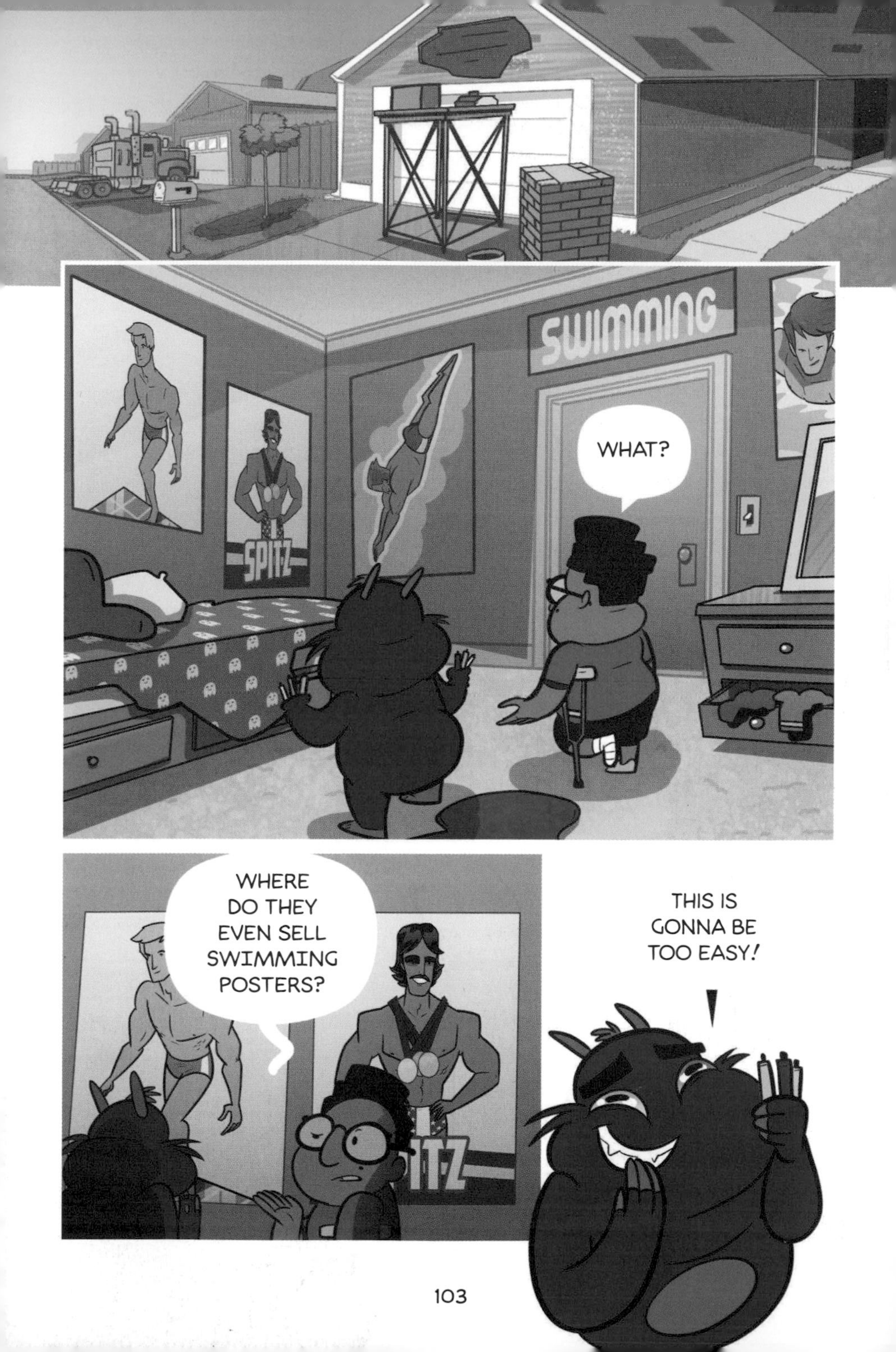
SWIMMING
SPITZ
WHAT?
WHERE DO THEY EVEN SELL SWIMMING POSTERS?
THIS IS GONNA BE TOO EASY!

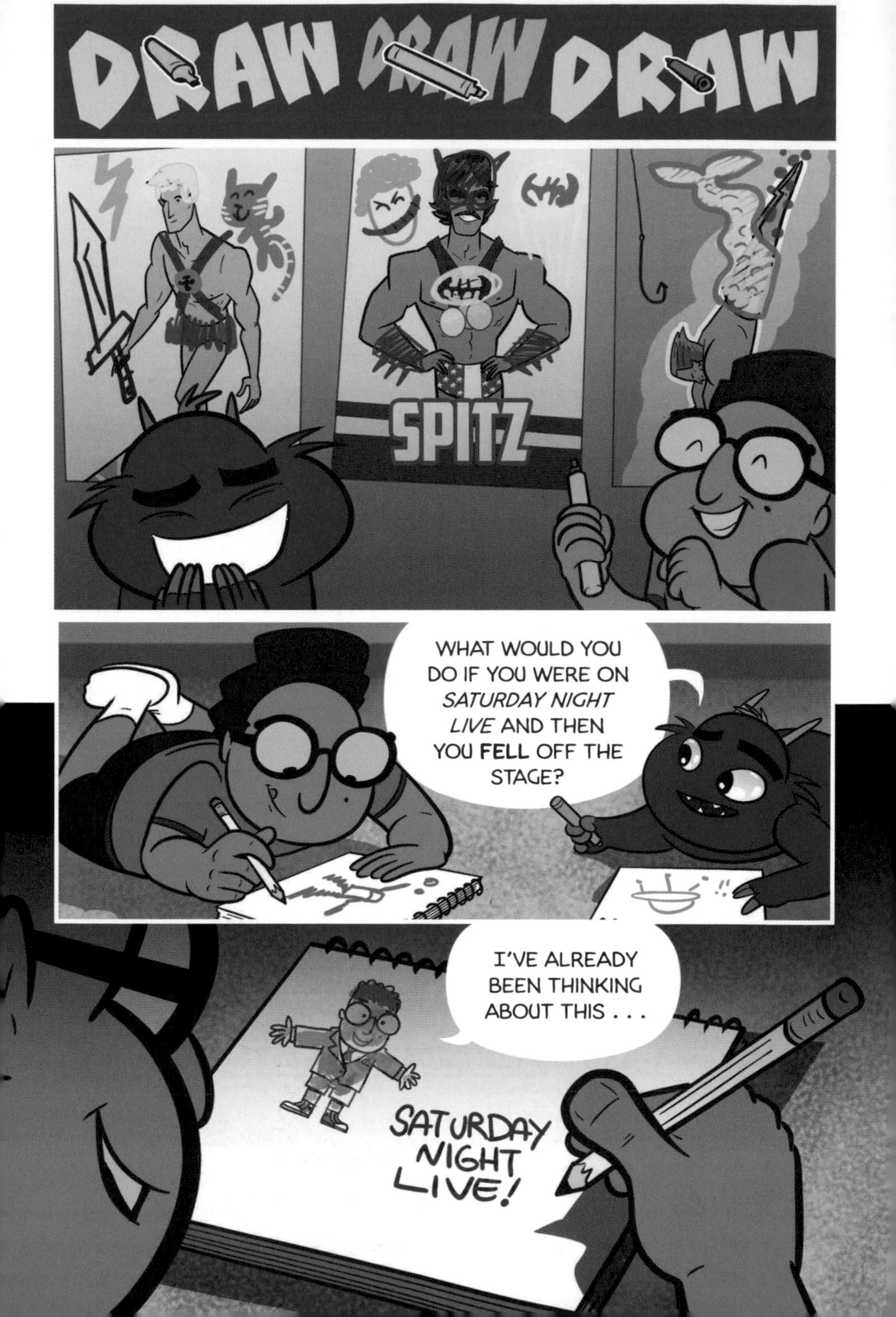
DRAW DRAW DRAW
SPITZ
WHAT WOULD YOU DO IF YOU WERE ON *SATURDAY NIGHT LIVE* AND THEN YOU **FELL** OFF THE STAGE?
I'VE ALREADY BEEN THINKING ABOUT THIS . . .
SATURDAY NIGHT LIVE!

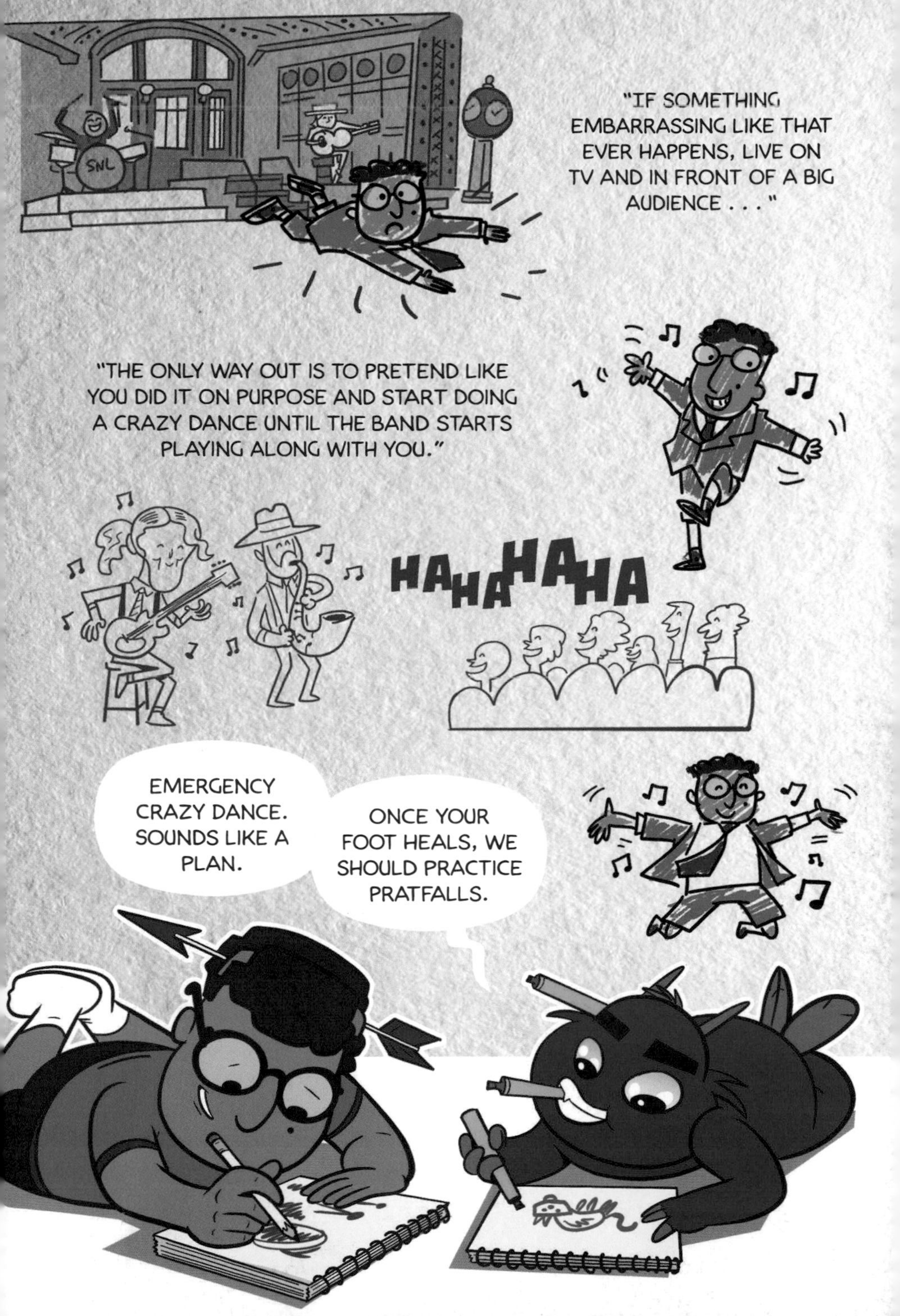
"IF SOMETHING EMBARRASSING LIKE THAT EVER HAPPENS, LIVE ON TV AND IN FRONT OF A BIG AUDIENCE . . ."
SNL
"THE ONLY WAY OUT IS TO PRETEND LIKE YOU DID IT ON PURPOSE AND START DOING A CRAZY DANCE UNTIL THE BAND STARTS PLAYING ALONG WITH YOU."
HAHAHAHAHA
EMERGENCY CRAZY DANCE. SOUNDS LIKE A PLAN.
ONCE YOUR FOOT HEALS, WE SHOULD PRACTICE PRATFALLS.

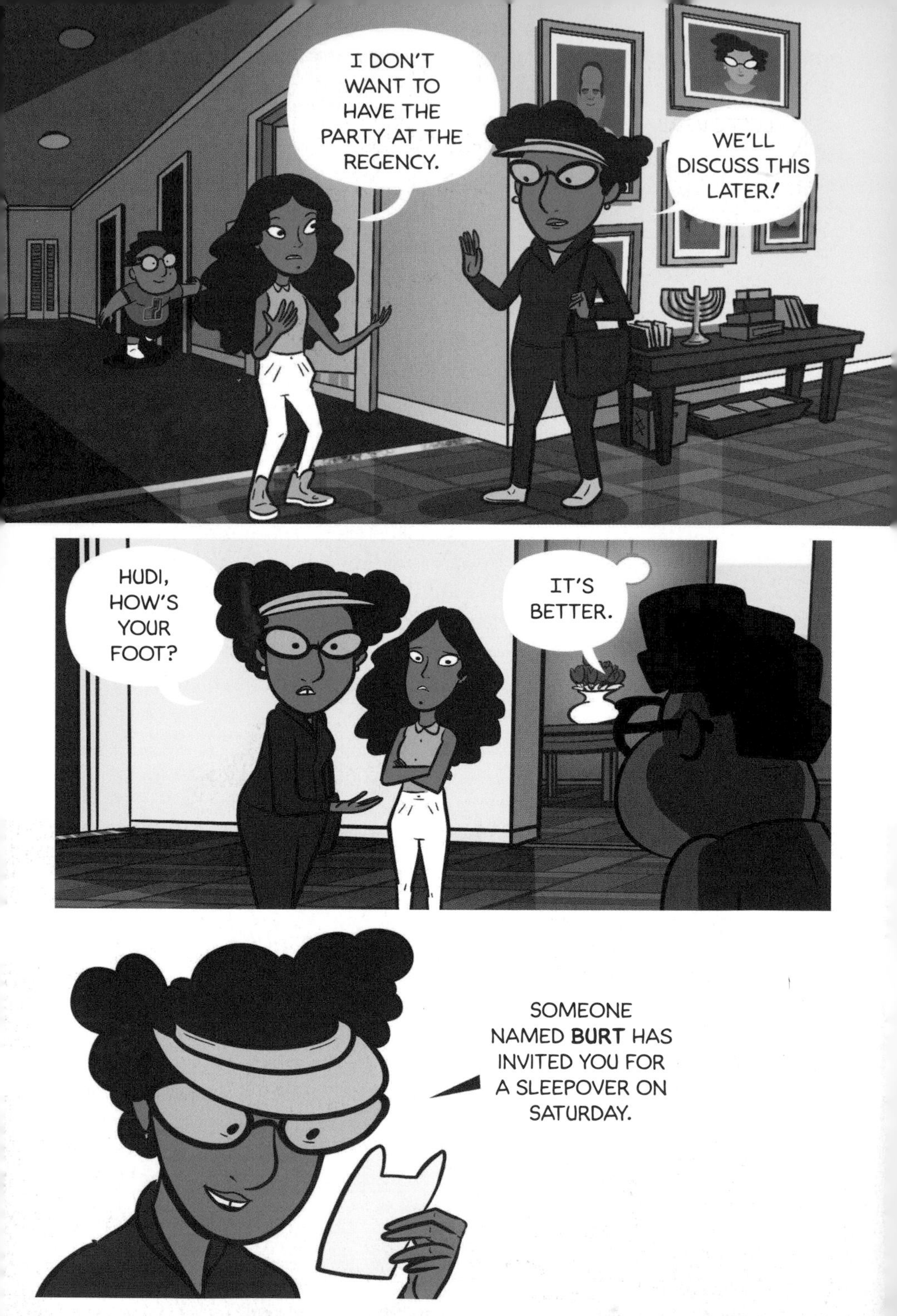
I DON'T WANT TO HAVE THE PARTY AT THE REGENCY.
WE'LL DISCUSS THIS LATER!
HUDI, HOW'S YOUR FOOT?
IT'S BETTER.
SOMEONE NAMED **BURT** HAS INVITED YOU FOR A SLEEPOVER ON SATURDAY.

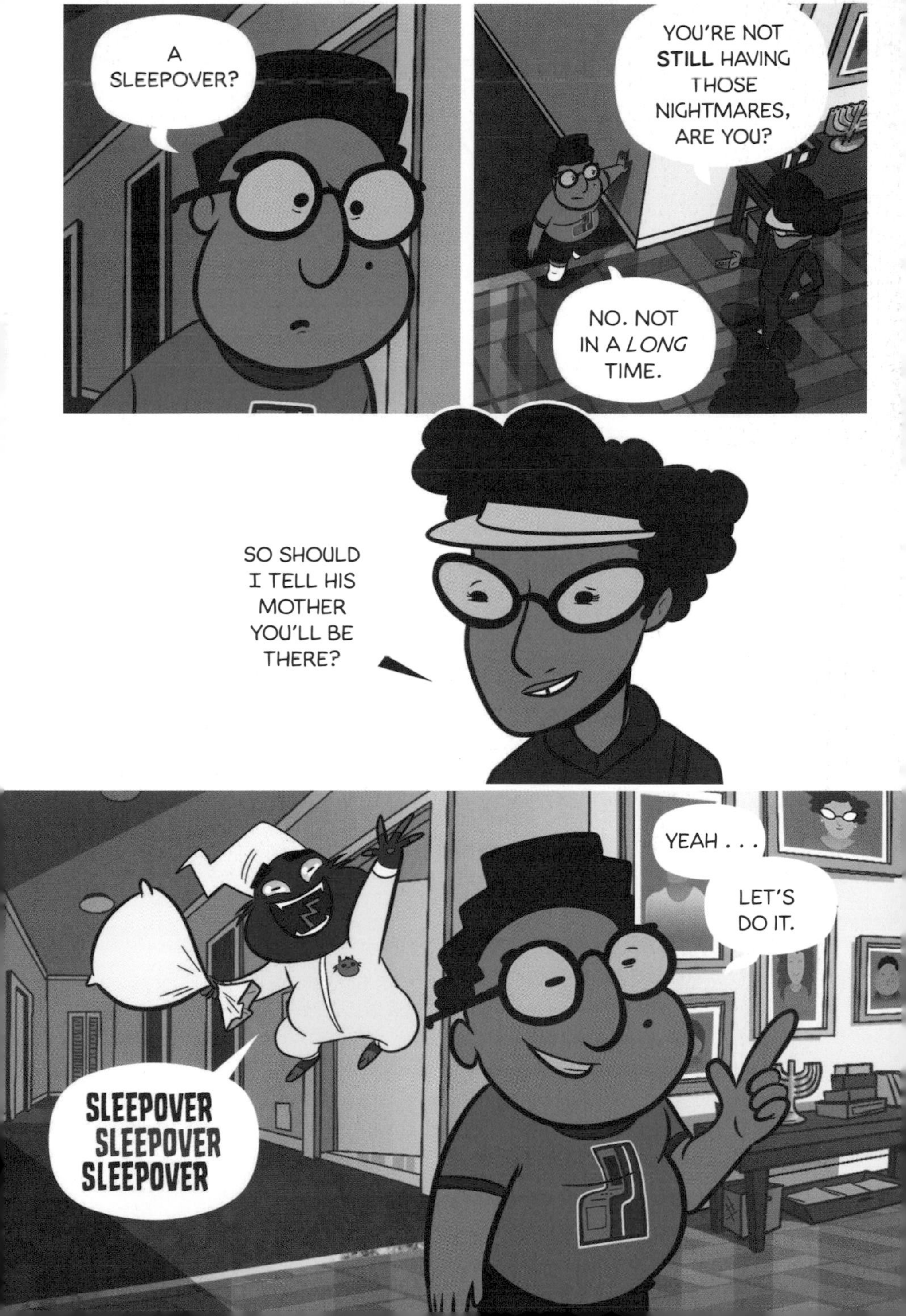
A SLEEPOVER?
YOU'RE NOT **STILL** HAVING THOSE NIGHTMARES, ARE YOU?
NO. NOT IN A *LONG* TIME.
SO SHOULD I TELL HIS MOTHER YOU'LL BE THERE?
YEAH . . .
LET'S DO IT.
SLEEPOVER SLEEPOVER SLEEPOVER

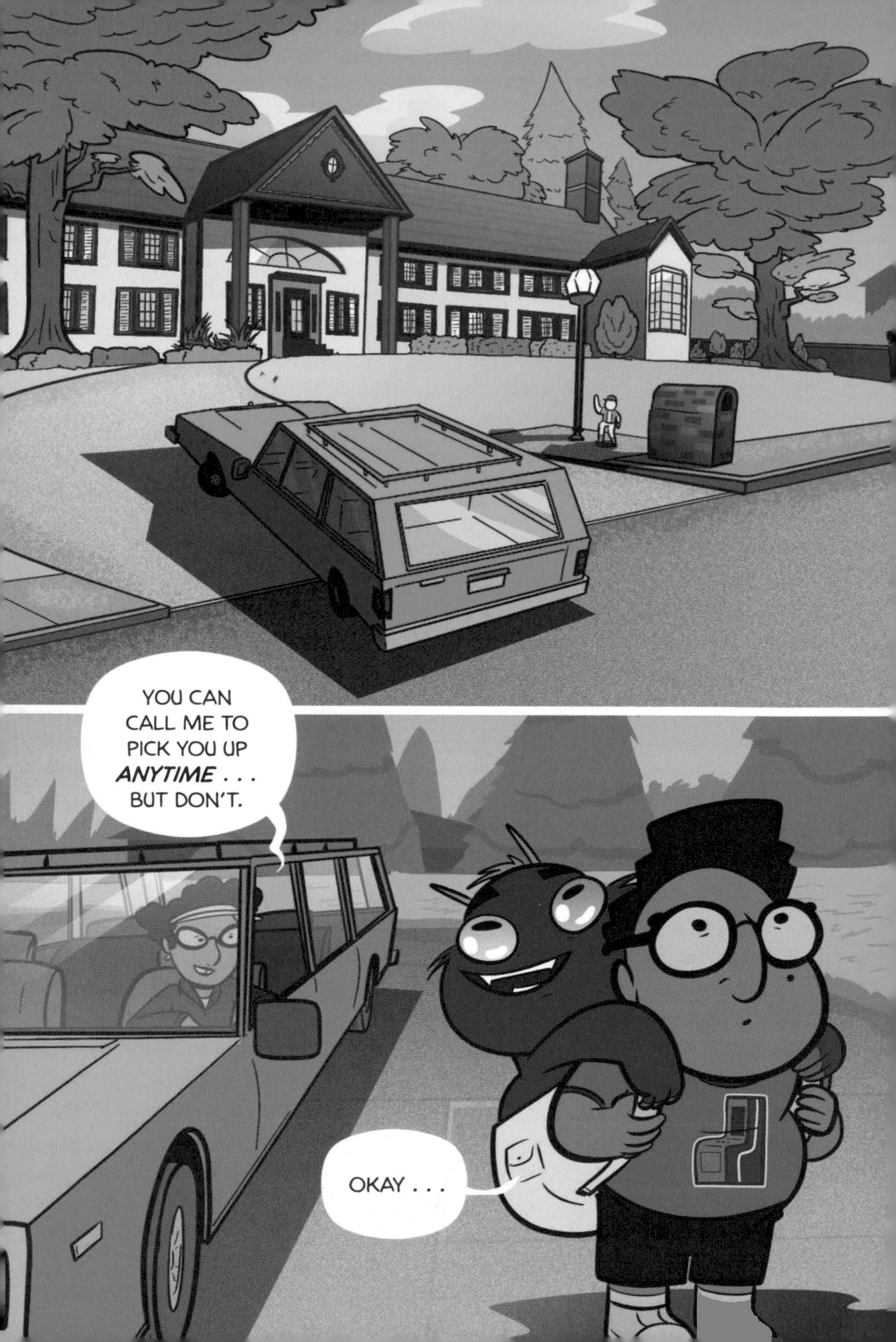
YOU CAN CALL ME TO PICK YOU UP *ANYTIME* . . . BUT DON'T.
OKAY . . .

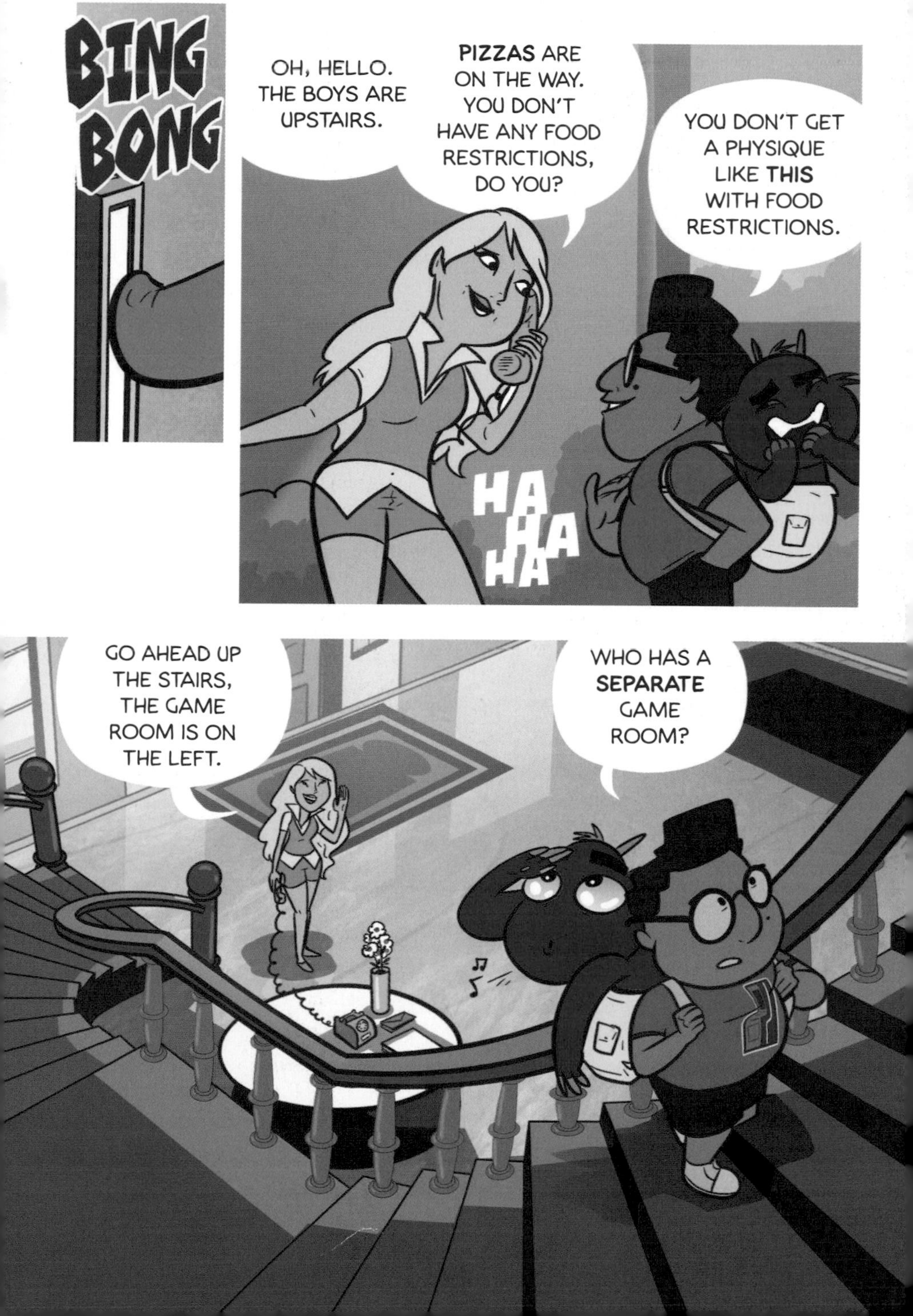
BING BONG
OH, HELLO. THE BOYS ARE UPSTAIRS.
PIZZAS ARE ON THE WAY. YOU DON'T HAVE ANY FOOD RESTRICTIONS, DO YOU?
YOU DON'T GET A PHYSIQUE LIKE THIS WITH FOOD RESTRICTIONS.
HA HA HA HA
GO AHEAD UP THE STAIRS, THE GAME ROOM IS ON THE LEFT.
WHO HAS A SEPARATE GAME ROOM?

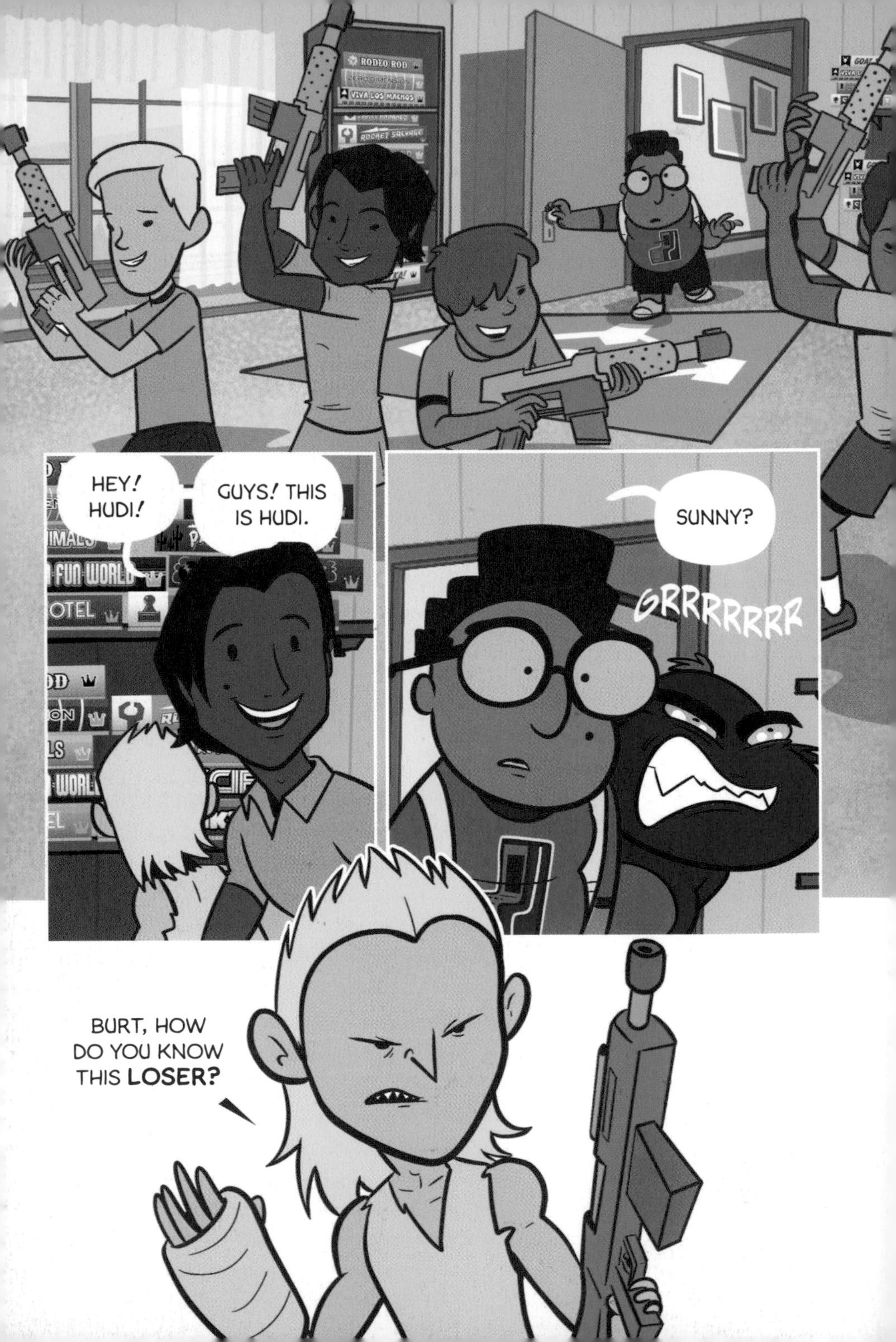
HEY! HUDI!
GUYS! THIS IS HUDI.
SUNNY?
GRRRRRRR
BURT, HOW DO YOU KNOW THIS LOSER?

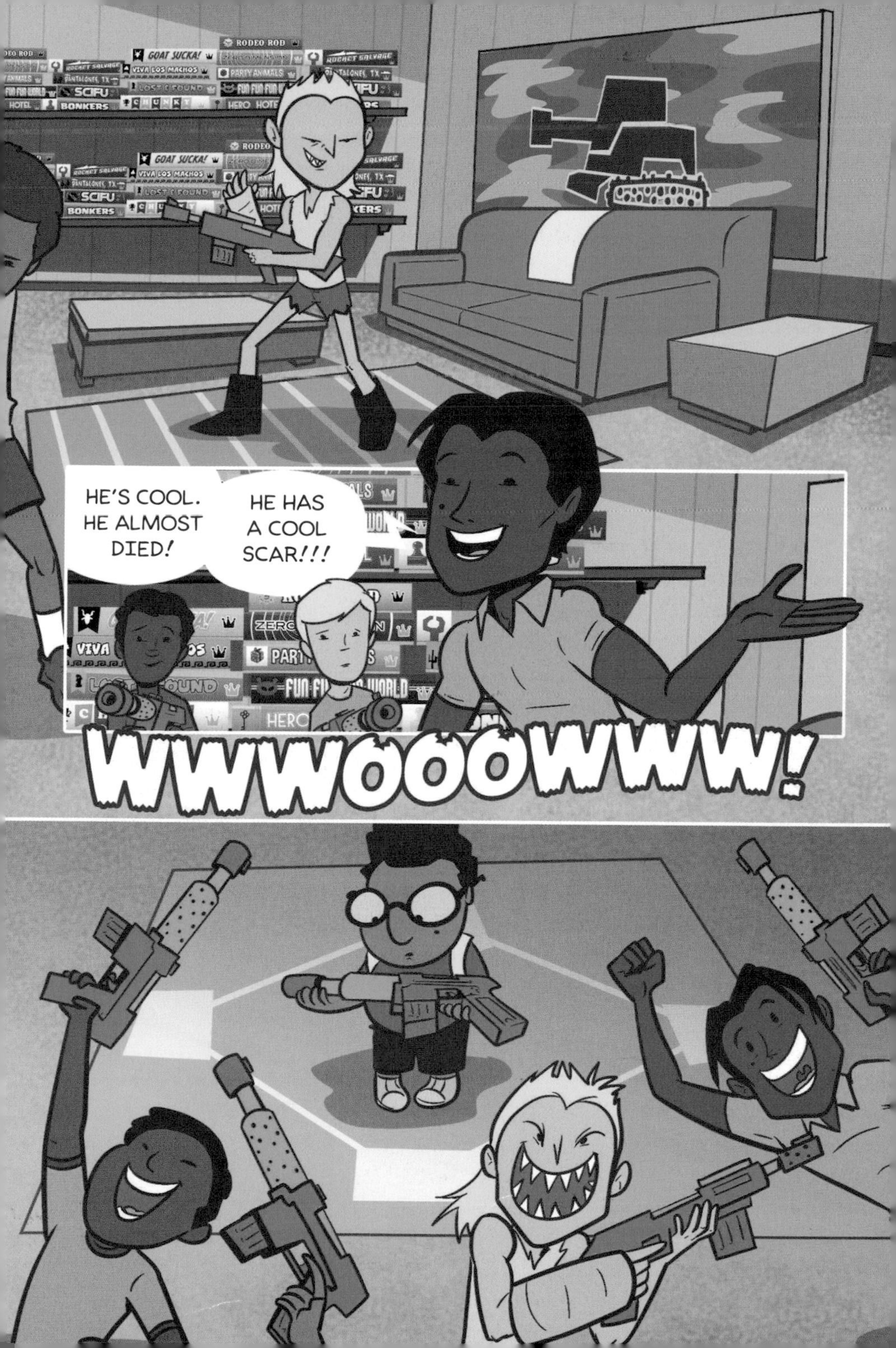
HE'S COOL. HE ALMOST DIED!
HE HAS A COOL SCAR!!!
WWWOOOWWW!

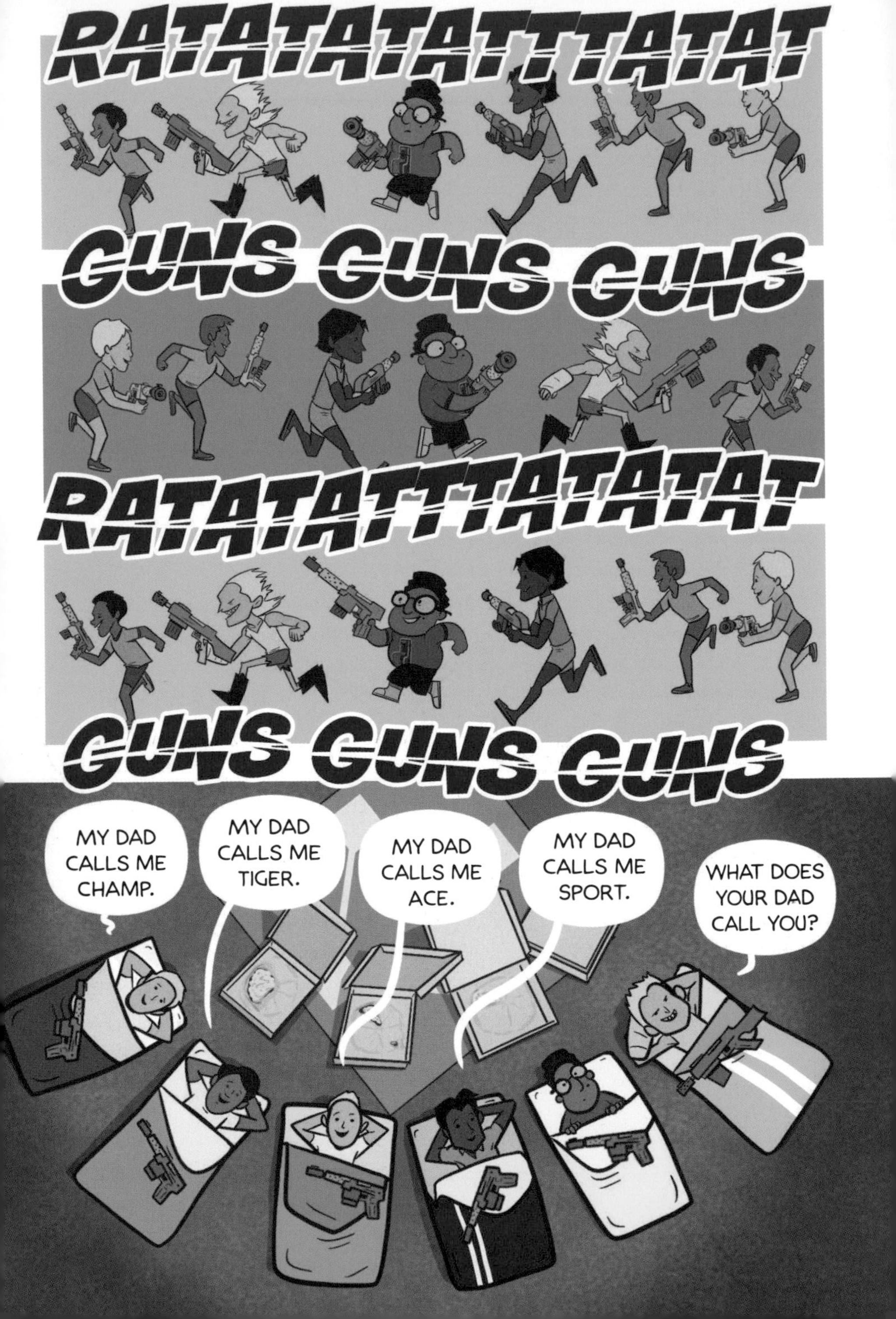
RATATATATTTATAT
GUNS GUNS GUNS
RATATATTTATATAT
GUNS GUNS GUNS
MY DAD CALLS ME CHAMP.
MY DAD CALLS ME TIGER.
MY DAD CALLS ME ACE.
MY DAD CALLS ME SPORT.
WHAT DOES YOUR DAD CALL YOU?

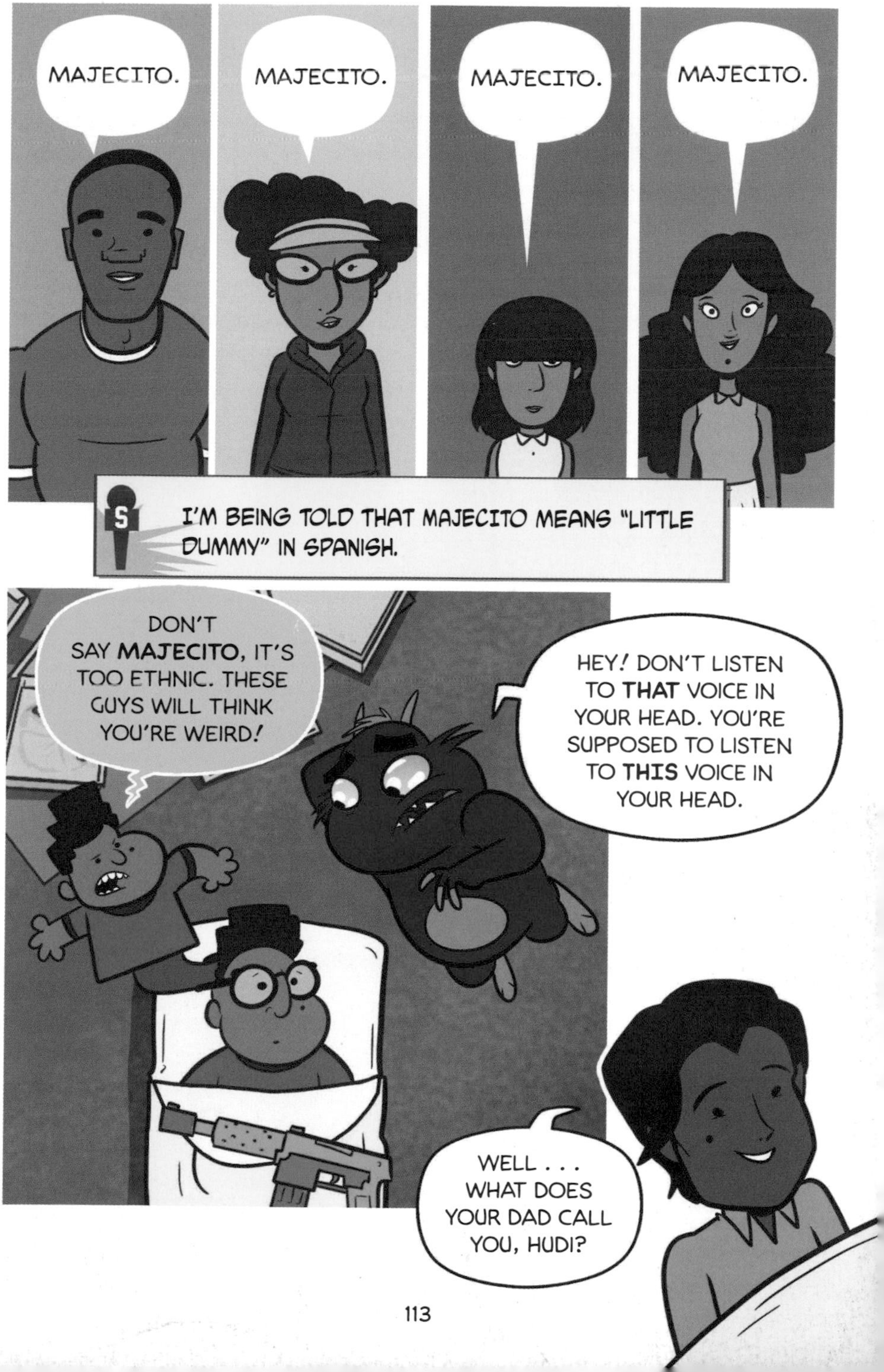

MAJECITO.
MAJECITO.
MAJECITO.
MAJECITO.
S
I'M BEING TOLD THAT MAJECITO MEANS "LITTLE DUMMY" IN SPANISH.
DON'T SAY **MAJECITO**, IT'S TOO ETHNIC. THESE GUYS WILL THINK YOU'RE WEIRD!
HEY! DON'T LISTEN TO **THAT** VOICE IN YOUR HEAD. YOU'RE SUPPOSED TO LISTEN TO **THIS** VOICE IN YOUR HEAD.
WELL . . . WHAT DOES YOUR DAD CALL YOU, HUDI?

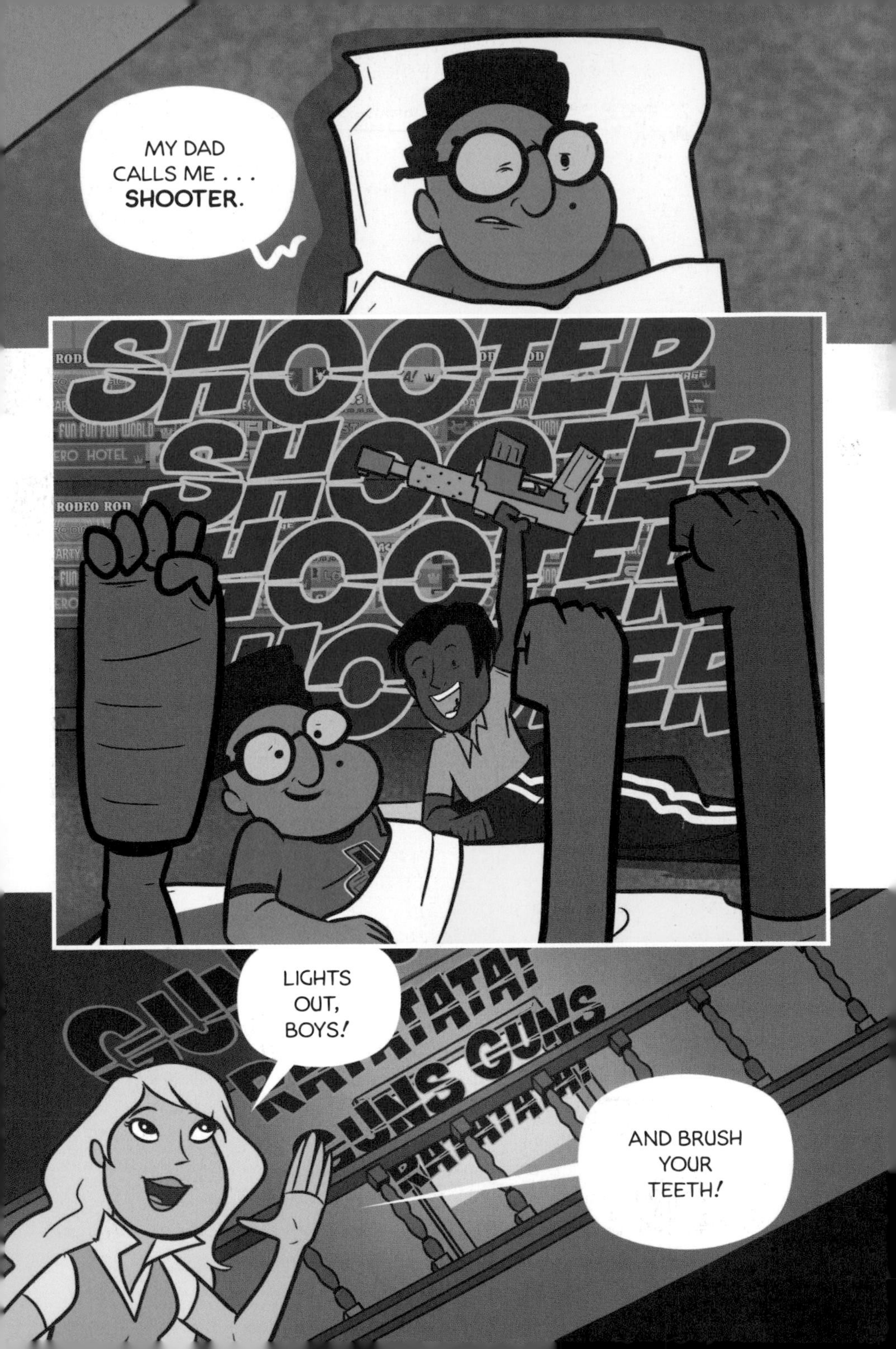
MY DAD CALLS ME . . . SHOOTER.
SHOOTER
SHOOTER
RODEO ROD
FUN FUN FUN WORLD
LIGHTS OUT, BOYS!
GUNS GUNS
AND BRUSH YOUR TEETH!

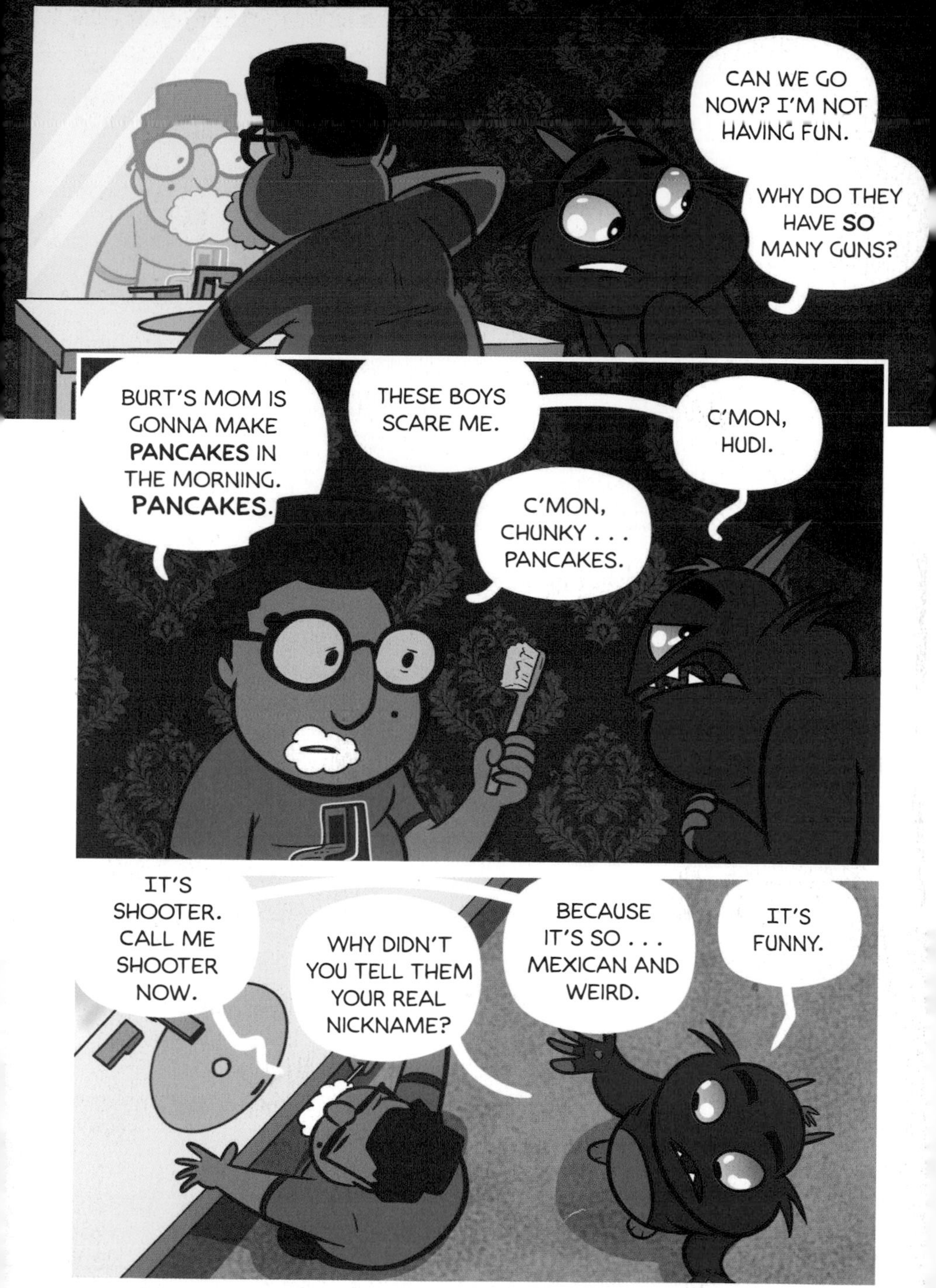
CAN WE GO NOW? I'M NOT HAVING FUN.
WHY DO THEY HAVE **SO** MANY GUNS?
BURT'S MOM IS GONNA MAKE **PANCAKES** IN THE MORNING. **PANCAKES.**
THESE BOYS SCARE ME.
C'MON, HUDI.
C'MON, CHUNKY . . . PANCAKES.
IT'S SHOOTER. CALL ME SHOOTER NOW.
WHY DIDN'T YOU TELL THEM YOUR REAL NICKNAME?
BECAUSE IT'S SO . . . MEXICAN AND WEIRD.
IT'S FUNNY.

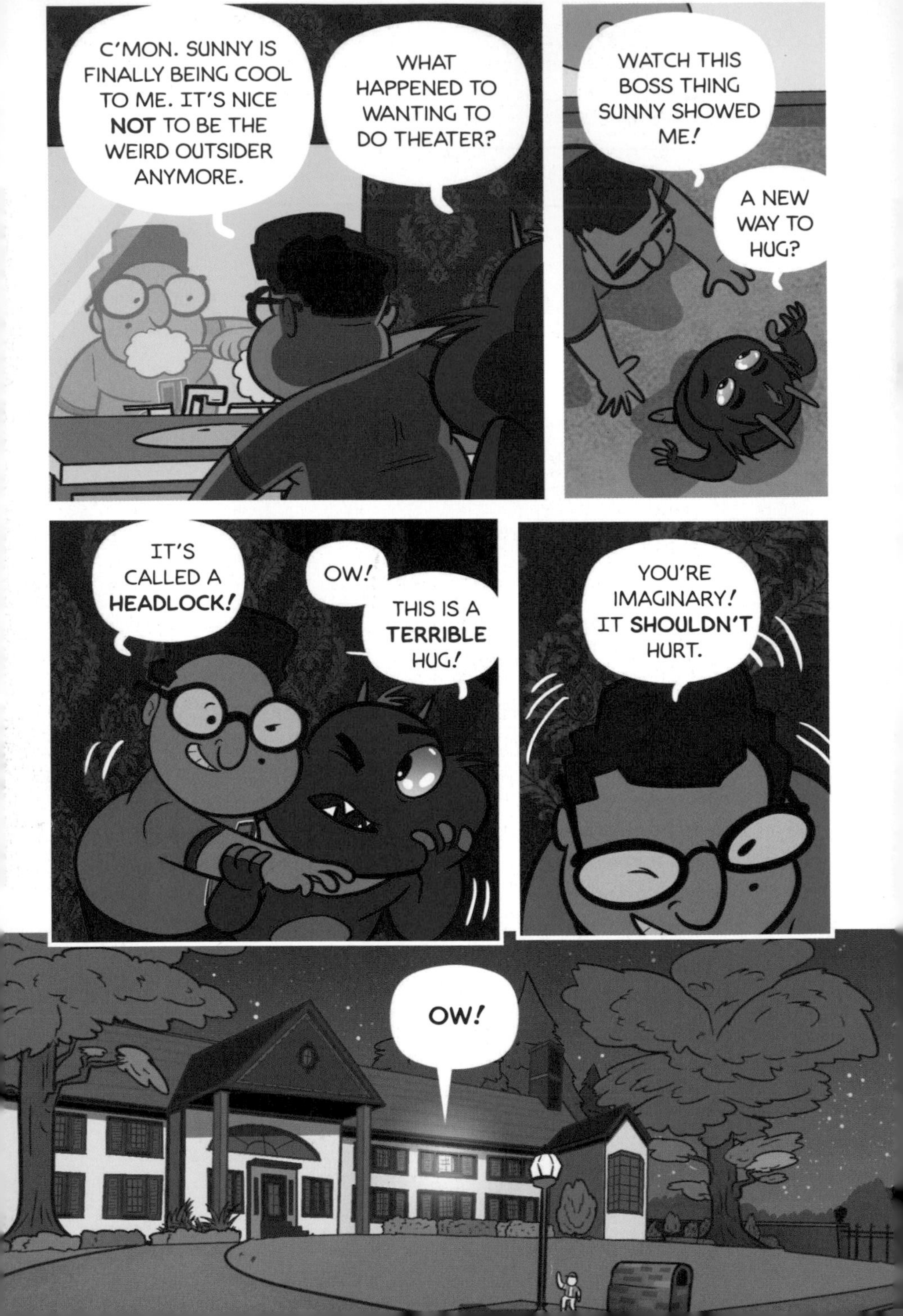
C'MON. SUNNY IS FINALLY BEING COOL TO ME. IT'S NICE **NOT** TO BE THE WEIRD OUTSIDER ANYMORE.
WHAT HAPPENED TO WANTING TO DO THEATER?
WATCH THIS BOSS THING SUNNY SHOWED ME!
A NEW WAY TO HUG?
IT'S CALLED A **HEADLOCK!**
OW!
THIS IS A **TERRIBLE** HUG!
YOU'RE IMAGINARY! IT **SHOULDN'T** HURT.
OW!

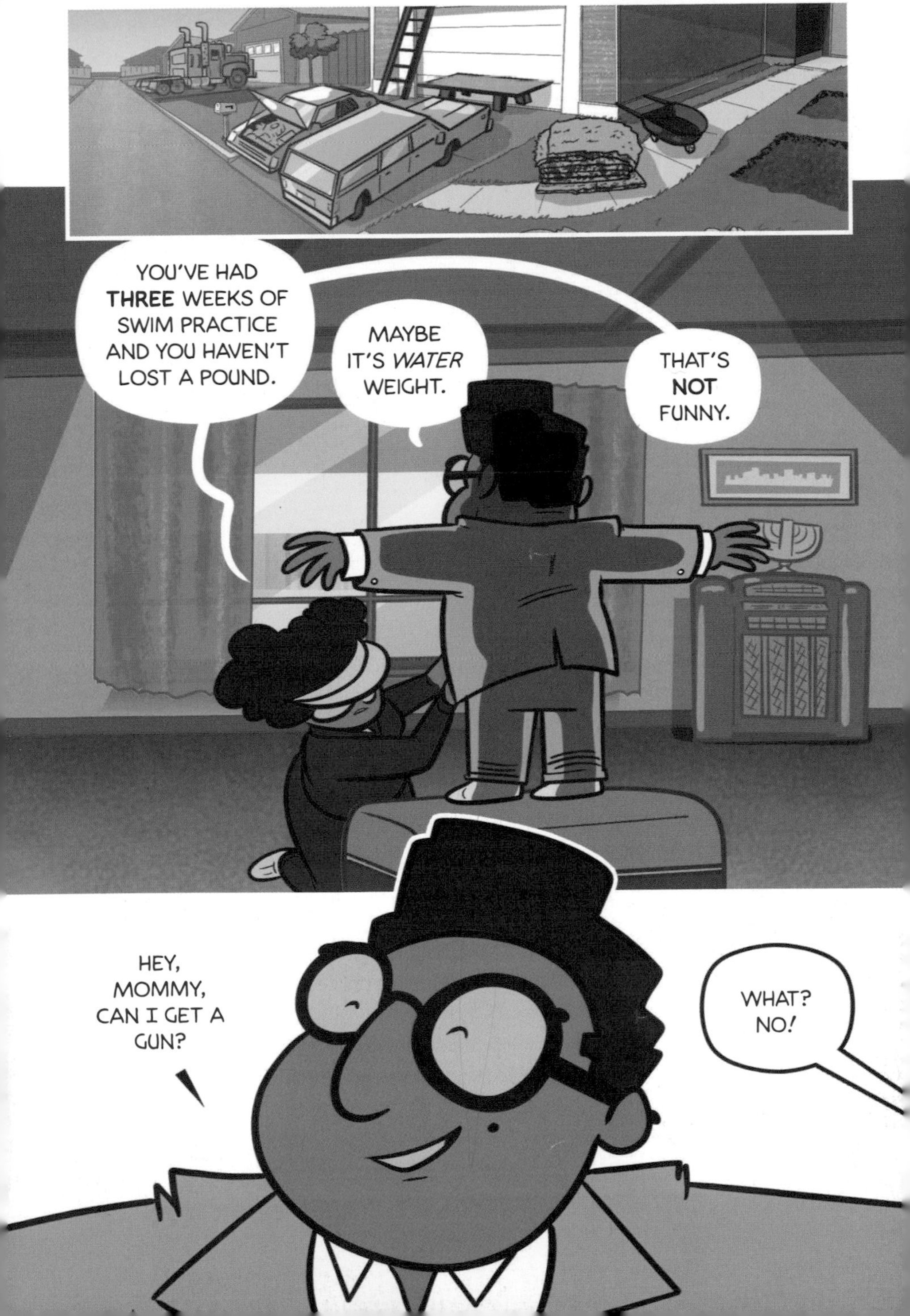
YOU'VE HAD **THREE** WEEKS OF SWIM PRACTICE AND YOU HAVEN'T LOST A POUND.
MAYBE IT'S *WATER* WEIGHT.
THAT'S **NOT** FUNNY.
HEY, MOMMY, CAN I GET A GUN?
WHAT? NO!

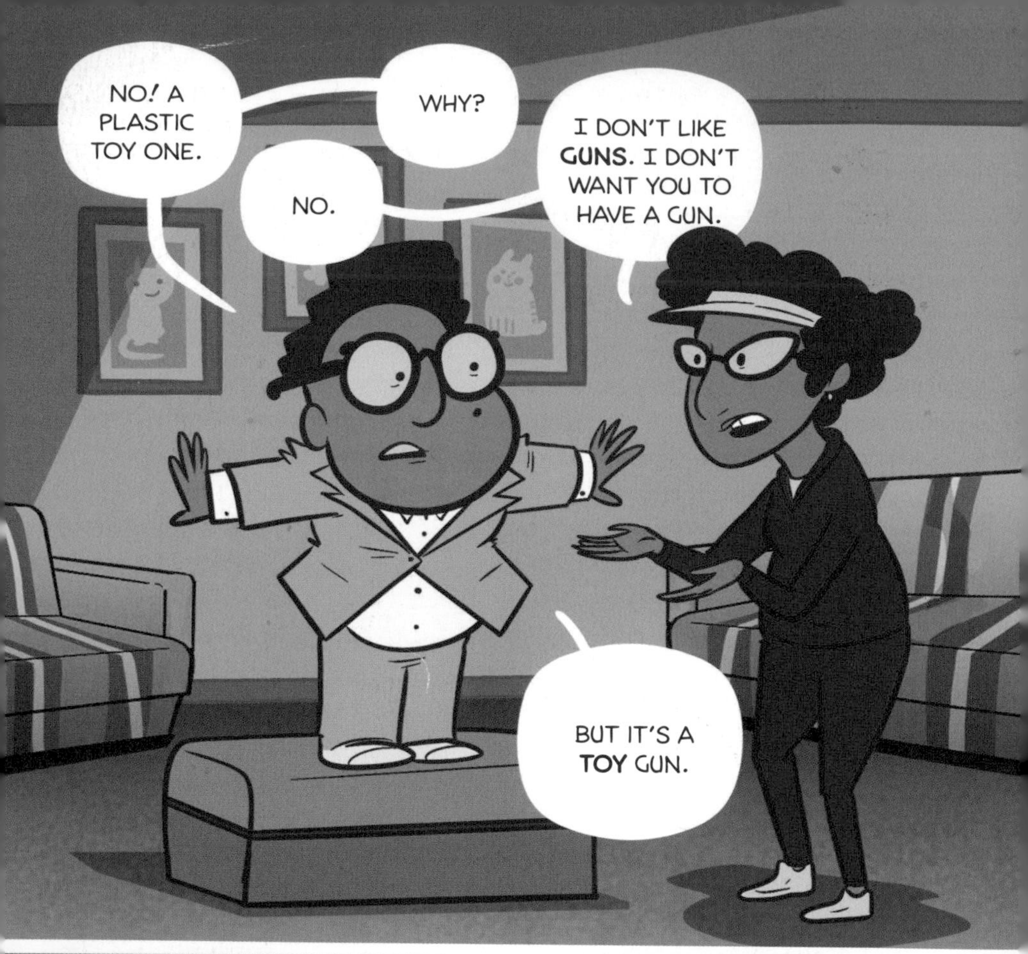
NO! A PLASTIC TOY ONE.
WHY?
NO.
I DON'T LIKE **GUNS**. I DON'T WANT YOU TO HAVE A GUN.
BUT IT'S A **TOY** GUN.

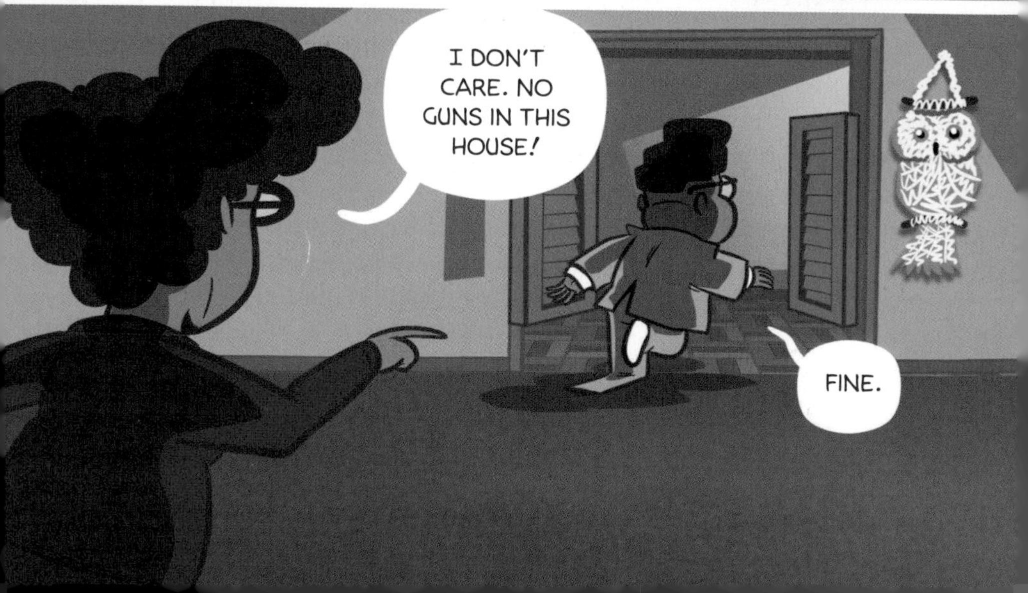
I DON'T CARE. NO GUNS IN THIS HOUSE!
FINE.

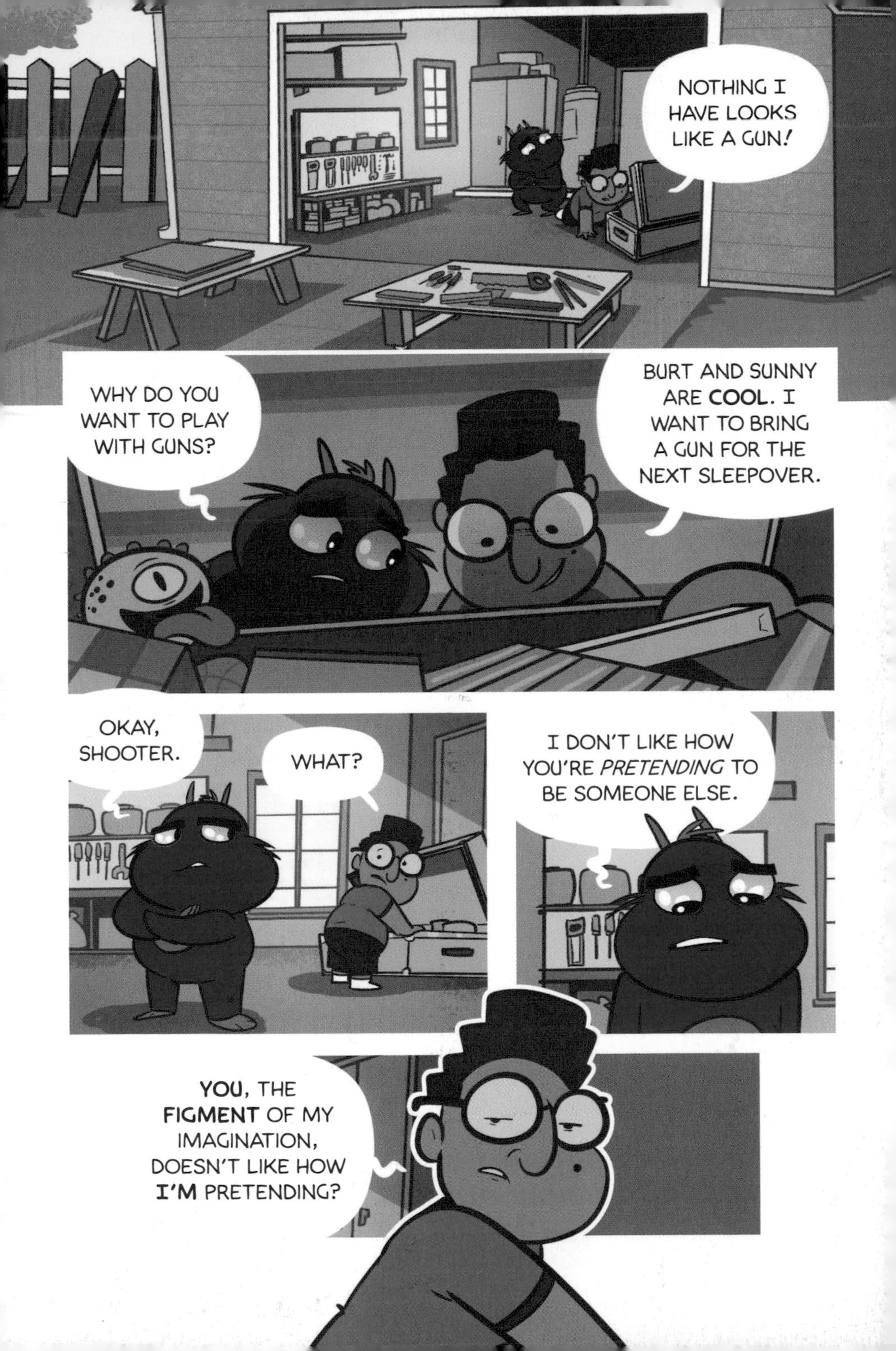
NOTHING I HAVE LOOKS LIKE A GUN!
WHY DO YOU WANT TO PLAY WITH GUNS?
BURT AND SUNNY ARE **COOL**. I WANT TO BRING A GUN FOR THE NEXT SLEEPOVER.
OKAY, SHOOTER.
WHAT?
I DON'T LIKE HOW YOU'RE *PRETENDING* TO BE SOMEONE ELSE.
YOU, THE **FIGMENT** OF MY IMAGINATION, DOESN'T LIKE HOW **I'M** PRETENDING?

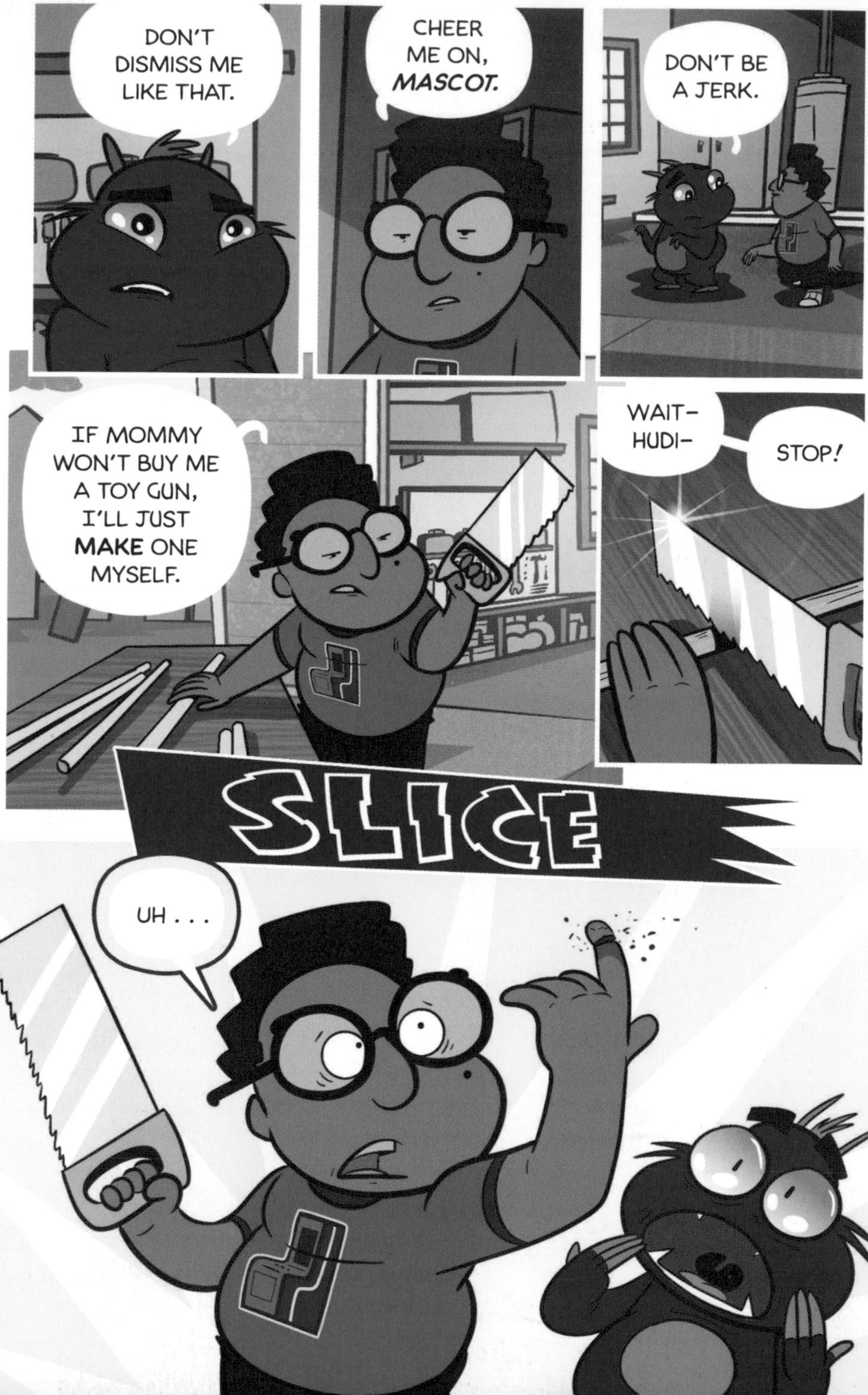
DON'T DISMISS ME LIKE THAT.
CHEER ME ON, MASCOT.
DON'T BE A JERK.
IF MOMMY WON'T BUY ME A TOY GUN, I'LL JUST MAKE ONE MYSELF.
WAIT— HUDI—
STOP!
SLICE
UH . . .

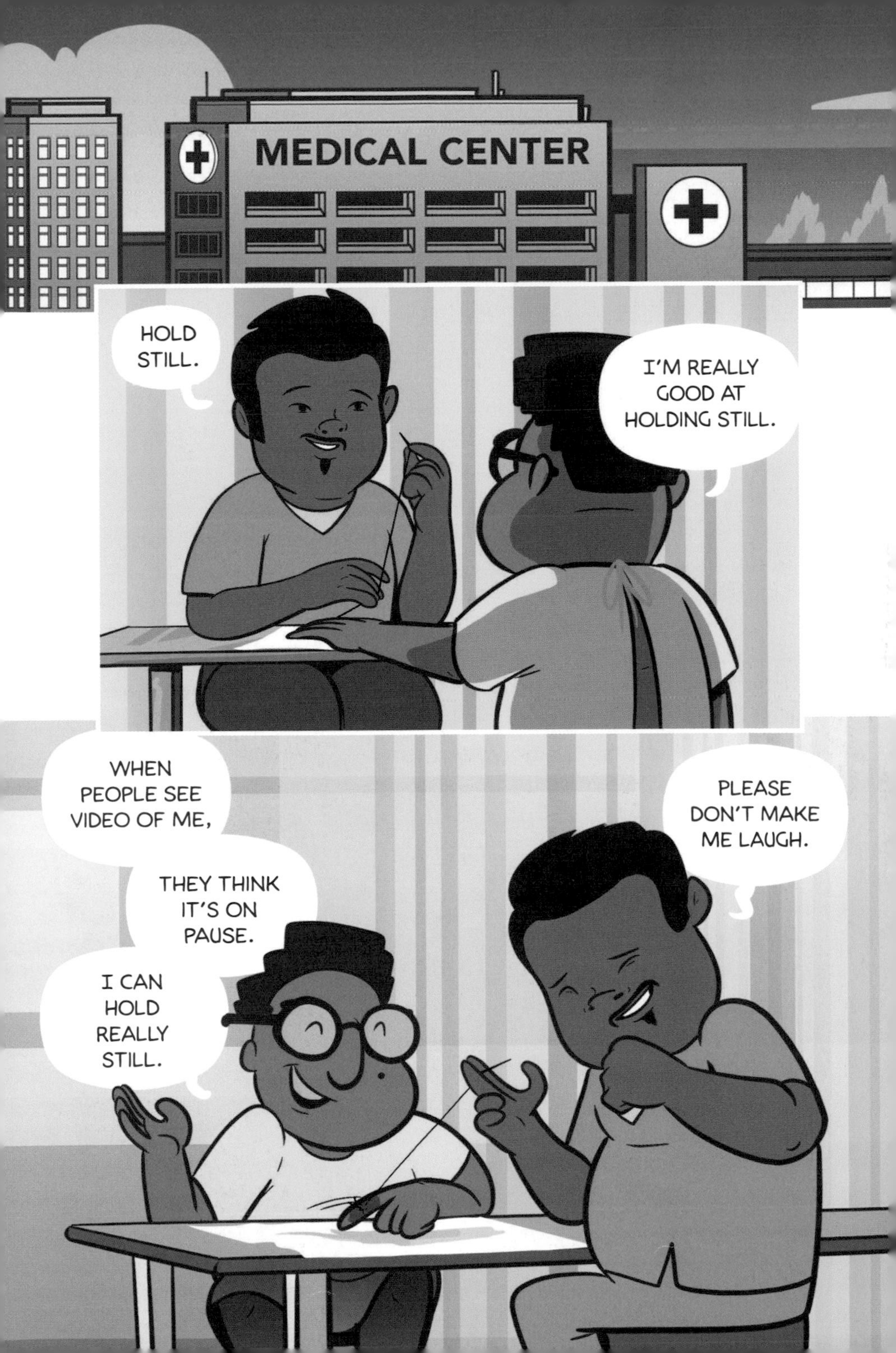
MEDICAL CENTER
HOLD STILL.
I'M REALLY GOOD AT HOLDING STILL.
WHEN PEOPLE SEE VIDEO OF ME,
THEY THINK IT'S ON PAUSE.
I CAN HOLD REALLY STILL.
PLEASE DON'T MAKE ME LAUGH.

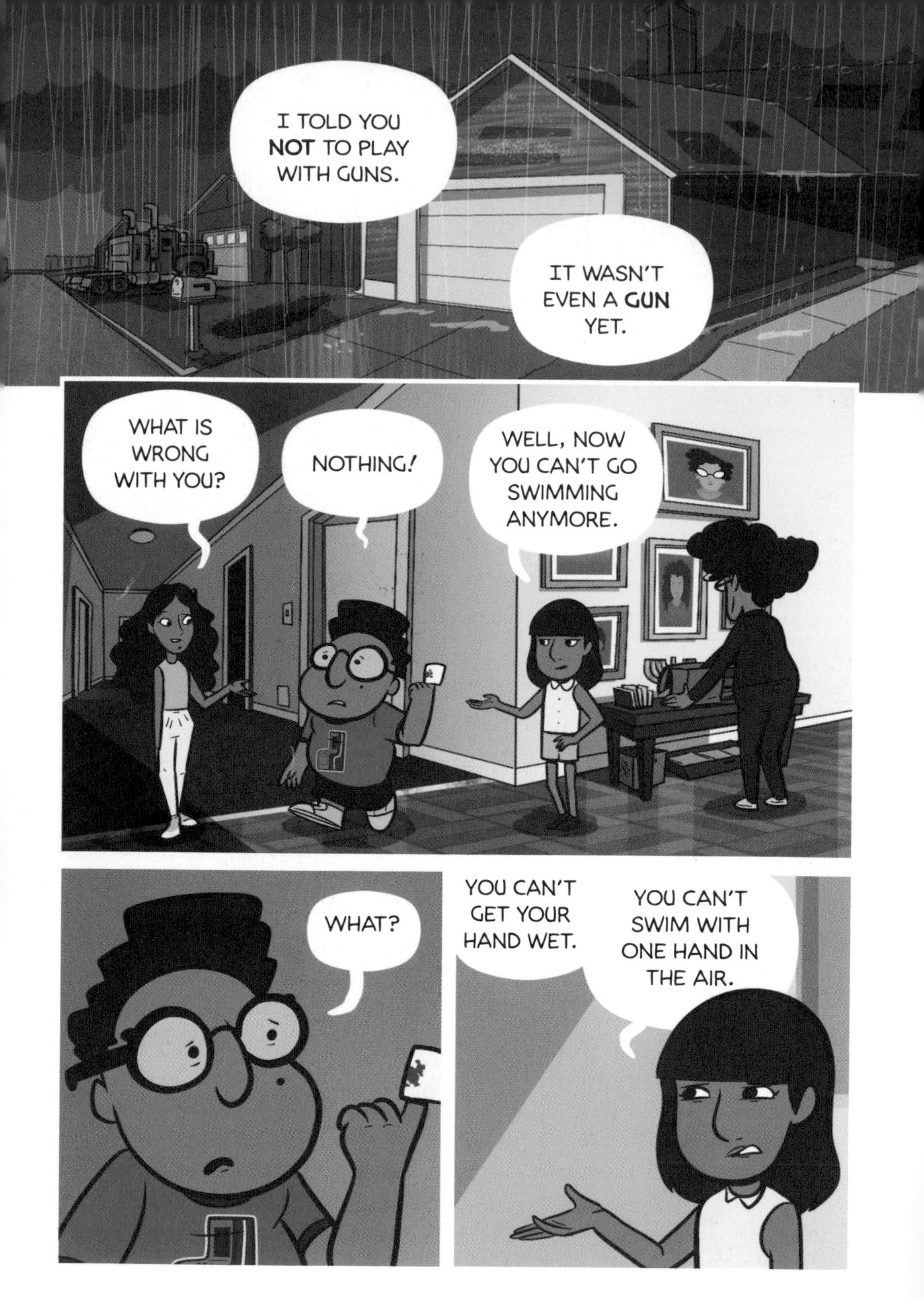
I TOLD YOU **NOT** TO PLAY WITH GUNS.
IT WASN'T EVEN A **GUN** YET.
WHAT IS WRONG WITH YOU?
NOTHING!
WELL, NOW YOU CAN'T GO SWIMMING ANYMORE.
WHAT?
YOU CAN'T GET YOUR HAND WET.
YOU CAN'T SWIM WITH ONE HAND IN THE AIR.

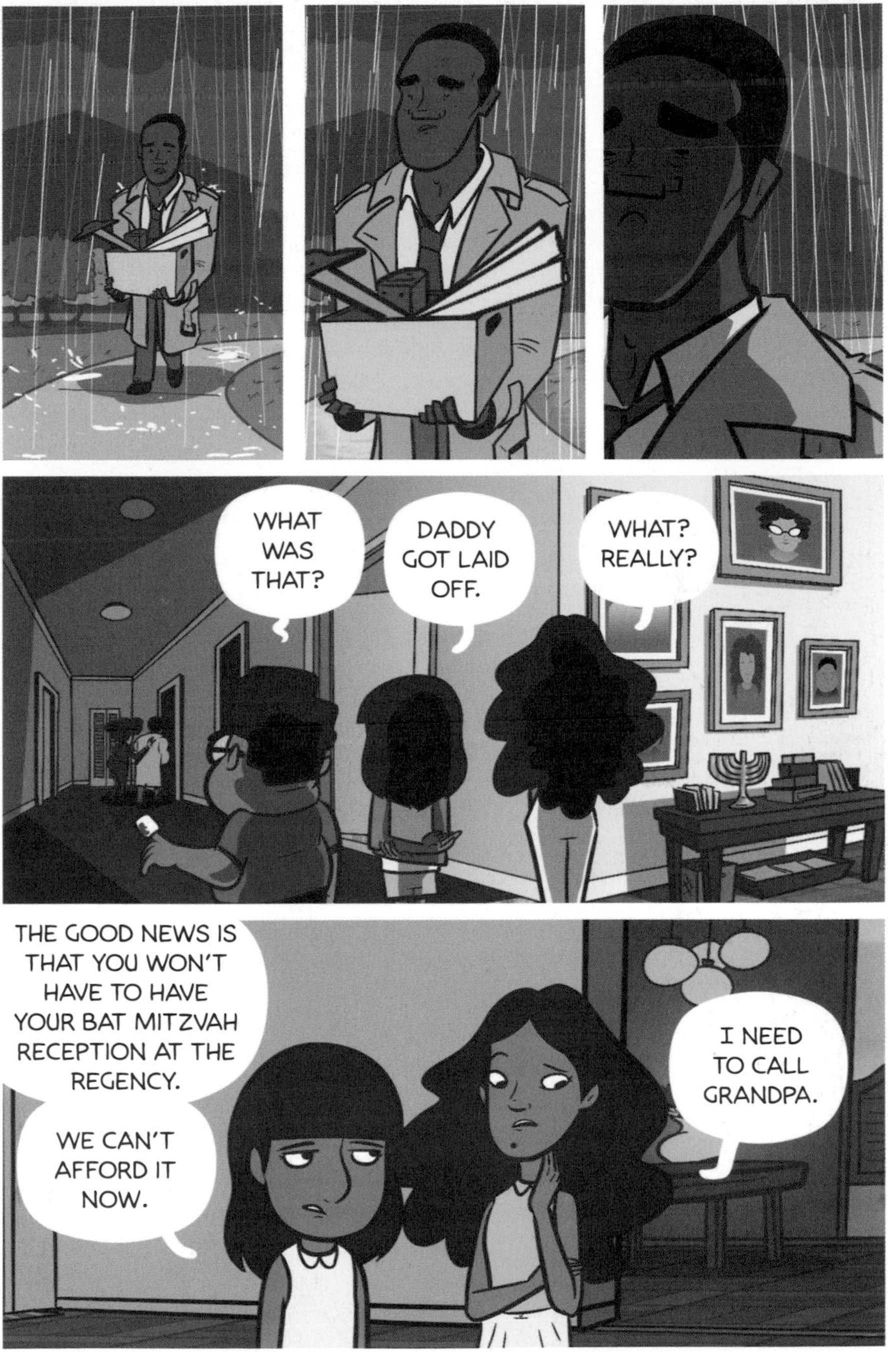
WHAT WAS THAT?
DADDY GOT LAID OFF.
WHAT? REALLY?
THE GOOD NEWS IS THAT YOU WON'T HAVE TO HAVE YOUR BAT MITZVAH RECEPTION AT THE REGENCY.
WE CAN'T AFFORD IT NOW.
I NEED TO CALL GRANDPA.

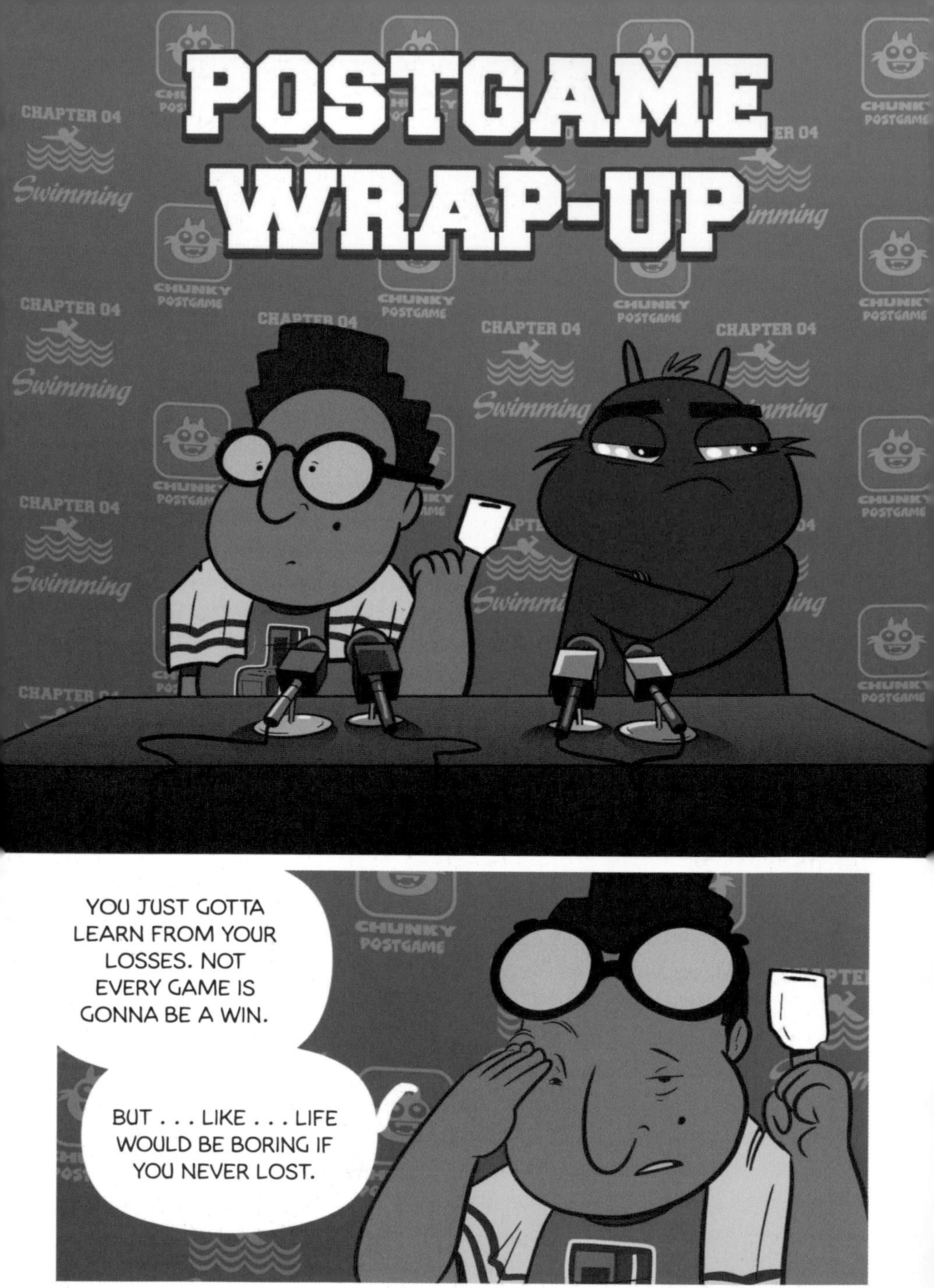
POSTGAME WRAP-UP
CHAPTER 04
Swimming
CHUNKY POSTGAME
YOU JUST GOTTA LEARN FROM YOUR LOSSES. NOT EVERY GAME IS GONNA BE A WIN.
BUT . . . LIKE . . . LIFE WOULD BE BORING IF YOU NEVER LOST.

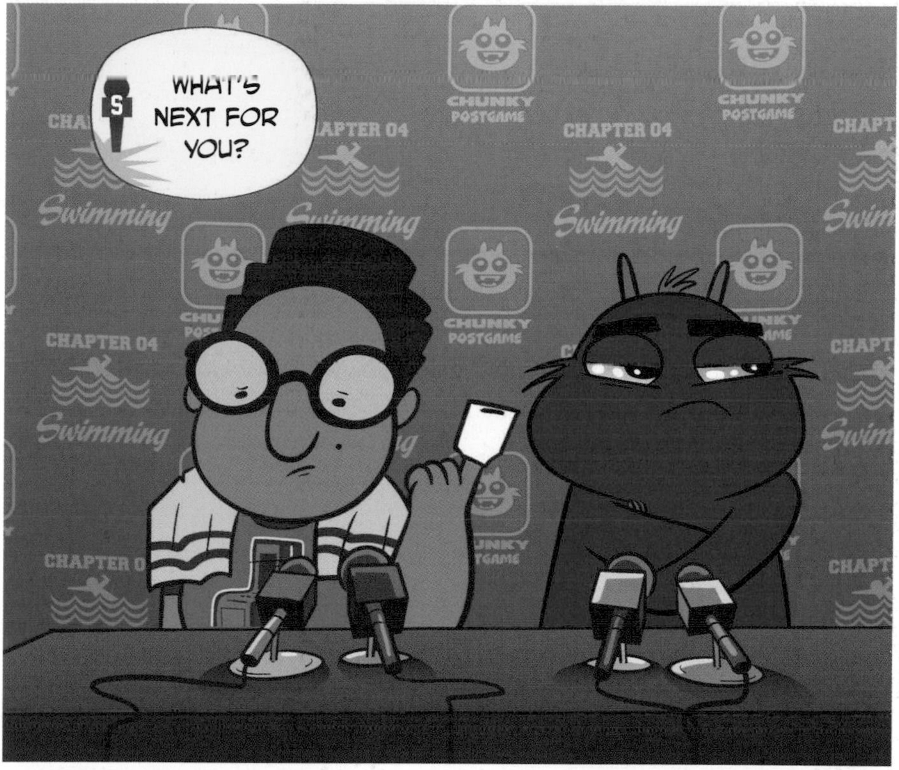
WHAT'S NEXT FOR YOU?
CHUNKY POSTGAME
CHAPTER 04
Swimming

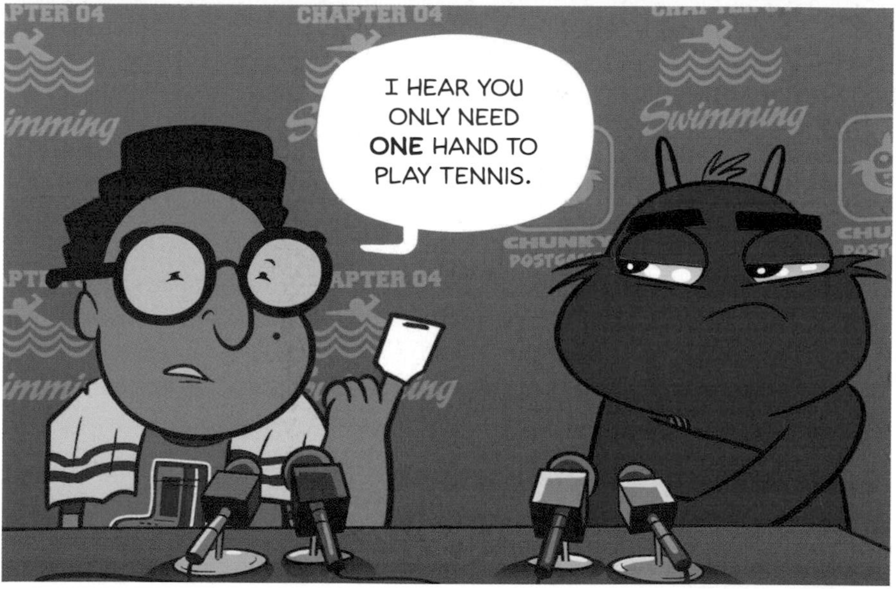
I HEAR YOU ONLY NEED **ONE** HAND TO PLAY TENNIS.
CHAPTER 04
Swimming

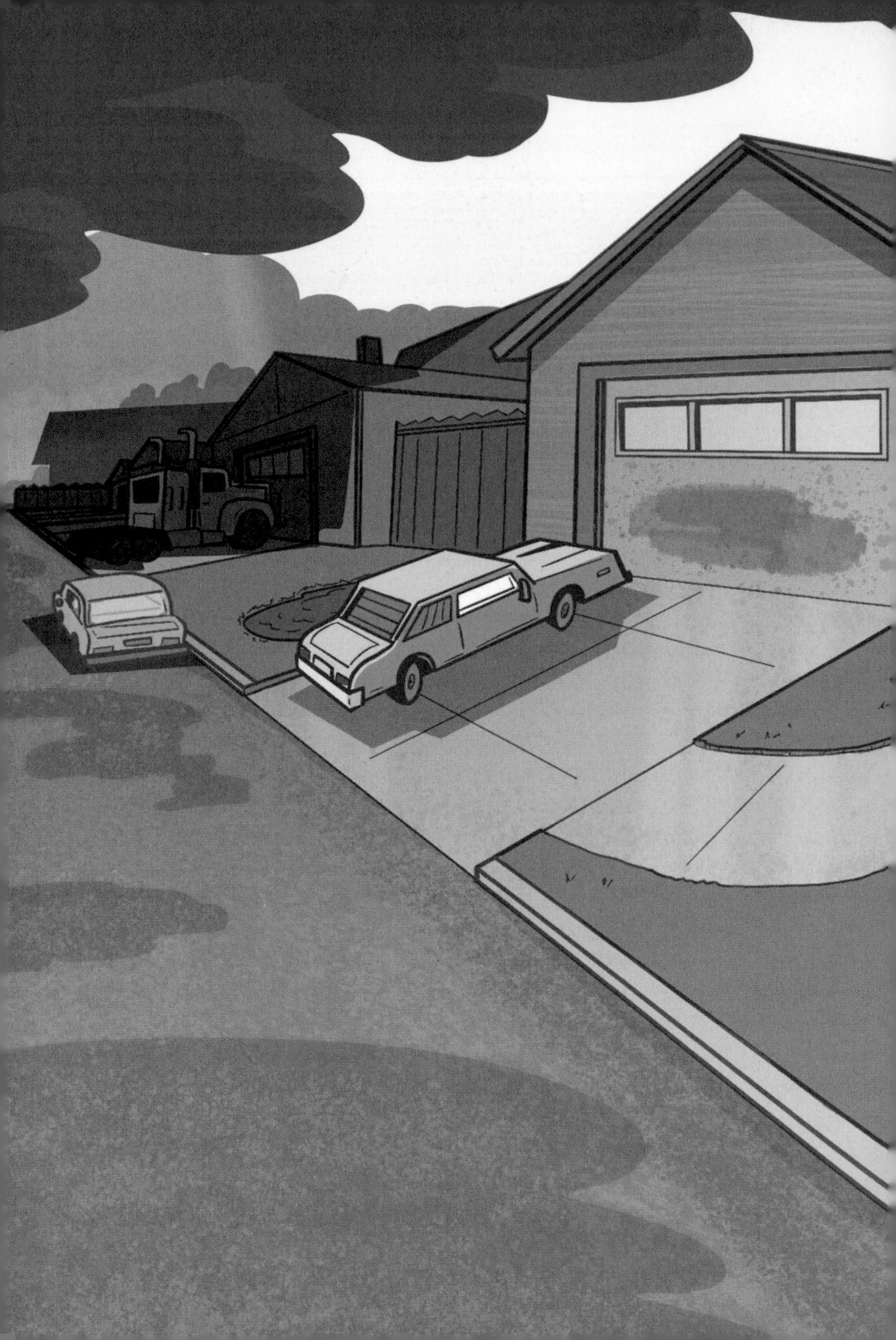

CHAPTER FIVE
Tennis

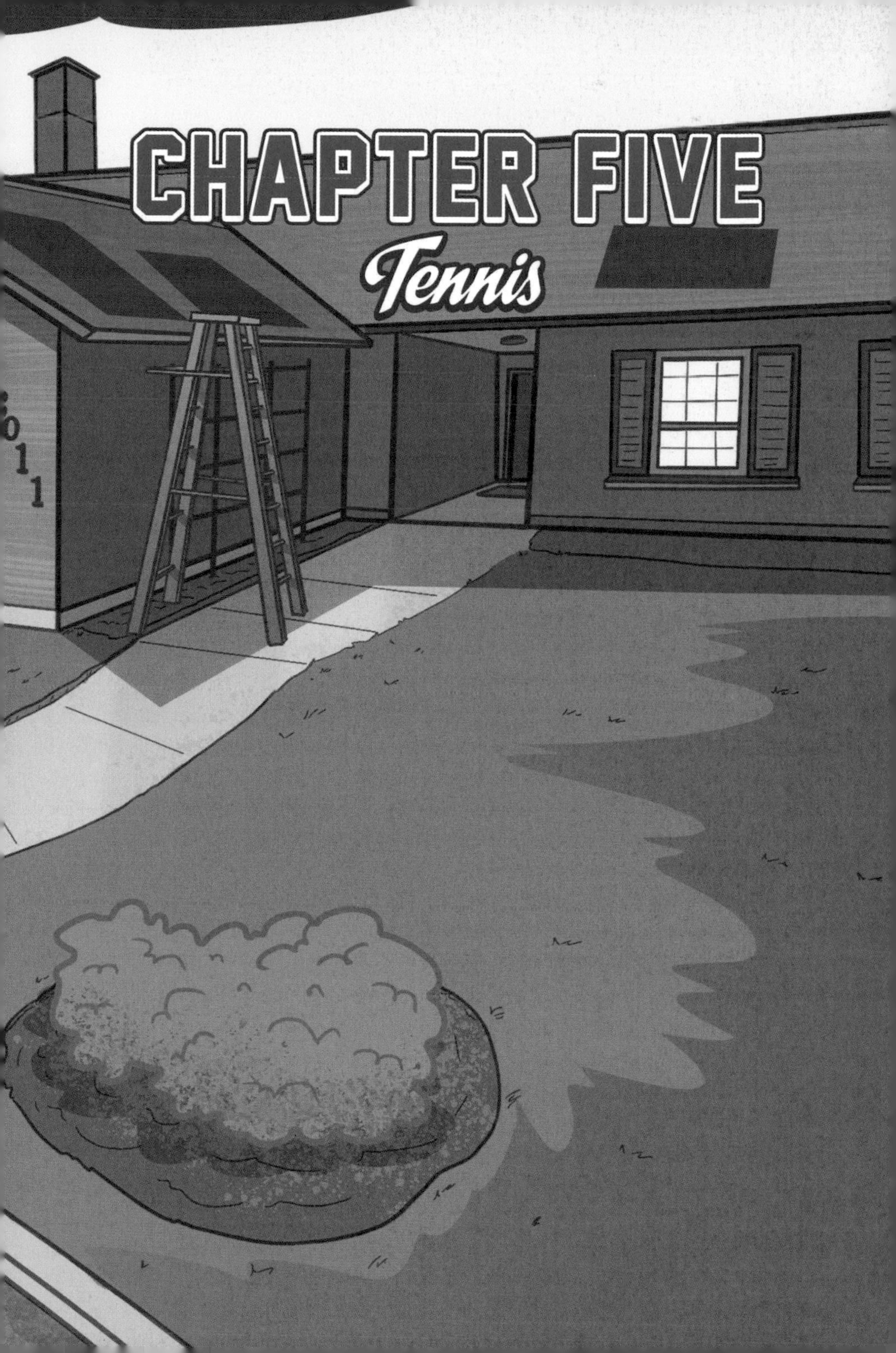
011

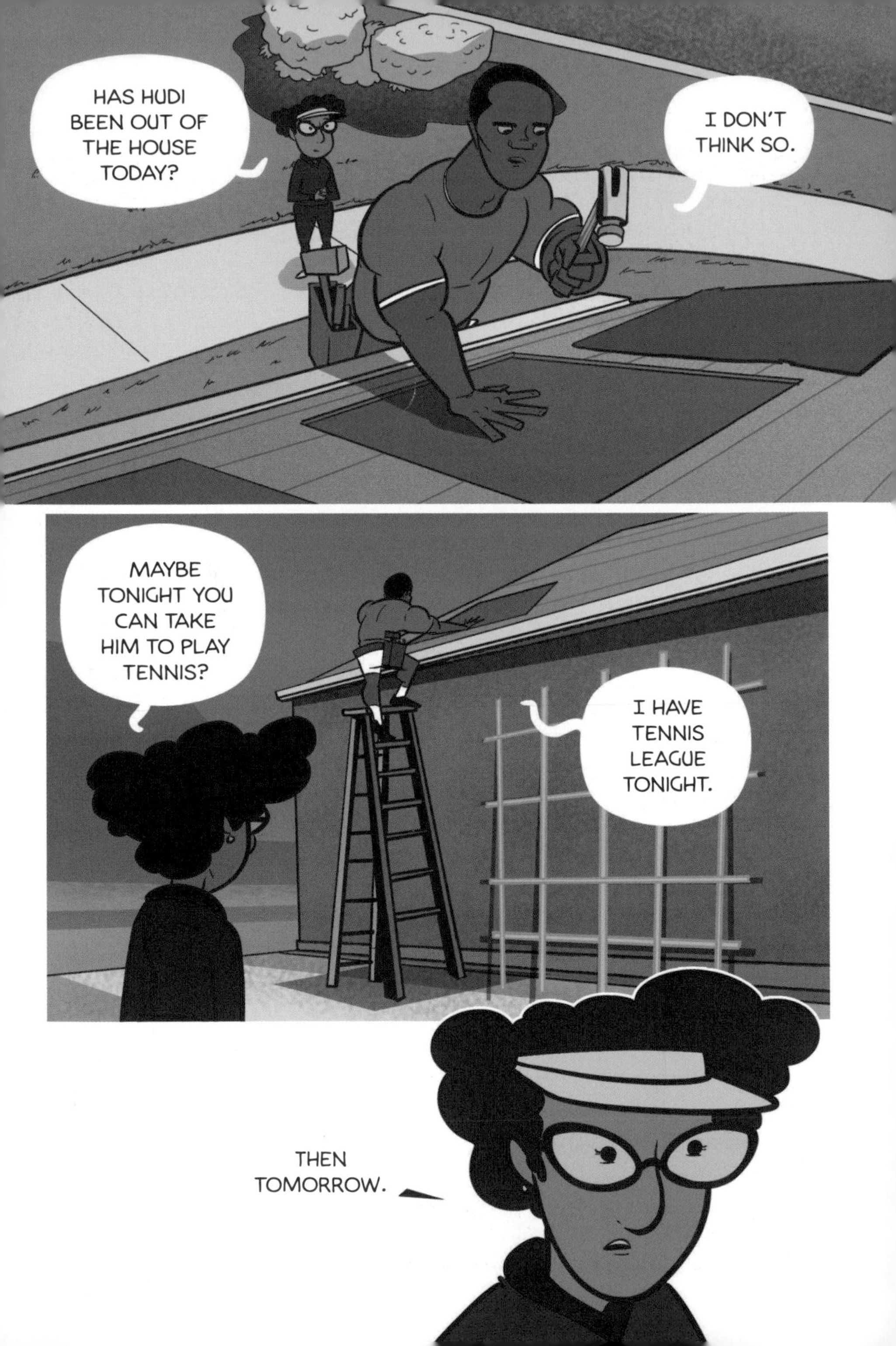
HAS HUDI BEEN OUT OF THE HOUSE TODAY?
I DON'T THINK SO.
MAYBE TONIGHT YOU CAN TAKE HIM TO PLAY TENNIS?
I HAVE TENNIS LEAGUE TONIGHT.
THEN TOMORROW.

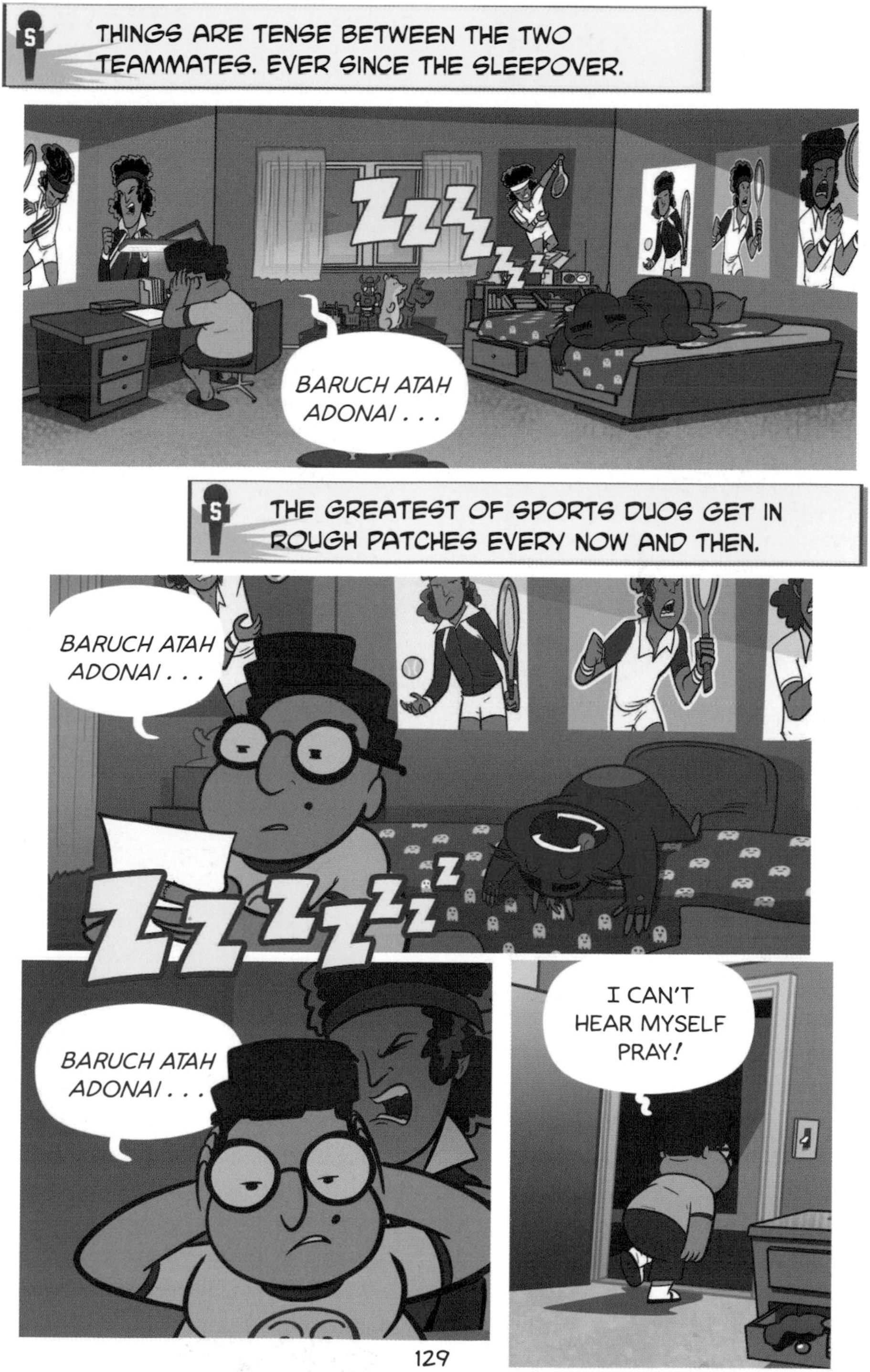
THINGS ARE TENSE BETWEEN THE TWO TEAMMATES. EVER SINCE THE SLEEPOVER.
ZZZZZZZ
BARUCH ATAH ADONAI . . .
THE GREATEST OF SPORTS DUOS GET IN ROUGH PATCHES EVERY NOW AND THEN.
BARUCH ATAH ADONAI . . .
ZZZZZZZZ
BARUCH ATAH ADONAI . . .
I CAN'T HEAR MYSELF PRAY!

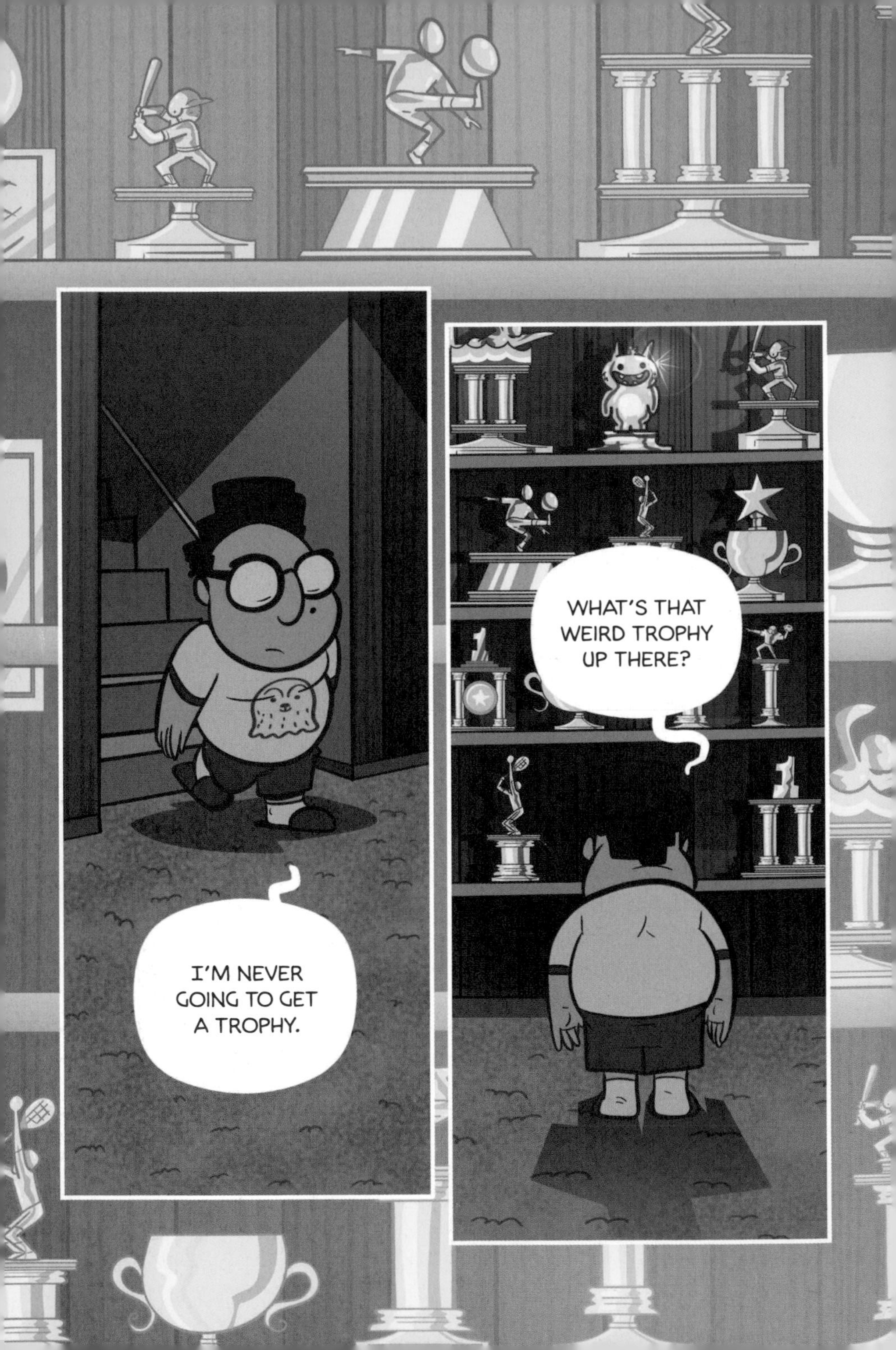
I'M NEVER GOING TO GET A TROPHY.
WHAT'S THAT WEIRD TROPHY UP THERE?

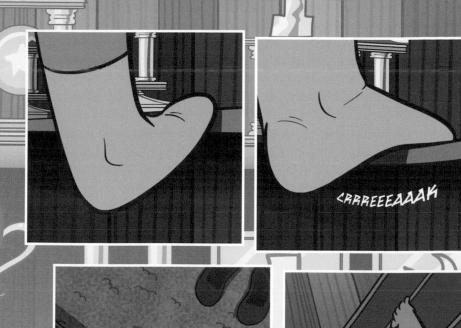

CRRREEEAAAK

CRACK

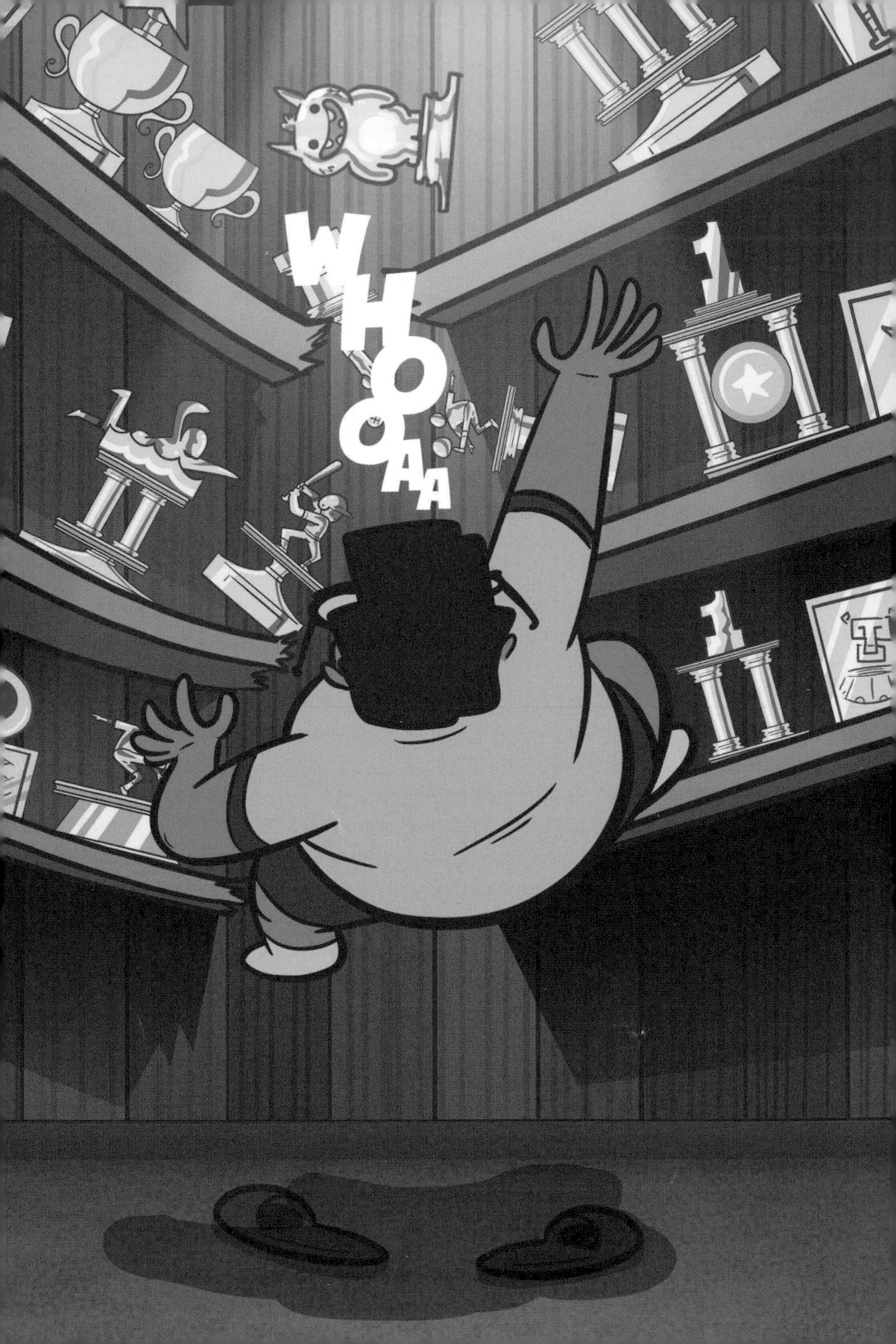
WHOOAAA

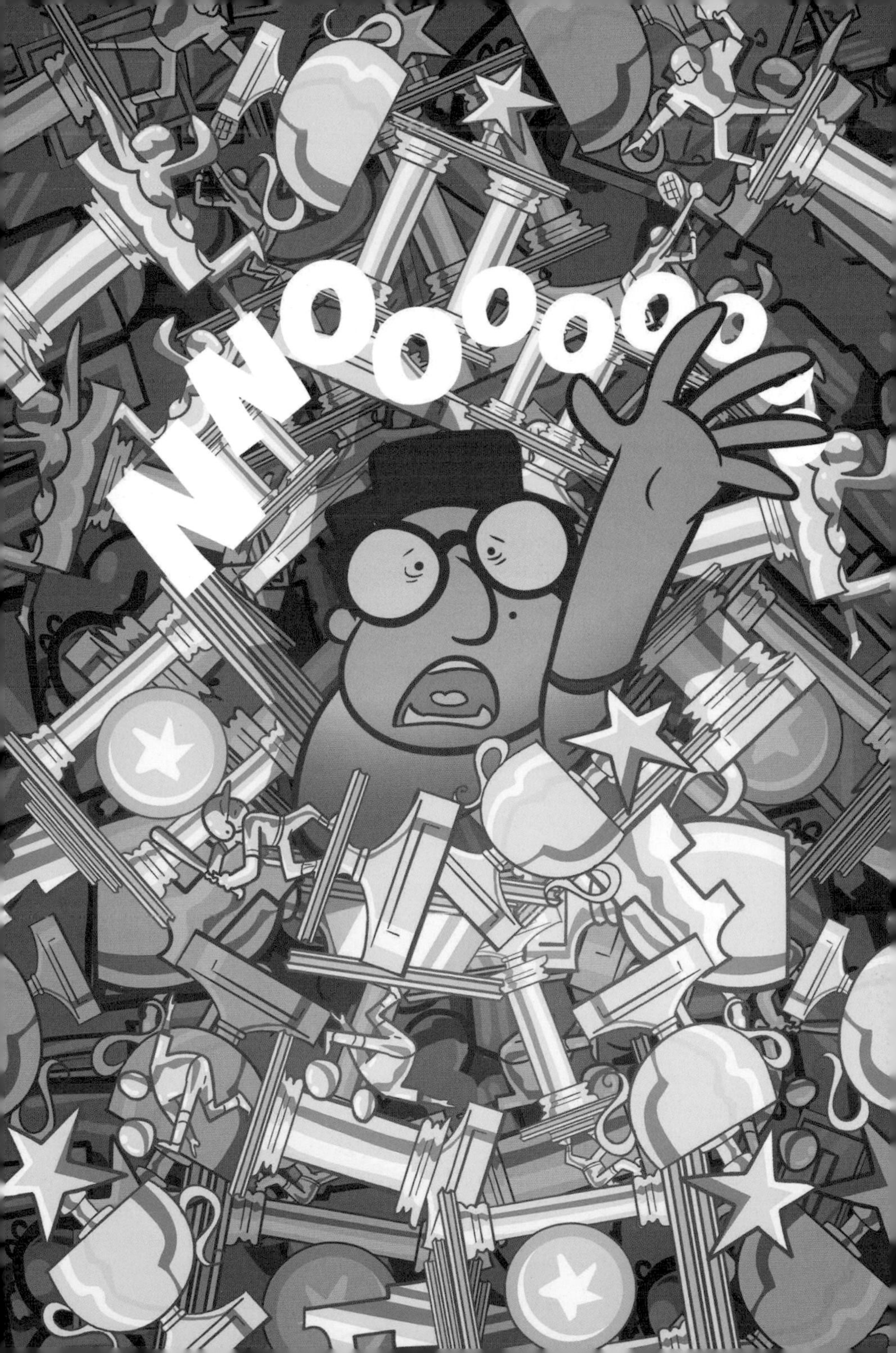
NOOOOOO

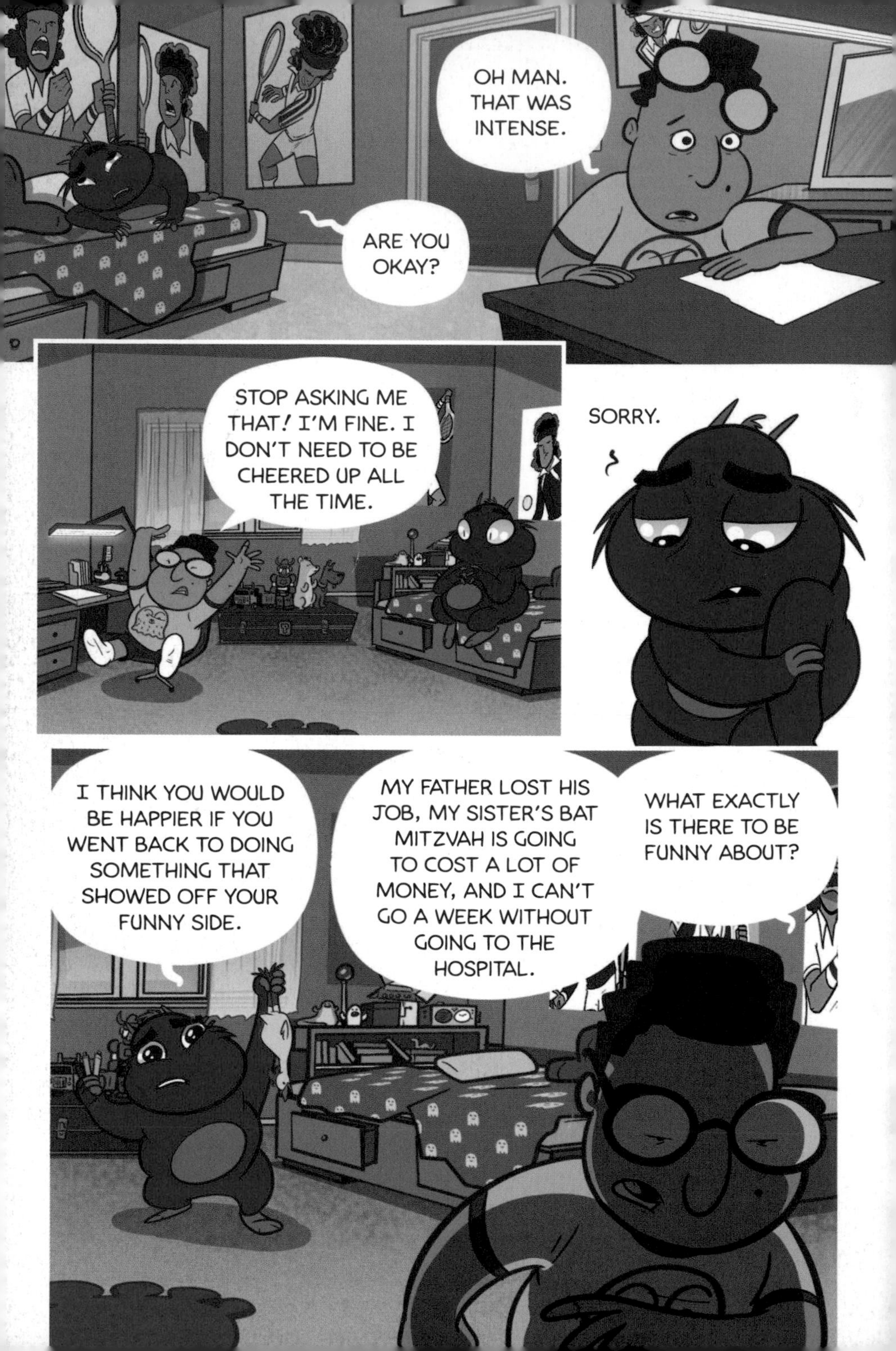
OH MAN. THAT WAS INTENSE.
ARE YOU OKAY?
STOP ASKING ME THAT! I'M FINE. I DON'T NEED TO BE CHEERED UP ALL THE TIME.
SORRY.
I THINK YOU WOULD BE HAPPIER IF YOU WENT BACK TO DOING SOMETHING THAT SHOWED OFF YOUR FUNNY SIDE.
MY FATHER LOST HIS JOB, MY SISTER'S BAT MITZVAH IS GOING TO COST A LOT OF MONEY, AND I CAN'T GO A WEEK WITHOUT GOING TO THE HOSPITAL.
WHAT EXACTLY IS THERE TO BE FUNNY ABOUT?

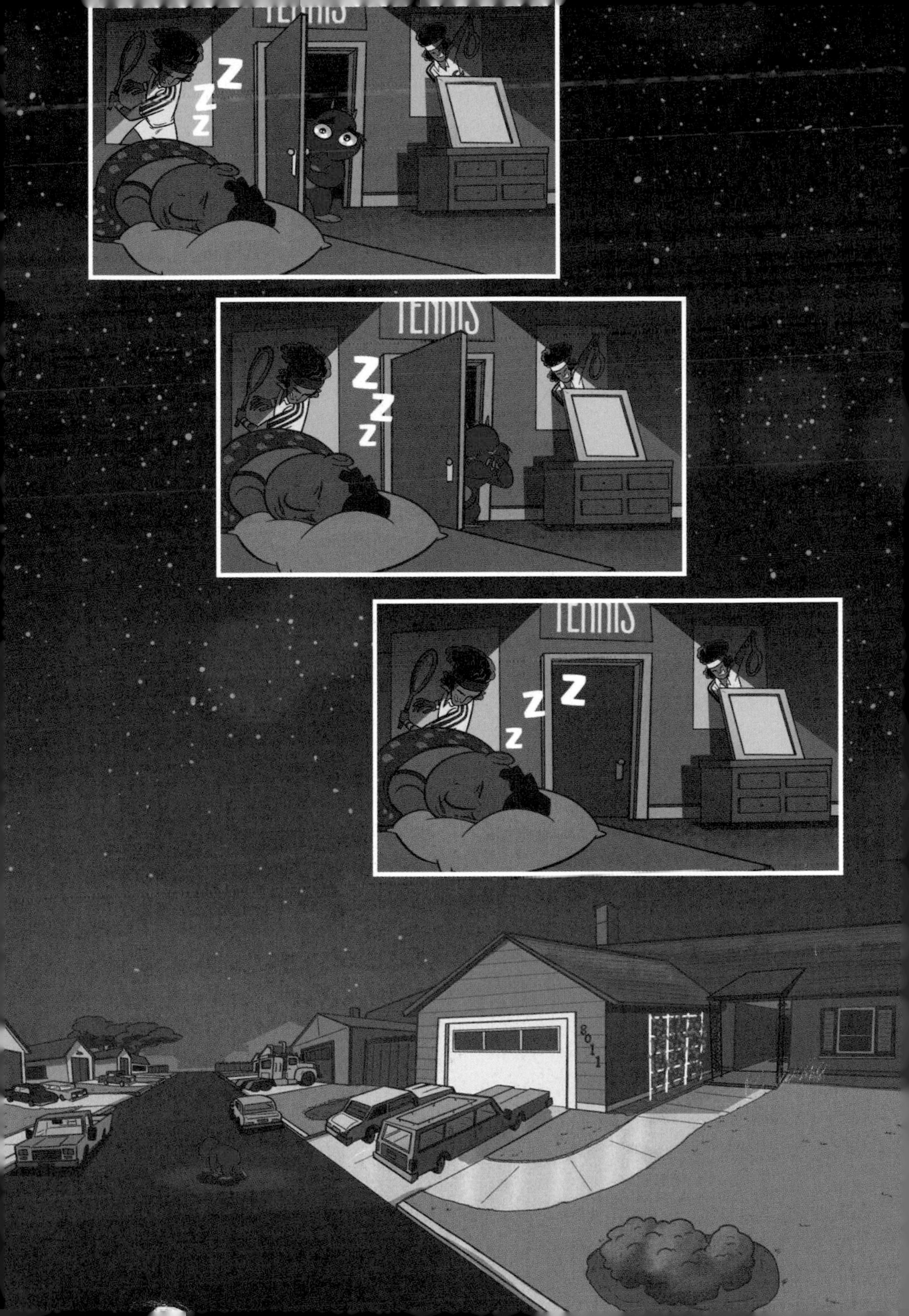
Z Z Z
TENNIS
Z Z Z
Z Z Z
8011

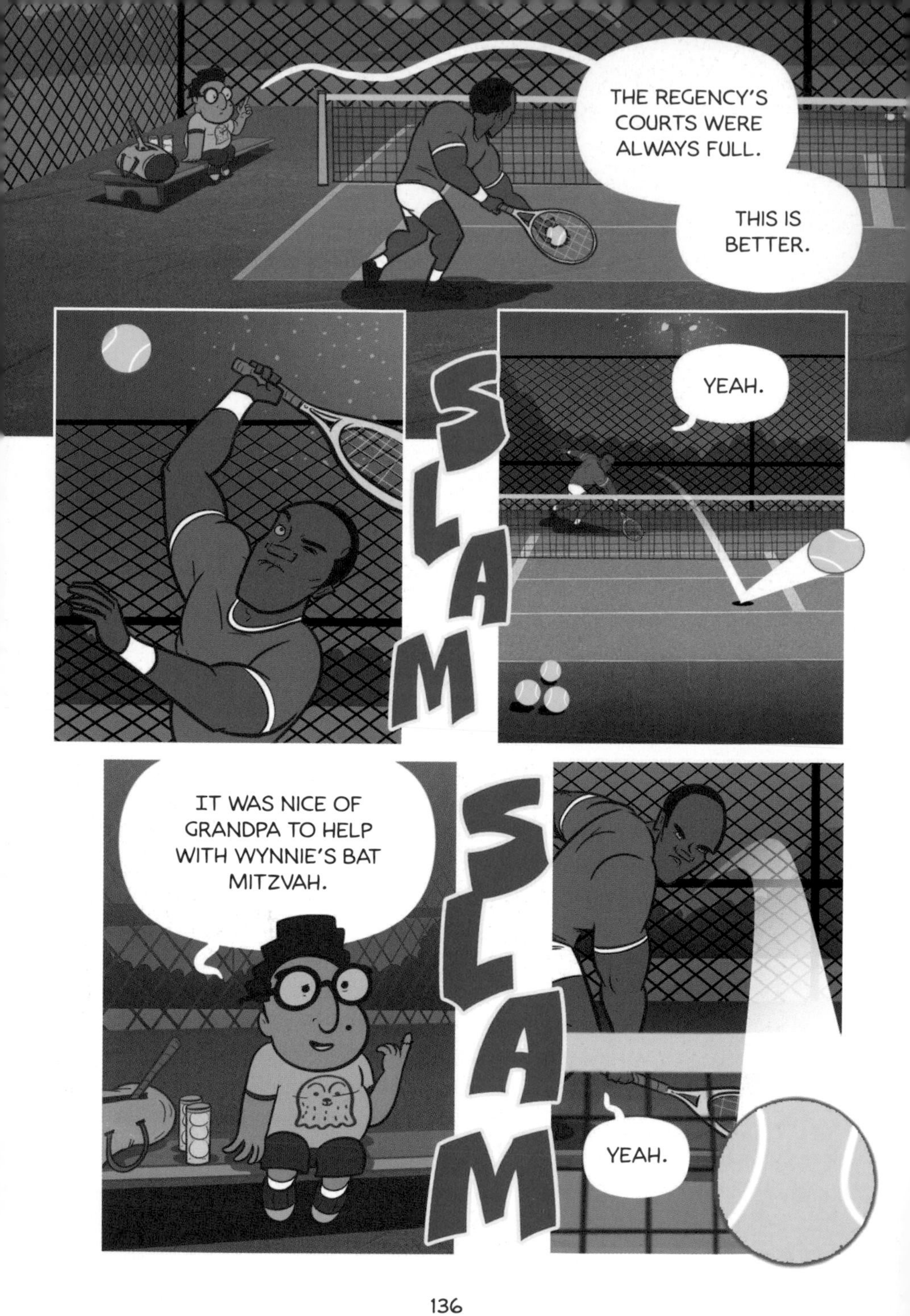
THE REGENCY'S COURTS WERE ALWAYS FULL.
THIS IS BETTER.
SLAM
YEAH.
IT WAS NICE OF GRANDPA TO HELP WITH WYNNIE'S BAT MITZVAH.
SLAM
YEAH.

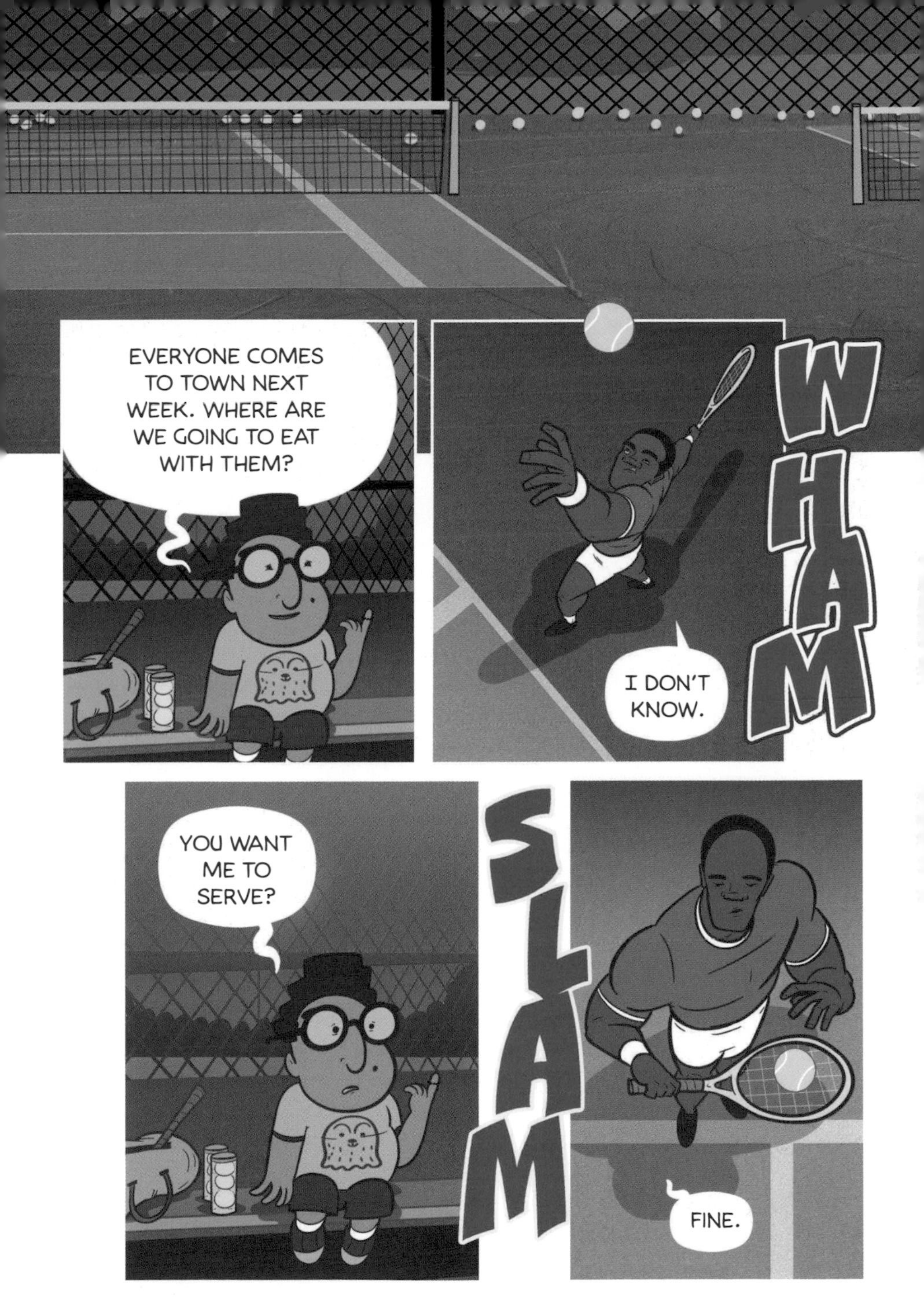
EVERYONE COMES TO TOWN NEXT WEEK. WHERE ARE WE GOING TO EAT WITH THEM?
I DON'T KNOW.
WHAM
YOU WANT ME TO SERVE?
SLAM
FINE.

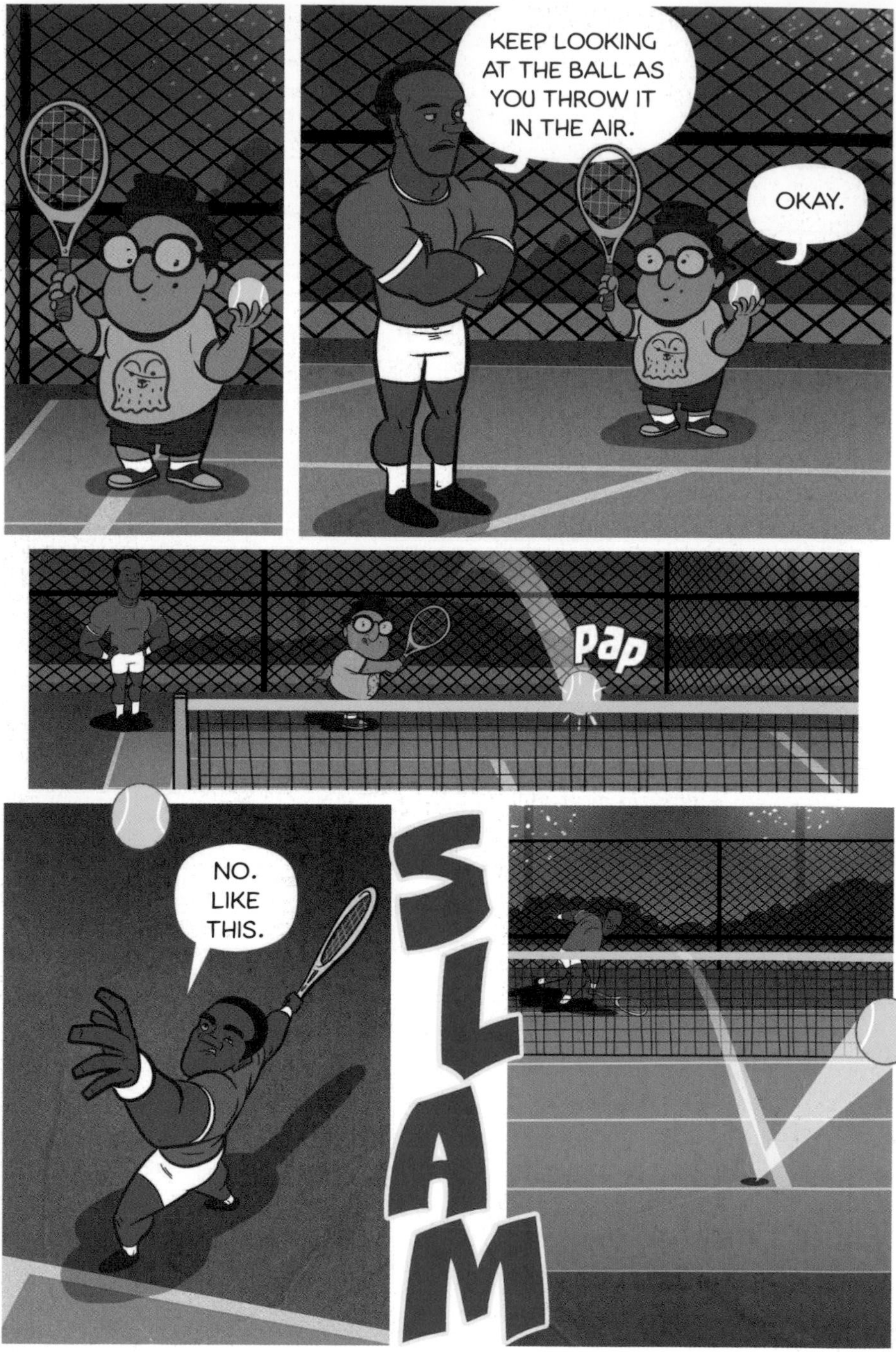
KEEP LOOKING AT THE BALL AS YOU THROW IT IN THE AIR.
OKAY.
PAP
NO. LIKE THIS.
SLAM

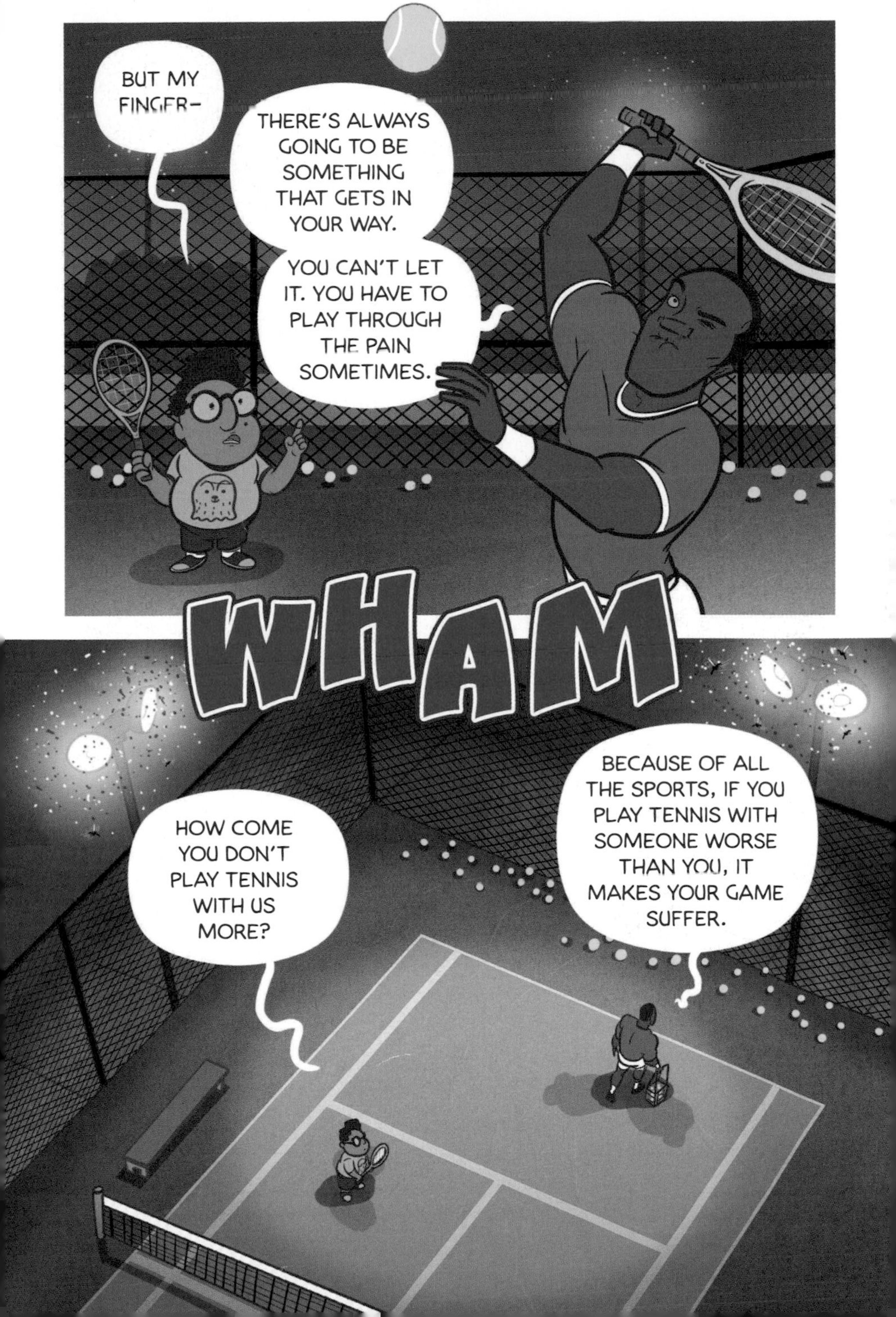
BUT MY FINGER–
THERE'S ALWAYS GOING TO BE SOMETHING THAT GETS IN YOUR WAY.
YOU CAN'T LET IT. YOU HAVE TO PLAY THROUGH THE PAIN SOMETIMES.
WHAM
HOW COME YOU DON'T PLAY TENNIS WITH US MORE?
BECAUSE OF ALL THE SPORTS, IF YOU PLAY TENNIS WITH SOMEONE WORSE THAN YOU, IT MAKES YOUR GAME SUFFER.

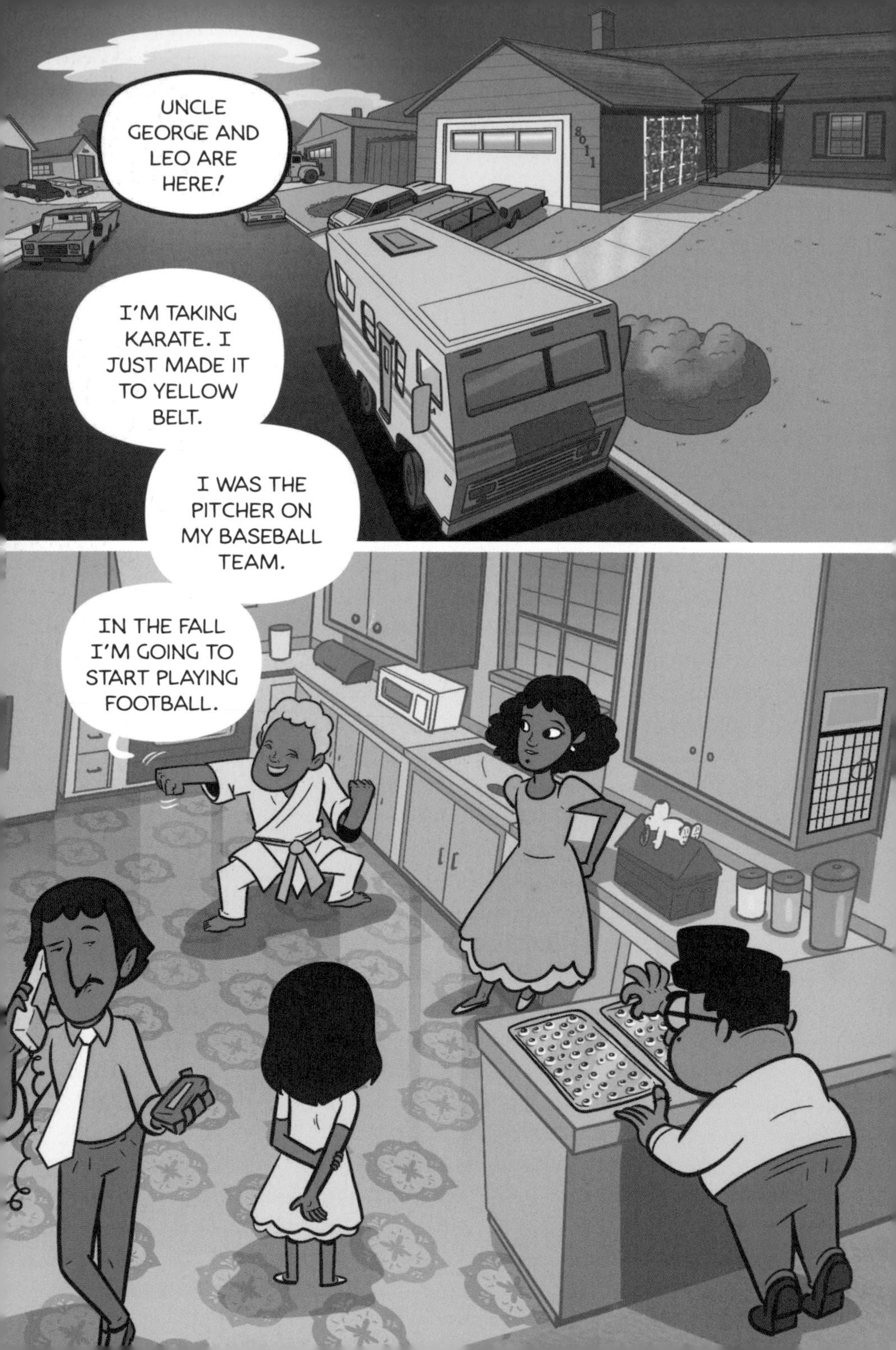
UNCLE GEORGE AND LEO ARE HERE!
8011
I'M TAKING KARATE. I JUST MADE IT TO YELLOW BELT.
I WAS THE PITCHER ON MY BASEBALL TEAM.
IN THE FALL I'M GOING TO START PLAYING FOOTBALL.

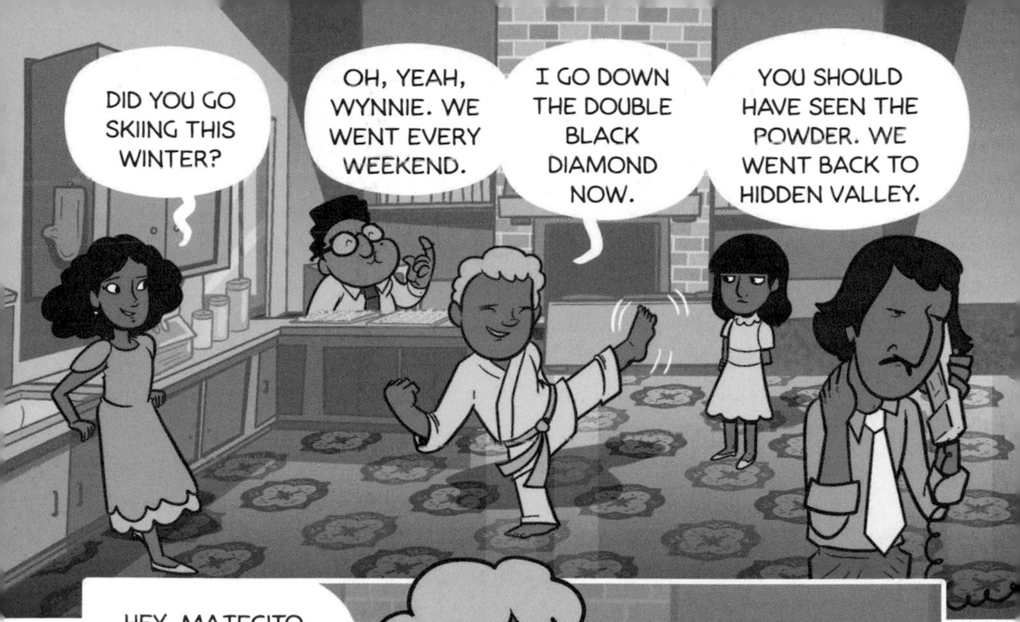
DID YOU GO SKIING THIS WINTER?
OH, YEAH, WYNNIE. WE WENT EVERY WEEKEND.
I GO DOWN THE DOUBLE BLACK DIAMOND NOW.
YOU SHOULD HAVE SEEN THE POWDER. WE WENT BACK TO HIDDEN VALLEY.

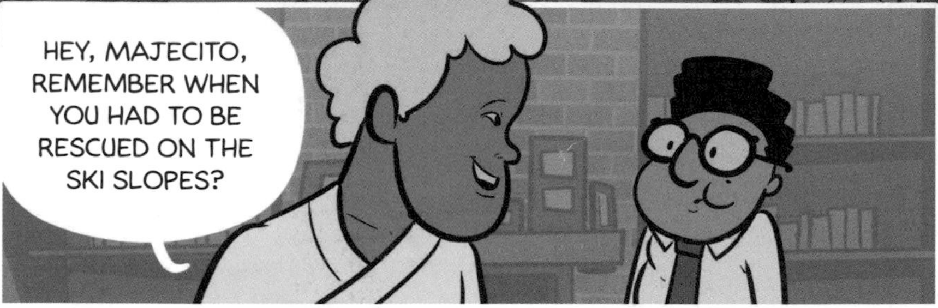
HEY, MAJECITO, REMEMBER WHEN YOU HAD TO BE RESCUED ON THE SKI SLOPES?

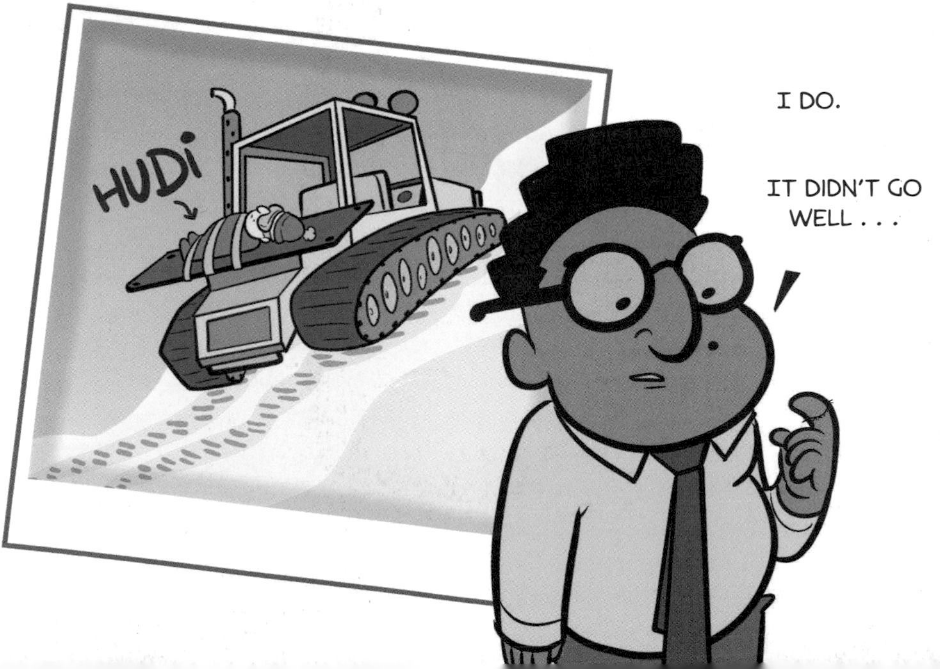
HUDI
I DO.
IT DIDN'T GO WELL . . .

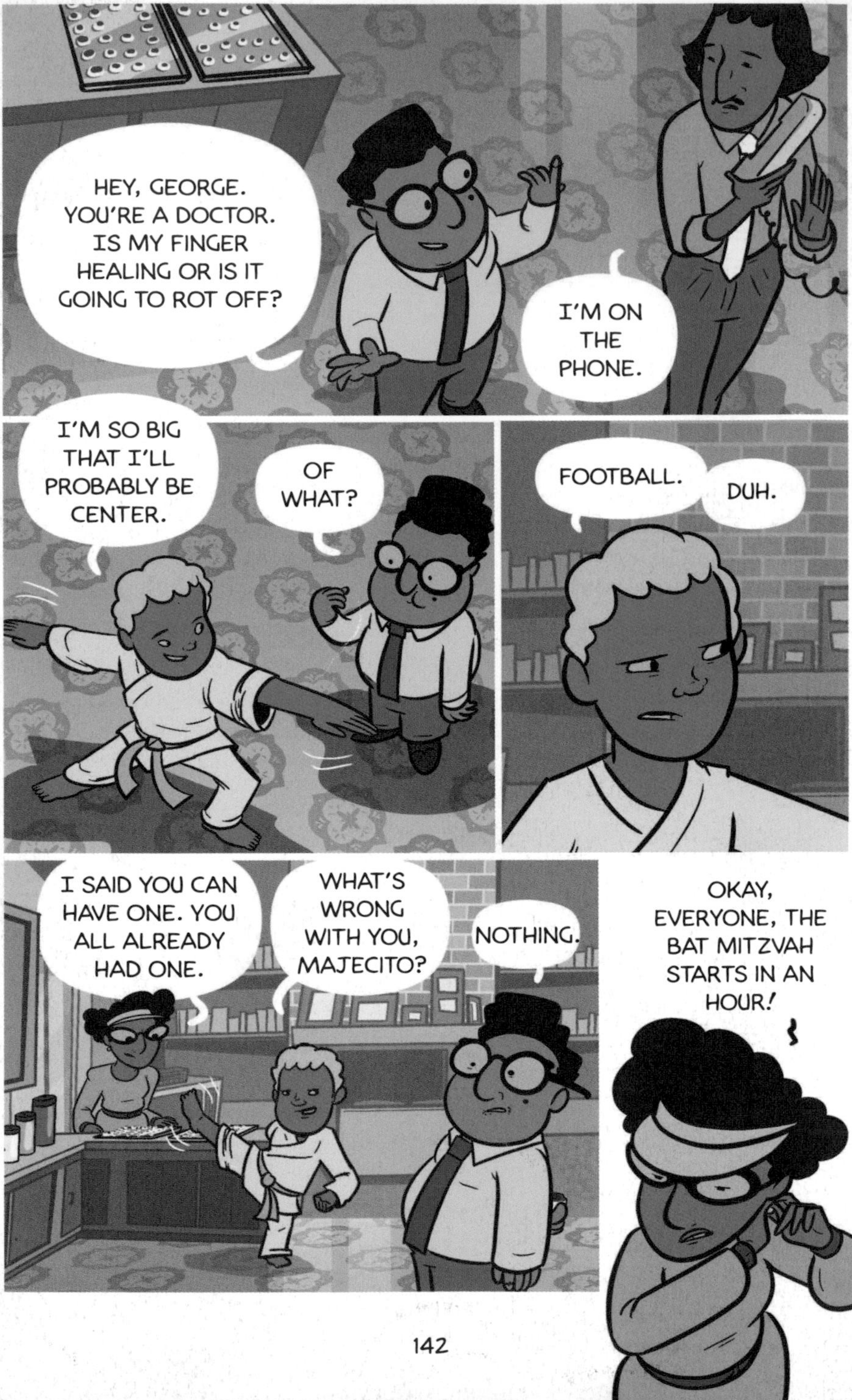
HEY, GEORGE. YOU'RE A DOCTOR. IS MY FINGER HEALING OR IS IT GOING TO ROT OFF?
I'M ON THE PHONE.
I'M SO BIG THAT I'LL PROBABLY BE CENTER.
OF WHAT?
FOOTBALL.
DUH.
I SAID YOU CAN HAVE ONE. YOU ALL ALREADY HAD ONE.
WHAT'S WRONG WITH YOU, MAJECITO?
NOTHING.
OKAY, EVERYONE, THE BAT MITZVAH STARTS IN AN HOUR!

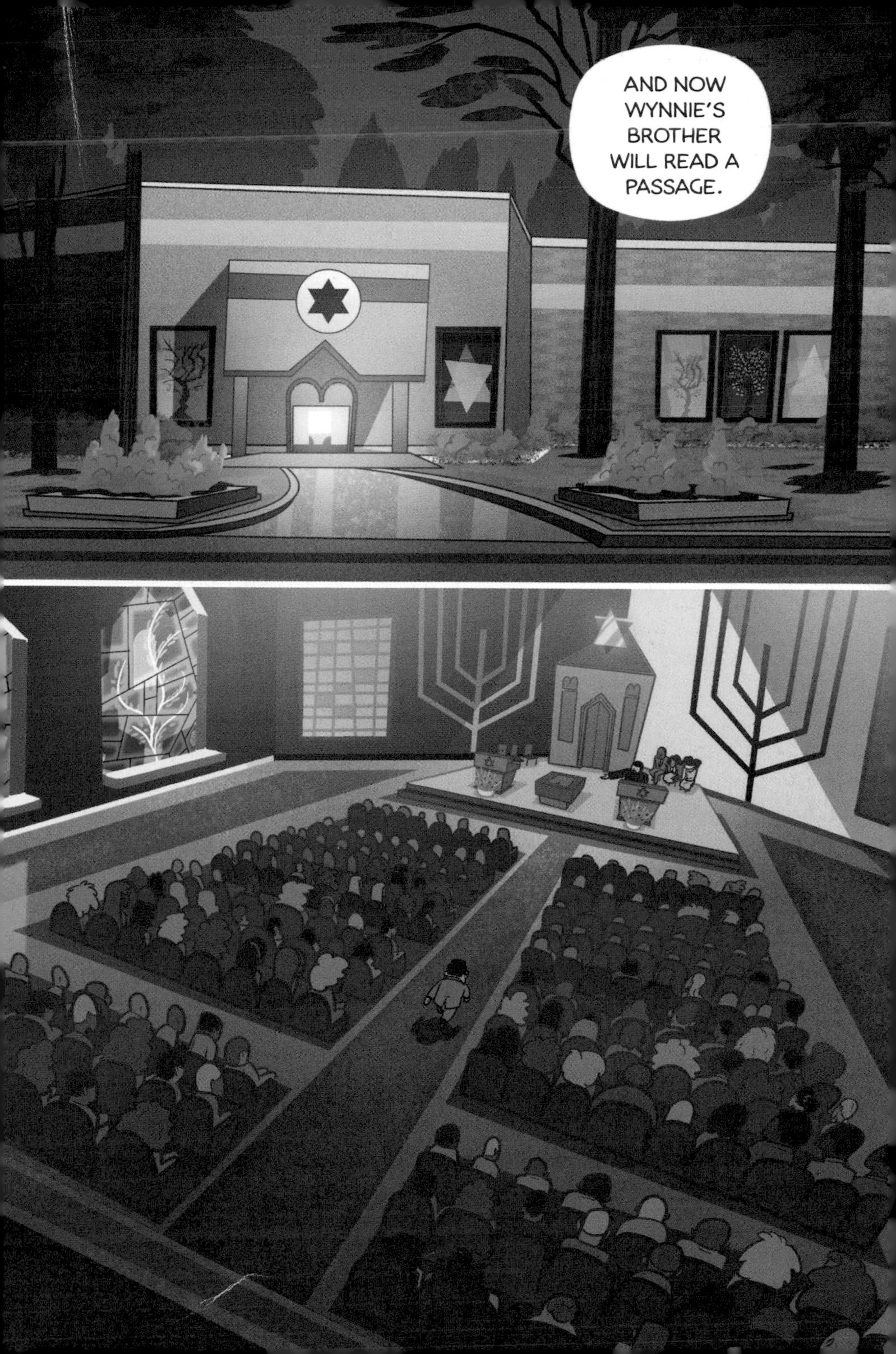
AND NOW WYNNIE'S BROTHER WILL READ A PASSAGE.

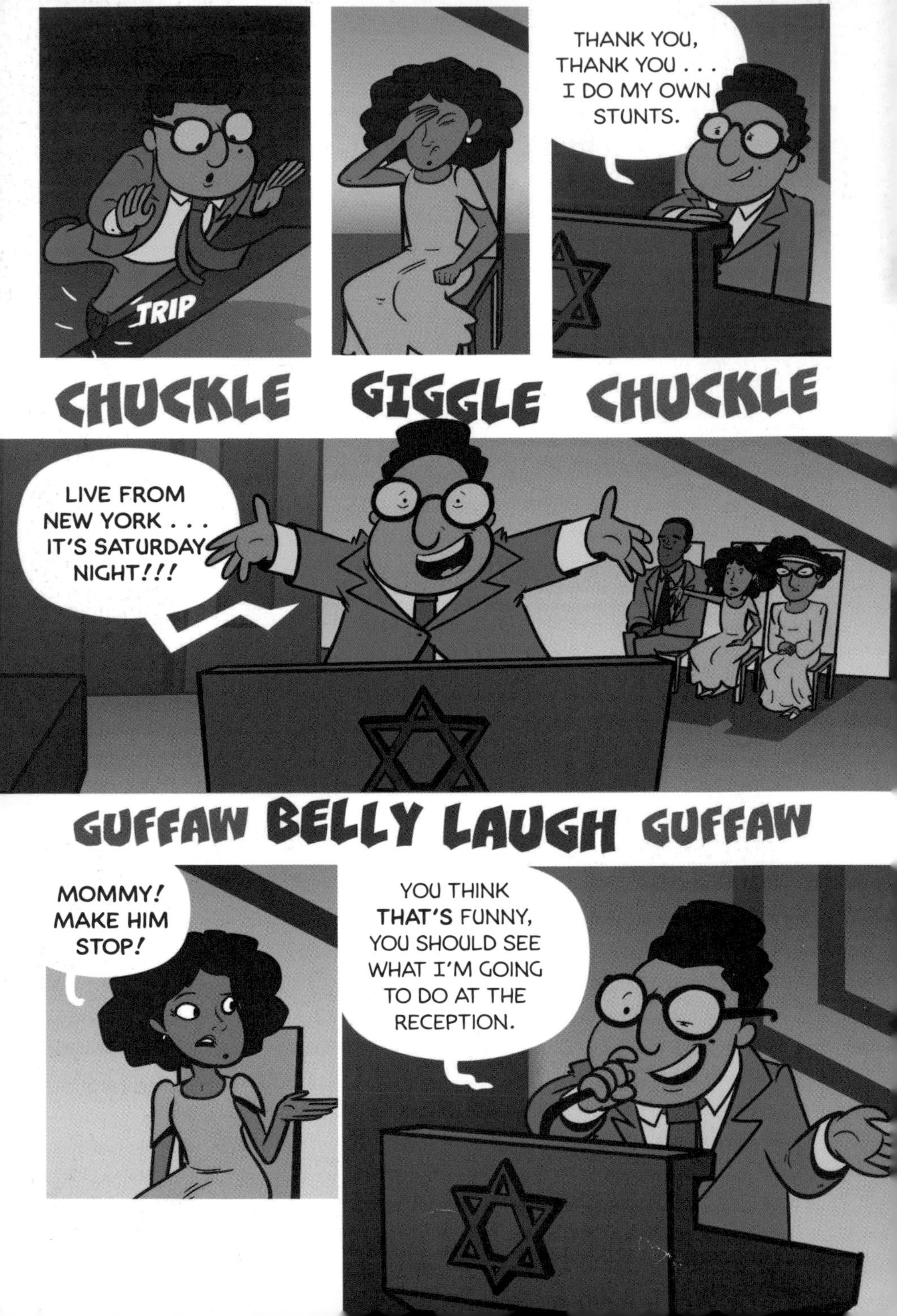
TRIP
THANK YOU, THANK YOU . . . I DO MY OWN STUNTS.
CHUCKLE GIGGLE CHUCKLE
LIVE FROM NEW YORK . . . IT'S SATURDAY NIGHT!!!
GUFFAW BELLY LAUGH GUFFAW
MOMMY! MAKE HIM STOP!
YOU THINK THAT'S FUNNY, YOU SHOULD SEE WHAT I'M GOING TO DO AT THE RECEPTION.

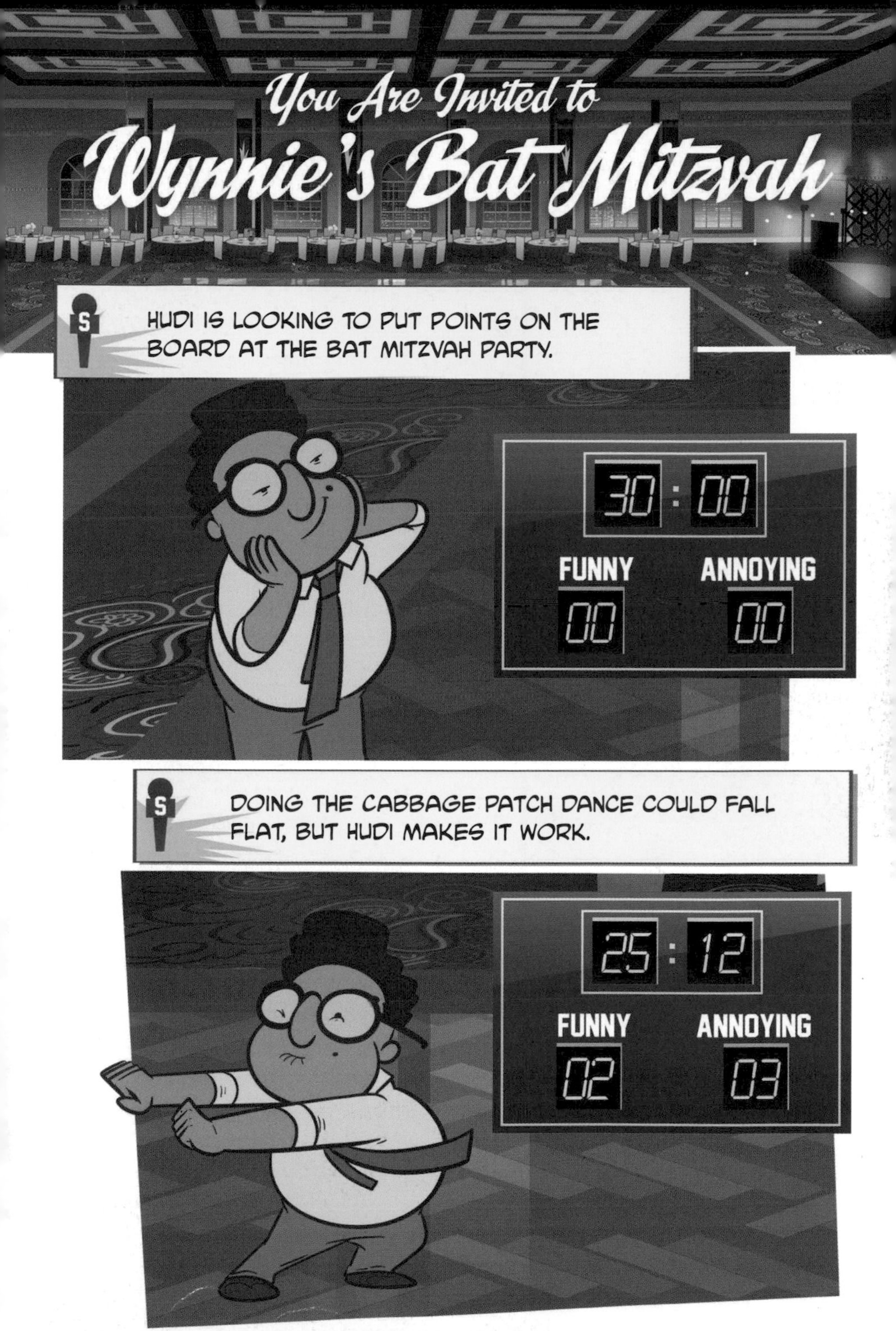
You Are Invited to
Wynnie's Bat Mitzvah
HUDI IS LOOKING TO PUT POINTS ON THE BOARD AT THE BAT MITZVAH PARTY.
30 : 00
FUNNY
00
ANNOYING
00
DOING THE CABBAGE PATCH DANCE COULD FALL FLAT, BUT HUDI MAKES IT WORK.
25 : 12
FUNNY
02
ANNOYING
03

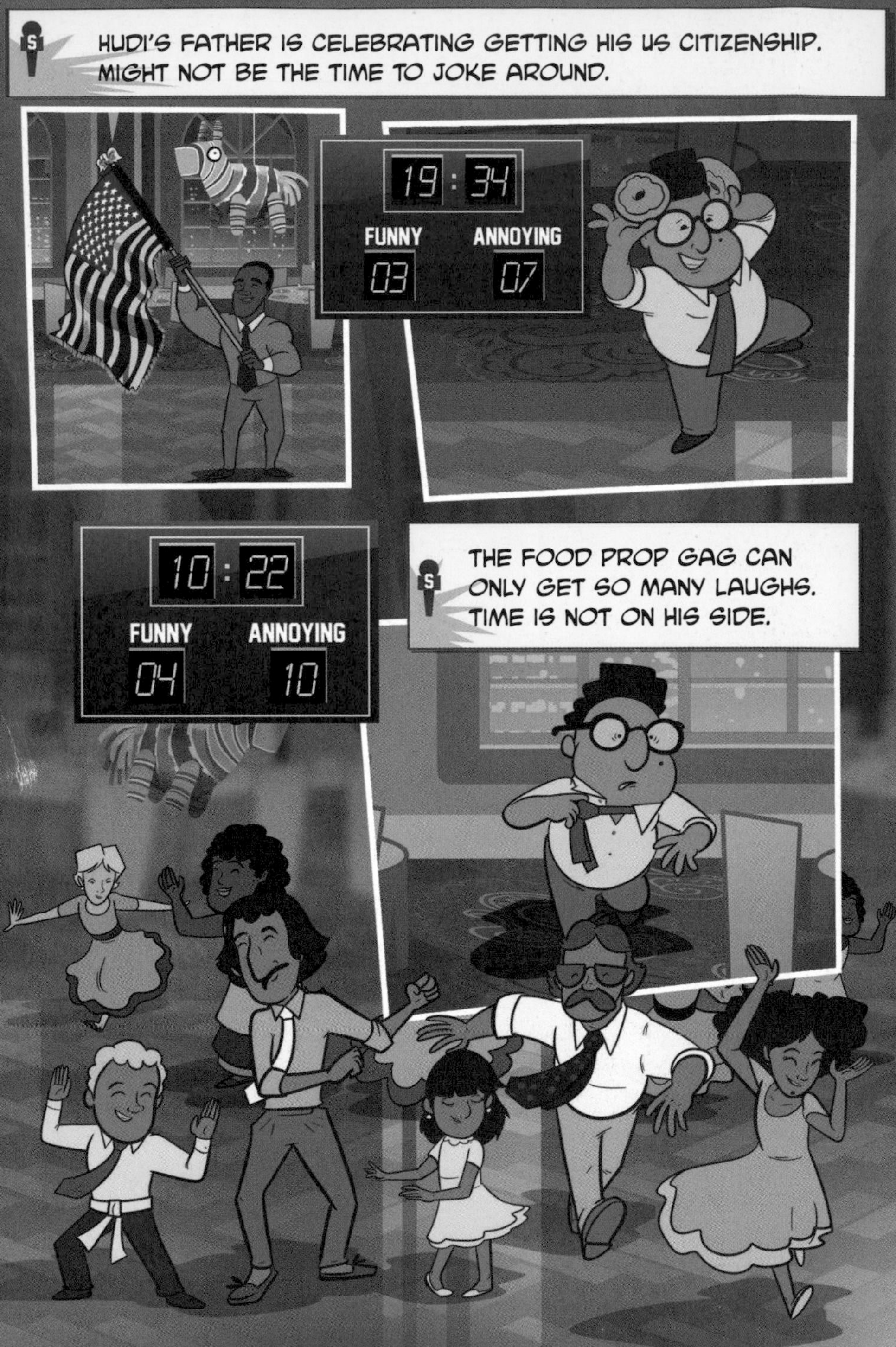
HUDI'S FATHER IS CELEBRATING GETTING HIS US CITIZENSHIP. MIGHT NOT BE THE TIME TO JOKE AROUND.
19 : 34
FUNNY
03
ANNOYING
07
10 : 22
FUNNY
04
ANNOYING
10
THE FOOD PROP GAG CAN ONLY GET SO MANY LAUGHS. TIME IS NOT ON HIS SIDE.

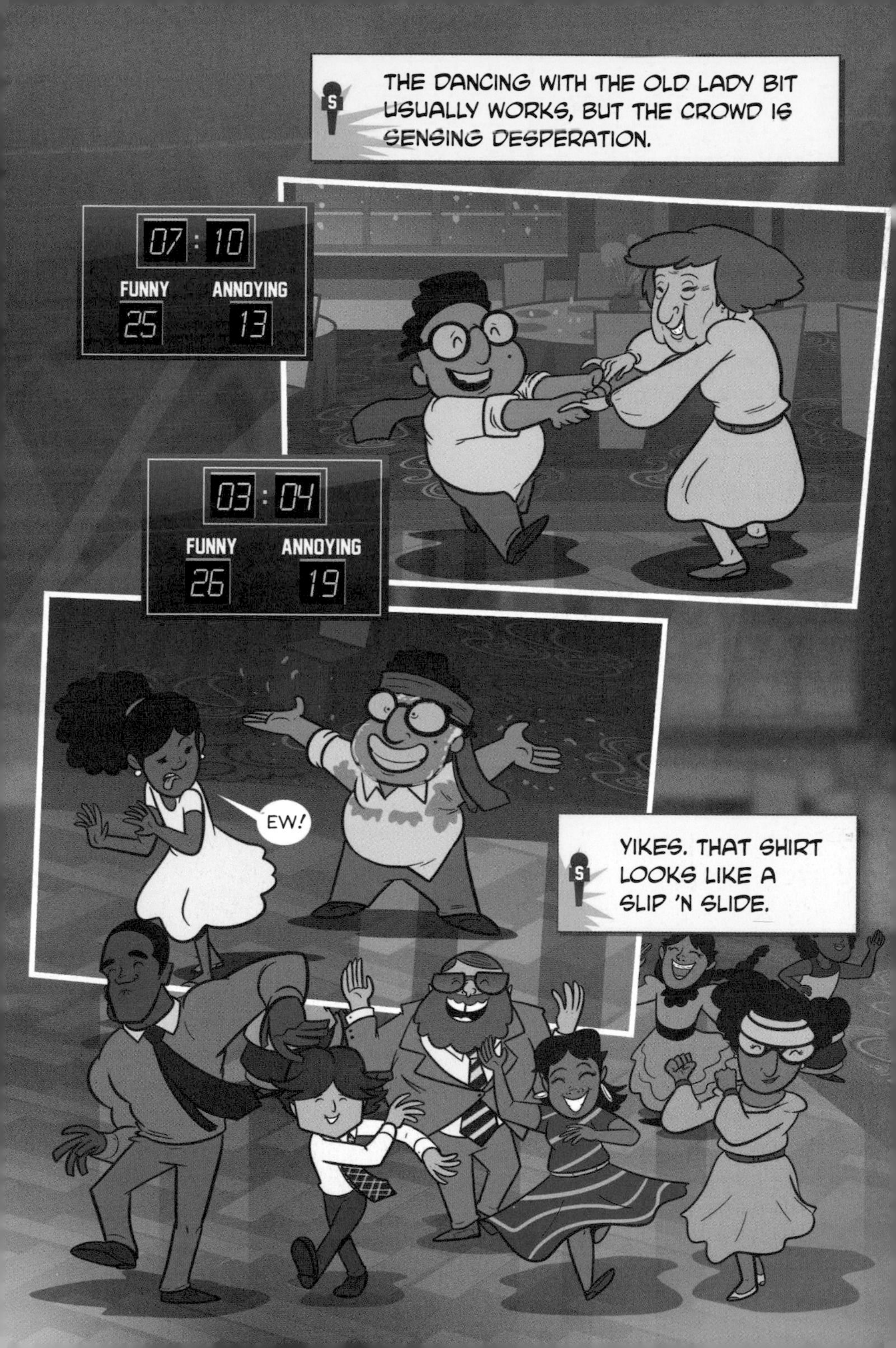
THE DANCING WITH THE OLD LADY BIT USUALLY WORKS, BUT THE CROWD IS SENSING DESPERATION.
07 : 10
FUNNY
ANNOYING
25
13
03 : 04
FUNNY
ANNOYING
26
19
EW!
YIKES. THAT SHIRT LOOKS LIKE A SLIP 'N SLIDE.

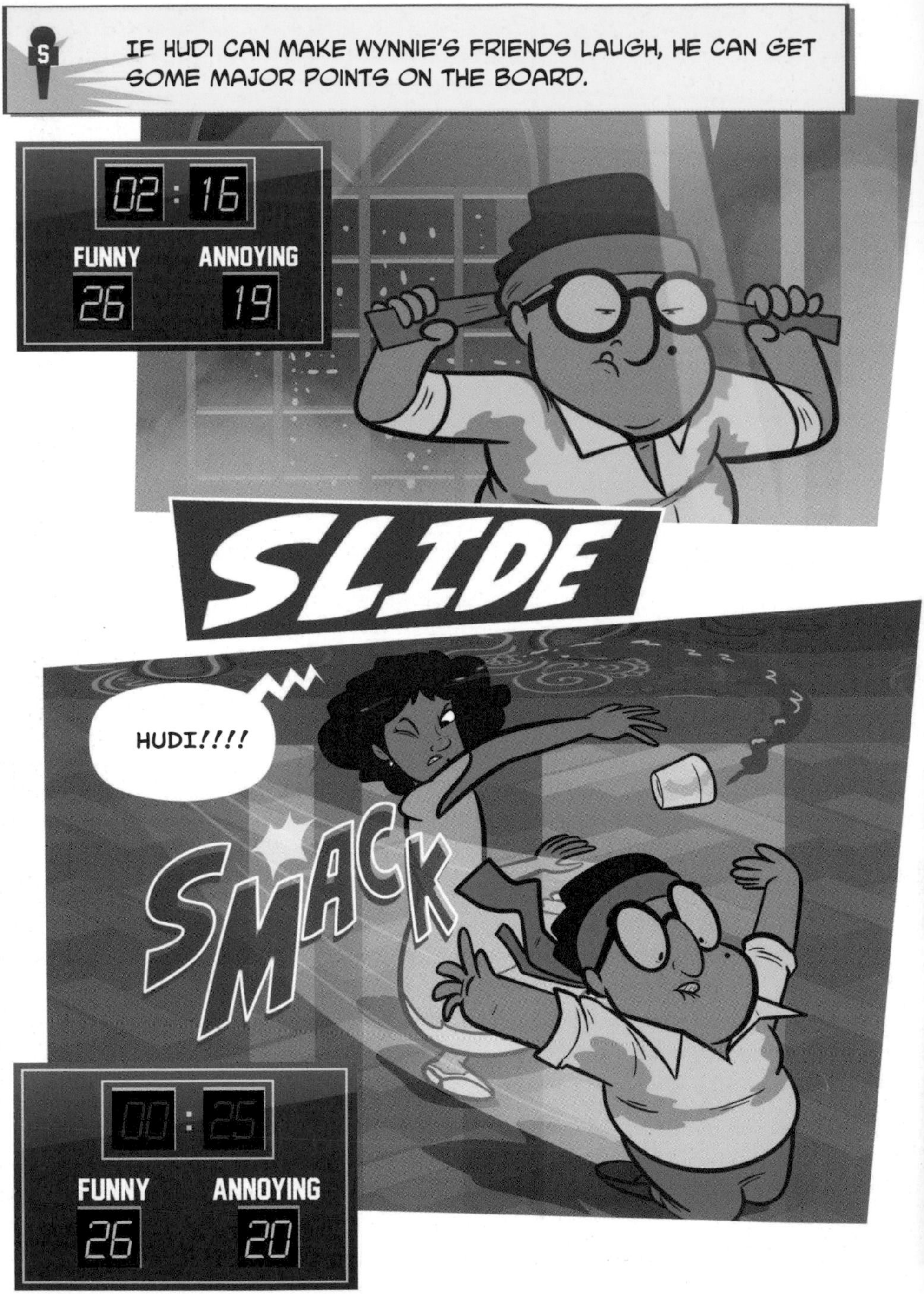
IF HUDI CAN MAKE WYNNIE'S FRIENDS LAUGH, HE CAN GET SOME MAJOR POINTS ON THE BOARD.
02:16
FUNNY
26
ANNOYING
19
SLIDE
HUDI!!!!
SMACK
00:25
FUNNY
26
ANNOYING
20

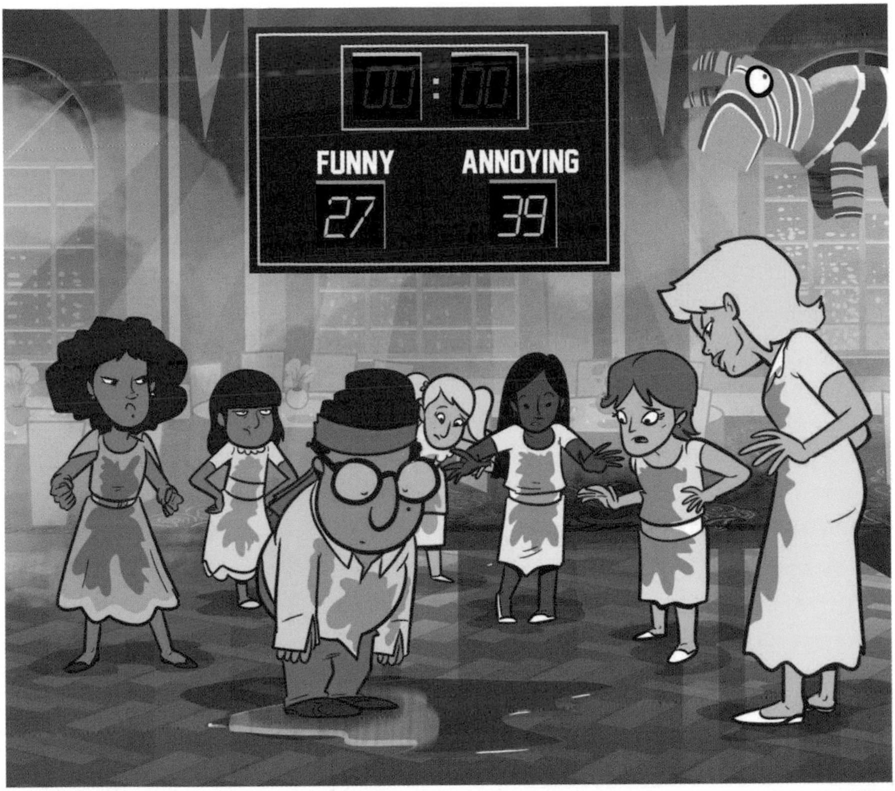
00:00
FUNNY
27
ANNOYING
39

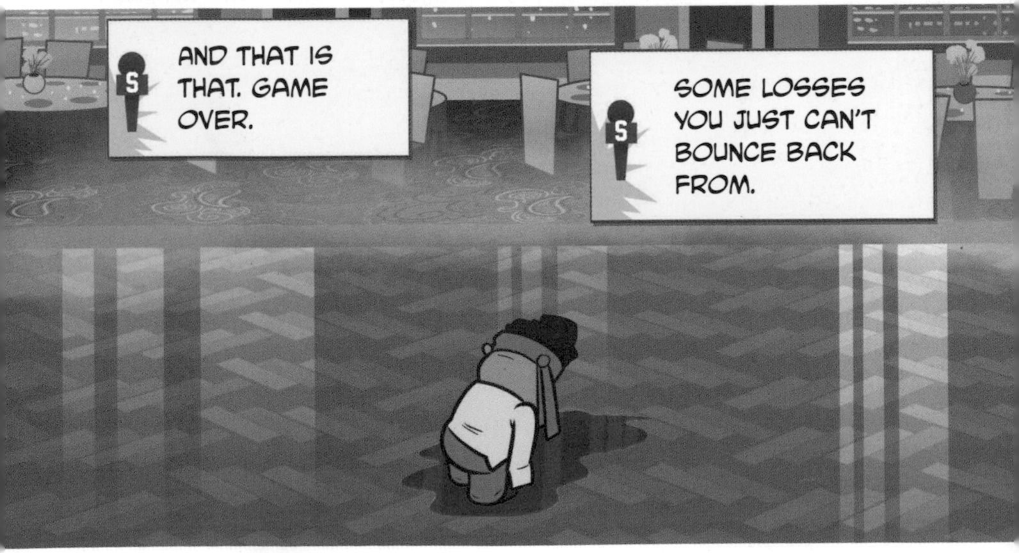
AND THAT IS THAT. GAME OVER.
SOME LOSSES YOU JUST CAN'T BOUNCE BACK FROM.

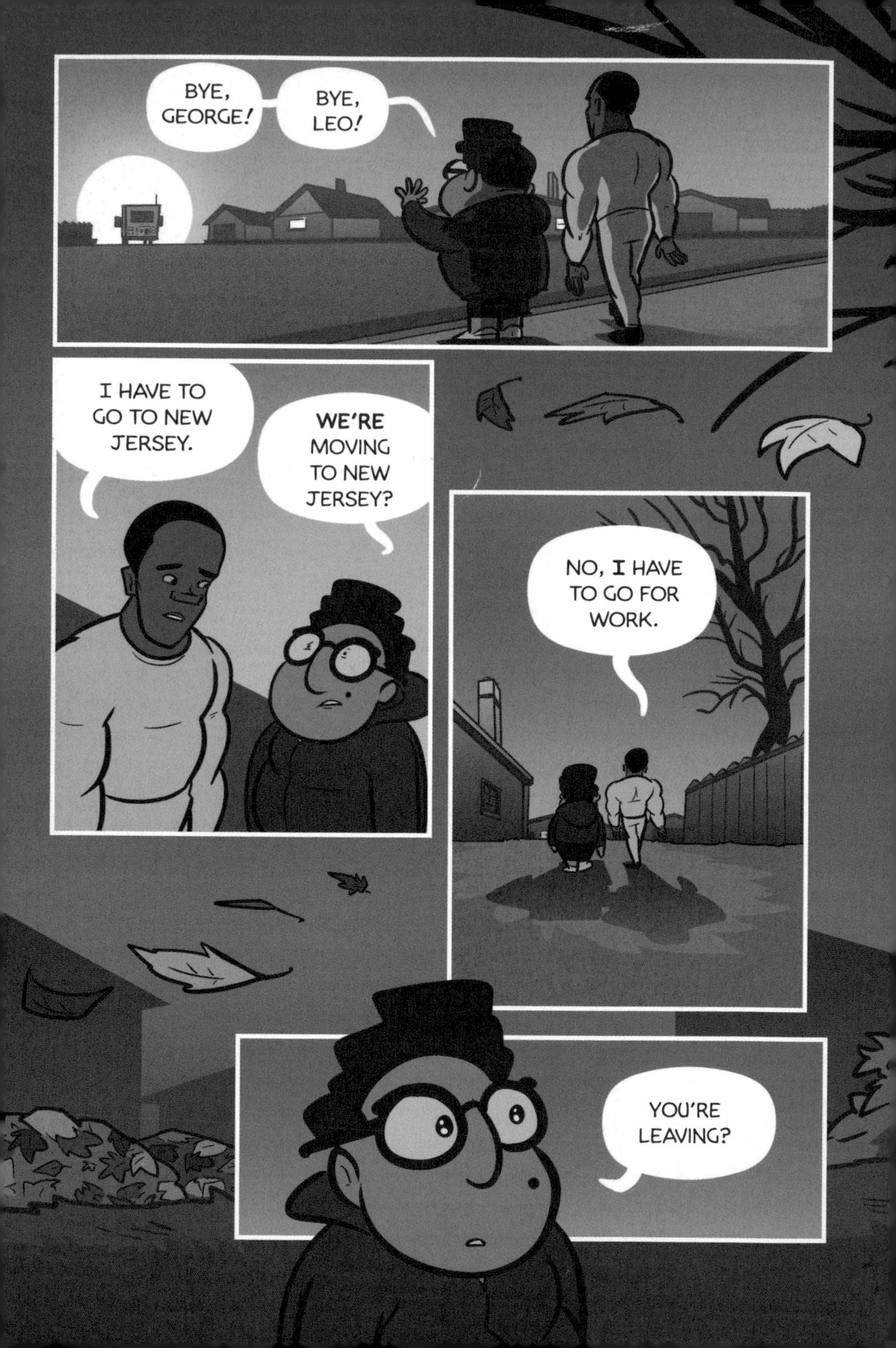
BYE, GEORGE!
BYE, LEO!
I HAVE TO GO TO NEW JERSEY.
WE'RE MOVING TO NEW JERSEY?
NO, I HAVE TO GO FOR WORK.
YOU'RE LEAVING?

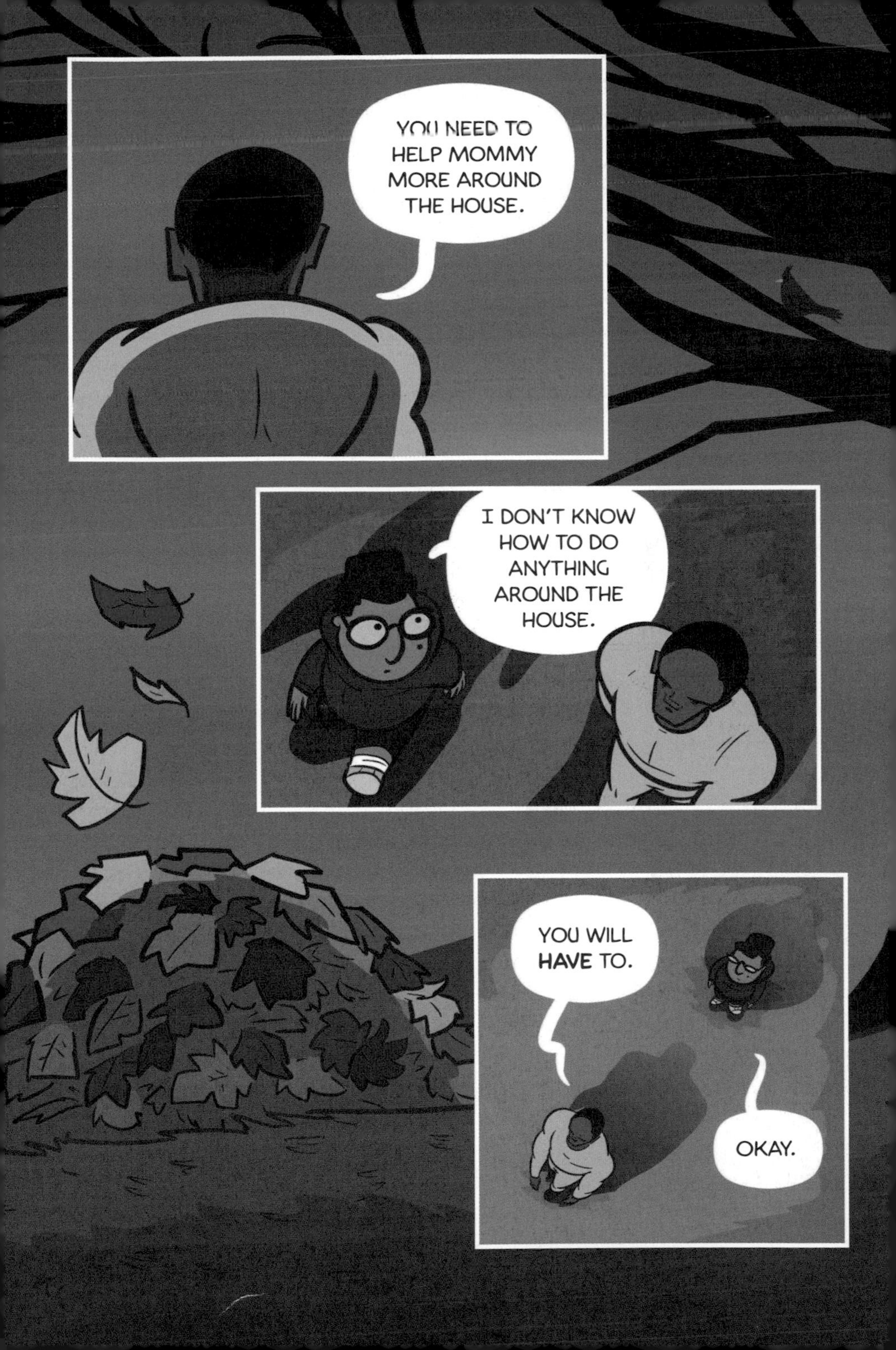
YOU NEED TO HELP MOMMY MORE AROUND THE HOUSE.
I DON'T KNOW HOW TO DO ANYTHING AROUND THE HOUSE.
YOU WILL **HAVE** TO.
OKAY.

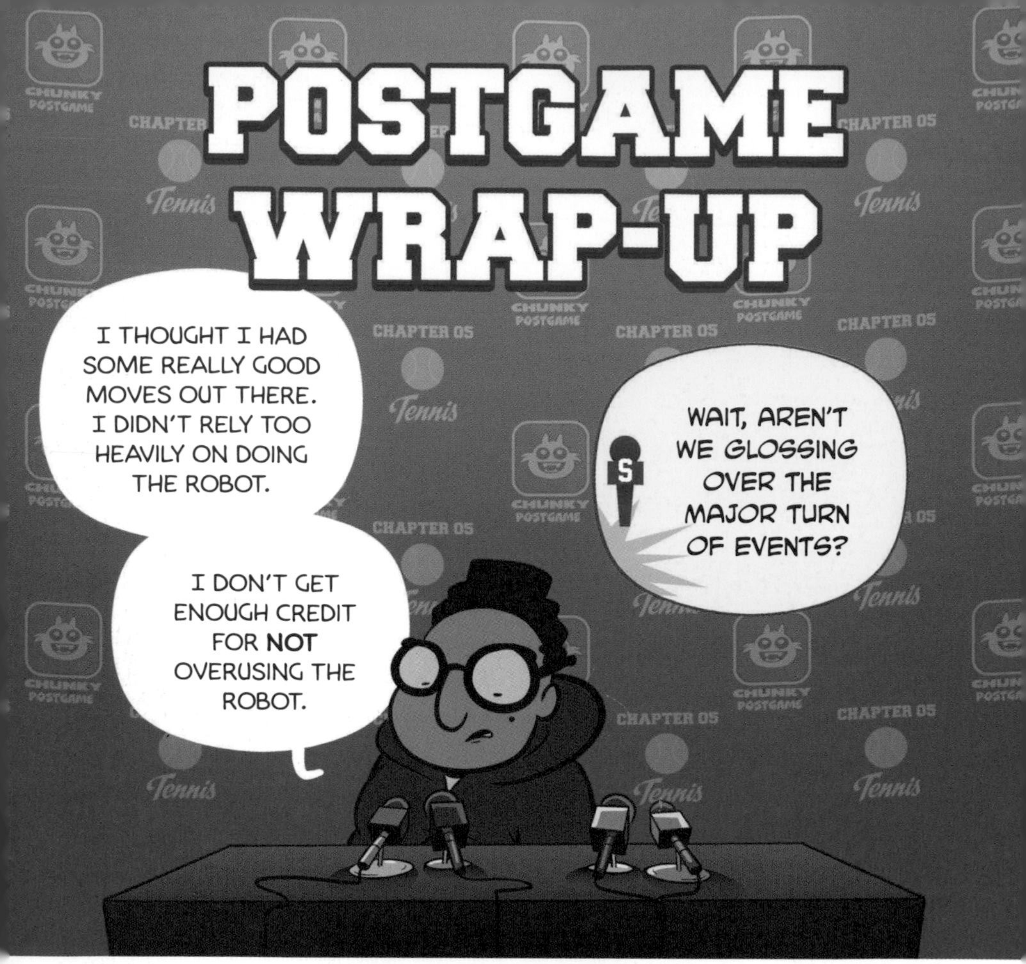
POSTGAME WRAP-UP
I THOUGHT I HAD SOME REALLY GOOD MOVES OUT THERE. I DIDN'T RELY TOO HEAVILY ON DOING THE ROBOT.
I DON'T GET ENOUGH CREDIT FOR **NOT** OVERUSING THE ROBOT.
WAIT, AREN'T WE GLOSSING OVER THE MAJOR TURN OF EVENTS?

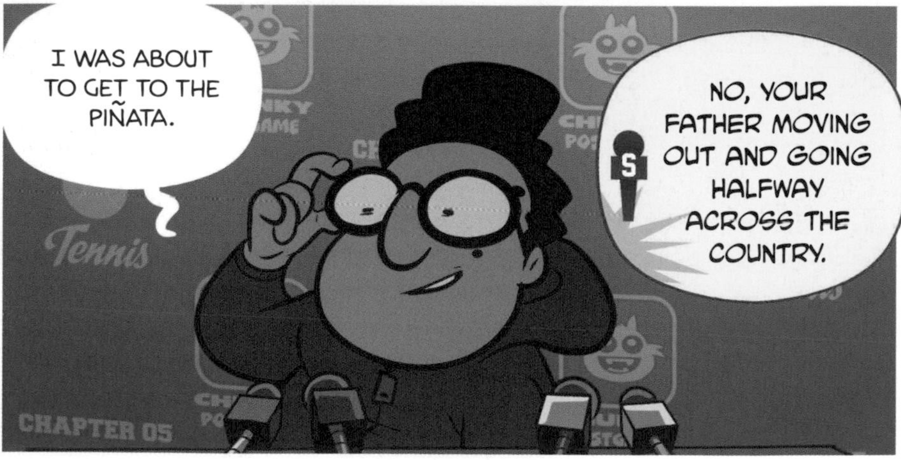
I WAS ABOUT TO GET TO THE PIÑATA.
NO, YOUR FATHER MOVING OUT AND GOING HALFWAY ACROSS THE COUNTRY.

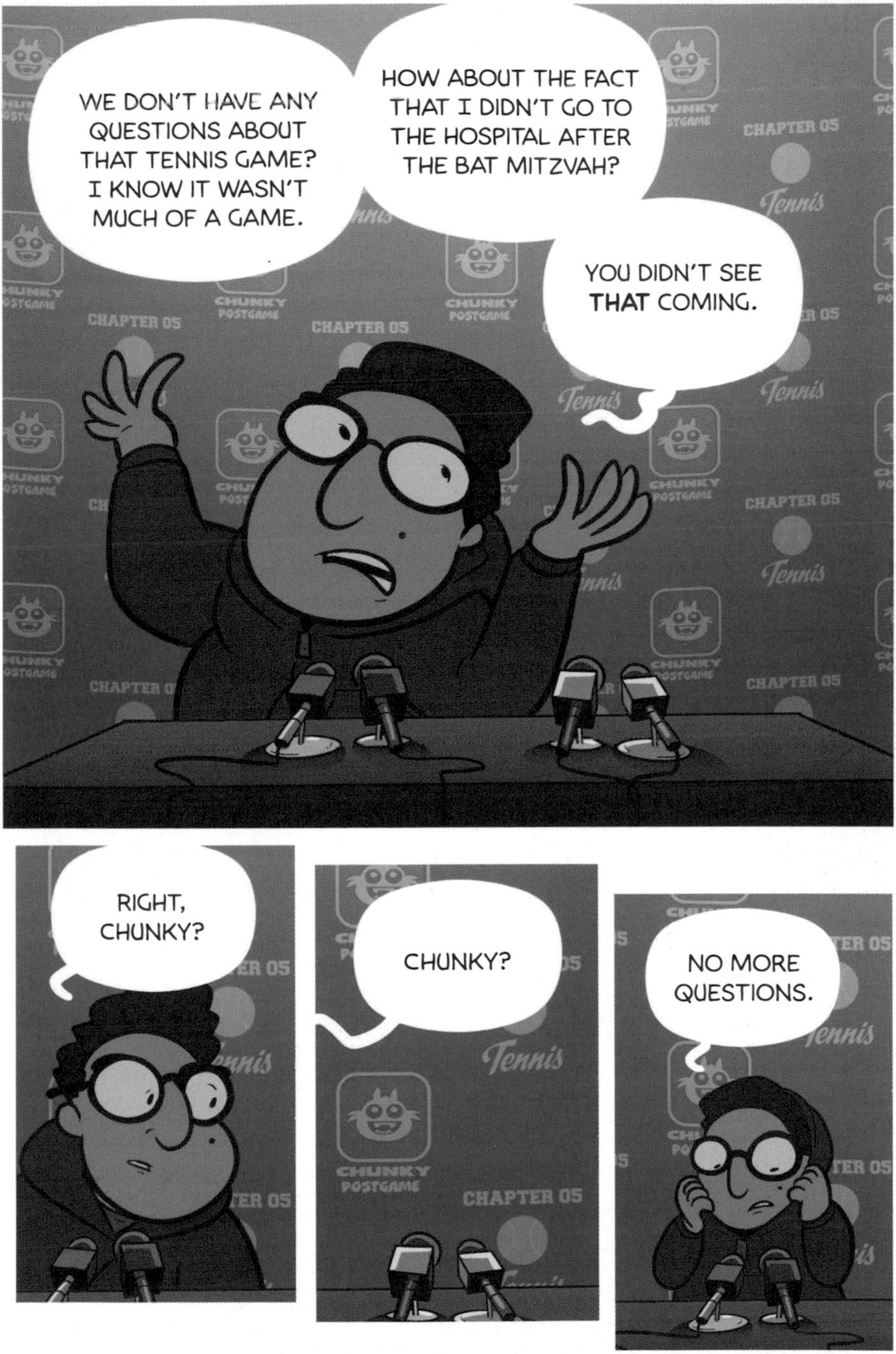
WE DON'T HAVE ANY QUESTIONS ABOUT THAT TENNIS GAME? I KNOW IT WASN'T MUCH OF A GAME.
HOW ABOUT THE FACT THAT I DIDN'T GO TO THE HOSPITAL AFTER THE BAT MITZVAH?
YOU DIDN'T SEE **THAT** COMING.
RIGHT, CHUNKY?
CHUNKY?
NO MORE QUESTIONS.

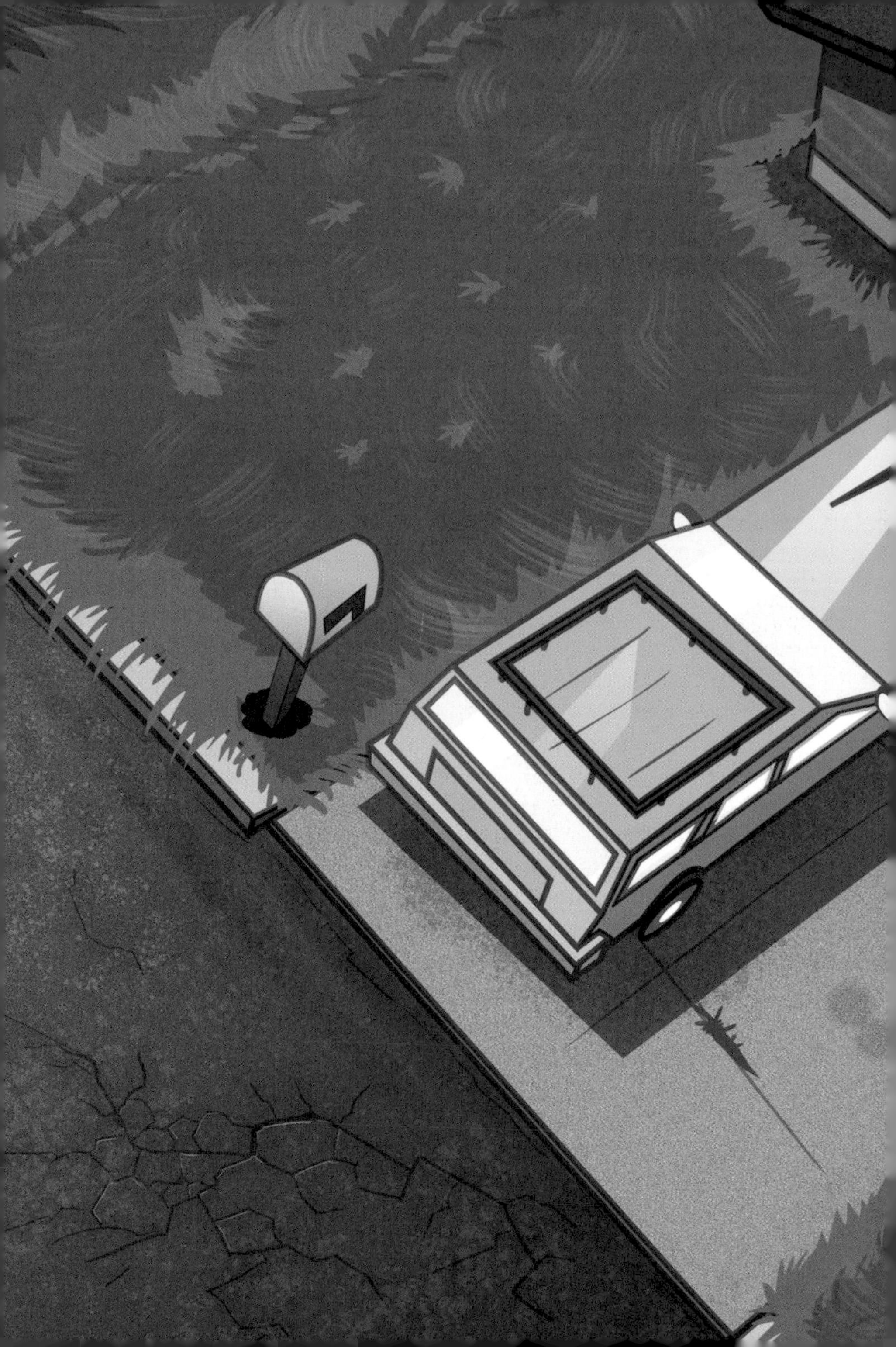

CHAPTER SIX
Football

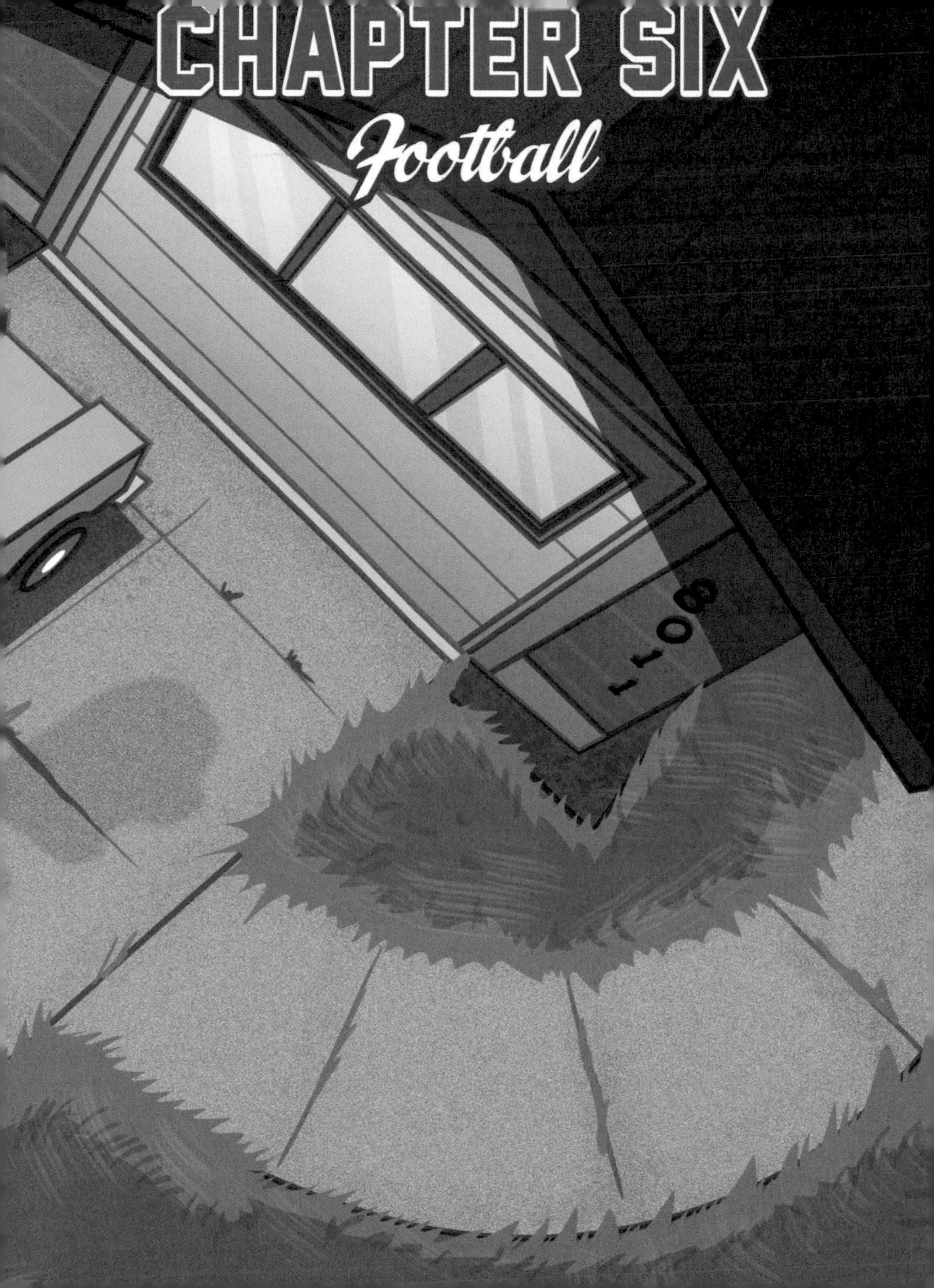

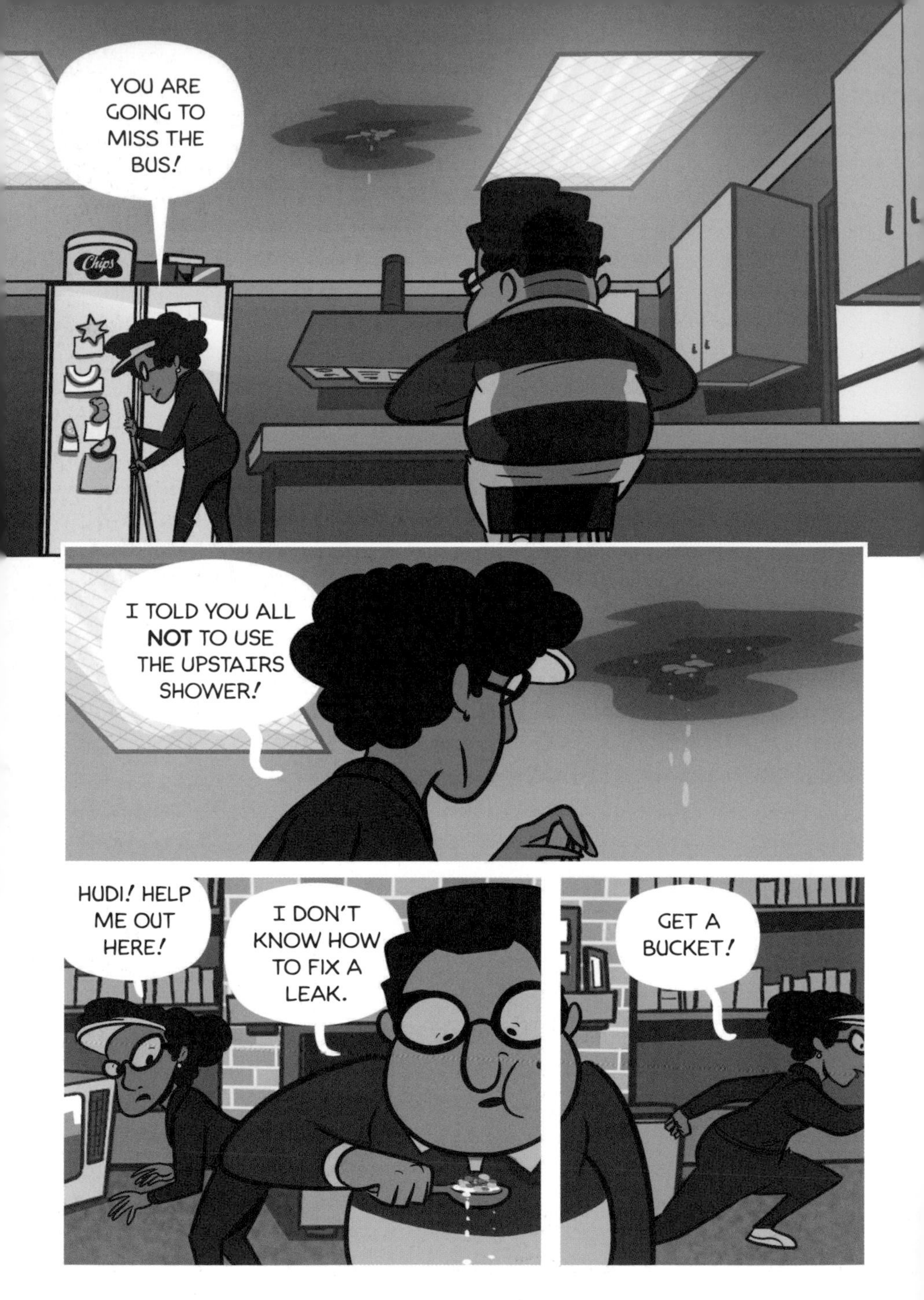
YOU ARE GOING TO MISS THE BUS!
I TOLD YOU ALL **NOT** TO USE THE UPSTAIRS SHOWER!
HUDI! HELP ME OUT HERE!
I DON'T KNOW HOW TO FIX A LEAK.
GET A BUCKET!
Chips

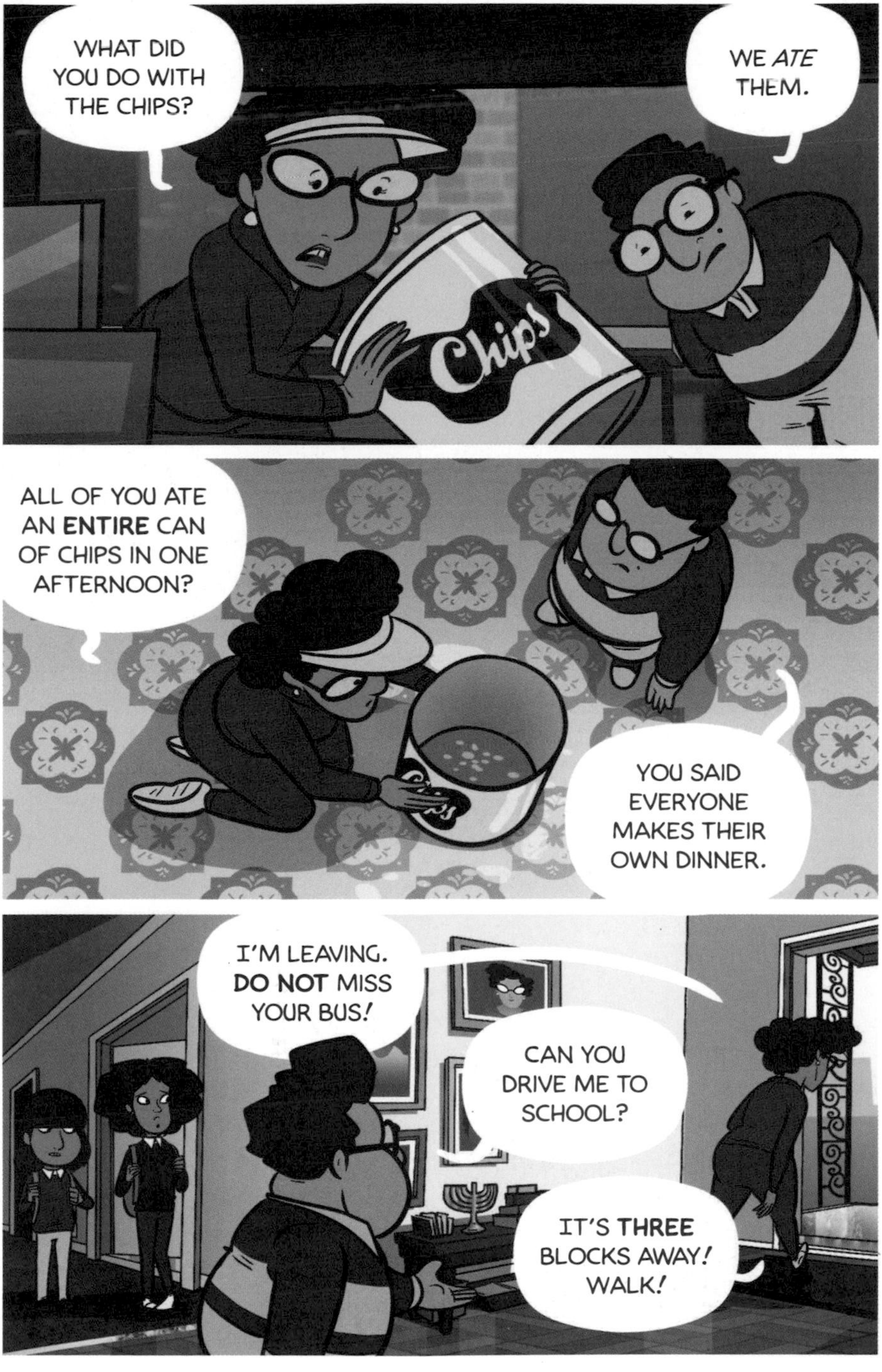
WHAT DID YOU DO WITH THE CHIPS?
WE *ATE* THEM.
Chips
ALL OF YOU ATE AN **ENTIRE** CAN OF CHIPS IN ONE AFTERNOON?
YOU SAID EVERYONE MAKES THEIR OWN DINNER.
I'M LEAVING. **DO NOT** MISS YOUR BUS!
CAN YOU DRIVE ME TO SCHOOL?
IT'S **THREE** BLOCKS AWAY! WALK!

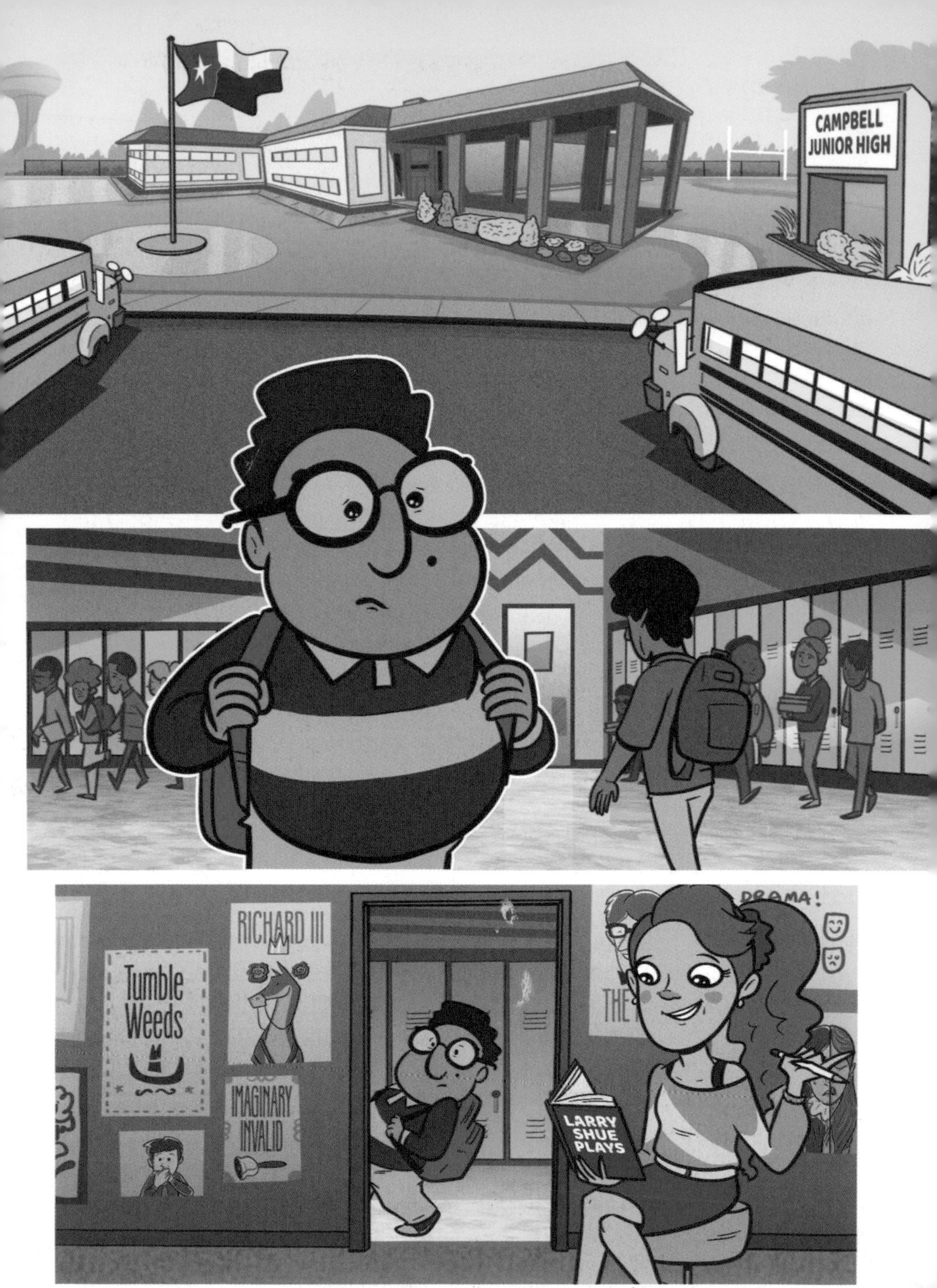
CAMPBELL
JUNIOR HIGH
RICHARD III
Tumble
Weeds
IMAGINARY
INVALID
DRAMA!
THE
LARRY
SHUE
PLAYS

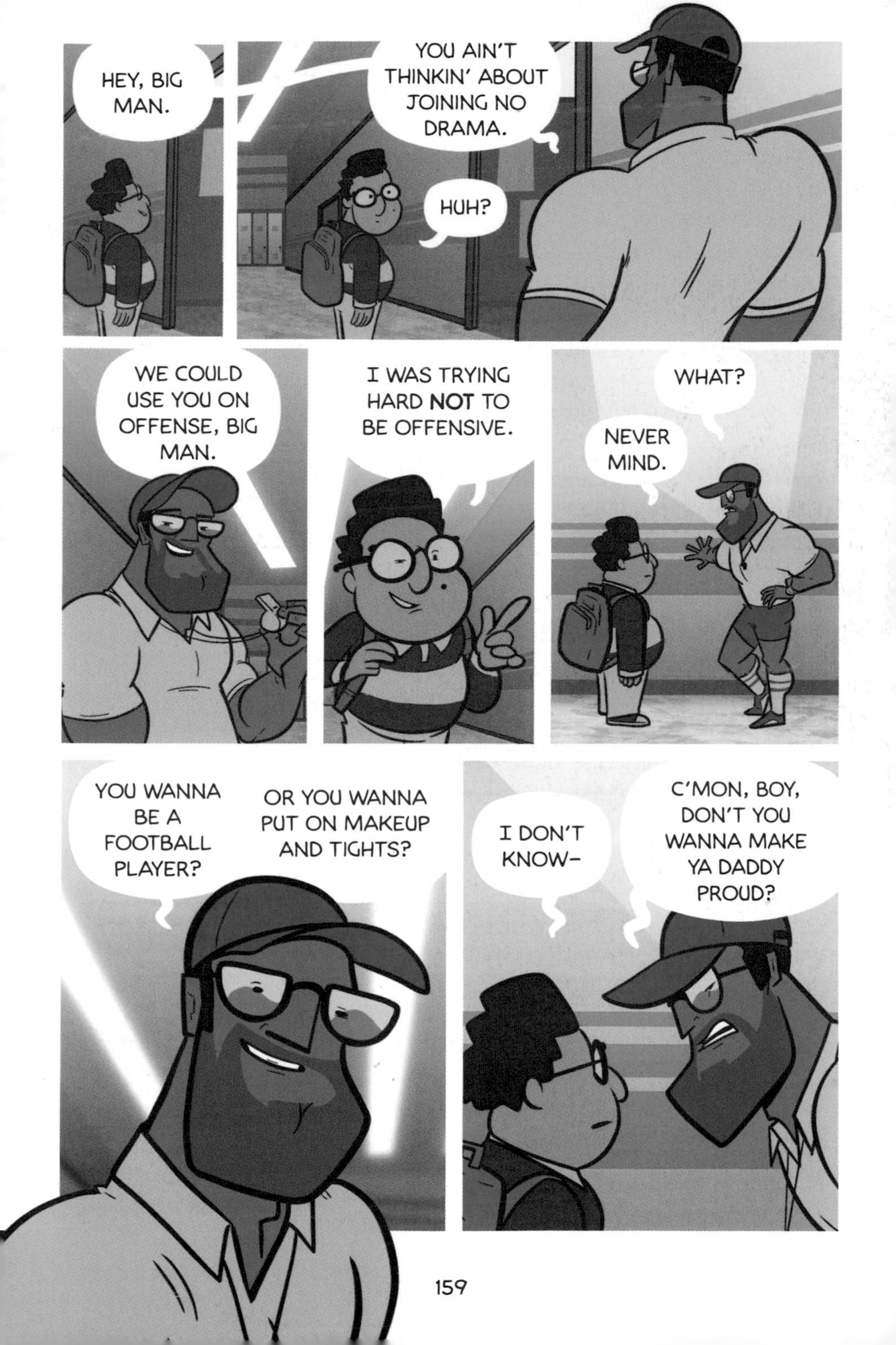
HEY, BIG MAN.
YOU AIN'T THINKIN' ABOUT JOINING NO DRAMA.
HUH?
WE COULD USE YOU ON OFFENSE, BIG MAN.
I WAS TRYING HARD **NOT** TO BE OFFENSIVE.
WHAT?
NEVER MIND.
YOU WANNA BE A FOOTBALL PLAYER?
OR YOU WANNA PUT ON MAKEUP AND TIGHTS?
I DON'T KNOW-
C'MON, BOY, DON'T YOU WANNA MAKE YA DADDY PROUD?

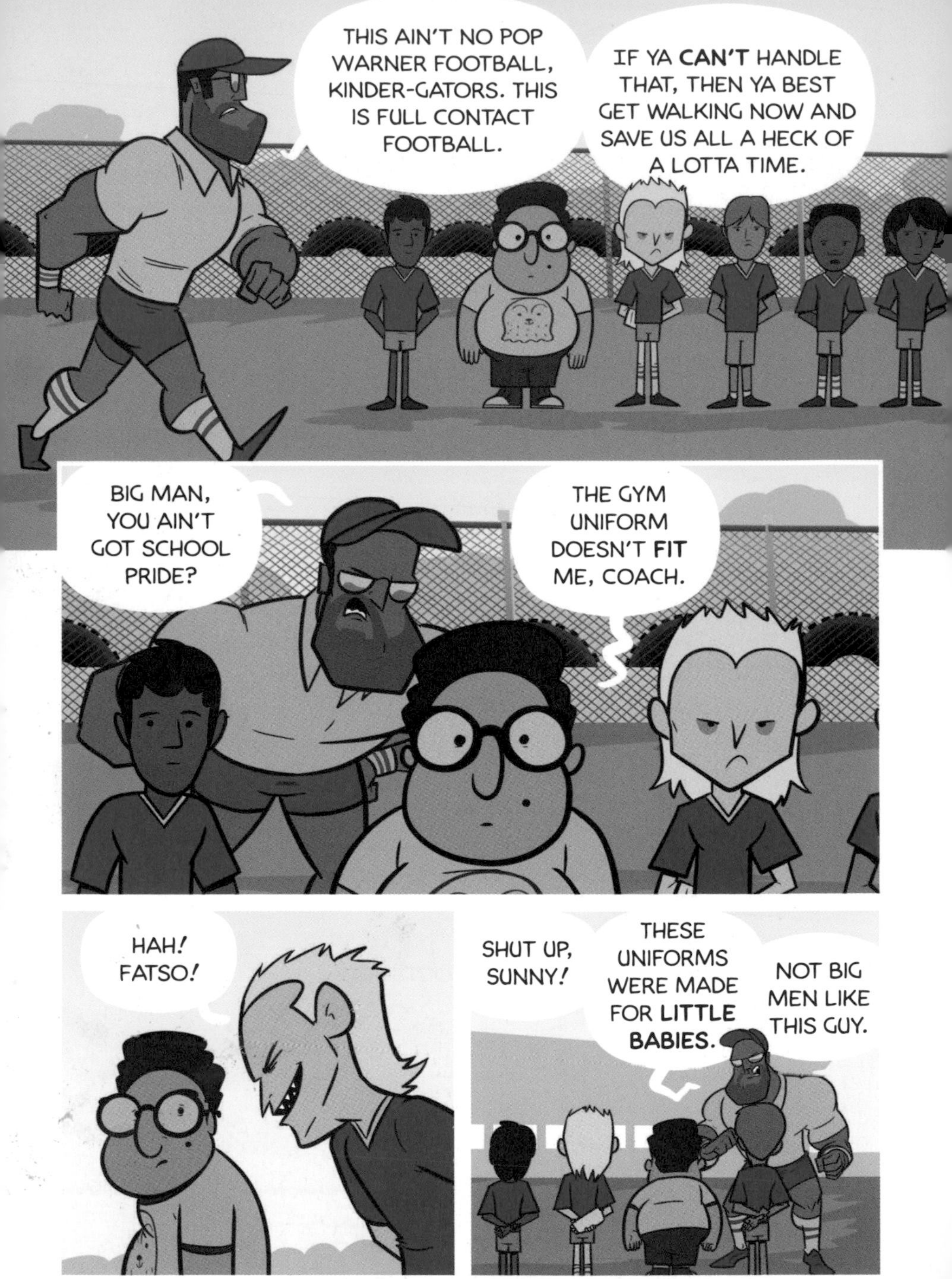
THIS AIN'T NO POP WARNER FOOTBALL, KINDER-GATORS. THIS IS FULL CONTACT FOOTBALL.
IF YA **CAN'T** HANDLE THAT, THEN YA BEST GET WALKING NOW AND SAVE US ALL A HECK OF A LOTTA TIME.
BIG MAN, YOU AIN'T GOT SCHOOL PRIDE?
THE GYM UNIFORM DOESN'T **FIT** ME, COACH.
HAH! FATSO!
SHUT UP, SUNNY!
THESE UNIFORMS WERE MADE FOR **LITTLE BABIES.**
NOT BIG MEN LIKE THIS GUY.

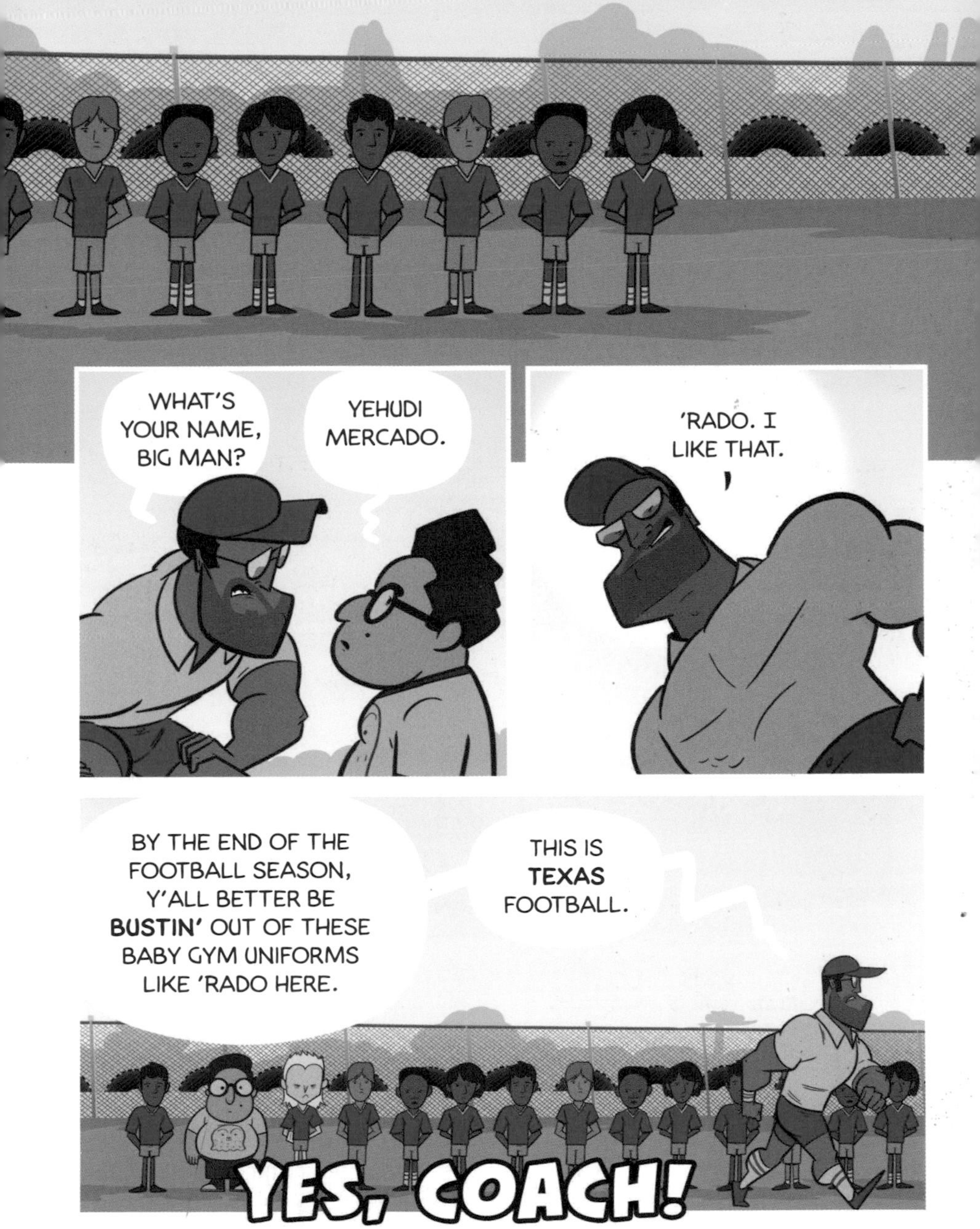
WHAT'S YOUR NAME, BIG MAN?
YEHUDI MERCADO.
'RADO. I LIKE THAT.
BY THE END OF THE FOOTBALL SEASON, Y'ALL BETTER BE **BUSTIN'** OUT OF THESE BABY GYM UNIFORMS LIKE 'RADO HERE.
THIS IS **TEXAS** FOOTBALL.
YES, COACH!

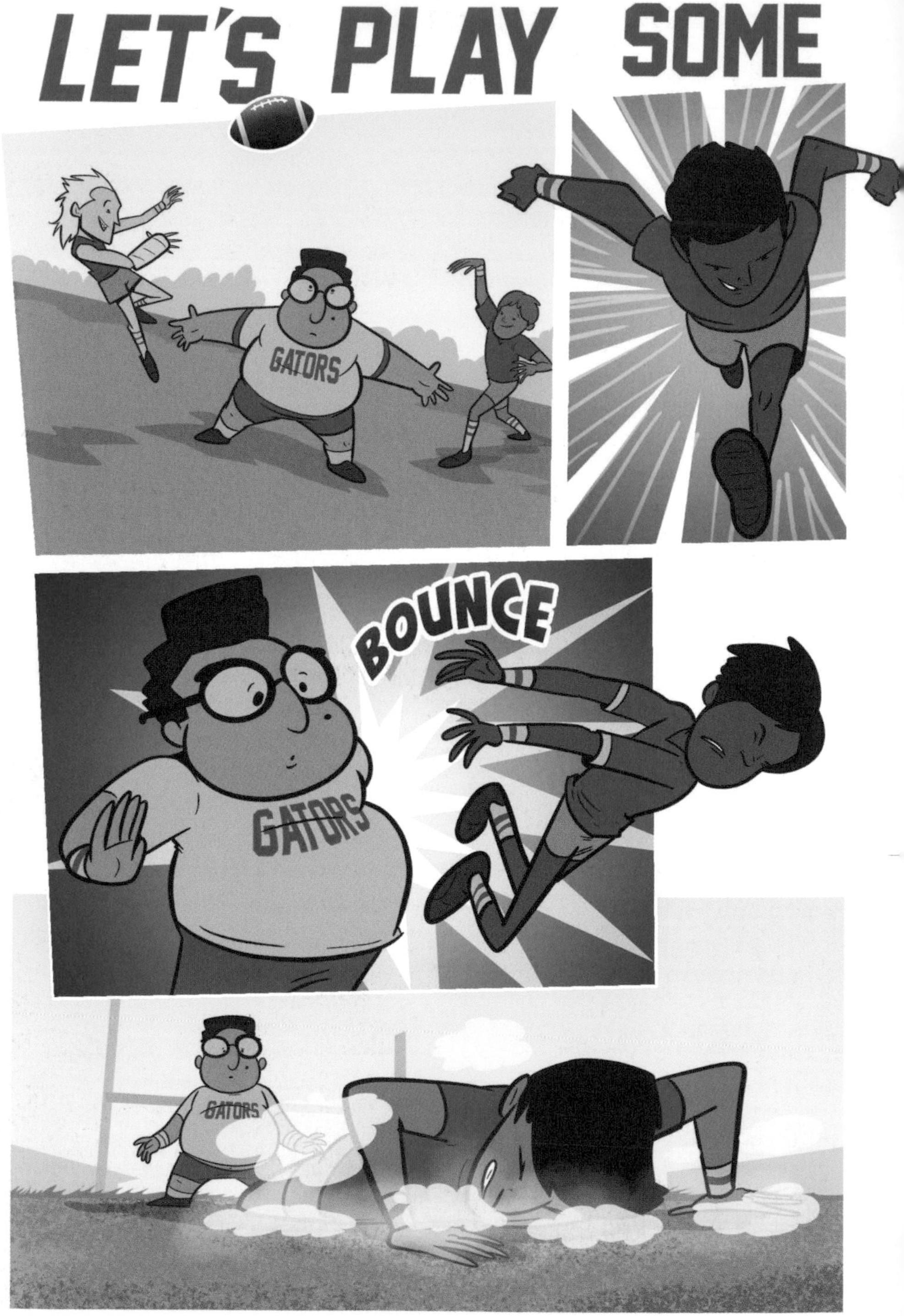
LET'S PLAY SOME
GATORS
BOUNCE
GATORS
GATORS

FOOTBALL

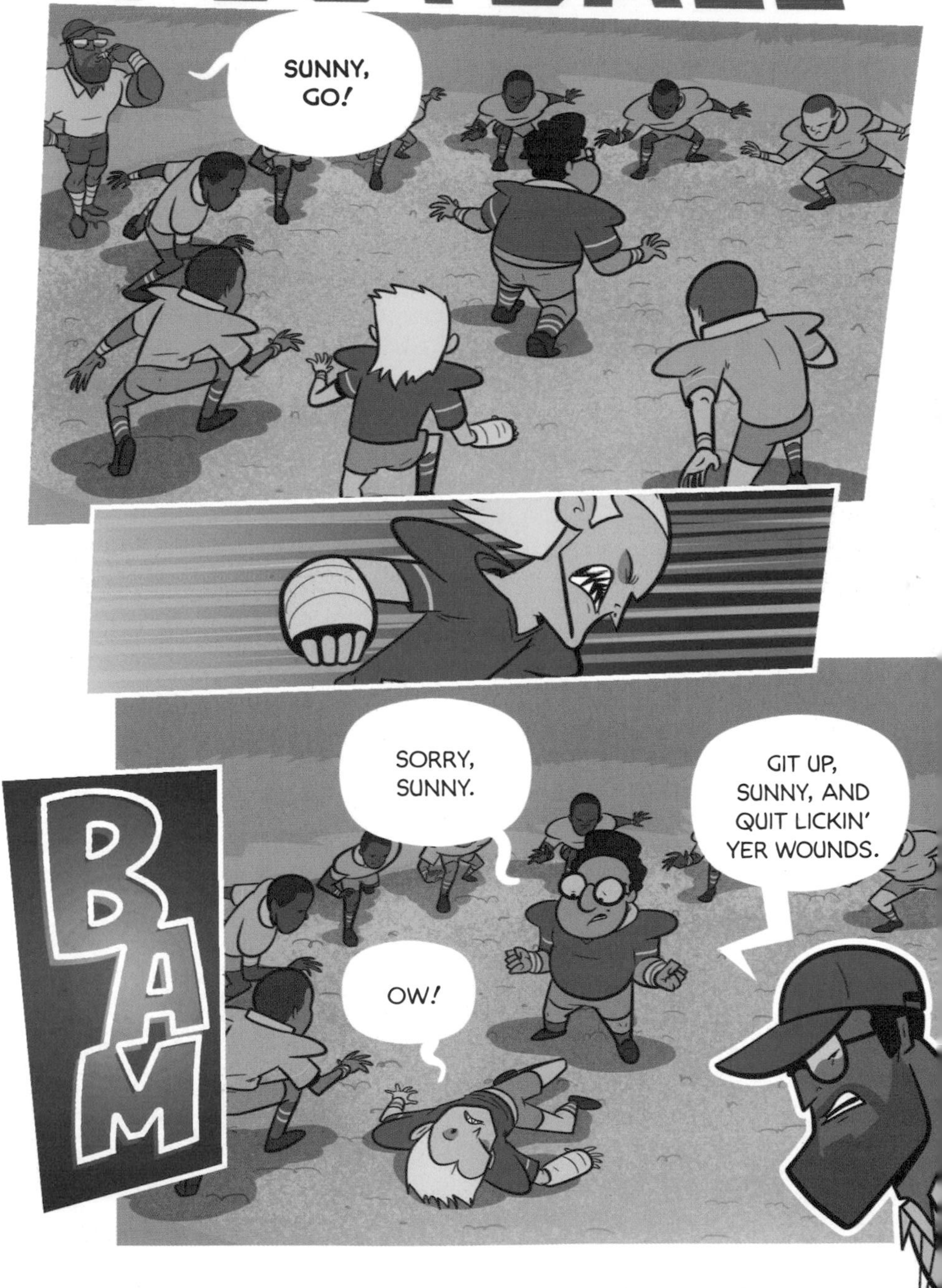
SUNNY, GO!
BAM
SORRY, SUNNY.
GIT UP, SUNNY, AND QUIT LICKIN' YER WOUNDS.
OW!

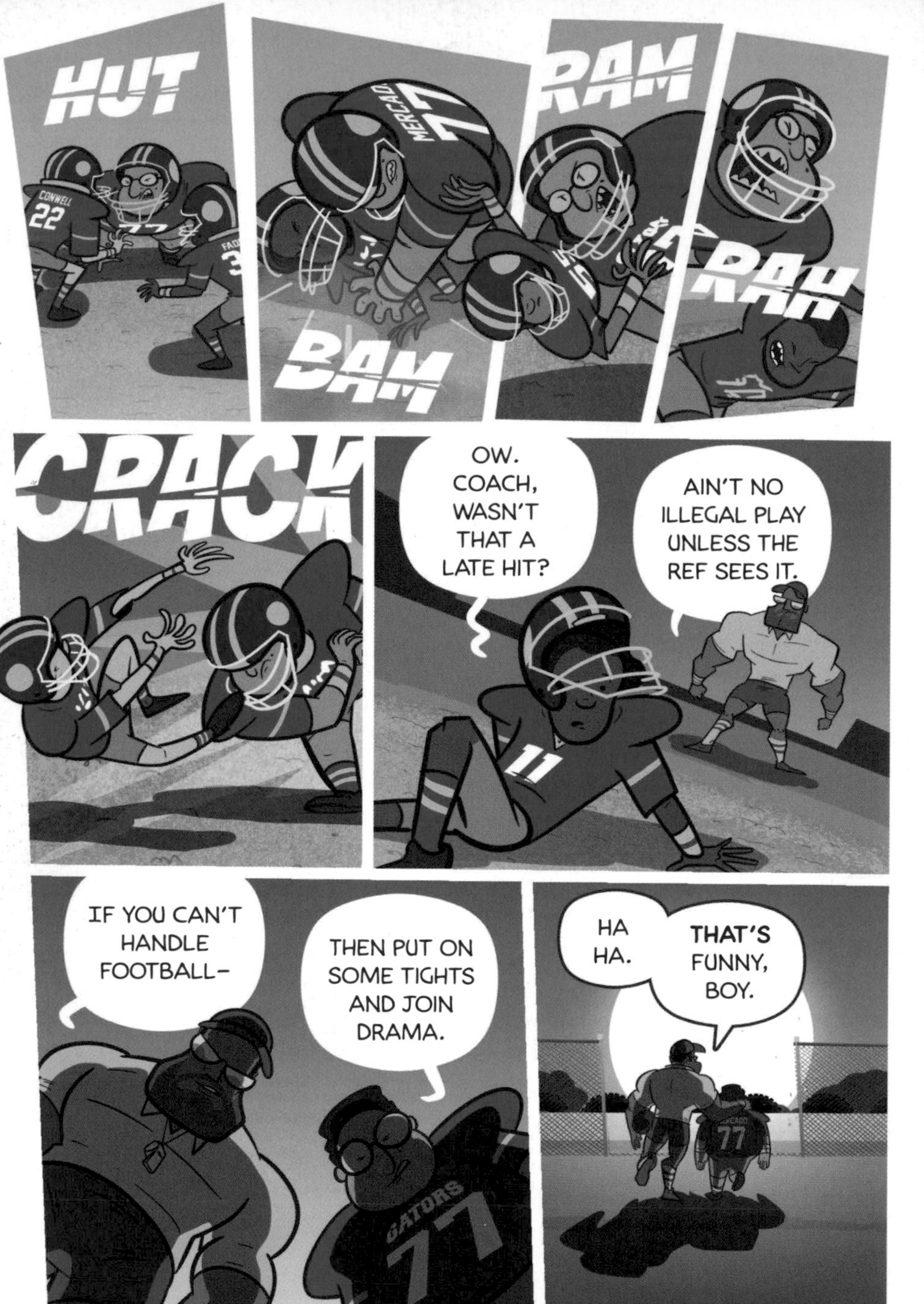
HUT
MERCADO 77
CONWELL 22
BAM
RAM
RAH
CRACK
OW. COACH, WASN'T THAT A LATE HIT?
AIN'T NO ILLEGAL PLAY UNLESS THE REF SEES IT.
IF YOU CAN'T HANDLE FOOTBALL—
THEN PUT ON SOME TIGHTS AND JOIN DRAMA.
GATORS 77
HA HA.
THAT'S FUNNY, BOY.

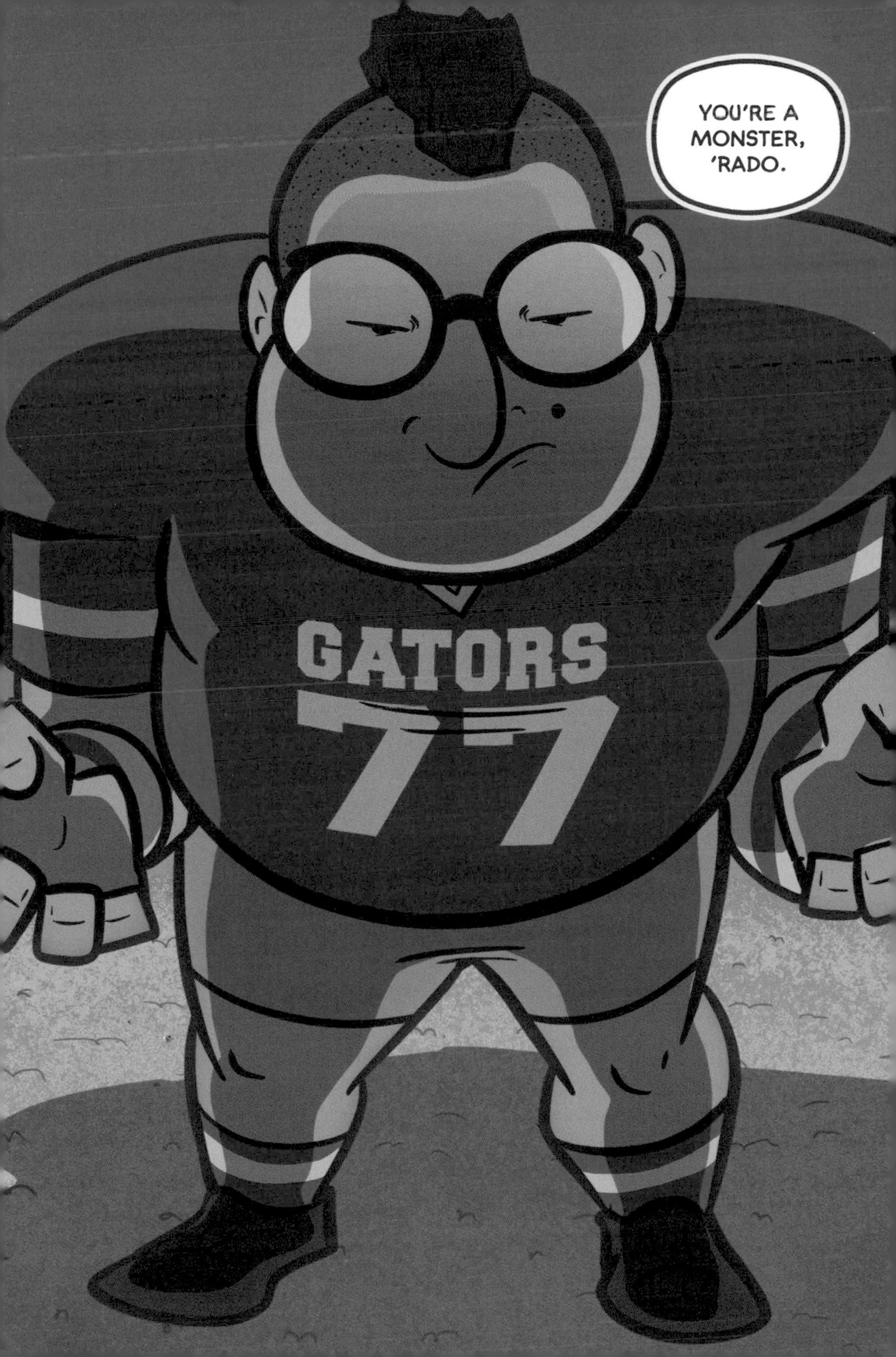
YOU'RE A MONSTER, 'RADO.
GATORS
77

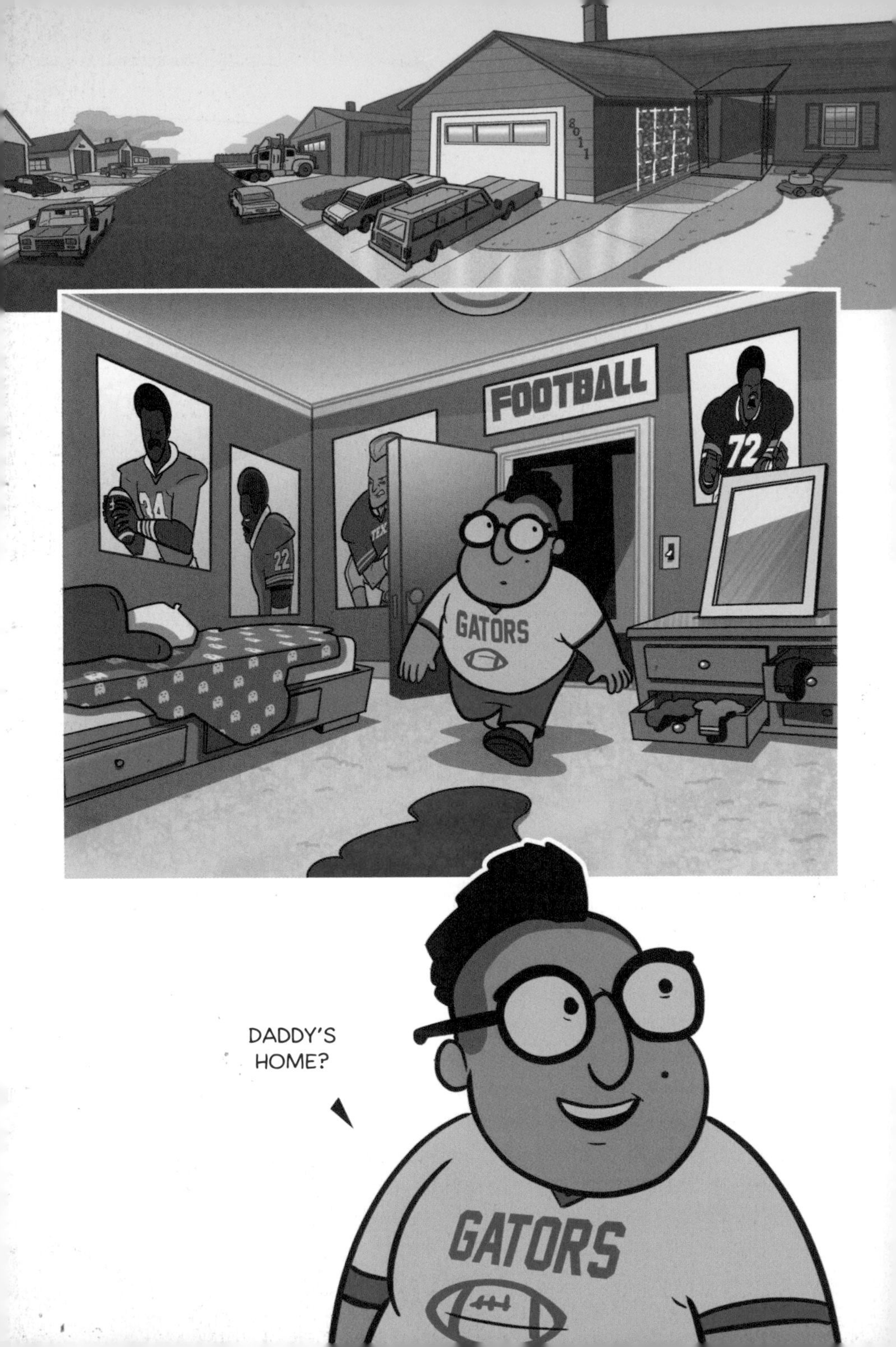
8011
FOOTBALL
22
72
GATORS
DADDY'S
HOME?
GATORS

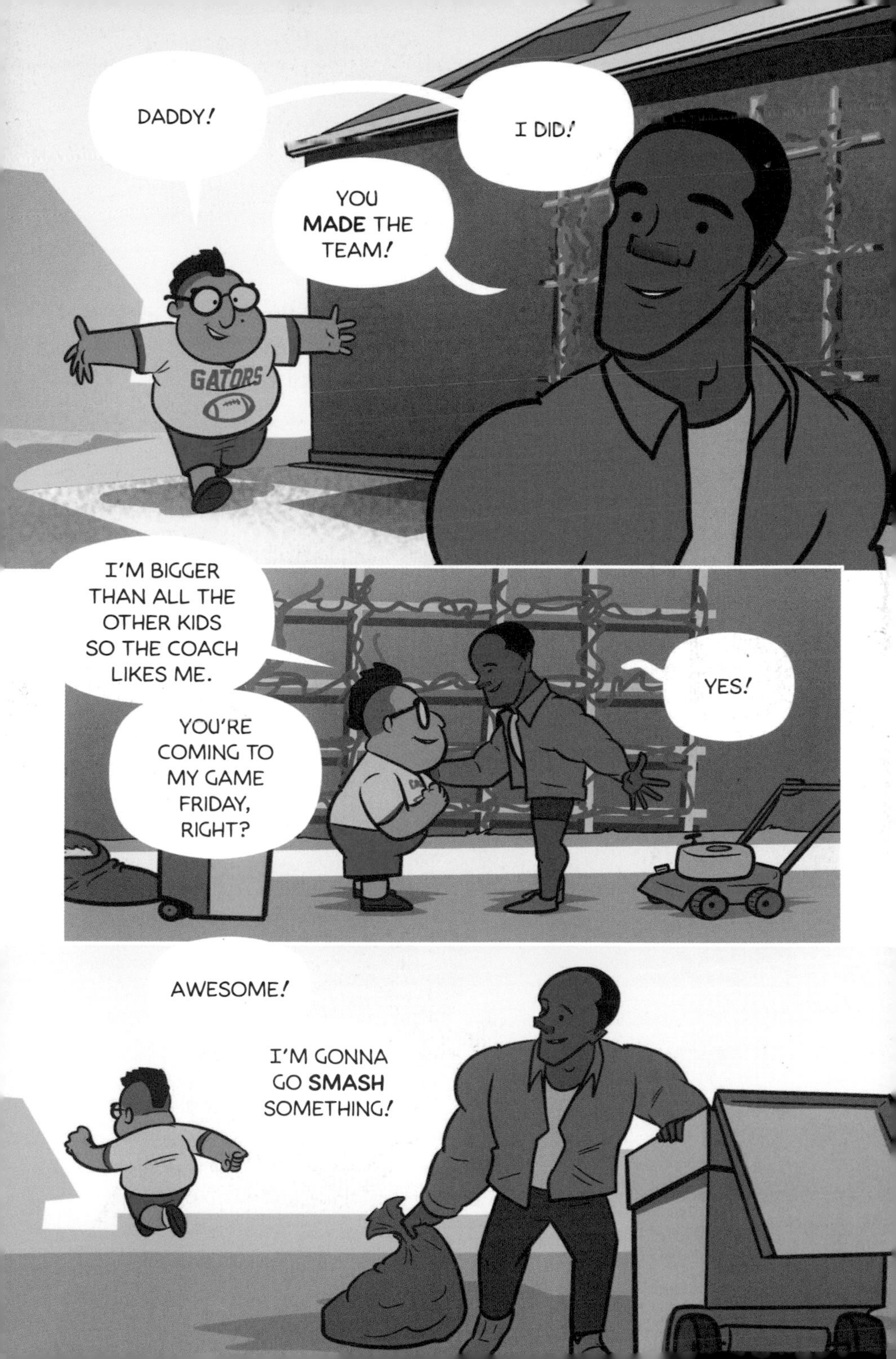
DADDY!
I DID!
YOU MADE THE TEAM!
I'M BIGGER THAN ALL THE OTHER KIDS SO THE COACH LIKES ME.
YES!
YOU'RE COMING TO MY GAME FRIDAY, RIGHT?
GATORS
AWESOME!
I'M GONNA GO SMASH SOMETHING!

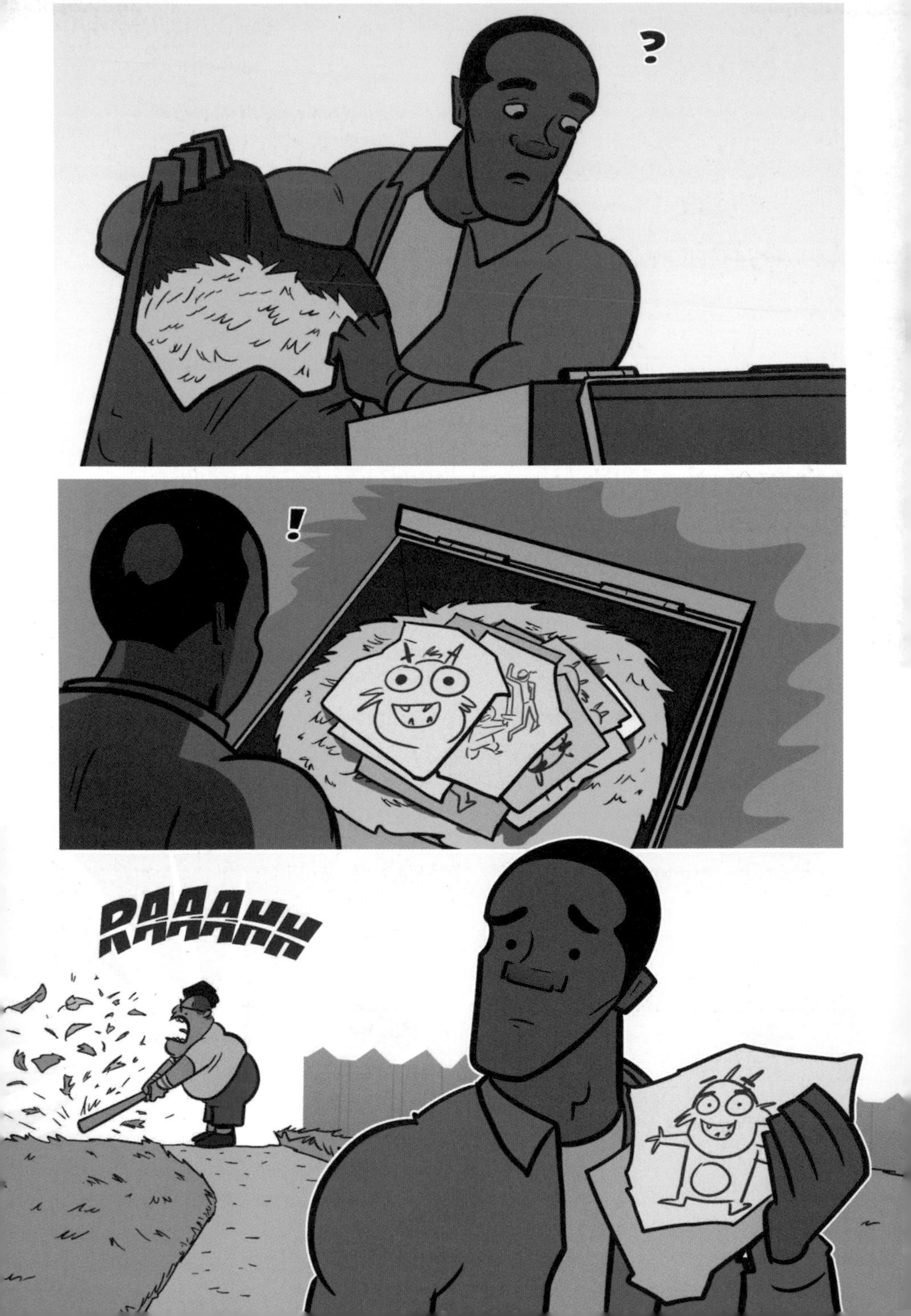
?
!
RAAAHH

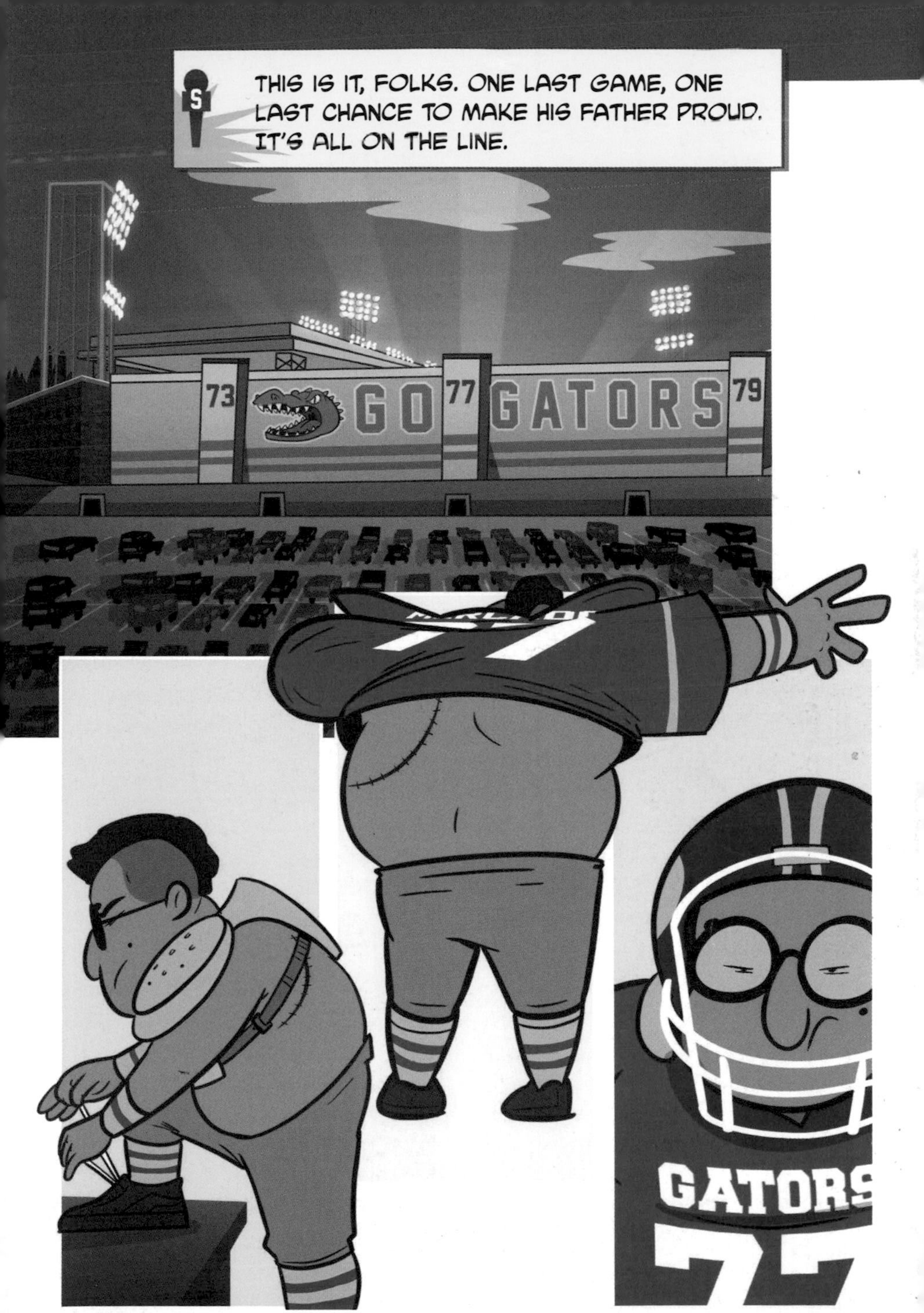
THIS IS IT, FOLKS. ONE LAST GAME, ONE LAST CHANCE TO MAKE HIS FATHER PROUD. IT'S ALL ON THE LINE.
73
GO
77
GATORS
79
GATORS

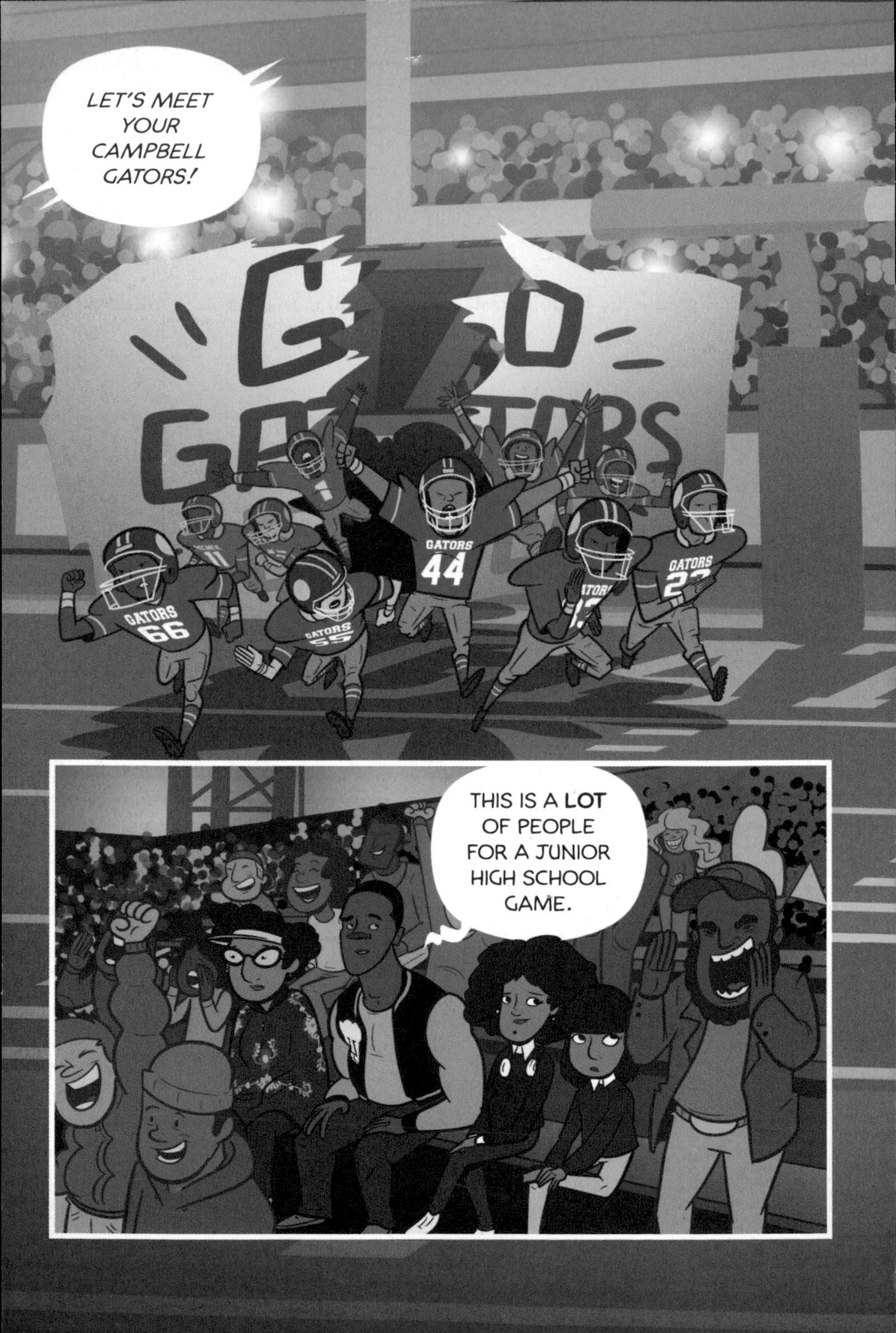
LET'S MEET YOUR CAMPBELL GATORS!
GO GATORS
GATORS 66
GATORS 55
GATORS 44
GATORS
THIS IS A **LOT** OF PEOPLE FOR A JUNIOR HIGH SCHOOL GAME.

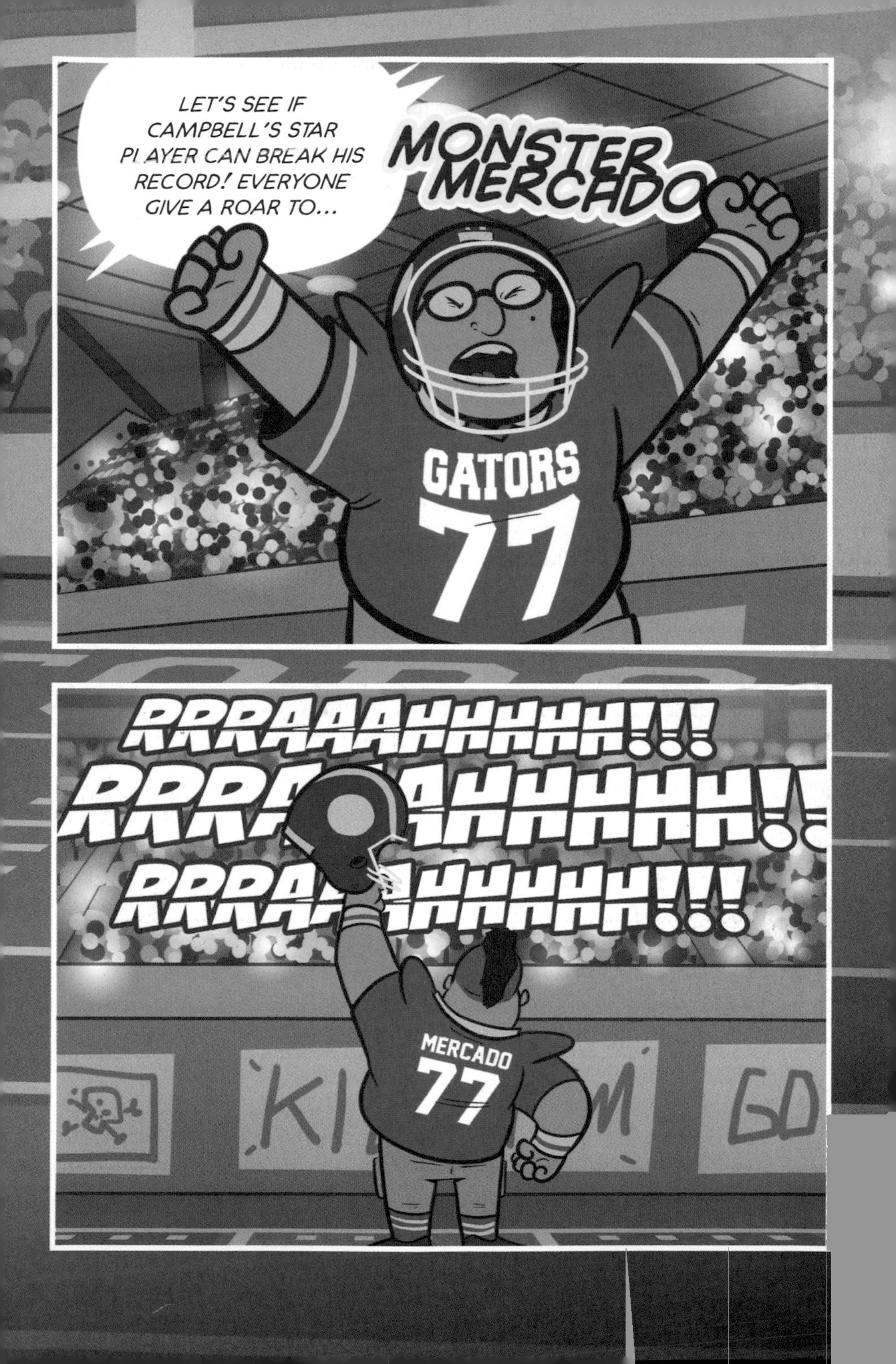
LET'S SEE IF CAMPBELL'S STAR PLAYER CAN BREAK HIS RECORD! EVERYONE GIVE A ROAR TO...
MONSTER MERCADO
GATORS 77
RRRAAAHHHHHH!!!
MERCADO 77

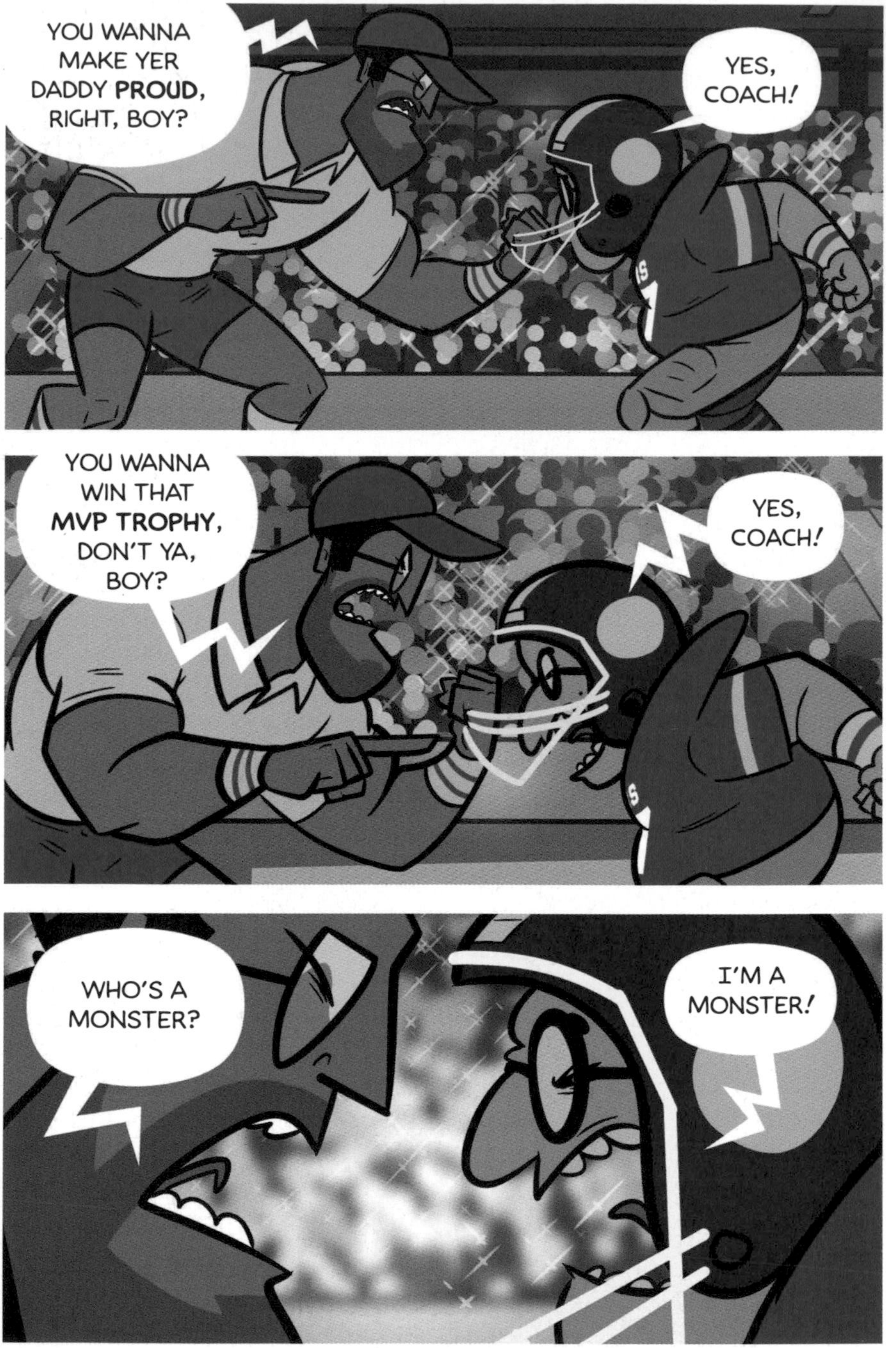
YOU WANNA MAKE YER DADDY **PROUD**, RIGHT, BOY?
YES, COACH!
YOU WANNA WIN THAT **MVP TROPHY**, DON'T YA, BOY?
YES, COACH!
WHO'S A MONSTER?
I'M A MONSTER!

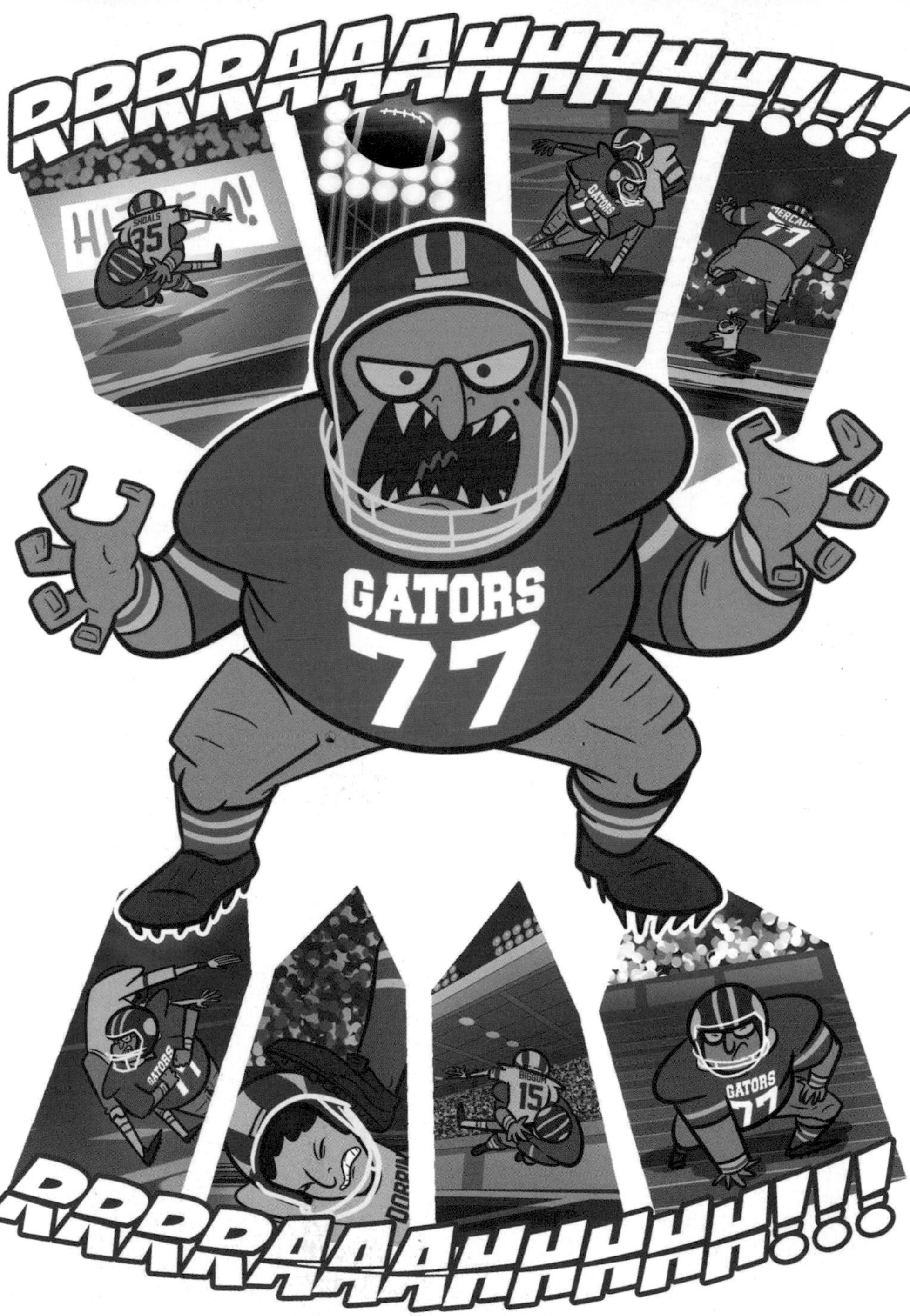
RRRRAAAAHHHHH!!!
SHOALS
35
GATORS
GATORS
77
GATORS
BIGGUM
15
GATORS
RRRRAAAHHHHH!!!

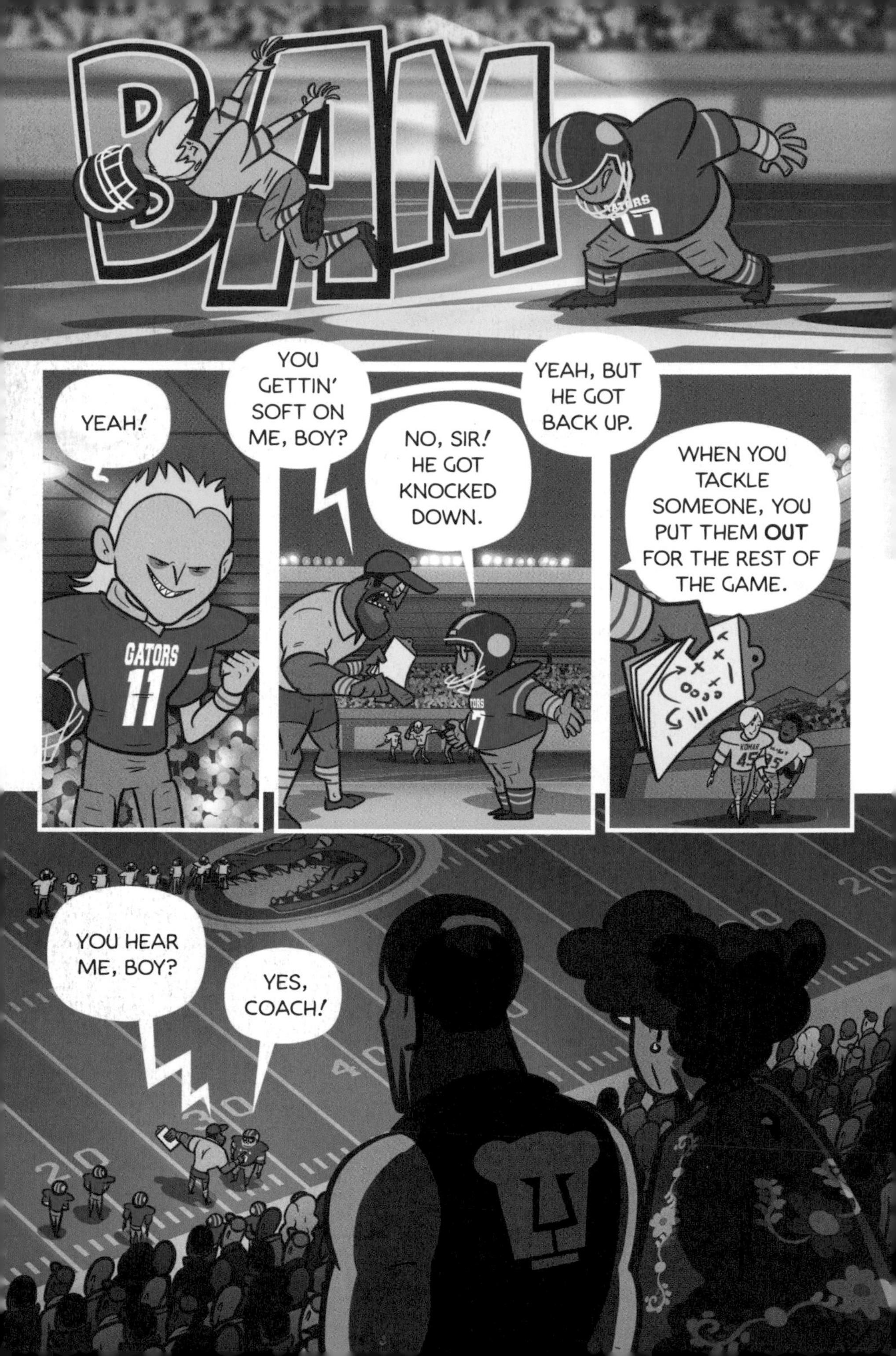
BAM
GATORS
YEAH!
GATORS
YOU GETTIN' SOFT ON ME, BOY?
NO, SIR! HE GOT KNOCKED DOWN.
YEAH, BUT HE GOT BACK UP.
WHEN YOU TACKLE SOMEONE, YOU PUT THEM **OUT** FOR THE REST OF THE GAME.
YOU HEAR ME, BOY?
YES, COACH!

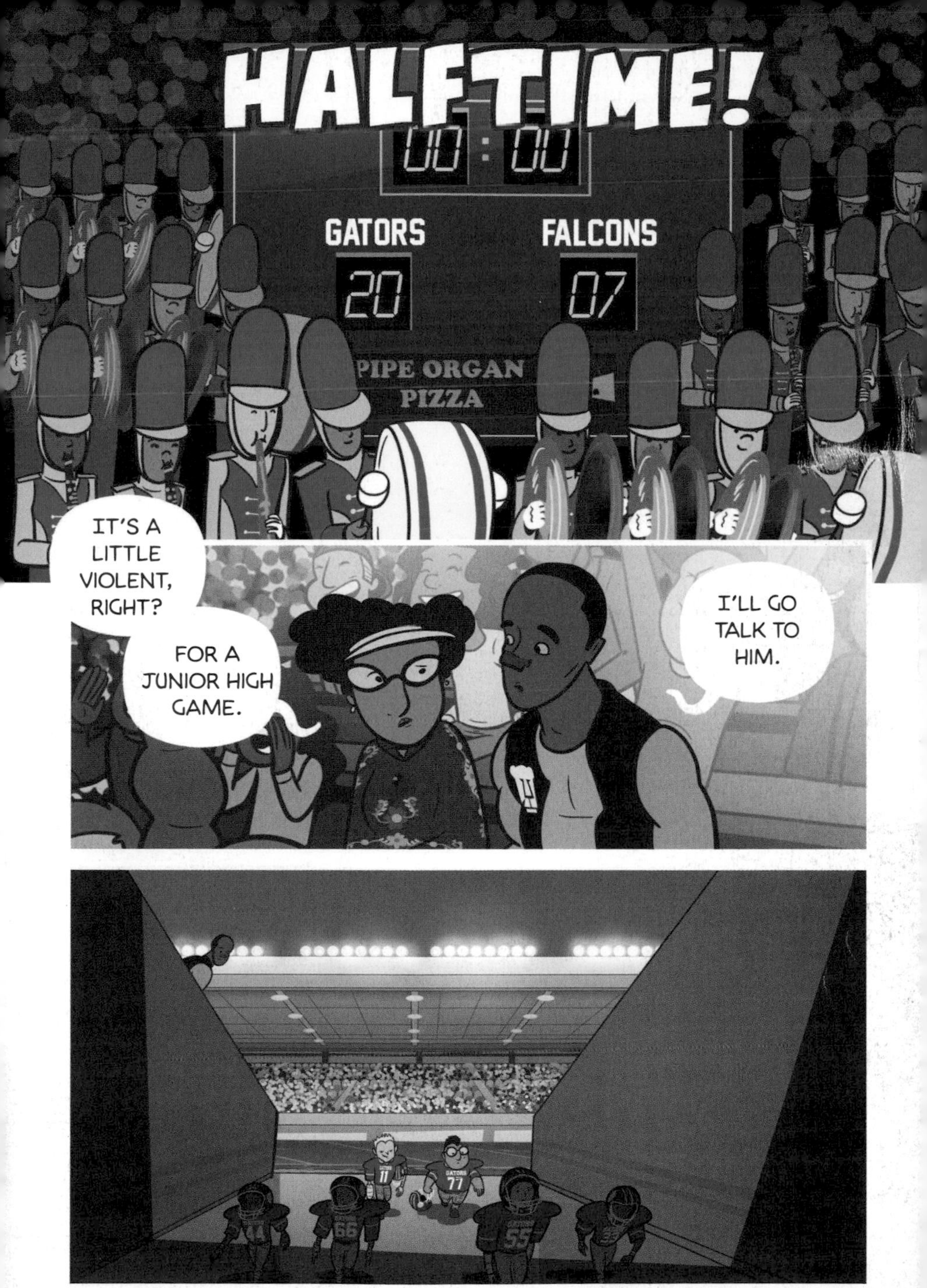
HALFTIME!
00 : 00
GATORS
FALCONS
20
07
PIPE ORGAN
PIZZA
IT'S A LITTLE VIOLENT, RIGHT?
FOR A JUNIOR HIGH GAME.
I'LL GO TALK TO HIM.

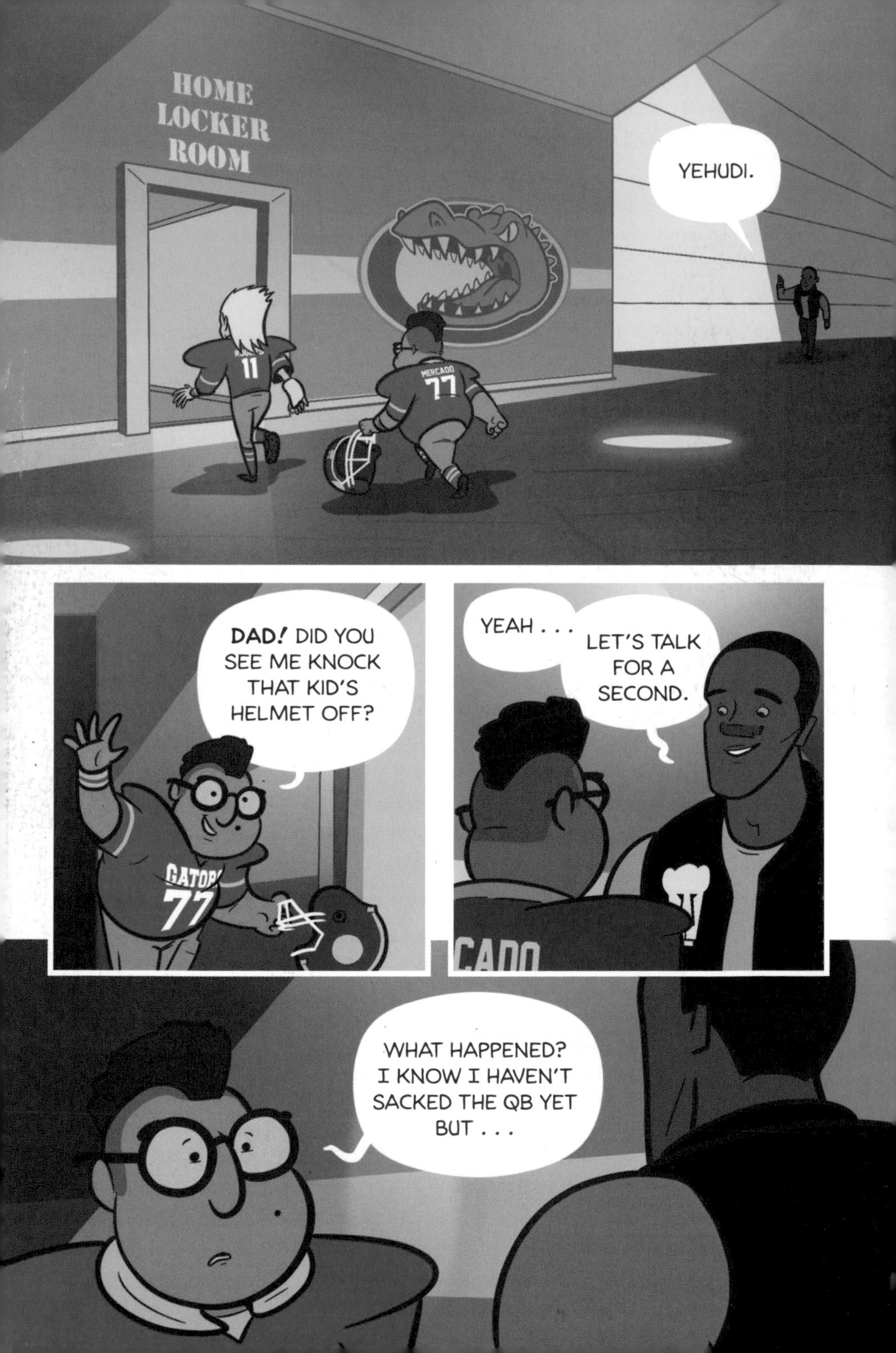
HOME
LOCKER
ROOM
11
MERCADO
77
YEHUDI.
DAD! DID YOU SEE ME KNOCK THAT KID'S HELMET OFF?
GATORS
77
YEAH . . .
LET'S TALK FOR A SECOND.
CADO
WHAT HAPPENED? I KNOW I HAVEN'T SACKED THE QB YET BUT . . .

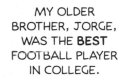

MY OLDER BROTHER, JORGE, WAS THE **BEST** FOOTBALL PLAYER IN COLLEGE.

JORGE WAS **SO GOOD** THAT HE WOULD PLAY **BOTH** OFFENSE AND DEFENSE AND THEN DURING HALFTIME HE WOULD ALSO PLAY IN THE MARCHING BAND.

AT THE UNAM. HE WAS THERE ABOUT FOUR YEARS BEFORE I STARTED.

WHAT? REALLY?

YEAH, HE WOULD PLAY IN THE BAND **IN** HIS FOOTBALL UNIFORM.

MERCADO

YOU REMEMBER MY FATHER, THE GENERAL . . .

YEAH.

KIND OF . . .

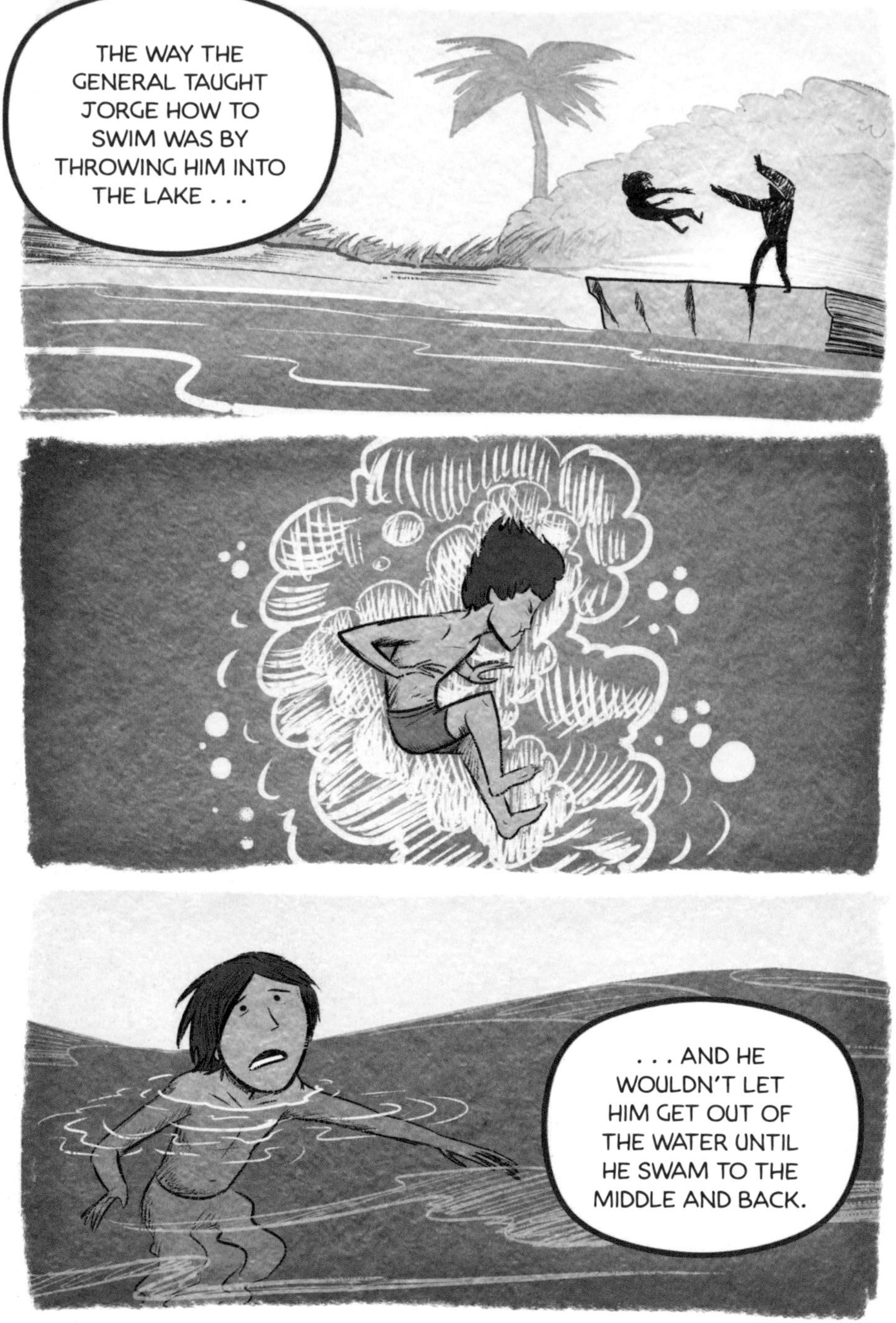
THE WAY THE GENERAL TAUGHT JORGE HOW TO SWIM WAS BY THROWING HIM INTO THE LAKE . . .
. . . AND HE WOULDN'T LET HIM GET OUT OF THE WATER UNTIL HE SWAM TO THE MIDDLE AND BACK.

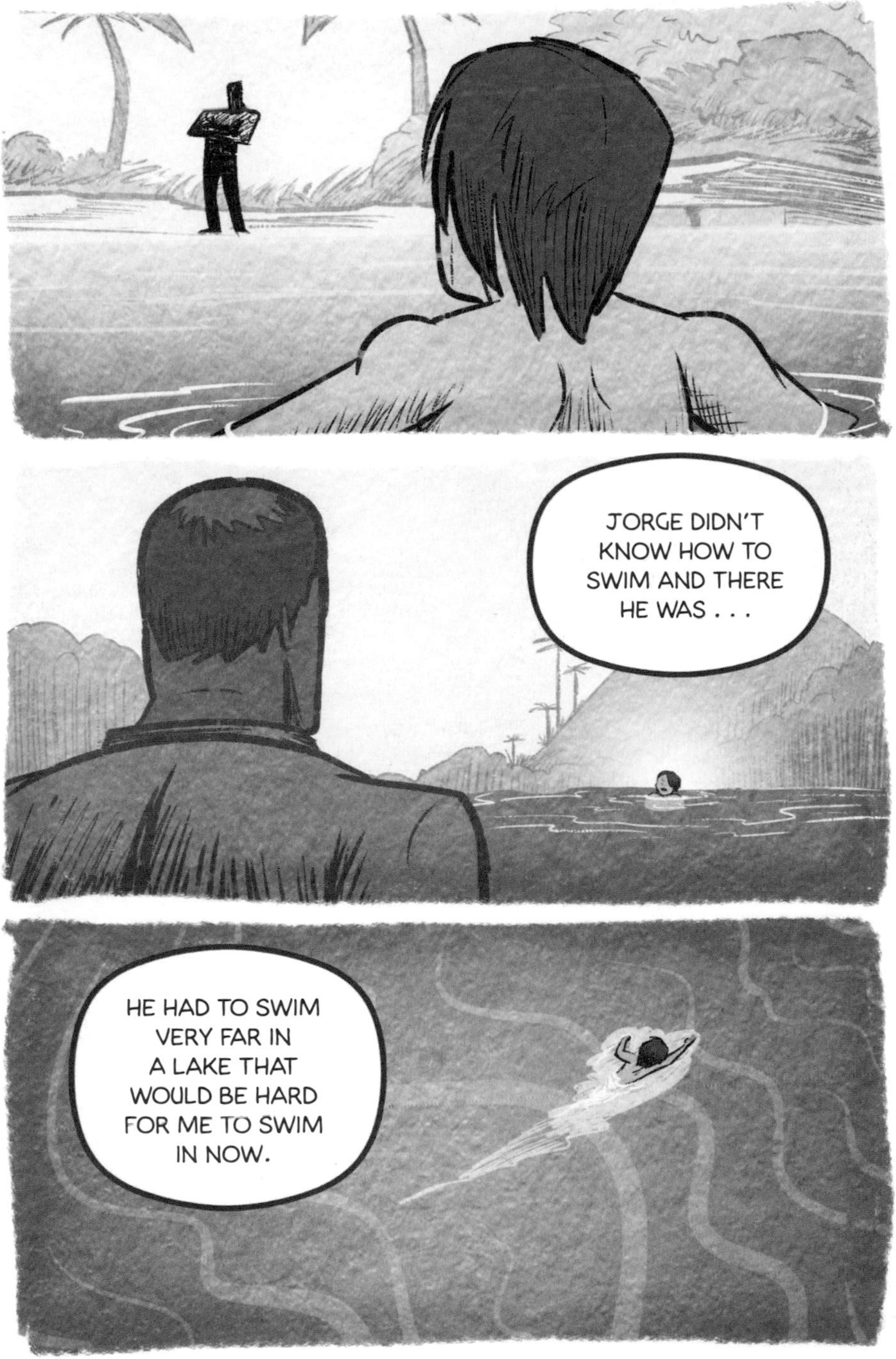
JORGE DIDN'T KNOW HOW TO SWIM AND THERE HE WAS . . .
HE HAD TO SWIM VERY FAR IN A LAKE THAT WOULD BE HARD FOR ME TO SWIM IN NOW.

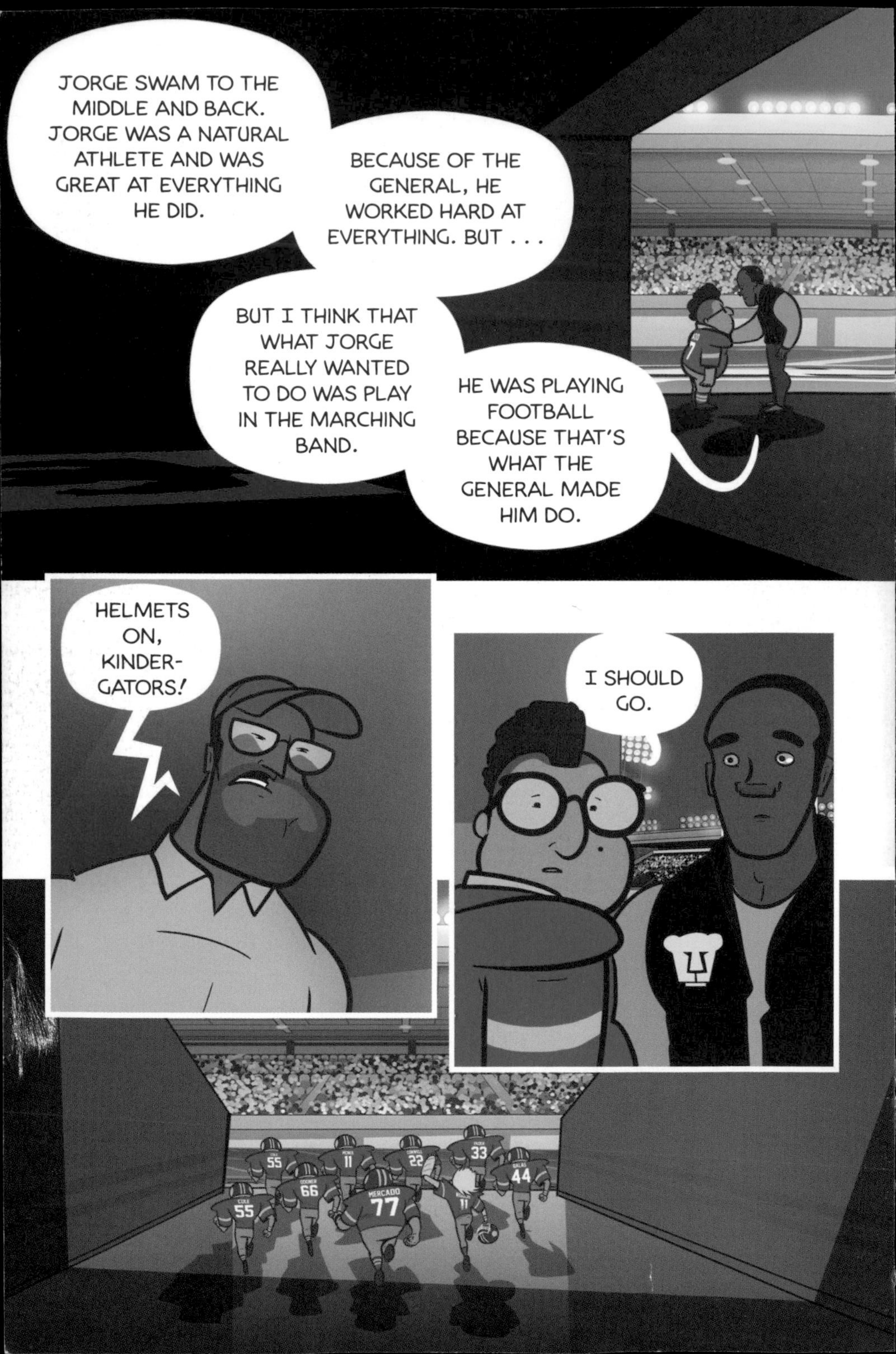
JORGE SWAM TO THE MIDDLE AND BACK. JORGE WAS A NATURAL ATHLETE AND WAS GREAT AT EVERYTHING HE DID.
BECAUSE OF THE GENERAL, HE WORKED HARD AT EVERYTHING. BUT . . .
BUT I THINK THAT WHAT JORGE REALLY WANTED TO DO WAS PLAY IN THE MARCHING BAND.
HE WAS PLAYING FOOTBALL BECAUSE THAT'S WHAT THE GENERAL MADE HIM DO.
HELMETS ON, KINDER-GATORS!
I SHOULD GO.
55
11
22
33
66
44
55
MERCADO
77
11

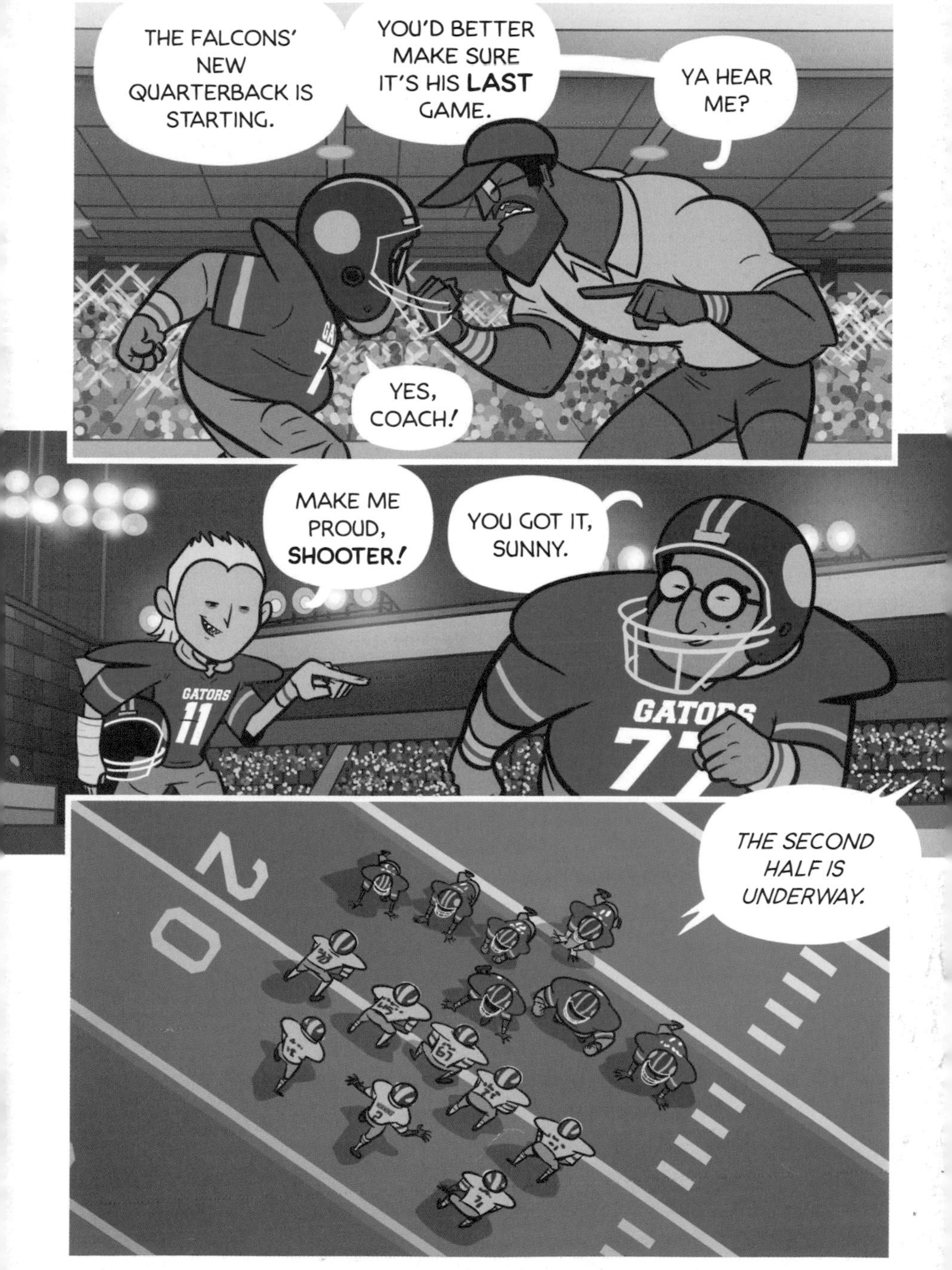
THE FALCONS' NEW QUARTERBACK IS STARTING.
YOU'D BETTER MAKE SURE IT'S HIS **LAST** GAME.
YA HEAR ME?
YES, COACH!
MAKE ME PROUD, **SHOOTER!**
YOU GOT IT, SUNNY.
GATORS 11
THE SECOND HALF IS UNDERWAY.

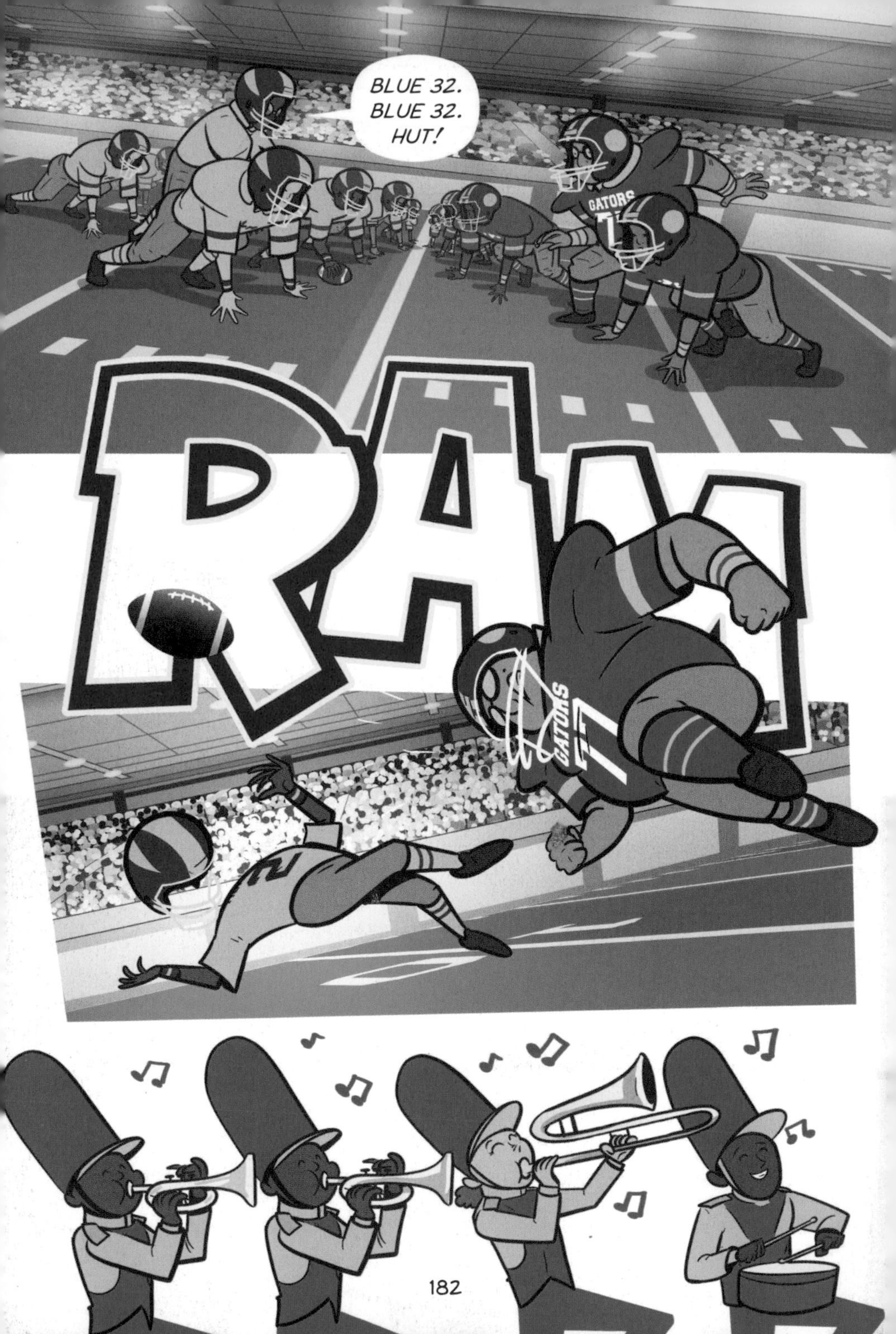
BLUE 32. BLUE 32. HUT!
RAM
GATORS
GATORS 77

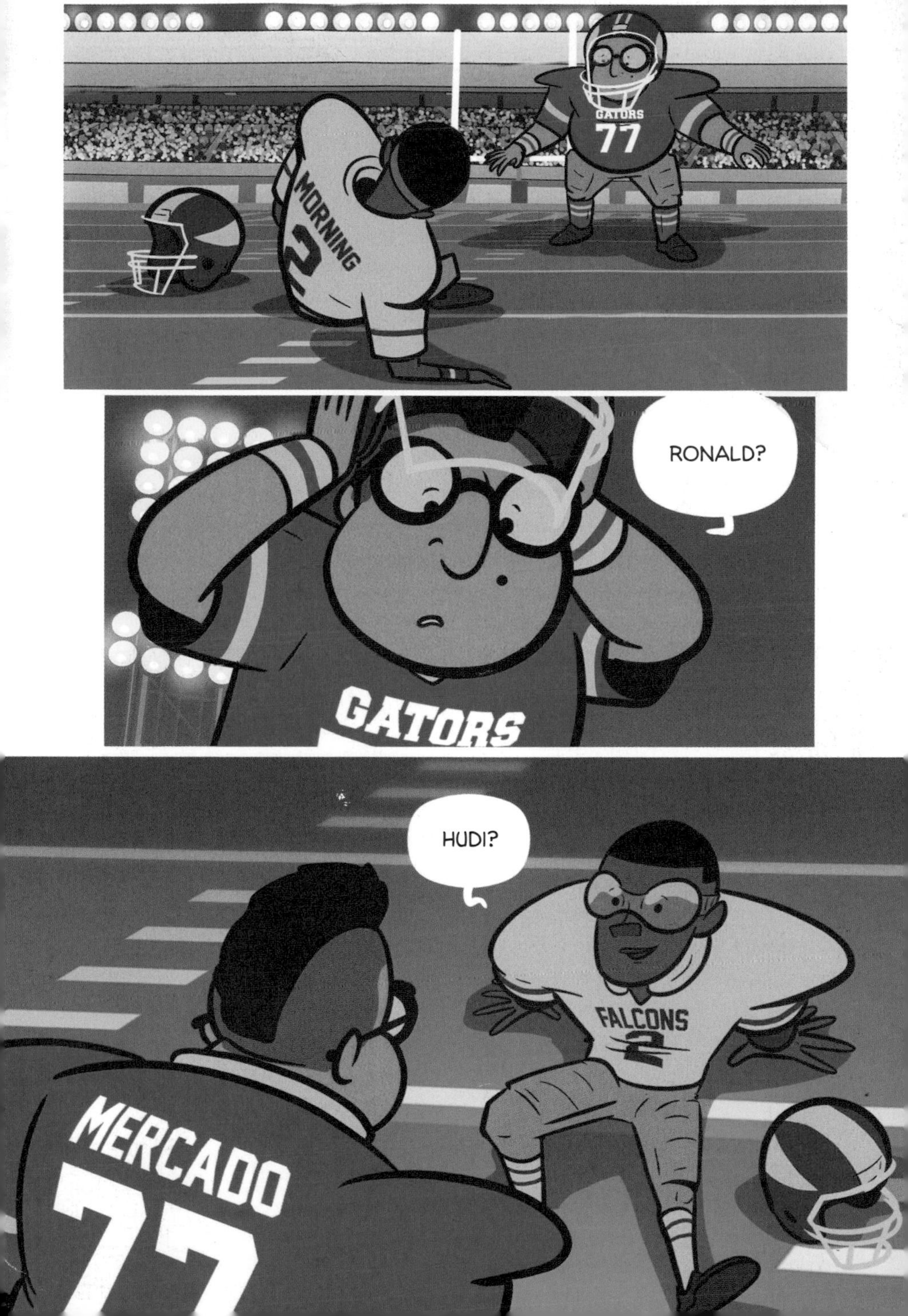
MORNING
2
GATORS
77
RONALD?
GATORS
HUDI?
FALCONS
2
MERCADO
77

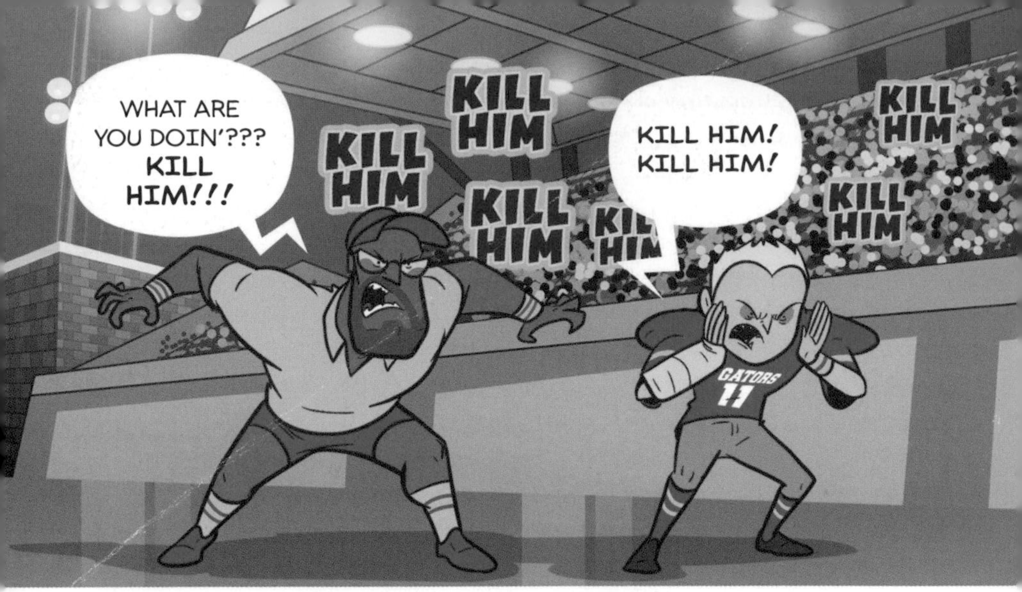
WHAT ARE YOU DOIN'??? KILL HIM!!!
KILL HIM
KILL HIM
KILL HIM
KILL HIM! KILL HIM!
KILL HIM
KILL HIM
GATORS 11

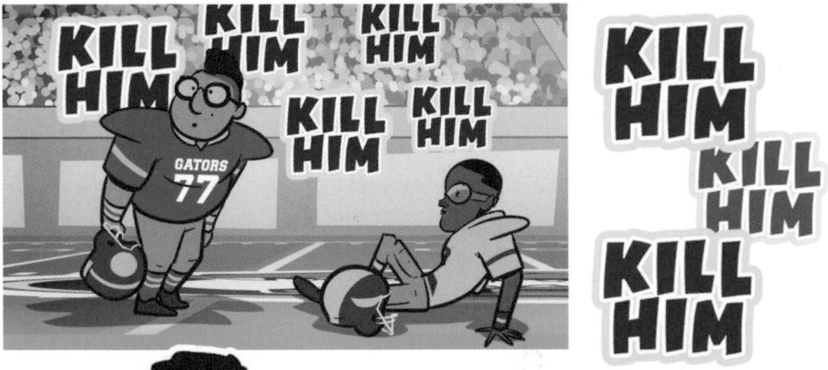
KILL HIM
KILL HIM
KILL HIM
KILL HIM
GATORS 77
KILL HIM
KILL HIM
KILL HIM

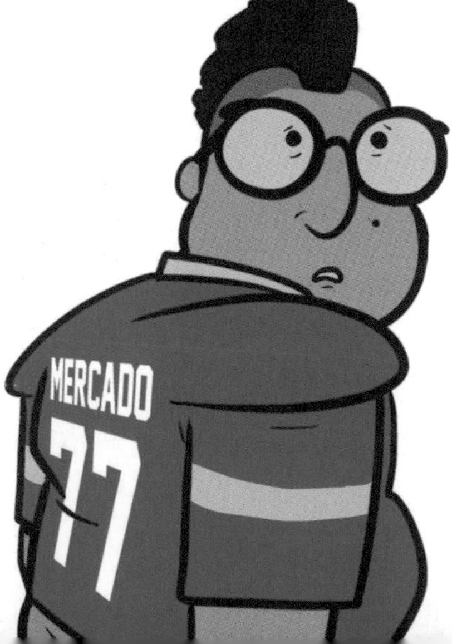
MERCADO 77

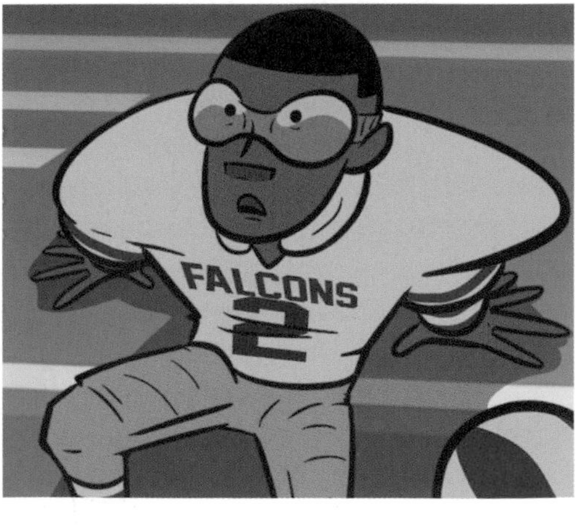
FALCONS 2

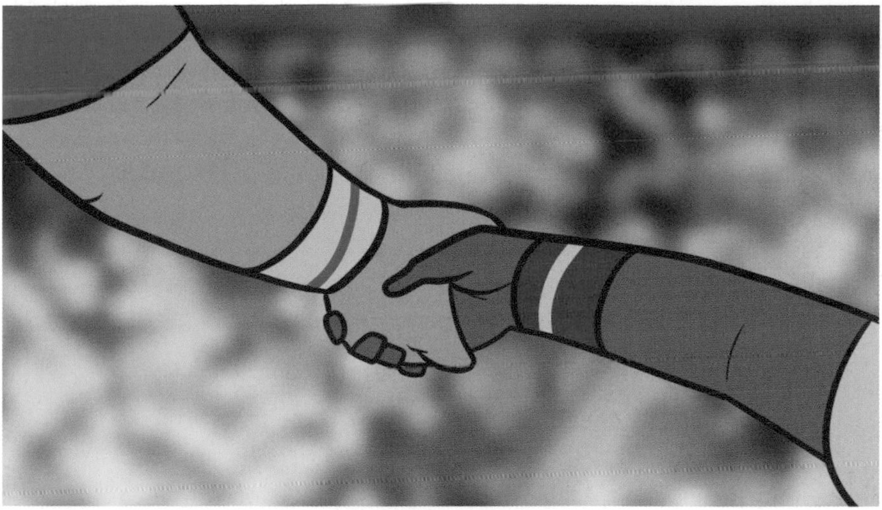

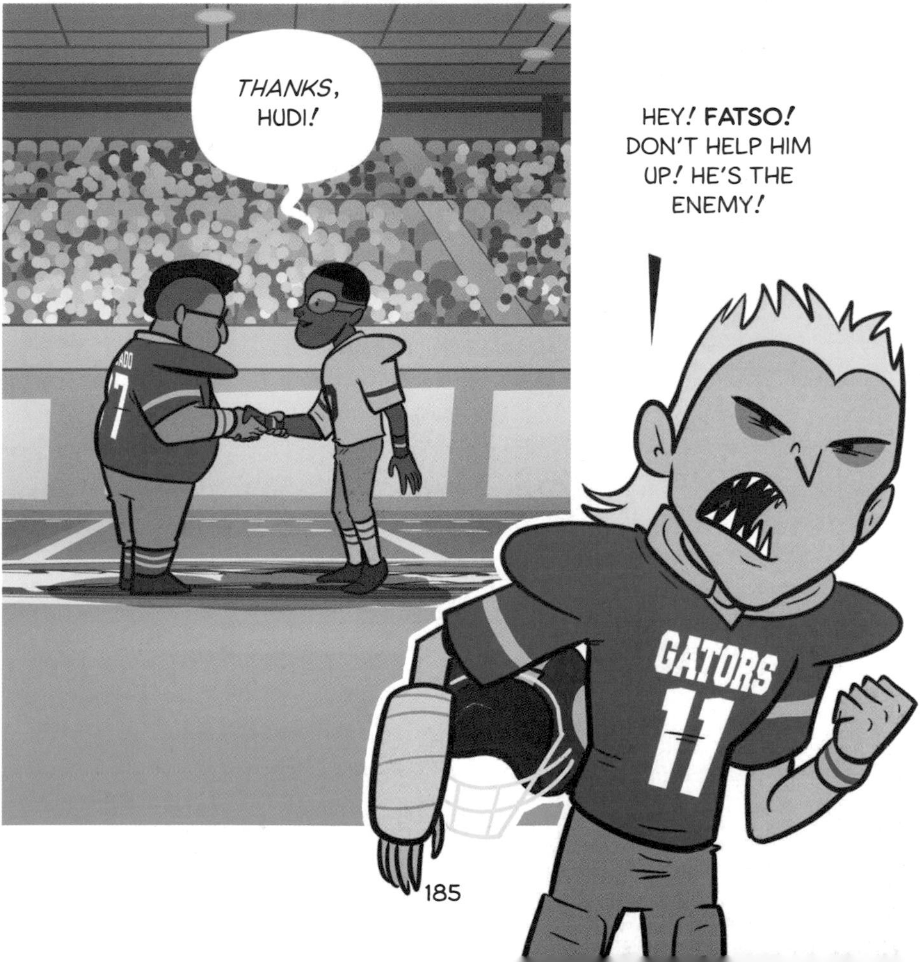
THANKS, HUDI!
HEY! **FATSO!** DON'T HELP HIM UP! HE'S THE ENEMY!
GATORS
11

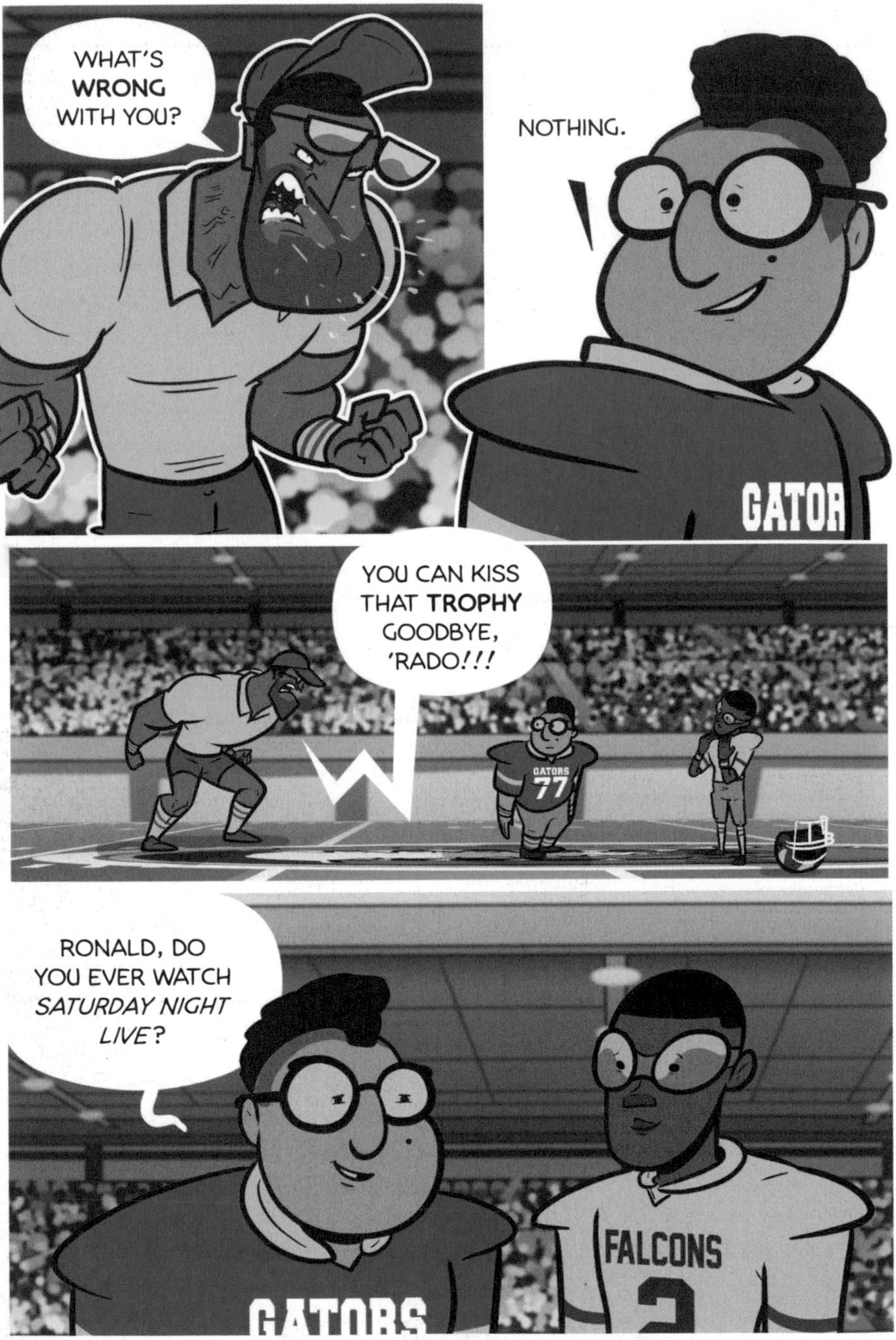
WHAT'S **WRONG** WITH YOU?
NOTHING.
GATOR
YOU CAN KISS THAT **TROPHY** GOODBYE, 'RADO*!!!*
GATORS 77
RONALD, DO YOU EVER WATCH *SATURDAY NIGHT LIVE*?
GATORS
FALCONS

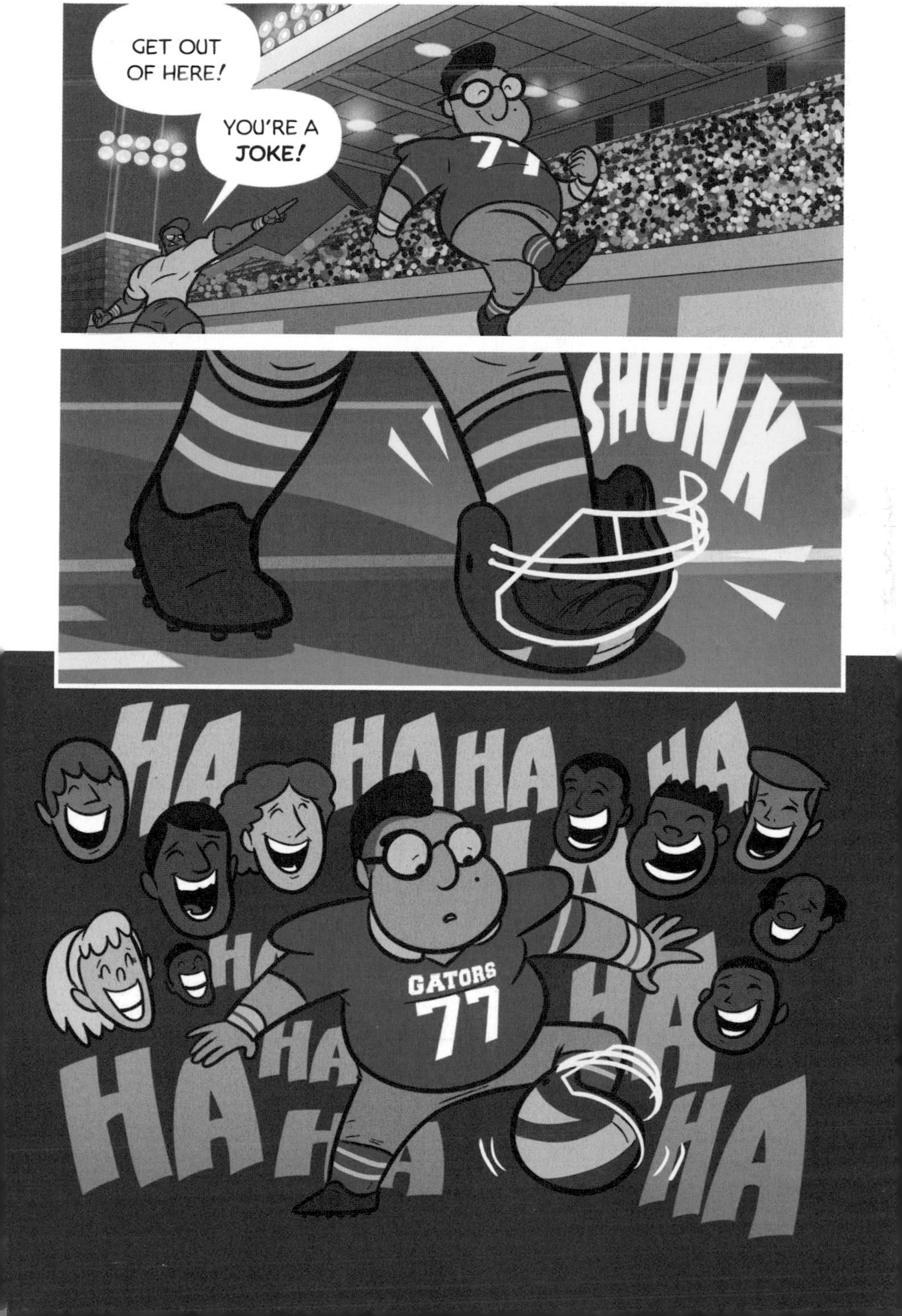
GET OUT OF HERE!
YOU'RE A JOKE!
77
SHUNK
HA HAHA HA
GATORS 77
HA HA HA HA HA
HA HA HA HA

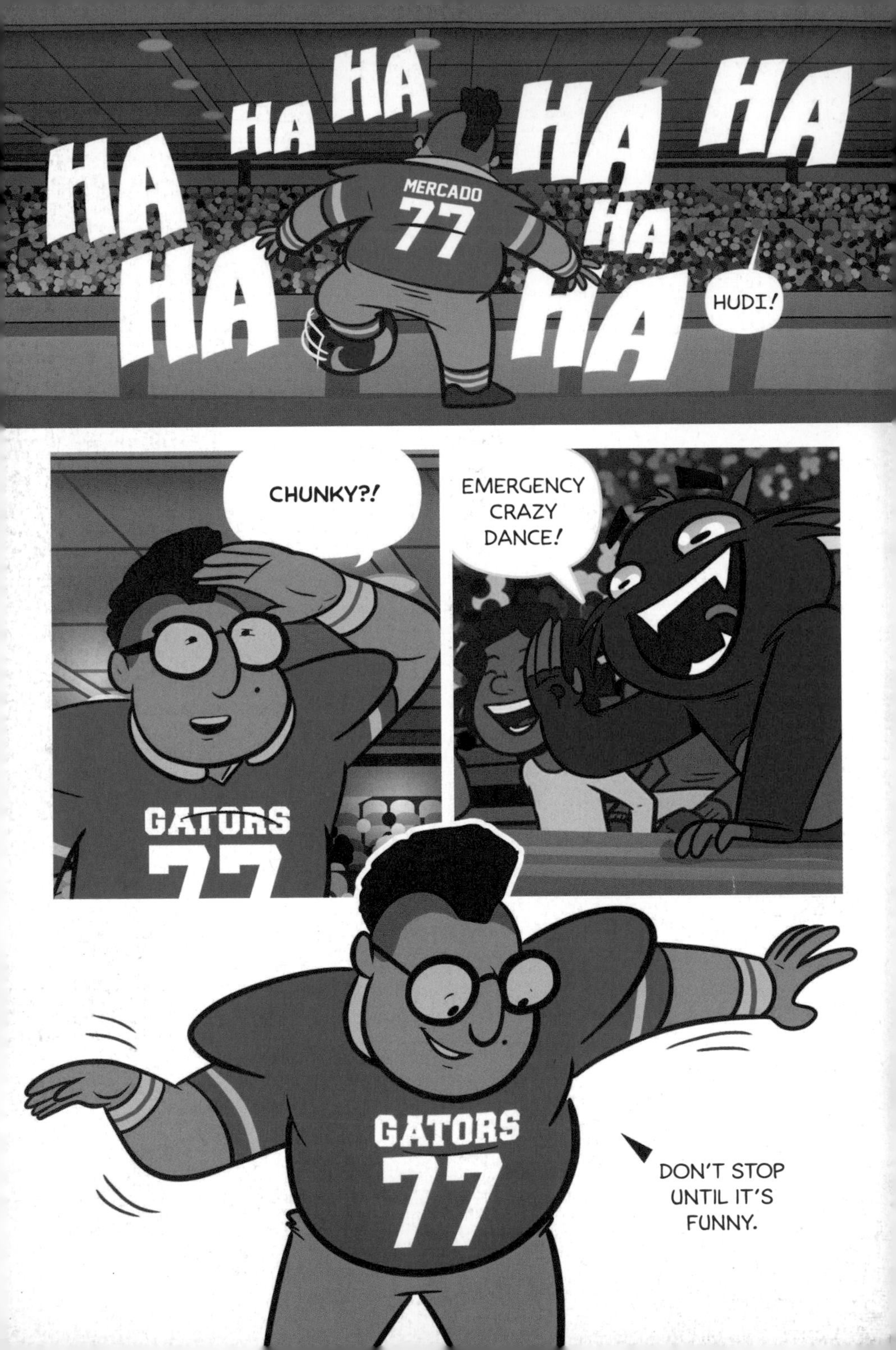
HA HA HA HA HA HA HA HA
MERCADO 77
HUDI!
CHUNKY?!
GATORS 77
EMERGENCY CRAZY DANCE!
GATORS 77
DON'T STOP UNTIL IT'S FUNNY.

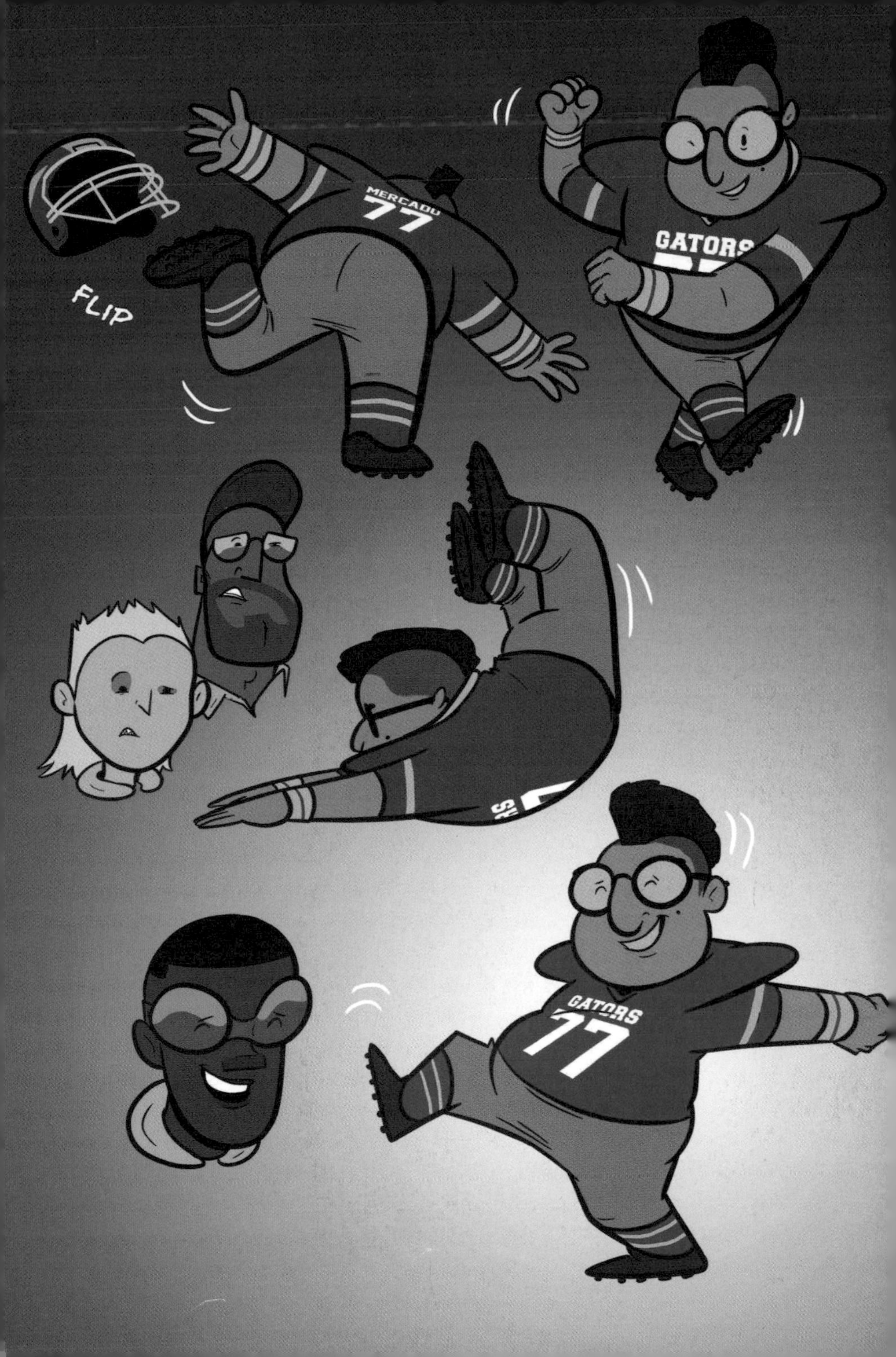
MERCADO
77
FLIP
GATORS
GATORS
77

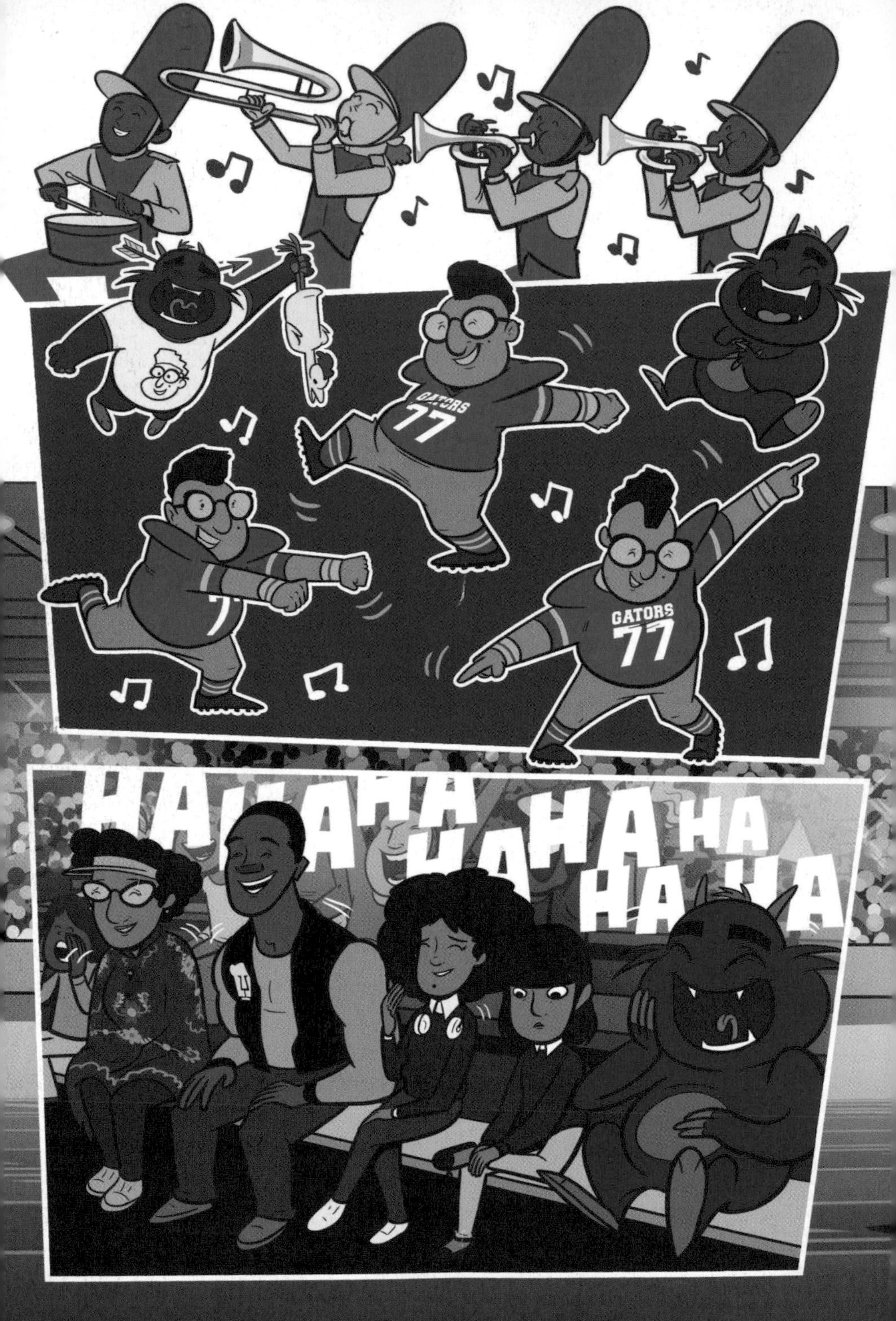
GATORS 77
GATORS 77
HA HA HA HA HA HA HA HA HA HA

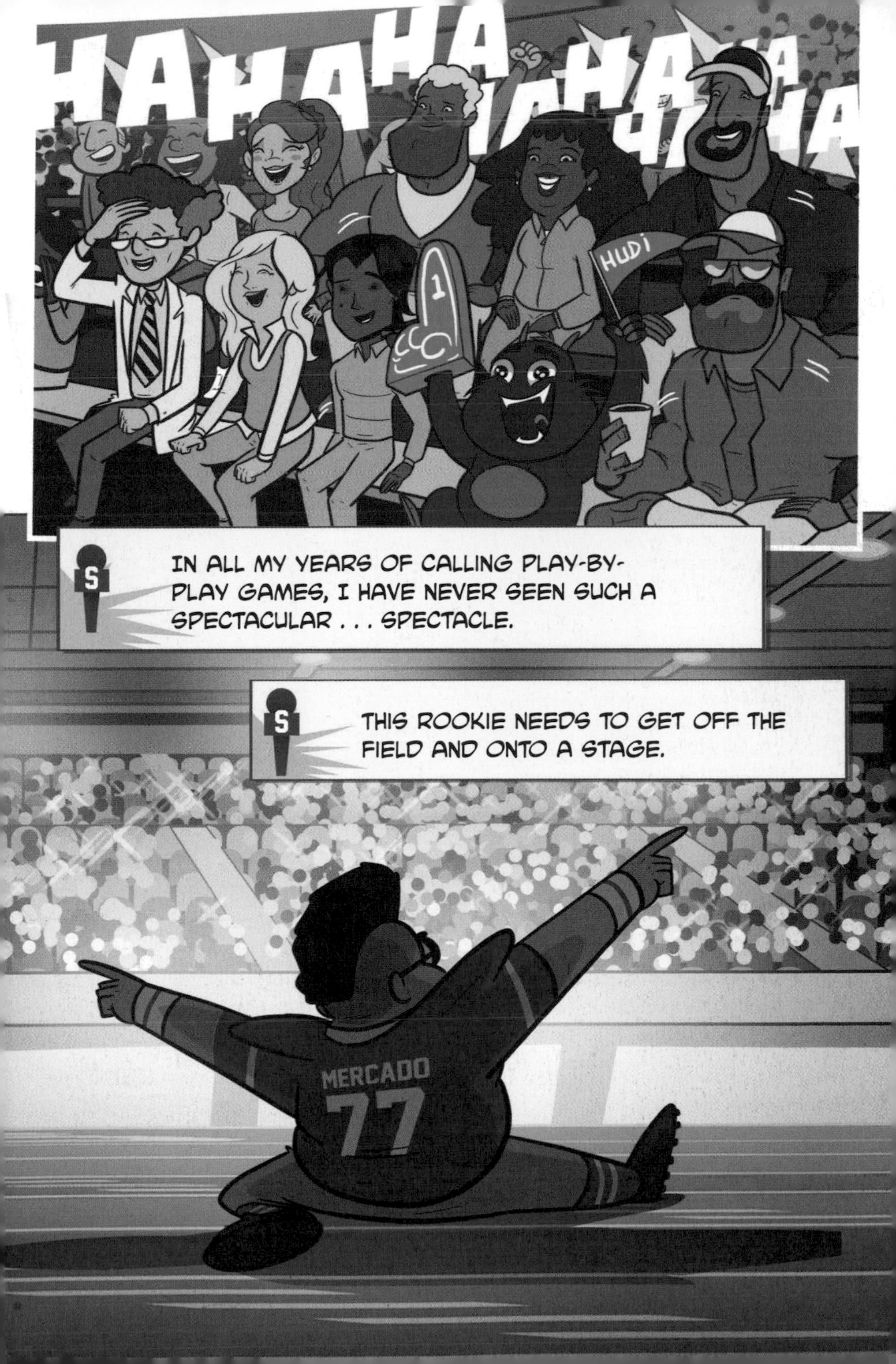
HAHAHA
HAHAHA
HUDi
IN ALL MY YEARS OF CALLING PLAY-BY-PLAY GAMES, I HAVE NEVER SEEN SUCH A SPECTACULAR . . . SPECTACLE.
THIS ROOKIE NEEDS TO GET OFF THE FIELD AND ONTO A STAGE.
MERCADO
77

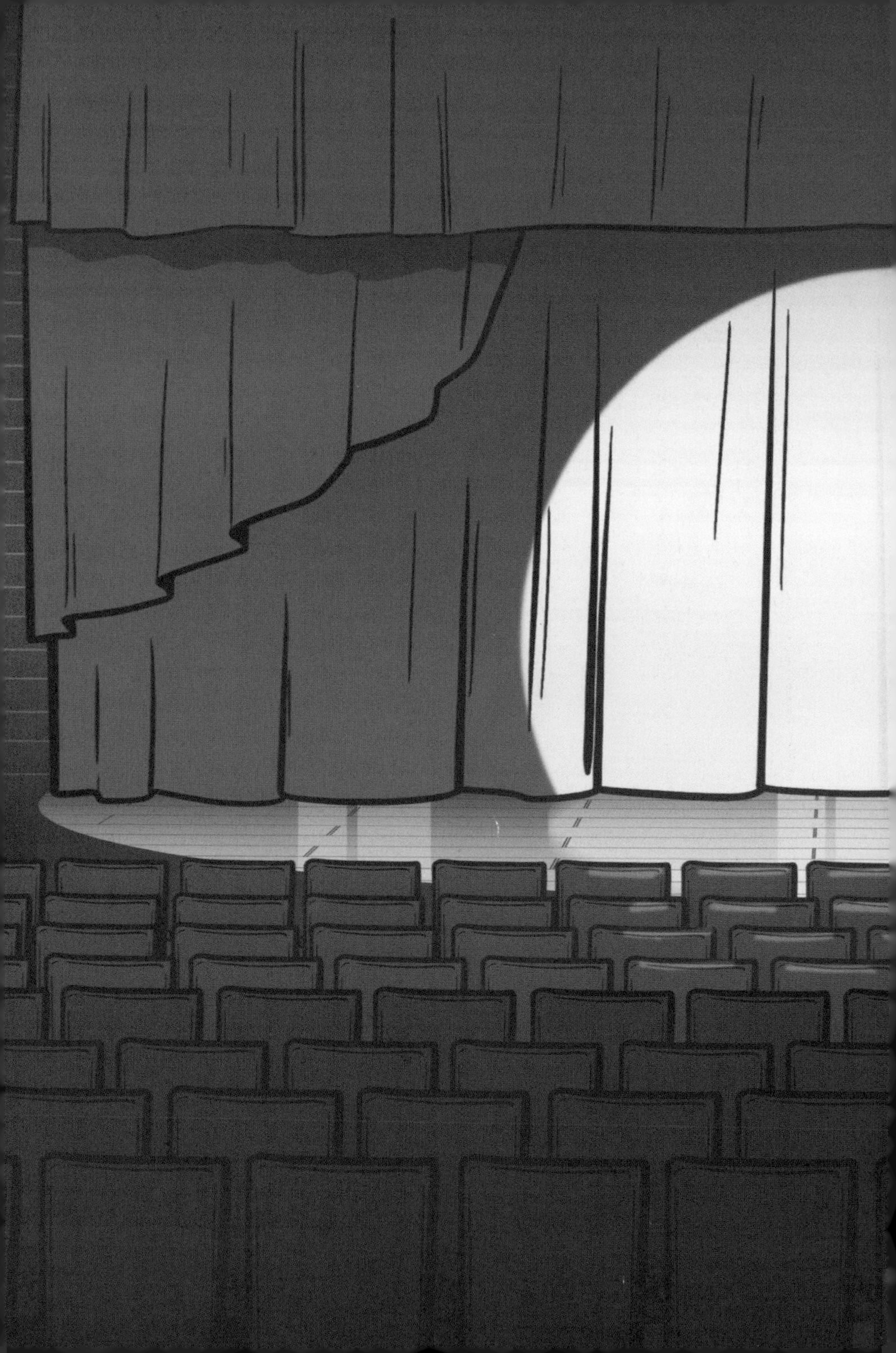

CHAPTER SEVEN

Theater

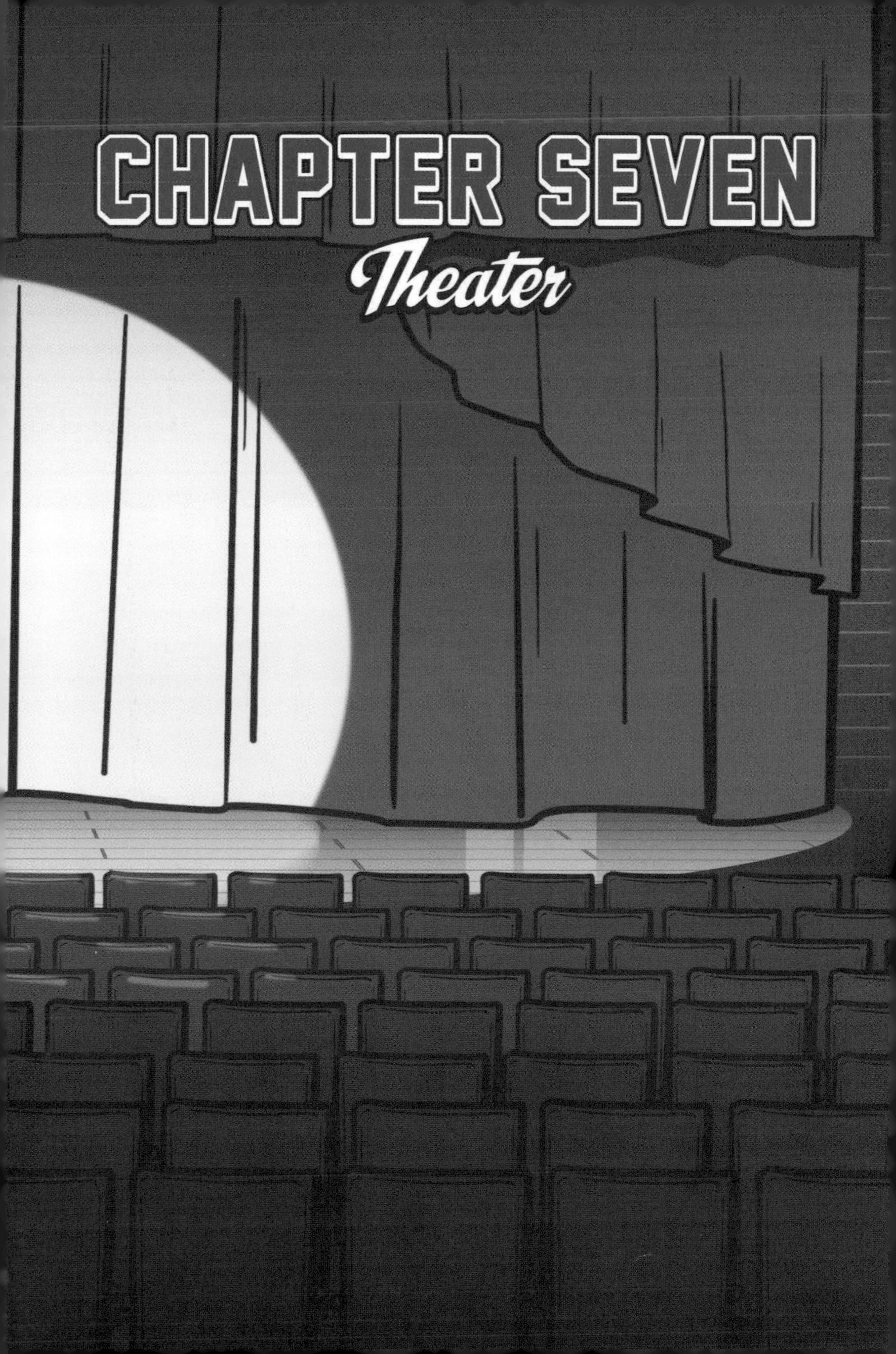

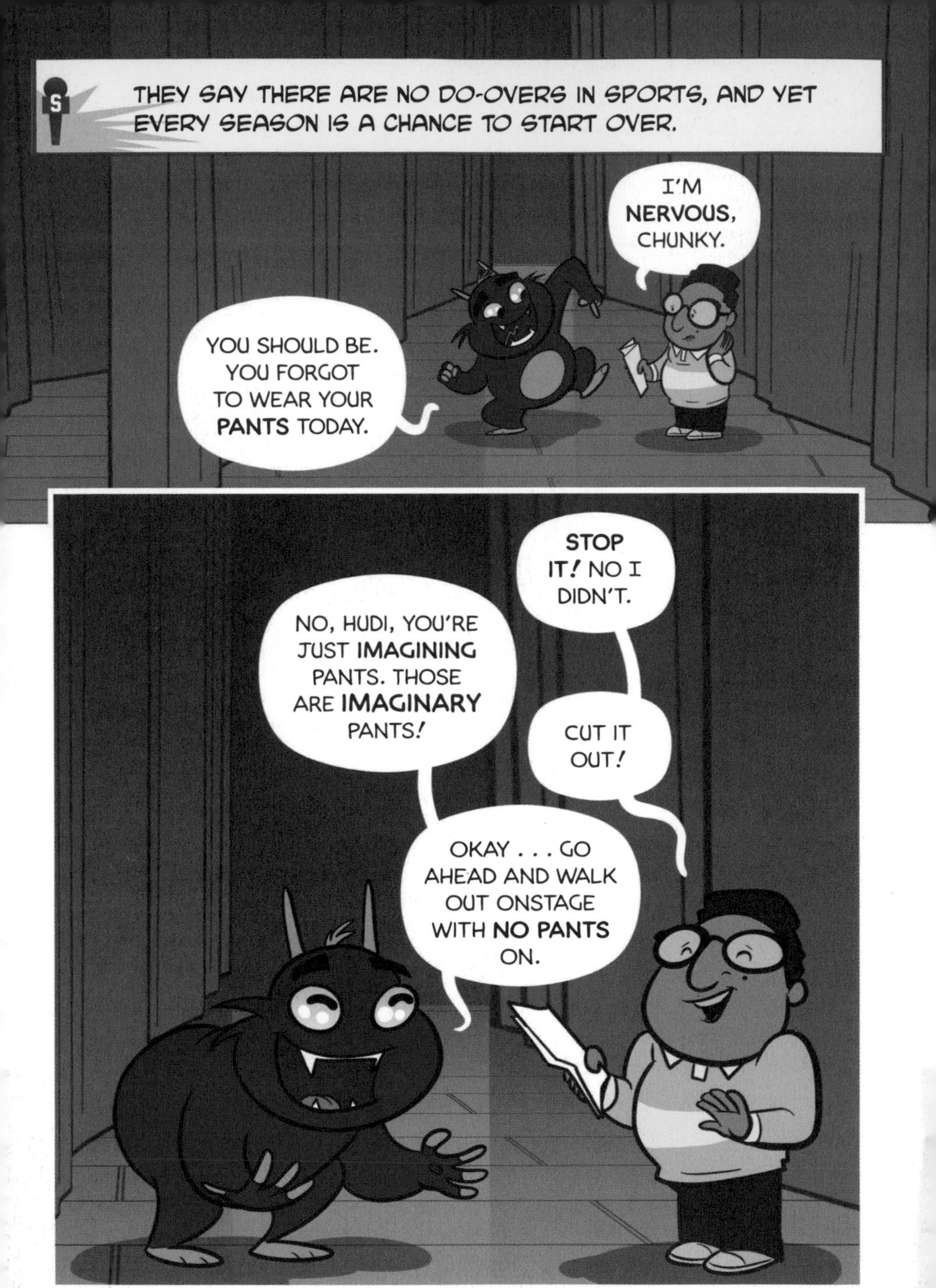
THEY SAY THERE ARE NO DO-OVERS IN SPORTS, AND YET EVERY SEASON IS A CHANCE TO START OVER.
I'M NERVOUS, CHUNKY.
YOU SHOULD BE. YOU FORGOT TO WEAR YOUR PANTS TODAY.
STOP IT! NO I DIDN'T.
NO, HUDI, YOU'RE JUST IMAGINING PANTS. THOSE ARE IMAGINARY PANTS!
CUT IT OUT!
OKAY . . . GO AHEAD AND WALK OUT ONSTAGE WITH NO PANTS ON.

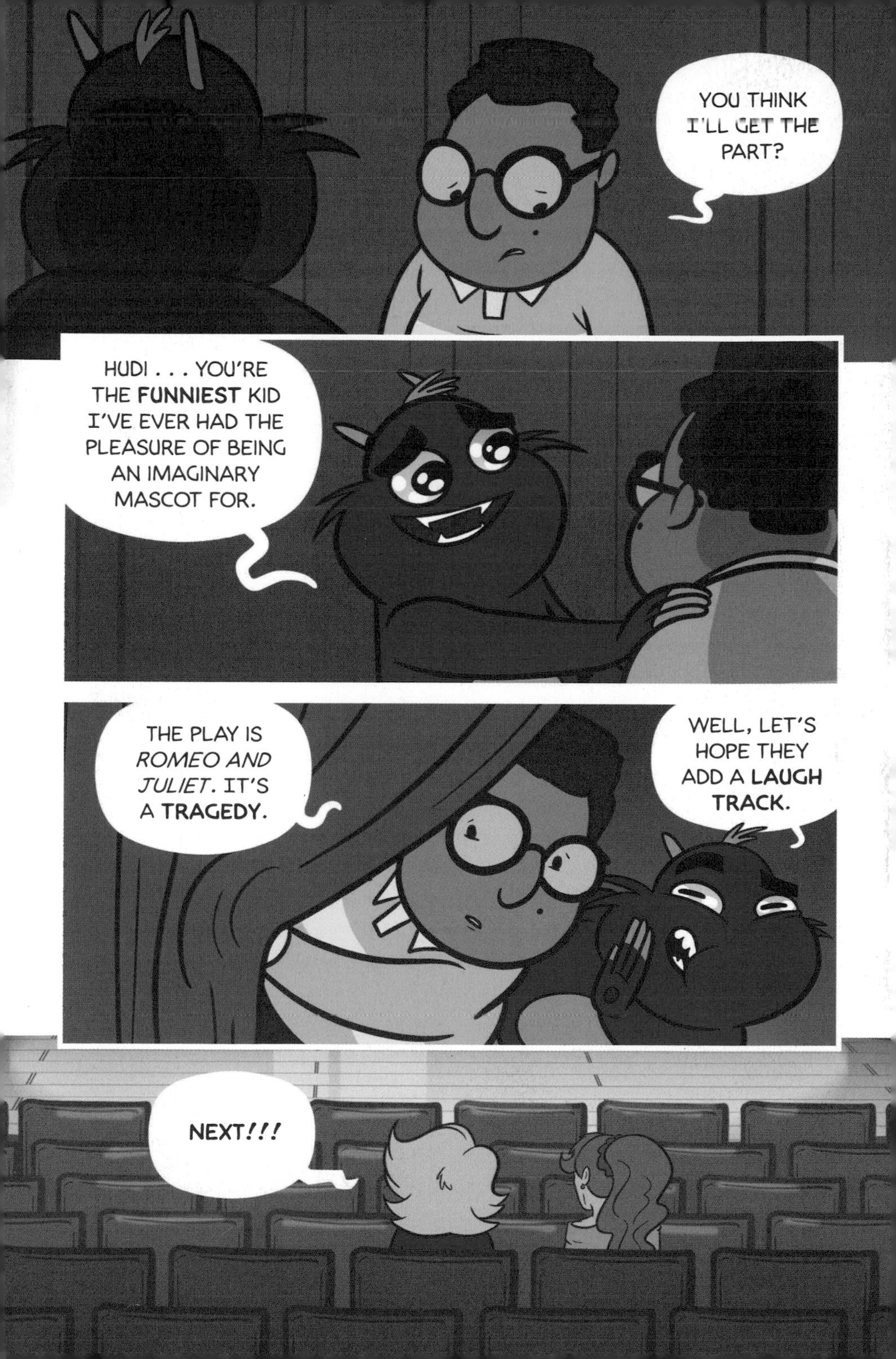
YOU THINK I'LL GET THE PART?
HUDI . . . YOU'RE THE **FUNNIEST** KID I'VE EVER HAD THE PLEASURE OF BEING AN IMAGINARY MASCOT FOR.
THE PLAY IS *ROMEO AND JULIET*. IT'S A **TRAGEDY**.
WELL, LET'S HOPE THEY ADD A **LAUGH TRACK**.
NEXT*!!!*

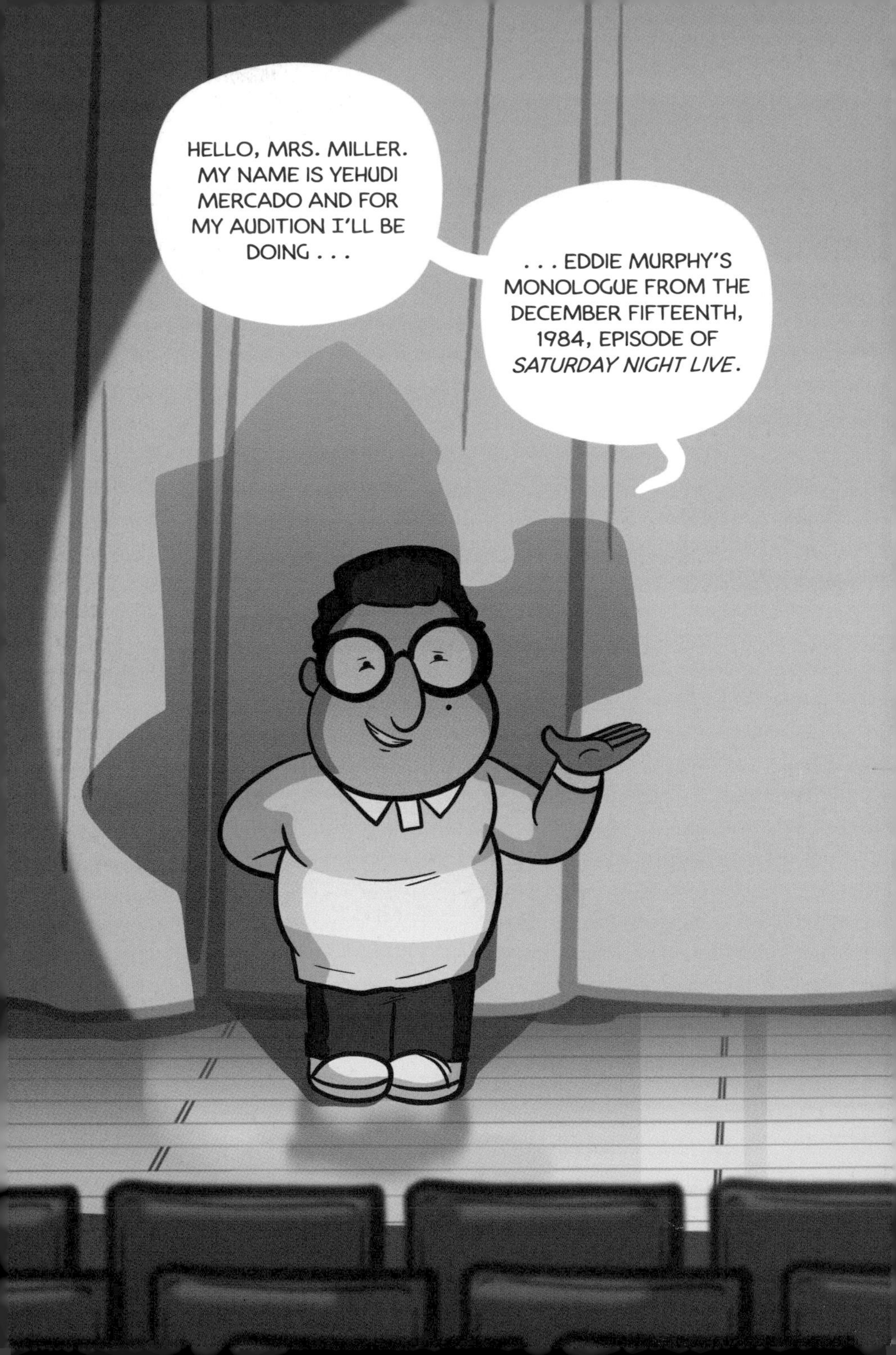
HELLO, MRS. MILLER. MY NAME IS YEHUDI MERCADO AND FOR MY AUDITION I'LL BE DOING . . .
. . . EDDIE MURPHY'S MONOLOGUE FROM THE DECEMBER FIFTEENTH, 1984, EPISODE OF *SATURDAY NIGHT LIVE*.

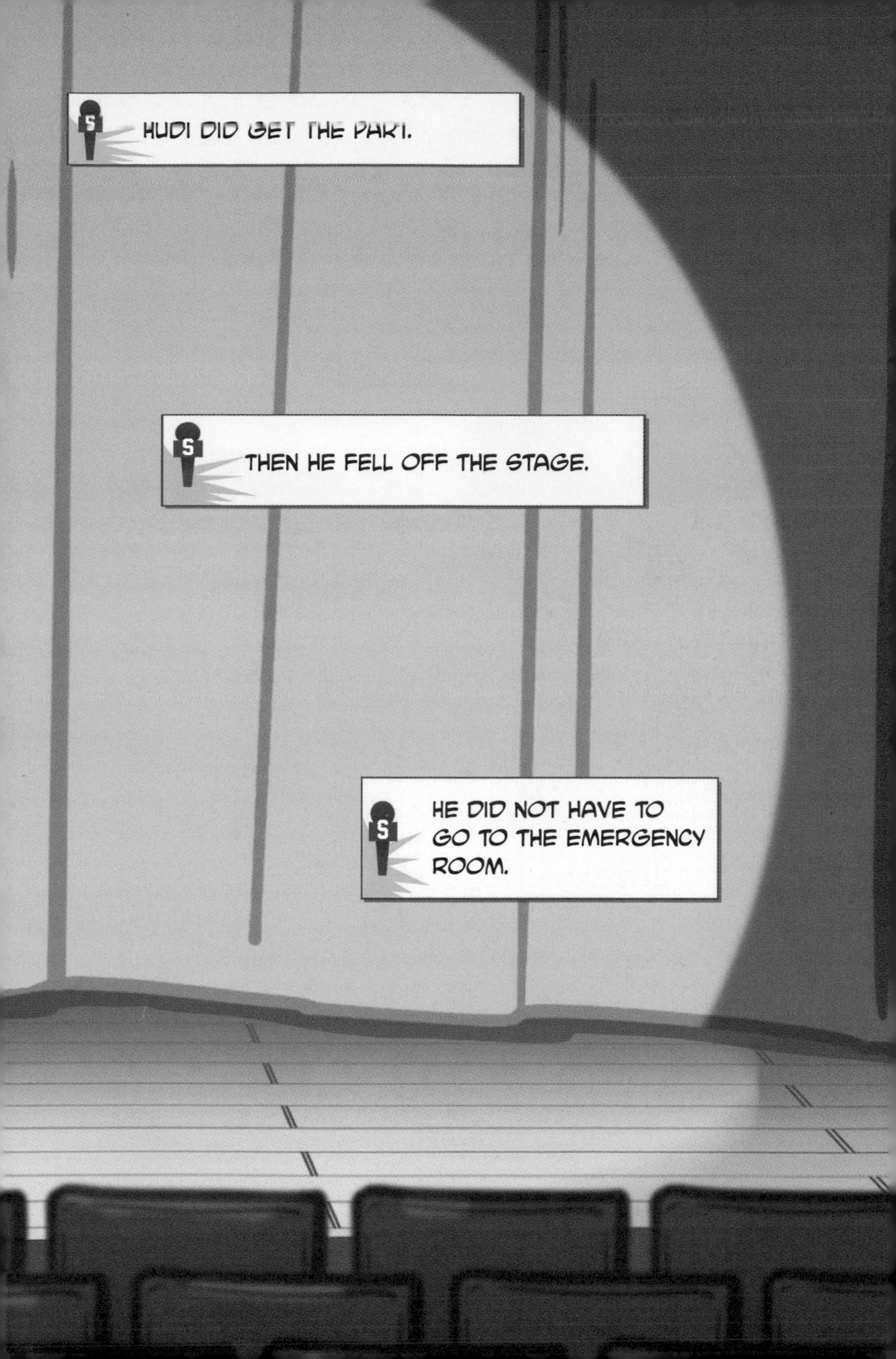
HUDI DID GET THE PART.
THEN HE FELL OFF THE STAGE.
HE DID NOT HAVE TO GO TO THE EMERGENCY ROOM.

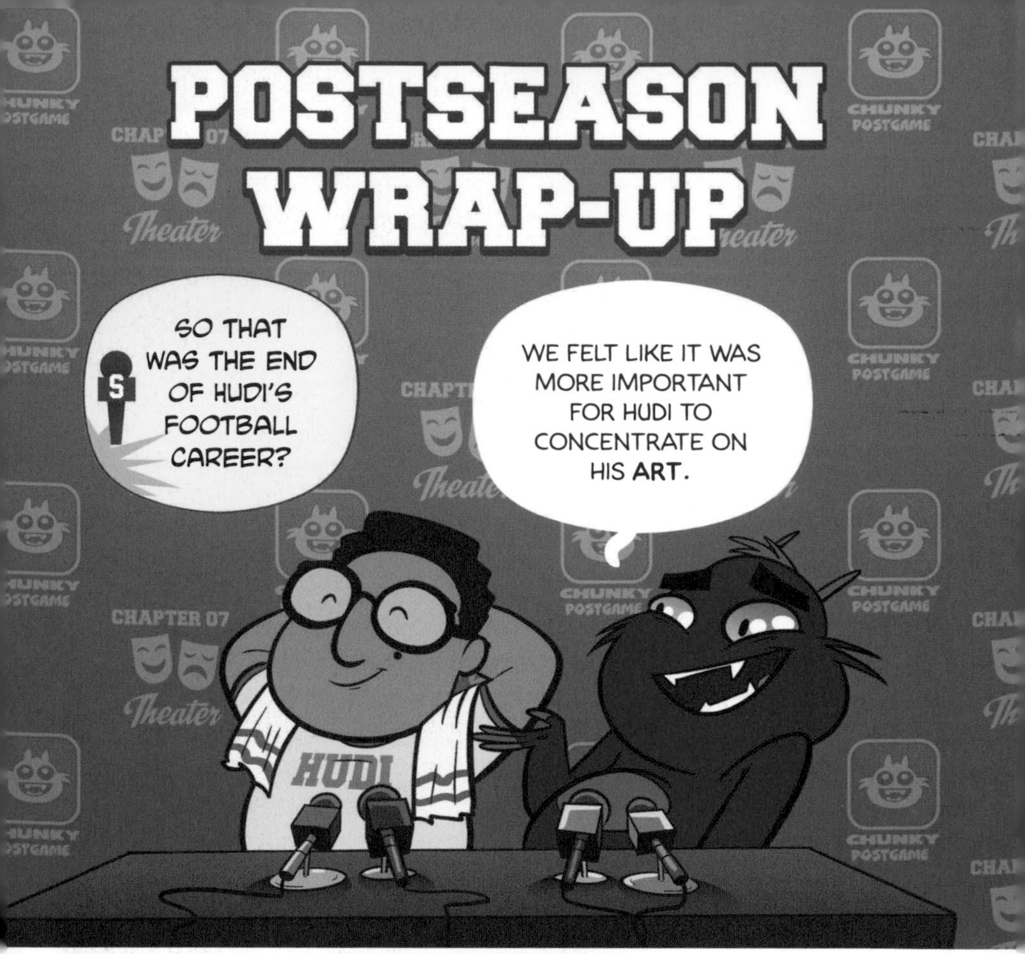
POSTSEASON WRAP-UP
SO THAT WAS THE END OF HUDI'S FOOTBALL CAREER?
WE FELT LIKE IT WAS MORE IMPORTANT FOR HUDI TO CONCENTRATE ON HIS **ART**.

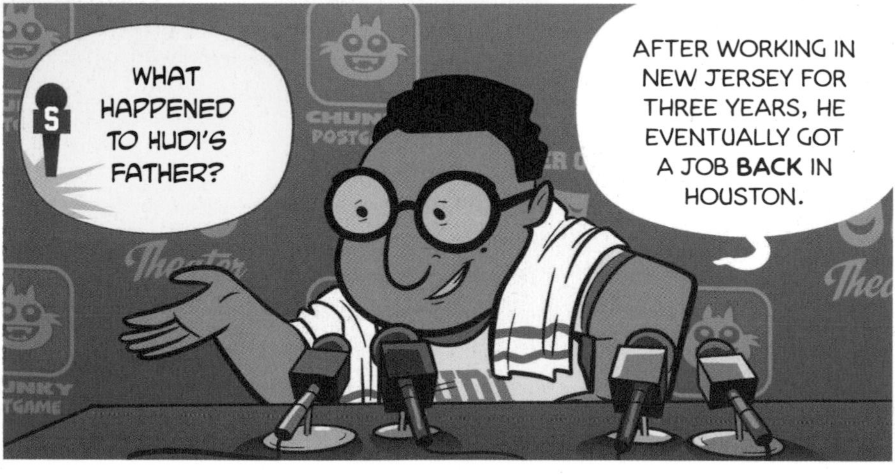
WHAT HAPPENED TO HUDI'S FATHER?
AFTER WORKING IN NEW JERSEY FOR THREE YEARS, HE EVENTUALLY GOT A JOB **BACK** IN HOUSTON.

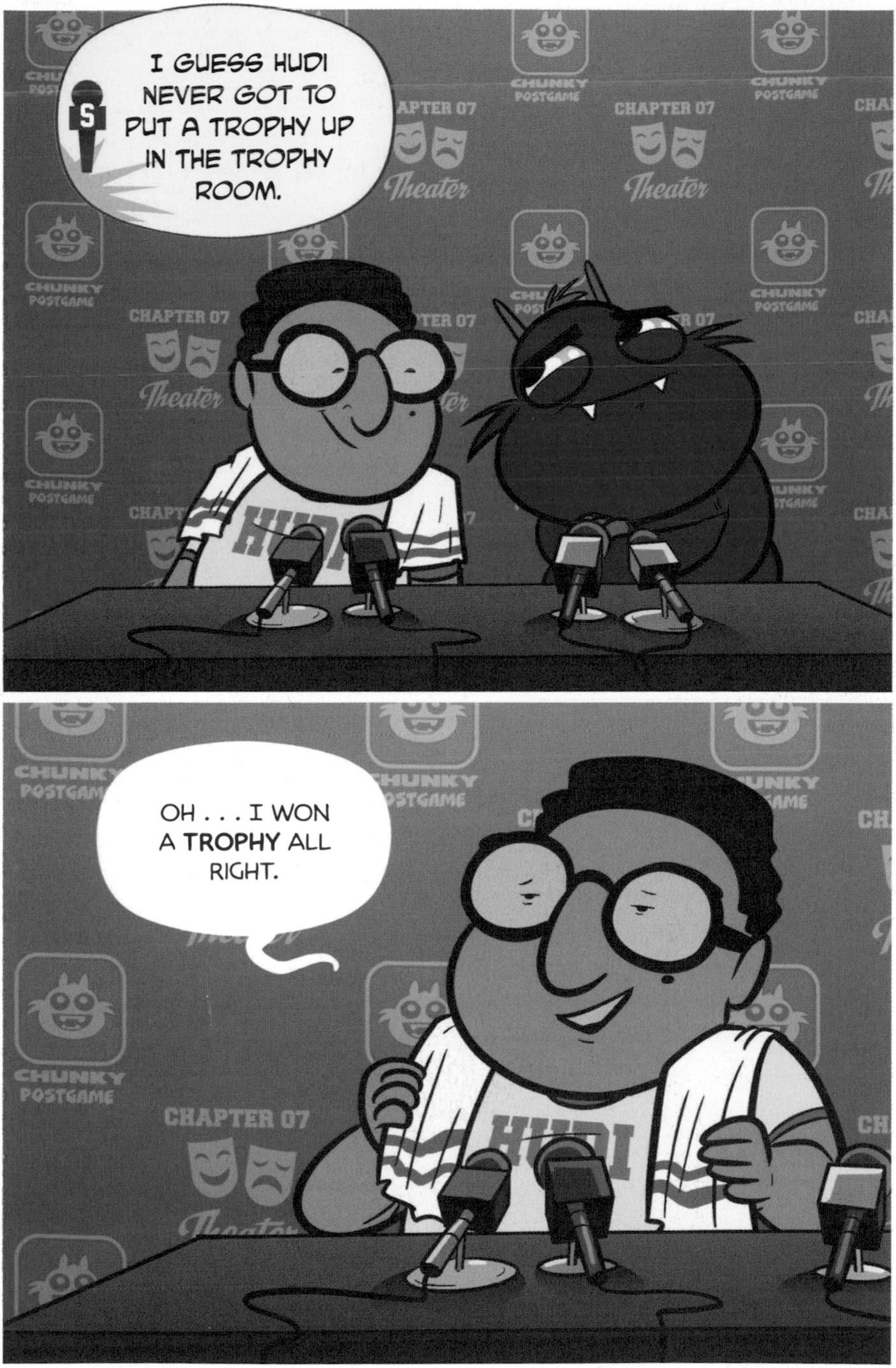
I GUESS HUDI NEVER GOT TO PUT A TROPHY UP IN THE TROPHY ROOM.
OH . . . I WON A **TROPHY** ALL RIGHT.

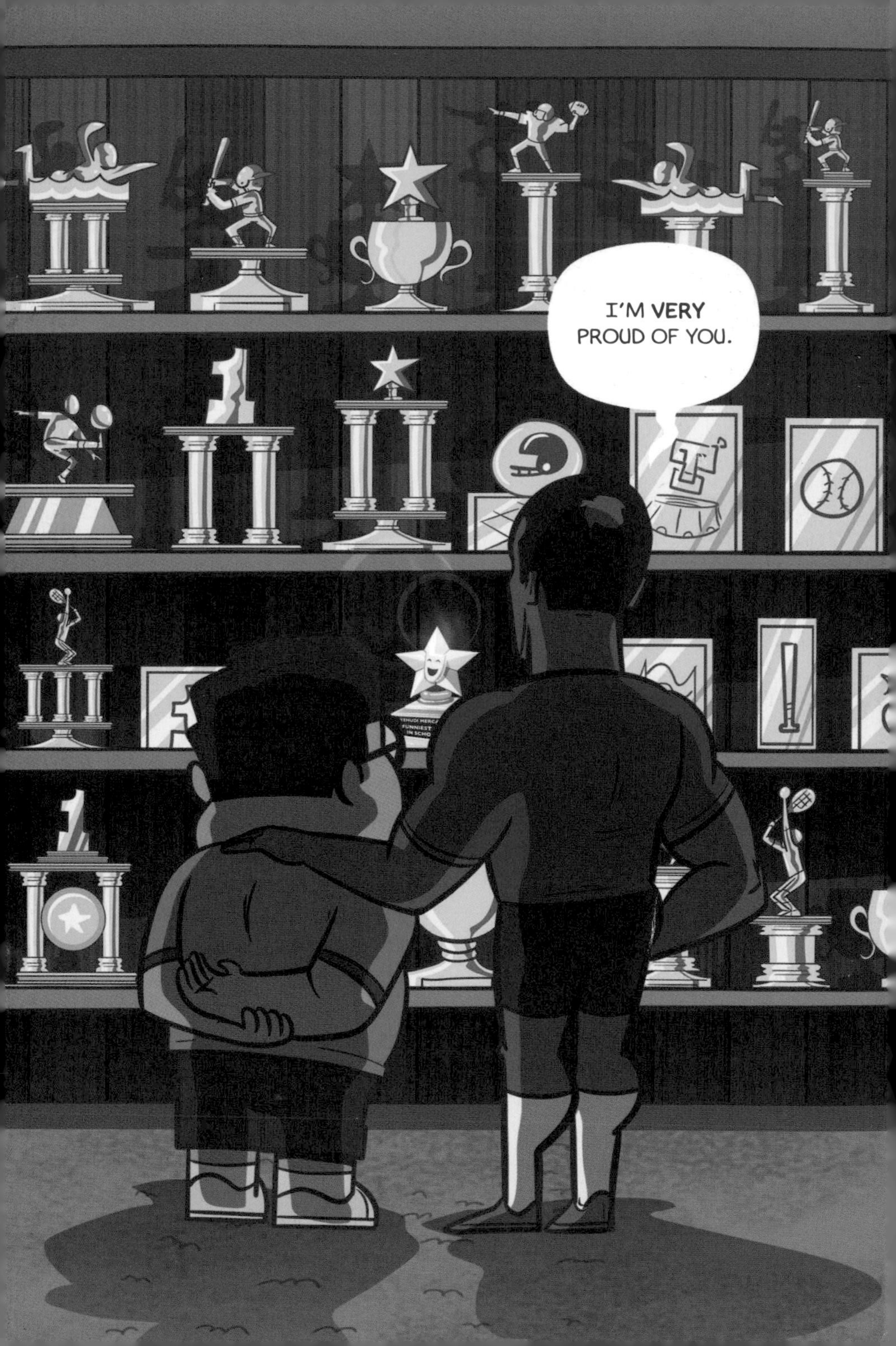
I'M VERY PROUD OF YOU.

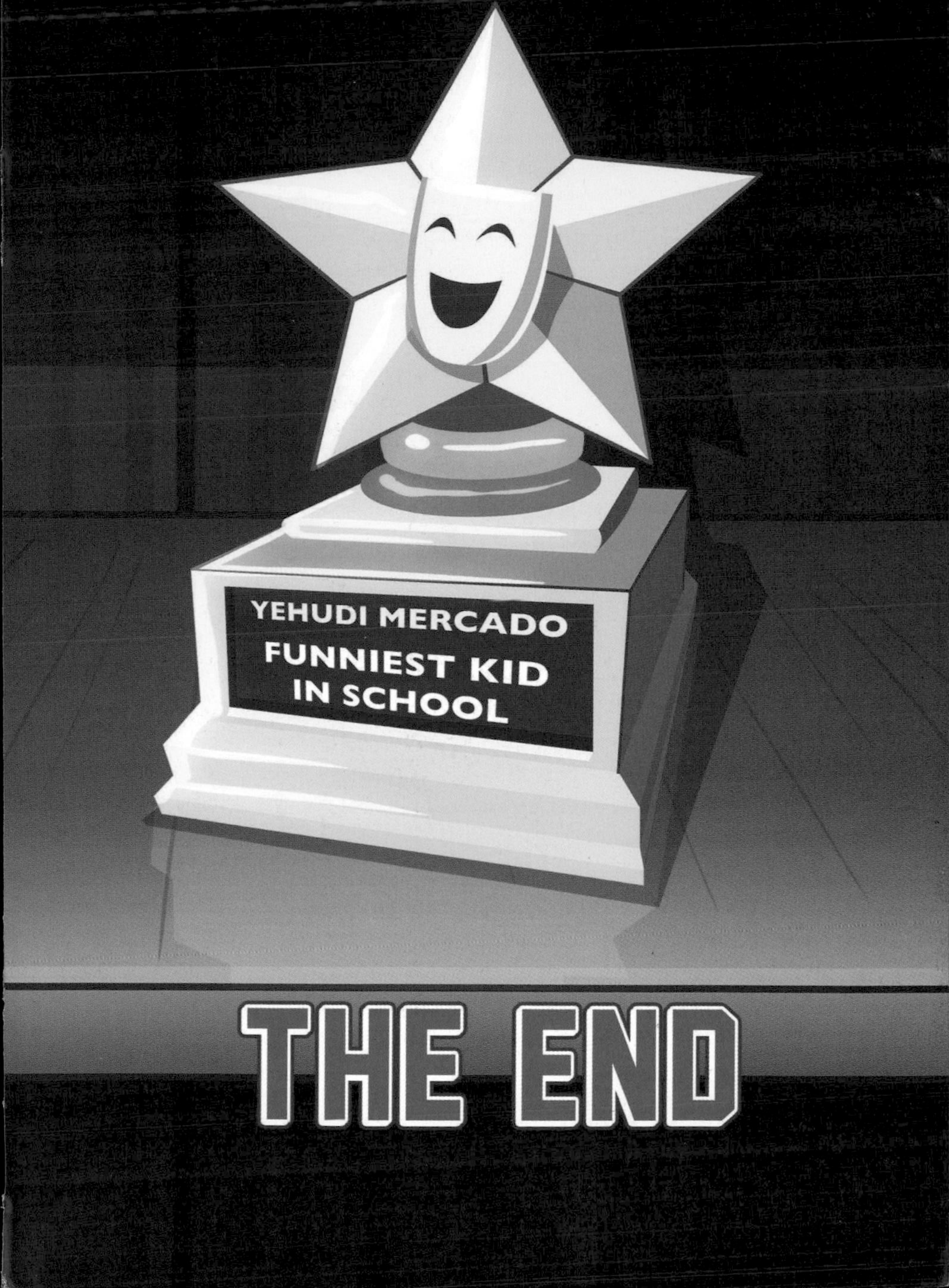
YEHUDI MERCADO
FUNNIEST KID
IN SCHOOL
THE END

AUTHOR'S NOTE

First of all, my parents want you to know that they weren't *that* pushy.

I want to thank them profusely for all the support they've shown me my whole life. They always encouraged my artistic pursuits. My father, while being a great athlete, is also an amazing artist. So we always had art supplies all over the house and I was never without a sketch pad or a fist full of markers.

All the health issues in the book are real. All the trips to the emergency room and the hospital really happened. Dr. Plumb was the doctor who performed my lung operation. I only remember flashes of that time. The whole operation and the recovery took me out of school for half a year. I actually had to repeat the first grade, which really bothered me, because I had done all the reading and homework from home— thanks to my mother, who was a teacher.

I continued with football until the eighth grade, but I never really loved it. Texas football was very brutal, and some of those drills are now outlawed. But there was one incident where I hurt my arm, and that's when it hit me. I didn't want to risk injuring my drawing hand because art meant way more to me than sports. I may not be a sports fan, but I do love sports movies.

Yehudi's father at Wynnie's Bat Mitzvah celebrating his US citizenship.

Being "Chunky" isn't about being fat. Being Chunky is about feeling like you don't fit in. As a Mexican Jewish kid with loads of health problems growing up in Houston, Texas, I never felt like I fit in anywhere. It wasn't until I discovered theater that I felt like I finally found my people. In high school I tried out for all the plays. I was playing leads by sophomore year. I went to speech tournaments and competed in various categories like mime, duets, and monologues. My senior year I played Richard III in the UIL (University Interscholastic League) One-Act Play Contest and we went all the way to state. I guess making theater into a sport was a very "Texas" thing to do.

This book is dedicated to my high school drama teacher, Mrs. Marylyn Miller. That's the back of her head on page 195. She passed away in 2012. She helped shape me into the person I am; she let me write and direct plays and always cheered me on. I never would have had the confidence to do what I now do for a living if it weren't for Mrs. Miller.

Find that thing that sparks your imagination. Find your people. Find your Chunky.

Special thanks to
Ben Rosenthal
Raina Telgemeier
Dave Scheidt
Charlie Olsen
Eileen Anderson
the Hoodis family
the Warfields
the Pueblitzes
and
Katherine Tegen

Yehudi in junior high on the Campbell Gators football team.